What they're saying about
The Huna Warrior: The Magic Begins

"*The Huna Warrior: The Magic Begins* unearths a treasure trove of secrets about ancient Hawaiian mysticism still used today by Huna practitioners worldwide. A great read! I highly recommend it."
—Lloyd Youngblood, certified Huna practitioner (retired)

"Experiencing Kat Romero's plunge into the Huna Way of Life is a way to vicariously dive into your own depths and your own possibilities. The Huna wisdom Kat embraces will open you up to a new and deeper understanding of your true nature as spiritual beings."
—Bud Gardner, author of *Chicken Soup for the Writer's Soul*

"Revealing. Beguiling. Entertaining. This first book of *The Huna Warrior* series delivers the goods. It's a well-written story which uncovers the ancient secrets of Hawaii with a wealth of unforgettable characters, plot twists and suspense."
—Barb Rogers, author of *Mystic Glyphs,* and *Feng Shui in a Day*

"Finally, a spellbinding novel that incorporates the secrets of the ancient Hawaiians is here. Don't miss *The Huna Warrior*, an intriguing page-turner to the very end."
—Ethel Bangert, Sacramento author and writing teacher

"*The Huna Warrior: The Magic Begins* leaves the reader with an understanding of how the spirit of Huna is received and delivered for the good of all. This thought-provoking story, along with the author's insightful prose, keeps the reader involved, motivated, and wanting to learn more about the magic of Huna."
—Rose Benson, author of *I of a Tiger*

The Huna Warrior™

The Magic Begins

By

Jennifer Martin

Published by Prairie Angel Press
5098 Foothills Blvd. #3-324
Roseville, CA 95747

Publisher's Note

Publisher's Cataloging-in-Publication
(Provided by Quality Books, Inc.)

Martin, Jennifer, 1945-
    The Huna warrior : the magic begins / by Jennifer
Martin. -- 1st ed.
    p. cm.
    LCCN 2005909788
    ISBN 0-9646975-1-3

    1. Supernatural--Fiction. 2. Women shamans--Fiction.
3. Shamanism--Hawaii--Fiction. 4. Hawaii--Fiction.
5. Occult fiction. 6. Fantasy fiction.   I. Title.

PS3613.A7795H86 2006   813'.6
                            QBI05-600209

Cover by Robert Howard

Printed in the United States of America: First edition

Dedication:

This book is dedicated to Huna practitioners worldwide who are keeping the magic alive.

Acknowledgements

My profound thanks to the following people whose input helped shape this work:

Marian Applegate, Ethel Bangert, Rose Benson, Charlotte Berney, Lois Brooks, Daniel Darms, Rose Gasser, Darlynne and Steve Giorgi, Robert Gunn, Evelyn Hess, John Karsten, Cael and Deana Kuhlman, Catherine Lanigan, Dahlynn and Ken McKowen, Dan Millman, Barb Rogers, Pam Rothwell, Sue Swift, Dr. Otha Wingo, and Lloyd Youngblood.

Deep appreciation to my husband, Bud Gardner, who not only brings to these pages an editorial pen, but enriches my life daily as a friend, mentor, and soul-mate.

Prologue

Tapered fingers of sunlight snaked their way through dead hibiscus and fading ferns, into the tiny cracks of the ancient temple wall. Undeterred, the dappled light crawled across the stone floor, flickering on the rusty shackles clasped around the old Hawaiian's thin, bowed legs.

Peering into a calabash bowl on the table in front of him, he grated a bit of yellow ginger root into the water swirling in the bowl, stirring the mixture with a smooth black stone. Images leapt into his eyes, pulsing phantoms that twisted and stretched, then melted away at the jagged periphery like film slowly burned by the lamp of a projector.

The old Hawaiian, his bloodshot eyes pleading and sorrowful, turned to a man sitting on a woven mat.

"It's not to be, son. It's not in the stars for you," he said, flinching in anticipation of his son's anger.

"Then make it so, Father. My destiny is in your hands, just as your life is in mine. No one knows you're here. No one can help you escape. And if you want to stay alive, I'm your only hope. I will not be denied any longer. Help me become the greatest kahuna on earth or die a slow and agonizing death. It's as simple as that."

The old man, weakened with hunger, carefully weighed his son's words, then trembled in silent defeat, sealing the pact between them. He turned his back to his son and began to chant, casting his arms out as if releasing doves.

"Bring back to me the faces of my son's enemies, little aka cord. Send out your finger and search the world over. Show me who dares to block his path."

In the vapors emanating from the crevices in the temple door, a thin, golden thread shot out, spiraling through the sky. Tiny brown birds chattered in the mango trees just outside the window where the old Hawaiian waited despondently for the answer to his soaring prayer.

Chapter 1

"What are you looking at, punk?" the new kid growled.

"You, psycho. What's up with the hair? You related to Don King or something?"

The new kid, Rudy Baker, shook his balled up fist at Mike Farnsworth who towered over him by a foot. "No, but you're gonna be related to this if you don't get outta my face."

"Ooh, I'm sooo scared!" Mike said, pulling money out of his pocket. "Here. Buy yourself a haircut."

Rudy smirked. "You just bought yourself a six-pack of whoop-ass."

Mike swung first, but Rudy dodged his fist, tripped him at the ankle, and kicked him viciously in the back. Mike fell face-first onto the floor, his money flying out of his hand into the crowd of students who had bolted out of their classrooms to see the fight.

Rudy picked him up by the back of his shirt and slammed his fist into his face. Blood spurted from Mike's nose as he dropped to his knees. Someone in the crowd shouted, "Kill him!"

"Ow! I can feel that punch from here! Where's my walkie-talkie?"

Vice-principal, Kat Romero, grimaced and stared into the video monitors in her outer office, watching two boys whaling on each other in the hallway of the upper

1

floor of the science building. She radioed the campus monitors about the fight and peered again at the monitor.

"Look, Mazie. It's Mike Farnsworth. You sure called that one."

Her beaded corn-rows clinking, Kat's secretary ambled over to the screen.

"Uh huh," Mazie said. "I told you he wouldn't last day one without steppin' in it."

"Great," Kat sighed. "First day of school, and I have to deal with Godzilla's mother. My ears hurt already."

"Ain't that the truth. That woman's voice can wake the dead."

Mazie plopped down in her swivel-backed chair, the air swishing out of the cushion from her bulk.

Kat returned to her office and looked out the window which faced into the quad of Susan B. Anthony High School, the newest high school built in Folsom, California. In its final phase of completion, SBAHS looked more like a college campus. Dotted with crape myrtles and gleaming buildings covering over sixty acres, the school sat between a busy freeway and Folsom Lake, reflecting the frenetic and tranquil qualities of both.

Kat shook her head, admiring the view: spacious, covered walkways, colorful murals splashing across the library walls, the impressive domed roof of the gymnasium in the distance, its Mediterranean blue tiles reflecting the hot August sun in shimmering bands of heat.

I wish my high school campus looked this beautiful when I was in school, Kat thought. *But then again, that was the Middle Ages.*

"Mazie, where do you keep the suspension notices?"

Mazie pulled her desk drawer open and rummaged through her folders, then handed Kat a stack of triplicate forms. "Here you go, honey," she drawled in a soft, Southern accent.

Built like an armored tank, Mazie Longer appeared taller than her five feet, ten inches and ran the VP office with a no-nonsense, "don't-even-think-about-it" attitude she had acquired during her previous years as a sergeant in the U.S. Marines. She stepped back to look at the surveillance monitors and squinted, accentuating the crow's feet on her ebony face.

"You can't miss Mike Farnsworth, but who's the other kid?"

Kat shrugged. "My guess it's the one from San Francisco. The one with all the hair."

"Oh, yeah. The new kid. Looks like he stuck his head in a wind tunnel."

She opened the student discipline file drawer and found Mike Farnsworth's file, already two-inches thick.

"Here's Dufus' file," Mazie said, laying it on the corner of her desk. "I bet it weighs five pounds by the end of the semester," continued Mazie, her alto voice lowering in a conspiratorial tone. "You wanna bet Mike started the fight?"

Before Kat could answer, the door next to hers flew open.

"Whatever you're betting on, I want in," said Serge Stafford, slicking back his auburn hair as he lurched into

3

the Vice-Principal's reception room. Serge, like Kat, was a newly appointed vice-principal at SBAHS.

"You don't want to bet with Mazie, Serge," said Kat. "She'll probably win and you'd probably want her to. Because if she loses, she'll want to arm-wrestle you to prove she's still a winner. Trust me. You don't want that."

Mazie dropped her head back and howled with laughter. "Girl, you ain't never lied," she guffawed, flinging her hand out at Kat. She pretended to glower at Serge, who raised his hands in mock surrender and retreated back to his office, then went back to her desk to sort through the stacks of mail that had accumulated over the summer break.

Kat flipped through Mike's file, then threw it back on her desk and turned on her computer. *No need to look in this file,* she thought. *I remember Mike from my first year as a vice-principal at the middle school. Gangly clown, always running his mouth, compulsivity brought about by Attention Deficit Disorder. Mother won't put him on meds.*

The outer VP office door jangled her back to the present. Kat looked up to see two members of campus security enter, each one securing one of the two fighters. The new kid, sullen and unruffled, sported a red bandana which circled his five-inch afro. He looked around disdainfully, then slumped into the chair Mazie pointed out to him. The second student, Mike Farnsworth, holding an icepack to his nose, steered his lanky frame into her office like it was a routine inspection.

"Hi, Mike," Kat said, wryly.

"Ms. Romero," he replied, a mischievous grin spreading over his face. "You're looking good, as usual."

Kat rolled her eyes and closed her office door behind him just as Serge opened his adjacent office door and stood towering in his doorway.

"Any referrals for me, Mrs. Longer?" he asked, formally addressing Mazie whenever students were present.

Serge had been an administrator in Arizona before coming to California six years earlier. Handling discipline was not just second nature to him. He actually looked forward to it, like a prize fighter getting into the ring with an opponent he knew he could whip.

"He's not in your part of the student alphabet, but you might want to talk to Rudy Baker," Mazie said, nodding in Rudy's direction. "He and Mike Farnsworth just got into a fight. Mike is in with Ms. Romero."

"Come in, Rudy. You'll need to take that bandana off. We don't allow gang paraphernalia here at school," boomed Serge. He eyeballed Rudy up and down as he held his office door open for him.

Unintimidated, Rudy slowly tugged on his bandana, hiked up his baggy jeans, and shuffled into Serge's office.

Twenty minutes later, both vice-principals had interviewed the students, filled out the paperwork for the fighters to each receive three-day suspensions from school, and put in calls to their homes for someone to pick the boys up. Kat kept Mike in her office, while Serge asked Mazie to escort Rudy to the front office to wait for his foster dad to arrive.

Mazie rose up to full height, looming over Rudy. "Sure thing, Mr. Stafford," she chirped brightly, then glared down at Rudy with molten eyes. "Follow me, young man."

He slowly trailed her down the hallway to the principal's office, dragging his feet in protest. Once there, he plopped into a seat near Denise Richards' desk. Denise, the principal's secretary, raised one eyebrow and stared at him suspiciously. Rudy flashed a fake smile at her and slouched deeper into his chair. Then he took a small ball out of his pocket and tossed it from one hand to the other, waiting impatiently for Denise to admit him to the principal's office so he could charm his way out of his suspension—something he was good at from years of practice.

When Mazie returned to the VP office, she knocked on Kat's door, barely opening it so Mike couldn't read her lips. "Broom alert," she mouthed.

That could only mean one thing. The formidable Becky Farnsworth had arrived at school and was heading to Kat's office. When Kat had called her about Mike's suspension, she sounded both irate and mortified. Once again, "Mikey" was in trouble.

Kat had no doubt Becky had only joined the Parents/Teachers/Students Association, both at the middle school and now at the high school, to ingratiate herself with the powers that be. She figured if she were personally involved at school, she could minimize the trouble her son managed to get into at regular intervals. She was bound and determined no one and nothing was going to get in the way of her son's high school diploma. He was going to cross that stage to graduate, by God, even if it killed her and everybody else at Anthony High.

6

Kat took Mike up to the front office to meet his mother who immediately snatched the suspension paper out of his hand. "Mikey!" she screeched as Mike's eyes studied the ceiling, trying to block out the amused looks of the students and teachers in the crowded office.

"Look at me! The first day of school isn't even over yet, and you're already in trouble. A three-day suspension! I hope you're proud of yourself. And if you think I'm going to let you play football after this, you better think again. You just wait until I talk to your father about this. After all I do for this school, and you embarrass me like this."

She seized Mike's left arm like she was pulling the arm on a slot machine, yanked it behind him and marched him, POW-style, out the door.

Kat saw some students milling near the parking lot and went out to shoo them into class. When she came back into the administration building, she noticed Rudy coming out of the principal's office, looking pleased and haughty, like he'd just pulled off a major bank robbery. He sneered at Kat triumphantly, then turned to stare out a large tinted window, all the while tossing a small ball in his hands.

Denise Dutra, the principal's secretary, looked up at Kat and smiled. "Just the person I want to see."

"Yeah? What's up, girlfriend?"

Glancing over at Rudy, Denise grabbed Kat's hand.

"Trouble. Come with me." She headed down the hallway to the vault.

Because of its thick reinforced walls, the walk-in vault for student records was the only sound-proof room in the main office of Anthony High and the perfect place to

7

gossip, which was Denise Dutra's specialty. She was the main school secretary assigned to the principal, Gabe Minelli, but it took a Herculean daily effort for Denise to fake even the slimmest pretense of loyalty to Gabe. Conversely, it gave her the greatest pleasure to rat on him to his wife, Angela, who happened to be a childhood friend of hers.

A blond pixie, brandishing rings on nearly every finger of her hands, Denise had worked with Kat at the middle school before transferring to the new high school, and they had bonded in a conspiratorial type of friendship.

Denise pulled Kat in and slammed the door shut. The insulated walls kept the small room much colder than the rest of the office, a welcomed contrast to the summer furnace outside.

"You know how loud Gabe's voice is, so I couldn't help but hear he just reduced Rudy Baker's suspension to a one-dayer," Denise said.

"He can't do that!" Kat exclaimed. "The discipline code calls for three days for a first offense fight for all parties involved. I just gave Mike Farnsworth three-days. Lord! If Becky finds out Rudy only got one.... Why would Gabe overturn the suspension, Denise? You know him better than I do."

"Gabe grew up without a father. It bothers him when he sees young boys get into trouble because there's no father in their lives. So he takes them under his wing. Tries to turn them around."

Denise pulled out a box of transcripts to sit on and motioned for Kat to do the same.

8

"Gabe takes home needy kids like you and I'd take in stray animals. He even put one kid through college. Angela tries to be understanding, but most of the time she resents the time and money she feels should be spent on her and their daughter, Brittany. Usually the boys end up doing something stupid so she has a good reason to kick them out. Gabe goes along with it for a while, then gets depressed. Starts looking for another kid to help out, like he's some kind of missionary. Rudy's just his newest prospect."

"But does he really think he has what it takes to save this kid? I did Rudy's intake interview last week. He's a sixteen-year-old with a mean right hook and lives with his foster dad. Now you and I both know a kid in a foster home has a host of problems which got him there in the first place. Plus, he was wearing a red bandana, so he's probably in a gang. No one in his right mind would willingly take on all that baggage until he had all the facts and could make a reasonable prediction whether the kid really wants to change," Kat said.

"Well, no one ever said Gabe was in his right mind," Denise said with a slow, Chestershire cat grin.

"When I was in graduate school, I did research on resiliency in kids who had overcome extreme adversity," Kat said. "There are a few predictors in a kid's life that will tell you if they'll be able to bounce up after a stressful childhood. One predictor is that they could read at grade level at fourth grade. The other is that at least one adult loved or mentored the kid during his or her lifetime. I wish

I had Rudy's cume folder right now. Sometimes teachers jot down notes on a kid's home life. It might have the answers we need to profile him."

"Hey, why don't we look in some of these record boxes?" Denise suggested. "These three all just arrived yesterday." She began searching through the box she'd just been sitting on while Kat rummaged through the other two.

Kat knew that a peek at Rudy's cumulative folder—cume, for short—would give her the data she needed to confirm her suspicions about him. Starting in kindergarten, cume folders followed students from school to school until they either graduated or dropped out of high school. Cumes held report cards, testing results, health records and year-end notes from teachers. They provided administrators and teachers a yearly snapshot of a student's academic and behavioral background.

After a while, Kat stood up to rub her aching neck. "Any luck?"

"Nope. I guess his isn't in yet."

"Hmmph," Kat muttered, worry lines forming on her forehead. "Well, I'm just going to have to rely on my intuition, which, right now, tells me Gabe's intervention won't be enough to turn Rudy around. If the kid's never been in counseling, then it's a matter of too little, too late. And the problem is, if Rudy's already decided to self-destruct, there's no doubt in my mind he'll take a few kids with him. Gabe's making a big mistake befriending Rudy without knowing much about him. My guess is he needs tough love, not a soft touch."

Denise nodded, then looked at her watch. It was time for them to go.

As they approached Gabe's closed door, Kat turned abruptly to Denise.

"Look, I know it's only our first day working together and he is my boss, but I just have to call Gabe on this. How do you think he's going to take it?"

"Not well," said Denise, grimacing. "Big hat, no cattle."

"That's what I thought," Kat replied. "But I have to do this."

Denise crossed her fingers and waved Kat on toward Gabe's closed door.

Chapter 2

Principal Gabe Minelli motioned abruptly toward the curious student squinting into his tinted office window. The student waved back and scurried off, embarrassed at being caught snooping. Gabe smirked and turned back to his computer. He glanced down at his hands on the keyboard, admiring his recently manicured nails as he finished up an email to the staff. His steely gray eyes checked for lint on his jacket sleeves as Kat knocked quietly on his door.

"Got a minute?" Kat asked, opening the door and forcing a smile.

"Why, sure!" Gabe said, gesturing for her to sit down. "You're looking well," he said, trying not to stare at Kat's chest.

"I hate to bother you because I know you're busy, but I want to talk to you about Rudy Baker. I understand you reduced his suspension," Kat said, sitting on the edge of her chair.

"Word gets out fast around here. Denise?" He frowned, making a mental note to lower his voice in his office.

"Does it matter?" Kat asked.

"Not really."

"Are you telling me Rudy gets one day and Mike gets three days—for the same offense? I'll get reamed by Becky Farnsworth, Gabe! What were you thinking?"

"Look, it's the first day of school, and we need to cut both boys some slack. They can't afford to be out that long at the beginning of a semester, or they'll get too far behind right away. Why don't you just reduce Mike's suspension to one day and tell him it's a welcome-back to school special?"

"Well, in the interest of fairness, I guess I have no choice," Kat said grimly. "But I've got to tell you, Gabe, I think it's important, from now on, all of us strictly follow the code and back each other up on suspensions."

"Absolutely. We're a team here," Gabe gushed. "And when school is really underway, I'll be leaving all the suspensions up to you and Serge." He stood up to let her know the conversation was over. "Listen, I'll be going off campus in a few minutes to take Rudy to get a hair cut, so I won't be able to work on our search for a temporary pool for the swim team. I'd really appreciate it if you could take care of that for me, okay, Kat?"

"Eh, yeah, sure," Kat said weakly, trying to show some enthusiasm for this new assignment, but not buying Gabe's ploy of changing the subject.

"But getting back to Rudy for a second. I just have a feeling about him that he's a really troubled kid. Maybe we should look in his school records to make sure he belongs here."

"He belongs here, Kat. He just needs a little fatherly guidance, and he'll be back on track," Gabe said, nostrils flaring.

"No offense, Gabe, but there's no guarantee your guidance"—Kat gestured quotation marks—"is going to instantly turn around his behavior or knock the chip off his shoulder. All the research says...."

Gabe cut her off. "Look, I don't care what the research says. I don't think it's ever too late to help someone turn his or her life around. You and I will just have to agree to disagree on this one," Gabe said, glaring at Kat.

Kat's eyes bored into Gabe's pinched face. "I think you are dead wrong. My gut feeling is Rudy is trouble. You need to be careful with him." She pivoted sharply and left the room, catching a glimpse of Rudy out of the side of her eye as he stared at her coldly, then went back to tossing his ball.

Gabe huffed as he returned to his chair. *That uppity bitch. What does she know? All Rudy needs is a little fatherly attention. She'll see.*

Pompous ass, Kat thought, as she hurried back to her office. She was so angry she almost collided head-on in the hallway with Kalani Kingston, a ninth grade student who had been in Kat's Language Arts class in the middle school. When Kalani saw Kat, her face lit up with a dazzling smile which amplified her Polynesian beauty and set off her long dark hair that trailed down her back in a French braid.

"Oh, hi, Ms. R.!" Kalani said. "I've been looking everywhere for you. I've got a hole in my schedule and wondered if you needed an office aide sixth period."

"I'd love that, Kalani. You're one of my all-time favorite students. Do you have the add slip?"

Kalani unzipped her backpack, found the paperwork and gave it to Kat to sign.

14

"How was your summer, Kalani?" Kat asked, digging in her pocket for a pen.

Kalani ran her hand over her hair and looked down at her feet. "Summer was fine until a few days ago. My mom had a nervous breakdown. She's in the hospital. Grandma's worried about her."

Kat reached out to hug the girl's shoulder, mindful of the school's policy for administrators not to physically touch students, but knowing full well this student was hurting.

"I'm really sorry to hear that, Kalani. Do you know what triggered it?"

"We don't know what was bothering her. I mean, it wasn't her job. It wasn't anything at home. We all got along. No fighting or anything. But she's always been a worrier and for some reason, got really nervous and anxious lately, you know? But we thought she'd snap out of it. Guess it was worse than we thought."

"Sometimes life has a way of becoming more worrisome to sensitive people like your mother than to those of us with thicker skins, Kalani. Just remember, she's doing the best she can," Kat said, knowing her words fell short of conveying the compassion she thought Kalani deserved.

"I know," Kalani said, finally glancing up at Kat. "Uh, Ms. R, do you think you could spare some time after school to help me with English? I have to write a three-page autobiography. You know me and writing."

Kalani shook her head, snorted a laugh and grinned.

"Yes, I know how you hate to write, but I'd like to help you change that attitude," Kat sympathized.

"Cool. Thanks, Ms. R. See you later."

"Give my best to your mom, Kalani. I hope she's better soon."

As Kalani walked away, Kat went back to the VP office.

"Hi, Kat," Mazie said, putting down the phone. "Just got a call from the Folsom Police Department. Looks like Officer Mark Matthews is our new liaison—in case we need to have kids arrested."

Kat's eyes twinkled. "Can you keep a secret?"

Mazie nodded and made a motion zipping her lips shut.

"Mark's my ex-husband."

Mazie's shocked expression provoked a giggle out of Kat. "But I have no problem with that. He and I made our peace years ago. Besides, he treats me better now than when we were married."

"Hmmph."

"I suspect he even requested this assignment."

"To see you?"

"No, to see our son."

Mazie gulped. "Your son?"

"Sean Matthews, the new counselor? He's our son. We have different last names because I went back to using my maiden name."

"Girl, you are just too full of surprises for one day." Mazie sat down with a thud and settled into her chair before picking up a folder to fan her face.

16

Kat leaned over Mazie's desk and stared into her face for emphasis. "But please keep all of this to yourself, Mazie. It's hard enough learning the ropes of being a high school administrator without the extra hassles I'd get if anyone else finds out about my personal life."

Mazie raised her hand and Kat followed suit in a high-five clap which sealed their secret.

Just as Kat had settled back in her office to answer email, her father, Henry, called to wish her a "Happy First Day at School," a tradition he had started when she was a small child.

"I knew you'd call, Dad."

"Well, you're my favorite daughter.'

"No wonder. I'm your only child." Kat giggled appreciatively into the phone.

Kat always laughed at her father's silly jokes. Since Kat's mother, Maxine, had been diagnosed the previous summer with advanced Alzheimer's disease, Henry's sense of humor had been curtailed a bit, but not totally diminished. Kat appreciated his effort to brighten her day.

"How's Mom doing?" Kat asked. "I haven't been able to see her much, with school starting and all."

Maxine was a patient in a health care facility which specialized in Alzheimer's disease and was located over eighty miles away. Kat had been very close to Maxine all her life, and it was emotionally taxing for her to see her mother's once vivacious personality unravel. The geographical distance just added to the burden Kat carried inside every time she prepared for a visit with her mother.

"She's hanging in there, Kathrine. And if she could speak, she'd tell you how proud she is of you. As I am. But you probably already know that."

"I know, Dad. It means a lot to me for you to say that." Kat said.

She noticed a few more students and their parents entering the outer VP office to register for school.

"Some new students just came in, so I've got to interview and admit them. But I really appreciate your call. You're the best. I'll talk to you soon."

Kat hung up the phone, pulled out her student intake binder, and invited one of the new students inside.

At the end of the day, Kat sat dejectedly in her office waiting for Kalani to appear. It was only the first day of school. She already wished it was the last. It didn't help she had spent a good part of the afternoon trying to find a pool the swim team could use for practice until the new pool was finished. The construction bid for the pool had gone to a company Gabe had fought for in long, drawn-out, closed negotiations with the school board. Because of the delay in securing the bid, the pool wouldn't be up and running for months.

At lunchtime, the pool work crew refused to shut down their dust-kicking rototillers and bone-rattling jackhammers, drills and buzz saws, generating a host of complaints from faculty, students and parents alike. Kat's head was beginning to pound.

Moodily, she scanned her tiny office, ten by twelve feet in area. It was crammed with two bookcases, three file cabinets, one long table, her desk with its computer and three chairs. Kat had brightened the ivory walls with paintings done in mauves, greens and blues and shelves of knickknacks she had accumulated over the years. Near her desk, her framed credentials circled a bulletin board plastered with dozens of autographed photos her students had given her.

A smile forced its way out when she looked at the small cactus plant sitting on the windowsill. Last year at Horace Mann Junior High School, she had tried to liven up the VP office with bushy Boston ferns and sprawling ivy, but the poor plants soon began to droop and turn brown, which Kat attributed to all the negative vibes from the angry parents and cussing students who flowed through her office on a regular basis. So she had taken her plants home where they bounced back within a week. This year she was prepared. "You can't kill a cactus," she had declared to a skeptical Mazie.

Mazie poked her head in the doorway, breaking Kat's train of thought.

"I'm heading out, girl. Got a doctor's appointment. Say, you okay? You're not your usual feisty self."

"I'm all right, Mazie. Just tired. First day on a new job."

"Kalani's here. You up to seeing her?"

"You bet. I've been waiting for her." Kat stood up to stretch, took in a big breath of air and forcefully blew it out.

Kalani bounded into Kat's office, threw her backpack on the floor and gave Kat a hug.

"How'd you know I needed a hug?" asked Kat, chuckling.

"Just guessed. I really appreciate you doing this, Ms. R. I've been dreading it all day."

"Now, Kalani. Just because you don't *like* to do it, doesn't mean you *can't* do it. You're a good writer. You just need a little confidence. I'll be your writing coach. Deal?"

"Deal. So… what could I possible say about my boring life that would fill up three pages?"

"You remember what I taught you about clustering? We'll start with that."

For the next half hour, Kat helped Kalani organize her ideas through clustering, a mind-mapping technique of brainstormed word associations and connections to the main subject, accomplished by drawing bubbles around topics and then drawing lines from these bubbles back to the main bubble. The page began to look like a sun with planets circling it.

Once the brainstorming was done, Kalani reorganized these scattered thoughts and put them into a logical, linear progression. By using the right side of the brain to access her creativity, and then turning to the left side of the brain to provide order and polish, the paper practically wrote itself.

Watching Kalani's mind work, Kat was impressed with her cognitive speed and intuition, as she wrote steadily for another hour.

"Gee, that was easier than I thought it'd be," Kalani said as she finished up her last sentence.

Kat helped her stuff her notepads and pens back into her backpack. "Ya done good, kid," said Kat in her best John Wayne imitation, patting Kalani's shoulder.

"Writing is just thinking on paper, and you've always been able to think well. You did a great job."

"Thanks, Coach."

Kalani's eyes widened when she spotted the clock near the file cabinets.

"Uh, Ms. R? You wouldn't by any chance be able to take me home, would you? I missed the bus, and my grandma will freak out if I don't show up right about now."

"Well, today must be your lucky day because I'm going home early. Want me to call your grandmother first to tell her we're on the way?"

"Can't," Kalani said, avoiding Kat's eyes. "No phone. Grandma doesn't want my dad calling me or even knowing where we live. It's a long story."

"I understand," Kat said, unlocking her file cabinet to retrieve her purse. "Let's go."

It took less than eight minutes for Kat to drive to Kalani's apartment. Kalani chatted the entire way about the latest summer romances, which kids were breaking up, who was cheating on whom—enough dirt to blackmail students for years, if either of them wanted to. Kat noticed Kalani pointedly avoided talking about her mother, Leilani. She walked Kalani to her front door, admiring the green wreath hanging in the window next to it.

"Would you like to come in?" Kalani's eyes pleaded. "It's probably better if you told my grandmother why I'm late."

21

"You're right. I'll come in for a minute," Kat said.

Key in hand, Kalani unlocked the door, holding it open for Kat to enter. The apartment was neatly decorated in a Polynesian motif, which was no surprise to Kat since she knew Kalani was Hawaiian. A simple vase filled with white lilies sat in the center of the dining room table set with tapa cloth placemats. A large portrait of King Kamehameha hung on the wall, giving Kat the impression of royalty presiding over all the meals.

Kalani's grandmother, Liana Kealoha, was sitting in a low recliner, feet propped up on a beige hassock, reading a book. When she saw Kat, she beamed at her. "What a lovely surprise!" she said as she struggled to stand.

"Oh, don't get up. I won't be a minute. It's good to see you again, Mrs. Kealoha. How are you?" Kat asked, extending her hand to the wizened woman.

"I'm just fine, Ms. Romero. It's good to see you, too." Placing both hands on Kat's, she patted her gently.

"Kalani should have told me you were coming. I would have prepared something special for dinner."

"Well, we were working on her English assignment after school, and the time just got away from us. I didn't want you to worry, so I brought her home as soon as I could."

Liana tilted her face and smiled. "I wasn't worried. I knew she was in good hands. And please call me Liana."

"Liana, I've always thought your name was beautiful. I've always loved the sound of the Hawaiian language," Kat remarked.

"Kalani tells me she's taught you a few words," Liana said, gesturing for Kat to sit in the easy chair next to her recliner.

"Just the basics, like *aloha*, *mahalo* and *Mele Kalikimaka*."

"Merry Christmas to you, too," Liana said, with a chuckle. "You'd be surprised at how many Hawaiians live in the Sacramento Valley. Some of them came with John Sutter in 1839 when he came here and built Sutter's fort."

"Really? I didn't know that," Kat said. "You'd think, since I've lived here for so many years, I'd know more about this area's history, but I must confess to being woefully ignorant, I'm afraid." She laughed at herself. "So much for being an educator."

"Well, we are all teachers to one another, dear. All of us have something to learn and something to teach. That's why we're here," Liana said. The tiny smile on her face grew larger.

Kat nodded, her body feeling heavy now that she was winding down from the enervating day.

Liana's eyes narrowed in discernment. "Why don't you sit back. I'll give you a *lomi lomi* massage."

Kat's eyebrows went up in surprise. "How'd you know I needed a massage?"

"Well, I know the person I met at Open House last year had pizzazz. And the person who is here before me is flat as last week's root beer. Must be the job. You're surrounded by people all day long who take your energy away. Energy vampires, I call them. Most of the time, they don't know they're doing this, but they suck up your energy anyway. Am I right?"

23

Kat cocked her head and thought back how earlier in the day she had been full of "piss and vinegar," as her father used to say, and now she was drooping like the plants she'd rescued from her office last year. She looked into Liana's soft doe-like eyes.

"You are so right. I'd love a massage."

Kat nestled deep into the easy chair and for the next ten minutes surrendered to Liana's powerful hands as they rubbed away the tension in her neck and shoulders. Streams of heat flowed out of Liana's hands into Kat's tight muscles, loosening the knots that had formed in them. Gradually, Kat could feel the circulation improving all over her body. Even her toes tingled.

"There. Doesn't that feel better, Ms. Romero?" Liana asked, returning to her recliner.

"Just what the doctor ordered. Thank you so much. And please call me Kat."

"Cat? As in c-a-t?"

"Kat as in short for Kathrine."

"It's a perfect name for you. Cats are very independent, and so are you."

"Right, again. You know, it's amazing how much you know about me, and we barely know each other."

"Oh, Kalani talks about you all the time. I feel like I've known you forever." Liana's eyes glowed with warmth.

Just then Kalani, who had gone to her room to change her clothes, bounced into the living room. "Grandma, you're not supposed to tell her that. She'll think I actually like her," Kalani teased.

"Too late. And the feeling's mutual, kiddo. But hey, it's getting late, and I've got to be on the road before traffic gets too heavy," Kat said, bending over to give Liana a hug.

"Thanks for everything, Liana. It was wonderful to see you again, and the *lomi lomi* did just the trick. I feel like myself again."

"Next time you come, I'll teach you how to put up a shield around you so that people don't steal your energy," Liana promised with a shy smile.

"Really? You can do that?"

"Sure. It's easy. When you have some time, come see me and I'll show you."

"Wow, you've really got me curious now," Kat said, mentally reviewing her calendar for the next few days. "We've got a three-day weekend coming up, you know, Labor Day. I'm moving into my first new house, but I probably could take a break Monday night. Would that be all right for you?"

"Come for dinner on Monday at six, and afterwards, I'll tell you all about energy shields," Liana said, her dark eyes twinkling.

"Okay, I'll be here. Next Monday. At six."

Kat backed up, toward the door, feeling a bit self-conscious for some reason. Kalani hugged her goodbye, then opened the door to see her out.

"Take care, Kalani," Kat said, rolling her shoulders to test for pain that was no longer there. "Tell your grandmother she has my endless thanks."

"I will," said Kalani as she returned to her door. *And you have her endless blessings,* she thought.

25

Locking the door behind her, Kalani rushed to her grandmother's side.

"Well, what do you think, Grandma? Is she the one?"

Eyes closed, Liana smiled with the greatest of satisfaction. "Yes, Kalani. I first suspected it when I met her two years ago, but now that I've held her hands again, I can really feel her power. She doesn't know it yet, but she's the one."

"Oh my God," gasped Kalani, as the full impact of her grandmother's words hit her. "She's the next Huna Warrior."

Chapter 3

Thousands of miles away in Maui, the old Hawaiian rubbed his arm where his son's strong grip had brought bruises.

"Did you bring the ring?" he asked, sweat mingling with blood on his split lip. He struggled to his feet, the chains around his ankles clanking hollowly in the sparsely furnished room.

His son, clad in a floral beach shirt and baggy cargo pants, dropped a shiny gold band in his father's trembling hand. A sneer broke across his lips as he studied his father's face.

The old man closed his eyes for a moment and took a deep breath. "I can feel her essence stored in webs of aka on the ring. Here, you feel it." He gave the ring back to his son.

Propping himself against the table, the son clasped his muscular hands around the ring and waited. Soon his foot began tapping against the stone floor and a scowl formed on his face.

"What exactly am I supposed to be feeling, Father?" he said, shooting the old man a look of disdain.

The old man sighed.

"When we touch an object, like this ring, we leave a tiny stream of our energy on it. The aka cord. It's like a spider's web. It sticks to everything we come in contact with."

27

"I already know that," the young man snapped. "Go on."

"In your mind's eye, see if you can sense the aka cord that's attached to the ring. Then transmit your message along its line, like a telegraph wire."

The son closed his eyes but soon lost his concentration.

"I can't do this right now," he said.

From his pants pocket, he took out a notepad and pen and dashed off a note, handing it to his father.

"Here. You do it. Just read it, Father, and send it to her with your mana."

The old man scanned the note and recoiled.

"I can't send this," he gasped. "That's not how we should use the magic. I should know. I learned it the hard way."

"But that's the way I choose to use it. Now say it out loud so that I can learn."

The old man darted his eyes, searching for a way out. "I need more mana, son. You haven't given me much to eat."

Opening a dusty duffel bag, the young man spilled its contents onto a small table. Bread, cheese, oranges, bananas and a roasted chicken brightened the old man's eyes.

"All right, Father, eat and grow stronger, then get to work."

"But I heard a mudhen croaking last night after dark. You know about our superstitions. Mudhens are always a sign of trouble."

The old man crammed fresh bread into his mouth and ripped a leg off the chicken.

"Oh, there's going to be trouble, all right. But not with me and not here. I'm counting on it," the son said with a sneer. "Now quit stalling and get to work!"

Chapter 4

A half hour after leaving Kalani's apartment, Kat arrived home, expecting to feel Caesar rubbing against her legs in his usual way of welcome as soon as she opened the door. Caesar was a black and white cat that she and her son, Sean, had found abandoned in a park six years before. A tiny ball of fur at first, Caesar soon grew into a fine specimen of feline ferocity, protective of his new home and the creatures in it. As far as he was concerned, he owned them, not the other way around. When strangers came over, they were subjected to his instant scrutiny. No one was spared his unpredictable reactions, which ranged from aloofness and snubbing to scratches and biting.

Tonight, however, he was seemingly on guard duty, perched on the back of the sofa, looking alertly out toward the apartment complex pool. His tail snapped in the air like a fly-fishing line.

Kat walked over to him and nuzzled his face, kissing him between his ears and scratching him under the chin.

"Hi, Caesar. How's my attack cat doing today, hmm?" She set him down gently.

Caesar arched his back, getting his claws in position to rip up the sofa, just as Kat scooped him up and carried him into the kitchen.

"Oh, no you don't. We had a deal, my friend. I give you that fowl-smelling cat food you like, and you leave the couch alone."

Caesar blinked languidly at her, not liking their deal one bit and squirming until Kat let him go.

Just then Kat noticed the red blinking light on her message machine. She tapped the play button, hoping it was from Sean confirming he'd be over to help her pack tonight. Instead, it was her dentist's office, reminding her of Saturday's appointment which she had made six months earlier.

When I made that appointment, I didn't know it'd be on moving day, Kat thought. *I'll have to cancel it. Ooh, I'm so excited! Moving into my first house. Caesar will finally have a decent yard to stalk birds in, and I'll finally have my own homegrown flowers. No more ugly marigolds foisted upon me.*

Kat opened the refrigerator door. "Caesar, this is your lucky night. Tuna casserole."

Always the multi-tasker, Kat opened her mail while she ate dinner, watched the evening news and packed her pots and pans. One of the envelopes was an invitation to her thirtieth high school class reunion which was holding its dinner/dance celebration at Jack London Square in Oakland, California, in November.

I wonder if my old boyfriend, Connor O'Sullivan, will show up? Kat thought. *I haven't seen him in twenty-eight years.*

Kat had gone to her ten-year reunion with high hopes of seeing Connor. Although he was a no-show, she'd still had a pretty good time with her old group of girlfriends, quickly falling into their familiar rhythm of teasing and repartee. But her husband, Mark, had gotten drunk at the bar and began hitting on Justine Stewart, her former rival in student government class, which was the final straw for Kat. For too long she had tolerated Mark's late night carousing, but he tried to be discreet and not flaunt it in her face. But, in public, with Justine of all people! It was too much for Kat to take. She made up an excuse to leave early, pushed Mark into their car, and arrived home so incensed, she immediately pulled out the phone book to scan the yellow pages for divorce attorneys. Enough was enough.

But, tonight, as she stared at the new invitation, for some sentimental or insane reason, she wanted to go to this one. Impulsively, she filled in the "Yes, I'm planning to attend" response, wrote out a check for herself and a guest and sealed it.

Now I'm forced to find a date for this, she thought. She looked at Caesar who was preening himself on the sofa. "Too bad you aren't human, Caesar. You'd come in handy right about now."

On her way to the outside mailbox, she saw Sean's black Chevy truck coming up the street.

"Hey, Mom!" Sean shouted, pulling over to stop.

"Hey, favorite son. I was hoping you'd still come by. How'd it go today?" Kat poked her head in to the open passenger window and gave him a kiss.

"Not bad, actually. I got forty-six kids' schedules straightened out, which is a minor miracle in itself," Sean deadpanned.

"Well, meet me at the house, honey. I have to mail this before I chicken out," Kat said, waving the reunion envelope in the air.

When she returned, she and Sean began packing the entire contents of her home office and filling each other in on all the nuances of their first day together at Anthony High School. Kat told him about her confrontation with Gabe over Rudy and how Liana had restored her energy through a *lomi lomi* massage.

"Being around Gabe must really drain me," Kat said, positioning a tape recorder into the packing box.

"Now that you mention it, he does look a lot like Count Dracula, doesn't he?"

As Kat struggled to lift a heavy box of framed photographs, the carton split, spilling them onto the living room carpet. Without saying a word, Sean grabbed the packing tape to reinforce the box while Kat began stacking the frames.

She liked that about him. He'd always been a partner as well as a son to her. If she needed help, she rarely had to ask him. He'd assess the situation and thoughtfully pitch in, no matter what it entailed.

As Kat was combing through the frames, a photo of her wedding day surfaced in her hands. She stared at the lovers in the picture, devotion and hope gleaming in their eyes. With a slow finger, she traced the outline of the bouquet, remembering how the gentle texture of the red roses felt in her hands that day.

Sean saw Kat's eyes mist up and took the photo away, quietly placing it back in the box. He turned toward Kat.

"You're not missing Dad. You're just missing the dream of what this picture represents."

"I know. Your dad apologized—years ago—for all the hurtful things he'd done, and I have long since forgiven him. We're both happier people since our divorce. But, sometimes I miss simple companionship. Especially now that you're on your own. I find myself talking to Caesar all the time like he's my longtime boyfriend." Kat laughed and tapped her forehead, as if to say "What was I thinking?"

With a tilt of his head, Sean grinned back at his mother. "Well, you haven't made it easy for anybody else *but* Caesar to keep you company. Remember Jerry Stranton? The television news anchor you bid on for that charity auction? He really had the hots for you."

"That egomaniac? He practically stalked me for months. I couldn't get rid of him fast enough," Kat said, flipping her bangs out of her eyes.

"And what about that actor who played Romeo in the "Plays in the Park" summer theater? When you congratulated him on his performance after the show, you'd have thought you'd given him an Oscar."

"He was a cutie pie, no doubt about it. But too young for me."

"Mom, you're forty-eight. He was forty. Eight years difference in age is no big deal anymore."

"What about Glen, my country western dance partner? We dated for almost a year."

"Yeah, that was a record for you. Why'd you break up with him?"

"I was an English teacher, honey, remember? He was a one-man language demolition team. After a while, 'I done this' and 'You is so perty' got really old."

"Not to mention embarrassing," Sean added. "The first time I introduced him to Chelsea, he said something clunky like 'Ain't you an all-day lollipop!'"

"Speaking of Chelsea, how are you two doing, anyhow? Let's see. It's been almost three years now. Time for some serious elevation in your relationship, not that I'm rushing you or anything."

Kat blushed, hesitant to break her personal code of minding her own business when it came to Sean's love life.

Sean shot her a wide grin, his eyes sparkling with excitement.

"I gotta tell you, Mom. She's got my heart. She's what I want in my life. Forever."

Kat bolted up and grabbed her son. She squealed with delight, squeezing him so tight, he could hardly breathe.

"I knew it! I knew you'd finally realize she's the one," she gushed.

"Whoa, Mom. I know you're happy for me, but you're breaking my ribs."

Sean pushed her playfully away, then thought better of it and clinched his mother tight once more.

"So, are you two getting engaged any time soon, or are you going to wait until she's out of law school? What about a ring? Have you picked out rings yet? Oh, listen to me! You haven't been able to get a word in edgewise. Okay, I'll shut up. You talk."

Kat cupped her hands over her mouth, gesturing like she was gagged. She sat back expectantly, wriggling with impatience.

Sean good-naturedly came through for her once more, quenching her curiosity and filling her heart and mind with precious details about his love for Chelsea. They talked and taped boxes into the night while Caesar dutifully gobbled Kat's half-eaten dinner that was forgotten in the excitement.

The next two days were a blur for Kat— supervising the cafeteria during lunch, helping the new teachers figure out the intricacies of the copier and scanning machines, and meeting with the student government class to plan for Homecoming Week.

Intermittently, she thought about her upcoming dinner with Liana and Kalani, wondering why she found it all so compelling. And she thought about moving day. Buying her own home had been at the top of her wish list for years. Now, it was a wish fulfilled which gave her considerable peace of mind.

Still, thoughts of Rudy Baker and her conflict with Gabe threatened Kat's hard-won serenity. Was Rudy the type of kid who could benefit from the principal's mentoring and attention? Would he change, or was he hardened by his earlier childhood to the point where no one and nothing could reach him?

If only that cume folder would come in, Kat thought with a shudder. She didn't want to prematurely judge Rudy without supporting evidence, but she couldn't ignore the sinking feeling in her stomach whenever she thought of him.

Later in the week during lunch supervision, she spotted Rudy eating lunch with other students in the middle of the quad. She was glad to see his chip-on-the-shoulder attitude had softened considerably. He'd gotten a haircut, thanks to Gabe, which seemed to lift and lighten him, making him fit in better with the other students. He was a bi-racial kid, inheriting attractive features from his African-American and Korean parents. He was about 5'6"—the same height as Kat—with an athletic body, buffed and toned like a body builder's. Although a pretty brunette had already staked her claim on him, other girls openly flirted with him, brushing back their hair and laughing loudly at his wisecracks.

I'm glad Rudy's happier, Kat thought, *and maybe Gabe's right. Maybe being cared about and accepted will change him. Maybe I should have given him the benefit of the doubt.*

On Friday morning, Kat met with Gabe and Serge for their first administrator's meeting of the semester. They went over a roster of duties that Gabe had drafted to divide the areas of responsibility up among them as equally as possible. They also filled out their respective calendars, selecting the extra-curricular activities that each would supervise over the next few months. At the end of their session, all three got up, stretched, yawned, looked at each other, and laughed.

"I don't know about you, but I'm looking forward to the three-day weekend," admitted Serge.

"Me, too," Kat said, "but not because I'll be resting. I'm moving. To my first house. I'm so excited! Which reminds me. Serge, do you two know of any students who

37

can help me move? I can't pay them much—fifty bucks for the day--but I could sure use some muscle power."

"How about Rudy Baker?" Gabe suggested. "He's got muscles, and I know he needs the money. Trust me, Kat, he's not a bad kid. He's coming around."

"Oh, yeah. Rudy," Kat said with a tight smile.

"Rudy lives with Blaze Amaro, Kat. Blaze could probably help you out, too," Serge added.

"Yeah, well, um," Kat stammered. "I guess I could see if they're available. Thanks, guys."

She walked out of the office, and slowly headed down the hall to her office which was teeming with students.

"Welcome back, Ms. Romero," Mazie said, relief clearly on her face. "We have a few new students here to register. You've got students whose last names begin with A through L, right? That means you'll see five of them."

"Well, send the first one in, Mrs. Longer," Kat replied, rolling her eyes at Mazie as she passed her desk.

"And while you're at it, could you send for Rudy Baker and Blaze Amaro? I need to see them about helping me move this weekend."

Mazie peered over her reading glasses and looked at Kat like she had just grown three heads. She let out a long sigh, reluctantly pulling up the computer screen for student schedules.

Kat noticed the blinking message light on her phone when she entered her office, but since she didn't want to put the students off any longer, she waited until school was out to retrieve her message. It was the voice of Dawn Silva, a Placer County probation officer she'd befriended during her first year as an administrator. Kat had called her earlier to enlist her help in providing more background information about Rudy. She punched the playback button.

"Hi, Kat. This is Dawn returning your call. Got your message and will have to get back to you on Rudy. There's a real shortage of staff here because of the dreaded B word. You know… budget. So I'm swamped. Can't get to it till next week. I'll call you if I find out something. Sorry it can't be any faster. Bye now."

Rats, Kat thought. *I was hoping to solve the riddle of Rudy. I just have a bad feeling about him I can't shake.*

Feeling more conflicted than ever, Kat locked up her office before heading out to supervise the boys varsity soccer match.

Early Saturday morning, Caesar kneaded his claws on Kat's head, waking her up at exactly 6:00 a.m. Good job, Caesar. It's moving day. Kat's eyes flew open. And I have to go pick up Rudy and Blaze.

Throwing back the covers, Kat jumped out of bed, wiggled out of her PJ's and hopped into the shower. She had pre-set the timer on her coffee maker to go off at 6:05 a.m., and it was hot and ready for her as she poured it into her favorite mug.

Kat put on a T-shirt and a wrinkled pair of shorts, then sat on some packing boxes to tie her tennis shoes. She found Caesar sitting on a batch of laundry she had done the night before.

"Caesar, you are such a brat," she scolded.

Caesar jumped out of the laundry basket and scrambled to the kitchen counter that held the electric can opener. He looked up at Kat and meowed non-stop until she opened a can of cat food and spooned it into his dish.

When she was ready, Kat picked Caesar up, grabbed a bag of dry cat food and dropped him off with her landlady, Mrs. Lambert, who'd agreed to watch him until the next day. Then she drove over to the nearest Krispy Kreme and bought a dozen assorted doughnuts, snatching a chocolate cruller up first, with the absolute certainty that the rest would be wolfed down by the two bottomless pits—in the guise of teenagers—that she'd soon be picking up.

She had familiarized herself with the directions Rudy had written down for her and pulled into his driveway fifteen minutes later. She could see him at the front window as he pulled the curtain aside to look for her.

The house was a duplex. Don Bass and the boys occupied the right side of it. The front yard was filled with brown and yellow splotches of grass, apparently watered mainly by dogs instead of sprinklers. A chewed-up hose, set too close to the sidewalk, managed to dribble water only onto the curb, which explained the sorry condition of the lawn.

Rudy opened the front door. "She's here," he yelled to Blaze. He descended the steps with studied deliberateness, pulling his sagging jeans up to avoid tripping.

"Hi, Ms. Romero," Rudy mumbled as he climbed in the back seat of her Camry.

40

"Hi, Rudy," Kat answered with a deliberate show of warmth. "Your directions were great. I had no problem finding this place."

"Good. Well, uh, Blaze should be here in a sec." Rudy forced a smile, picking up on her friendliness and showing a little of his own.

"It's going to be hot today," Kat said. "Like ninety-eight in the shade. Don't you think you'd be more comfortable in a pair of shorts?" She looked at Rudy in the rear view mirror.

"Never wear 'em," Rudy replied, looking cagily out the side window.

"Oh. Well, I have lots of cold drinks on ice for you two. That'll help keep you cool today."

Just then, to Kat's relief—Rudy still made her a bit nervous—Blaze came running down the stairs and opened the passenger door.

"Hi, Ms. Romero. Sorry I'm late. Had to tell Dad where we were going. He's sleeping in today. Like I wish I was doing," he said, stifling a yawn with his fist.

"I know what you mean," Kat sympathized, trying to stop her own yawn from surfacing.

"Hey, I really appreciate you guys helping me out today," she said. "There's a box of doughnuts in the back to jumpstart you two. It's going to be a long day."

By the time she got to the first freeway on-ramp, two lonely doughnuts rattled around in the box in the back seat.

When she pulled up to her apartment complex, Kat could see her son, Sean, and his girlfriend, Chelsea Scott, waiting in the parking lot in a big U-Haul van.

41

"What's he doing here?" Rudy demanded. "Isn't he a counselor from school?"

"Yes, he is, but he's also a friend of mine. He volunteered to help me move. That's his girlfriend Chelsea."

"Oh," Rudy said, relaxing his tone of voice. "I thought maybe he was spying on me."

Whatever for? Kat thought as she got out of the car with the boys. Her stomach did a sudden flip as doubts about Rudy began to surface once more. She was glad Sean had alerted Chelsea to keep his relationship to Kat a secret from anyone at school. *No sense in making Rudy privy to any bigger part of my life. It's bad enough he'll know where I live.*

Kat assembled the group together in the living room and handed out copies of a blue print of her new house, with all of its rooms colored in to match the colorful adhesive stripes she had put on the packed boxes.

"Okay, team, listen up. Here's a layout of the new house. All the boxes are color coded, so you'll know which rooms they go in by following this map. Let's start by moving everything out of the front of this place first, so it can be stacked in the back of the van. That way, everything from the back rooms will leave the van first, and we'll be able to fill up the back rooms of the new house without tripping over boxes in the front half. Dollies are in the van to move the heavy furniture, and I have gloves if anybody needs them. Any questions?"

"Yeah," Sean whined in a playful voice. "Are we there yet?"

Kat smacked him on the shoulder, while everybody else grinned and chuckled. Then, they all went to work.

At noon, Kat went out to the closest fast food restaurant and brought back an assortment of hamburgers, chicken nuggets, fishburgers, fries, and drinks. As she walked in the house, the aroma followed her to the kitchen, making everyone drop what they doing and dug in to eat. Everyone except Rudy.

Kat looked around the house and found him in the back of her walk-in bedroom closet. He was kneeling in front of a four-foot, oak, jewelry chest and had a deer-in-the-headlight look which Kat attributed to embarrassment at being caught struggling with her heavy furniture.

"Oh, there you are, Rudy. Your lunch is here," Kat said. Just then, a gleam of gold caught her eye. Kat's sapphire and diamond necklace—her only piece of expensive jewelry—lay on top of the chest.

"What's my jewelry doing out like this?" Kat puzzled aloud. She eyed Rudy dubiously, but he maintained a look of innocence, and she good-naturedly dismissed her suspicions.

"I must have forgotten to put it away," she said. She snapped up the necklace and stuffed it in her pocket.

"Need some help with that?"

"No, thanks. I got it," Rudy replied, beads of sweat running down his forehead.

Like a weight-lifter at an Olympic try-out, Rudy bent his knees, wrapped his arms around the bulky chest and lifted it cleanly. Kat watched him wrestle it to the moving van, his taut muscles rippling and bulging through his thin t-shirt. *No wonder the girls like him,* Kat thought.

At Pete's Pizzeria later that night, the tired moving crew eased their sore limbs into a large booth and ordered four different kinds of pizza. Everyone was dusty, exhausted and very glad the ordeal of moving was over.

After the waitress brought their drink orders, Sean started showing them the scrapes and bruises he'd acquired during the move. The conversation quickly escalated into a fest of bragging rights, as each person showed off their gouged elbows and scraped knuckles. By the time the food arrived, the table talk had escalated into one-upsmanship over who had the most injuries from prior exploits.

"How'd you get that scar by your right eye, Mr. Matthews?" Blaze asked, squinting at Sean from across the table.

Blaze needs glasses, Kat thought.

"I got it when I was two. Playing in the backyard. I pushed one of those two-sided swings and turned around just in time for it to bash me in the eye. Got two stitches and a black eye that day. And a lesson in physics. Of course, I usually tell people I got it from my days as a pro wrestler on the circuit with Steve Austin. That's the version I want you guys to pass around at school, okay?"

"You got it, Mr. C.," Blaze said. "Hey Rudy, show 'em your bullet hole."

All eyes shifted to Rudy.

Bullet hole? The hair on the back of Kat's neck stood up.

Rudy grinned. "Oh, yeah. Here. Let me show you guys." He stood up and planted his left foot on his chair, then rolled up his pant leg to expose his thigh. A purple

44

blotch, the size of a quarter, presented itself, to Rudy's immense pride and everyone else's amazement.

"How'd you get that, Rudy?" Kat asked, her throat tight with dread.

"I used to be in a gang in L.A. Me and my homies got ambushed one night in a drive-by. Got another hole in my butt, but you're just going have to take my word on that one." Rudy laughed and looked around to see if everyone had gotten the joke.

"Was anybody else hurt in this drive-by?" Sean asked, not seeing the humor in Rudy's anecdote.

"Nope, just me. There was a bunch of us standing outside of a house where a party was going on, but it was just me that got hit," Rudy said. He sat back down and adjusted his pant leg.

"Wow, you're lucky to be alive, Rudy," Chelsea blurted, aghast at Rudy's cavalier attitude about his injuries.

"Yeah, I know. But, I did get even," Rudy admitted, thrusting his chin out, his lips twisted in a sadistic smirk.

Sean leaned forward in curiosity and asked, "And how, exactly, did you do that, Rudy?"

Rudy surveyed the group one by one and started to say something, thought better of it, then finally answered.

"I turned 'em in to the cops," he said with a forced grin. "Got 'em busted. What else?"

"Good for you, Rudy," Chelsea said.

"Yeah," Kat chimed in. "It takes a big person not to want to give them a dose of their own medicine."

Rudy looked at Kat quizzically, but said nothing, and the conversation soon turned to the latest Mel Gibson movie which showcased similar gore.

Thirty minutes later, pizza devoured and stories all told, Kat called it a night and thanked them all for their help. She handed sealed envelopes of cash to Rudy and Blaze whom Sean and Chelsea offered to drive home. Kat dragged herself to her car, eyelids at half-mast, and called Mrs. Lambert from her cell phone to check on Caesar. Then she headed for home. Her own new home.

As she walked in the door and surveyed the mountain of boxes and thought of all the work still ahead, she realized that the best part of the day had not been the move at all.

She had come to know a side of Rudy she had not known, and her admiration for Gabe had grown as well.

Truly, it was a victorious day.

Chapter 5

The old Hawaiian pulled himself up from his filthy blanket and stood by his son who dumped beef jerky, walnuts, an assortment of fruits and a gallon of water onto a small table. Dust billowed up from the impact, filtering the dingy room with a yellow haze.

The son eyed his father up and down. "After you eat, I want you to show me how to materialize objects from one place to another," he said, a malevolent grin spreading across his face.

"What day is this?" the old man asked, hungrily stuffing chunks of pineapple into his mouth.

"It's the 30th. Why?"

"*Muku*. Means cut off. Not a good day to send a prayer."

"But then it's not a good prayer, now is it?" Hukui replied with a laugh which echoed eerily off the crumbling walls of stone.

The old man gulped water from the plastic jug, washing down the barely chewed food that stuck in his parched throat. "You're determined to do this, aren't you, son?"

"We've been through all this before," the son said wearily. "It's my destiny as the son of a kahuna. I will not be denied." He peered out of the grimy window at the sugar cane blotting out the sun which was now peeking over the horizon.

"But I am not a *kahuna nui* or a *kahuna po'o*," the old man insisted.

"I know you're not an expert in everything, father. But you are a *kahuna pule* and a *kahuna ho'opi'opi'po*. You're an expert on prayer and in causing sickness and distress."

"But it took forty years for me to master these things."

"Well, I don't have forty years to learn, and you don't have forty years left to live, so you'll have to find a way to shorten my learning curve."

The old man could not see his son through the tears that filled his eyes. "Hukui, I don't understand why you have such hatred in your heart," he said, sobbing openly. "What happened to the sweet boy I once knew?"

Good question, Hukui thought. Through an open window, he looked out at the crumbling wall of the ancient temple. Faded flowers drooped over the stones which served as a backdrop upon which layered images of his troubled childhood seemed to surface. His eyes narrowed as the memories, fresh and hurtful, burst upon his consciousness.

He was ten years old, listening to his father, Kahili, chanting secret Hawaiian prayers inside his private office. Locked out, always locked out, Hukui strained to catch a word or phrase of the ancient magic which his father practiced. Kahili's powers as a kahuna were well-known in the Hawaiian community, and seldom did a day pass when there were no visitors seeking his help. Sometimes Kahili would scold Hukui for listening outside his door. More often than not, he pushed him aside or insisted that he go outside and play.

Going outside, though, felt tantamount to a death sentence to Hukui. The neighborhood bullies targeted him as an easy mark. In their eyes, he was a skinny, sniveling loser with no redeeming social values. So what if his father was a kahuna? Kahili never once chewed them out for teasing Hukui. Or for throwing rocks at him. Or for ambushing him after school and beating him up. If Kahili didn't care what happened to Hukui, why should they?

In his early teens, Hukui got even with the bullies by lifting weights every day. Once he developed some muscles and filled out, his confidence grew proportionately. Soon, all it took was one punch to flatten his enemies whose numbers dwindled with each passing day. He liked how he looked and how the girls eyed him approvingly. Eventually, he got interested in showing off his body at diving competitions, taking top honors in the local, county and state meets.

As much as he begged him, though, Hukui couldn't get his father to come to see him dive. Kahili always begged off, telling him other matters were too pressing, but Hukui knew the real reason. His father didn't love him. His mother had, but she had died when Hukui was small. He desperately wanted his father's love, and, when it wasn't forthcoming, Kahili's indifference grated on him. He would look at himself in the bathroom mirror, studying himself from every angle. He liked what he saw. Why didn't his dad? *I'm really here,* he'd say to himself. *I exist. I live. I'm not invisible. Why doesn't he see me? I'm the only son of a kahuna. Why won't he teach me the ancient secrets?*

Hukui blinked his eyes and came back to the present. He fought back the angry tears that threatened to fall. "What happened to the sweet boy you once knew?" he snapped. "Still standing by your locked office door. Still looking for you after school to save me from a beating. Still waiting at the pool to see you in the stands. There is no sweet boy anymore. You killed him a long time ago!"

Hukui's hands flew up to his father's neck, but he caught himself before his emotions could get away from him. He released the old man with a sudden shove. "If you value your life, you'll give me what has been denied me all my life. I will be the greatest kahuna in the world."

The old man massaged his aching throat and nodded his head. "Then there are others you must learn from. *Kahuna ha ha, kahuna la'au lapa'au,* and *kahuna nana uli.* They specialize in powers I don't have." The old man rubbed his sunken eyes.

"In time, I'll go to them. But first let's start with this small step."

"This is not a small step, son. You're asking me to commit murder. "

Hukui's eyes gleamed in the dark. "Oh, like you've never done that before. Our heiau at home was right next to my bedroom, remember? Many nights when you thought I was asleep, I listened to you, father. I know what you're capable of."

"You don't understand. I'm not like that. I never...."

"Shut up! How dare you deny you've never killed anyone. I know you!"

Outraged, Hukui grabbed his father by the shirt and hoisted him off the floor.

"I could snap you like a twig, you filthy liar, but you're worth more to me alive than dead. For now."

The old Hawaiian winced, then bowed his head, his body sagging in surrender.

"All right," he sighed, "you win." *For now*, he thought.

Chapter 6

Kat arrived at Kalani's door at precisely six o'clock on Monday evening. The aroma of freshly baked bread greeted her as she stepped into the living room. Hawaiian music played softly in the background. Liana, dressed in a muu muu swarming with plumeria, had her long salt and pepper hair tied back in a bright purple scarf. She held out both arms to Kat, and they embraced like long-lost friends. Kalani slipped a pink carnation lei over Kat's neck.

"In honor of the occasion, Ms. R. I made this for you."

"Ooh, beautiful." Kat fingered the flowers draping her shoulders. "*Mahalo*, Kalani. This is so sweet of both of you."

"The pleasure is ours. We thought we'd eat right away if that's all right with you."

"Are you kidding? I've been looking forward to this all week."

Kat sat at the dining table, now adorned with velvety gladiolus crammed in a cobalt blue vase and positioned off-center so that Kat could see her hosts without obstruction. Three tiny flames, dancing from candles floating in a deep, crystal bowl, illuminated the cozy scene.

Kat smelled the succulent pork roast before Kalani brought it to the table. While Kalani went back to the kitchen for the sweet potatoes, Liana returned to the dining room, carefully balancing a hot dish of seasoned wild rice in one hand and a tossed green salad loaded with mandarin oranges and macadamia nuts in the other. A pineapple upside-down cake topped off the feast.

While they ate, Kat pointed to the imposing portrait of King Kamehameha and the portraits surrounding it. "Are those your family members, Liana?" she asked.

Liana laughed. "Not King Kamehameha that I know of, but, yes, the others are my ancestors. My great-grandfather on the upper right was a kahuna."

"Weren't the kahuna like native sorcerers or something? I remember reading something about them having magical powers," Kat said.

"We considered them more like masters in the ancient Hawaiian mystic arts," Liana explained.

"Kahuna are really cool, Ms. R.," Kalani said. "They could walk on hot lava and not get burned. Before it was outlawed in the 1900's, they did it all the time. First they'd throw heavy stones on the lava to test if it had cooled enough to hold their weight. Then, they'd wrap ti leaves around their feet, say a prayer to Pele, the goddess of volcanoes, and they were good to go." She beamed, happy to explain her family history to her former teacher.

"Wow, that *is* cool, kiddo. But weren't they also able to heal illness and disease?"

Liana smiled. "You *do* know about kahuna, Kat. Yes, their prayers carried a special power that could heal a fractured ankle instantly, make a cancerous tumor shrink and disappear, even cure insanity and other mental illnesses. And some kahuna had the power to pray a person to death—much like voodoo."

53

Kat sat spellbound, listening as if she were in a trance. She could picture the black, jagged cliffs of hardened lava, the turquoise waves pounding in the surf, the drums beating as the kahuna chanted their prayers to Pele. She finally surfaced enough to ask a question.

"Why were their prayers so powerful? How did they get them to work?"

"Because they were taught the secret way for a prayer to get through to God. Once God hears a prayer, it is always answered."

"But Huna's no longer a secret, Ms. R.," Kalani said. "A man named Max Freedom Long who lived in Hawaii in the 1930's researched the kahuna magic and told the world what he'd found in a series of books he wrote. He's the one who called it Huna which is the Hawaiian word for 'secret.'"

"But we've never called it that. To us, it's just our way of life." Liana poured iced tea from a silver pitcher and passed a glass over to Kat.

Kat acknowledged the tea with a quick smile. "The kahuna sound like miracle workers, but you say they learned the magic, so who taught them?"

"The secret way was passed down word of mouth from parent to child or adopted child to the select few who were chosen to use it. It was never written down."

"And your great-grandfather was a kahuna?"

"Yes, he was, although he would never publicly admit it. A few years after the Christian missionaries arrived in Hawaii, they outlawed all kahuna practices, saying it was a type of sorcery. Anyone even claiming to be a kahuna could be fined up to a thousand dollars and sent to prison for a year."

"Wow, the missionaries must have really been intimidated by them." Kat helped herself to more salad.

"Being a kahuna is no longer a crime," Liana added, "but you could see how over the years people were more and more reluctant to practice openly. So they went underground."

I wonder how many are left, Kat thought.

"It's believed there are only about twenty or twenty-five genuine kahuna left in Hawaii today," Liana said. "Outside of Hawaii they're rare and very much concealed."

Suddenly, Kat felt thunderstruck. "I was just wondering how many were left, and it's like you read my mind. *You're* a kahuna, aren't you, Liana? Your great-grandfather passed the knowledge on to you, right?"

Liani and Kalani laughed at Kat's sudden outburst.

Kat blushed self-consciously and grinned back at them, but she was eager to know more. "Tell me about your great-grandfather, Liana. What kinds of things did he teach you?"

"Well, for one thing, when I was five years old, he showed me how to put energy into a stick and float it across a creek through the air."

"No way."

"Yes, way," Kalani piped up. "I've seen Grandma do it."

Kat's mouth gaped as she studied both women in astonishment.

"And he taught me the energy shield technique that I'm going to teach you tonight," Liana said.

"I've got so many questions to ask you, Liana. You know, Huna sounds like magic, but if it can be taught and duplicated, then it's more like a science, isn't it? Are the Hawaiians the only people to practice it? How long has it been going on, anyway?" Kat felt like she couldn't spit out her thoughts fast enough, her mind toggling between incredulity and fascination.

"It's been around for a long time in various parts of the world," Liana answered patiently. "The particular magic that the kahuna practiced is based on the belief that there is energy all around us. In the air. In food. The energy, or mana as we call it, can be stored internally in the body or externally in objects for future use. When they need it, the kahuna are able to use mana to create any desired outcome."

"Why does it need to be stored up?"

"Think of it like the chemicals you need to develop a Polaroid picture, Ms. R.," Kalani explained. "If you have enough of the right kind of chemicals, you're going to have a beautiful, clear photo, right? Well, in order for your prayers or mind-pictures to become real, lots of energy is needed to bring about what you envisioned or asked for."

Kat shook her head in amazement. "So they pictured what they wanted and sent energy out to make it happen, right?"

"Pretty much," Liana agreed. "During times of war in ancient Hawaii, the kahuna chief would gather people on the steps of the temple and breathe in the mana. He or she—yes, Kat, there were women kahuna called *kahuna wahine*—would get emotionally worked up, breathing deeply, all the while holding a mental picture of energy flowing up through them like a water fountain. Once they had enough energy, they'd transfer it into heavy sticks or clubs which they would throw during skirmishes."

"Wham, you're knocked out!" Kalani erupted, supplying the audio to Kat's mental video. She glanced over to the portrait of King Kamehameha as if he could verify everything they'd been saying was true.

"Sounds like a form of electrocution," Kat muttered.

"The energy does act like electricity in a way," Liana answered.

"Actually, it reminds me of Luke Skywalker in *Star Wars* and how he learned to tap into the force," Kat said, laughing. "Except in that movie, the Jedi Knights were the group selected to learn how to access the energy which could be used for either good or evil. Is that why the kahuna have been so secret and selective? To protect the knowledge from getting in the hands of people who could use it in evil ways?"

"Right on, Ms. R.," Kalani said, delighted that her favorite teacher was catching on so fast.

"The kahuna were supposed to use Huna magic only for good. To improve someone's situation. Make life better for them," Liana said. "So they tried to pass it on only to those who would use it for good."

"Oh, come on," Kat said, eyes wide and searching. "There've got to be some evil ones loose in the world."

Liana and Kalani glanced at each other knowingly. "Yes, there have been times when the knowledge has

57

gotten into the wrong hands," Liana agreed softly. "And, believe me, it can be used for destruction and evil. But most of the time the kahuna have been very careful who they pick to share the secret with."

Kalani quickly changed the subject. "The Huna motto is: Hurt no one. The kahuna believed that something was a sin only if it hurt another human being. If it didn't hurt someone, it wasn't a sin."

"And they didn't believe in sins against God, either, Kat," Liana said, piggybacking on the sin concept. "They thought that God was too far above in the hierarchy of things to ever be hurt by something we mere humans could say or do."

Kat's face registered astonishment, then glee. "So using the Lord's name in vain is really not a sin because we can't hurt God, right?"

"Right. The kahuna also don't believe in original sin."

"Really?" Kat shook her head as if trying to clear a sudden fog that had seeped into her brain. "This is all so mind-boggling."

Liana reached over to rearrange the gladiolas and studied Kat's face to see if she had more questions. She did.

"But you said earlier that a kahuna could pray someone to death. That's not exactly living up to the "Hurt no one" motto, now, is it?"

Liana smiled grimly. "The death prayer, the 'ana'ana, was only used if the kahuna was convinced that someone deserved it."

"That's a scary thought," Kat said. "All it'd take would be some type of sleaze bag with the gift of gab or a lot of cash to talk a kahuna into it and, bam, somebody gets snuffed out." She looked off in the distance, her own version of this drama playing in her head.

Liana pushed herself away from the table. "Enough history for now. Time for your first lesson in Huna. Let's go sit in more comfortable chairs, shall we?"

Kat started to pick up her dishes to carry them to the sink, but Kalani stopped her.

"No, Ms. R., let me do that. You go with grandma," she said smiling mysteriously.

"Come sit with me, Kat," Liana said, walking back into the living room. She put her tumbler of iced tea on a small side table and patted the small brown sofa, fluffing up one of the back pillows for Kat.

"Before we begin the lesson on energy shields," Liana said softly, "I need to explain a little more about the Huna way of seeing things. While it may seem magical, it's not. Just like magic isn't really magic, either, if you know what I mean. Huna is a system that views human beings as having three distinct souls or selves in one physical body."

Liana scrutinized Kat cautiously, looking for skepticism, but seeing none, continued. "The three souls or selves are called the low self, the middle self, and the High Self. The low and middle selves live in the physical body, and the High Self hovers above it. Together, they run the human being."

"It's like having three motors which operate one vehicle, right?" Kat asked.

Liana nodded. "Very much like that. Now, the low self is thought to reside in the solar plexus of the body. That's why it's called "low" because that's its location in the body. The other selves reside above it. It's the seat of all emotions and memory and relies on the middle self for knowledge and direction. Like a puppy relies on its master. It wants to please the middle self, but it's its own person. It has its own likes and dislikes. And it's very stubborn. Once it decides upon something, it's difficult to get it to change its mind."

"Like Caesar, my cat." Kat stretched her legs out in front of her, crossing them at the ankles, to make herself comfortable.

"Uh huh," Liana agreed. "Now the middle self, the conscious mind, is thought to reside in a person's head and uses the brain to think. It's the logical, linear thinking part of a human."

Kat sat up. "Oh, I get it. If the middle self is the conscious mind, then the low self must be what we call the subconscious mind."

"Precisely. The low and middle selves work together as a team. The middle self uses all of its senses to send messages to the low self—everything it experiences, sees, touches, says, hears and so on. Then, in turn, the low self stores all these messages, grouping them together in similar meanings to be recalled later as memories."

"Sounds like the clustering technique I used with Kalani to help write her paper the other day," Kat said excitedly. "We brainstormed different random ideas. One thought led to another, and pretty soon we had tons of information that we then gave some rational order to."

"Correct. When you were working with Kalani, she used her low self to help her remember details and incidents about her life, then she used her middle self to put these facts and examples into a sensible order. That's a perfect example of how the low and middle selves work together."

Liana beamed at Kat like she had just discovered the most beautiful rose in her garden and continued. "Okay, now let me explain the High Self. Which by the way Mr. Long called the *Aumakua* and...."

"What are the Hawaiian names he used for the low and middle selves?" Kat interrupted, hoping Liana would overlook her impetuosity.

"The low self is called the *unihipili*. Oo nee hee pee lee." Liana slowly sounded out the word.

"Unihipili," echoed Kat.

"And the middle self is pronounced oo ha nay."

"Uhane."

"Very good. Back to the High Self, the Aumakua. This word translates as the 'utterly trustworthy parental pair.' The kahuna believed that the High Self, or superconscious mind, was composed of both masculine and feminine sides. The Aumakua acted like a pair of loving parents or what we like to think of as guardian angels, watching over the human being. If we need intervention like physical healing or financial help, it's the Aumakua, the High Self, who could then go to the Supreme Being or God to ask for the change to happen."

Kat mulled over the information ricocheting in her brain.

"The three selves, then, work together to make a person's life work well. They talk to one another, right? Well, the big secret that the kahuna knew was...," Liana said, gazing intensely into Kat's saucer-eyes, "they knew how the selves communicated with each other to get a prayer answered. It involved a transfer of energy."

"Okay, now you've lost me," Kat admitted.

"When you ask for something in prayer, your middle self comes up with the idea and the words, you see. But the big secret is that the low self delivers the prayer as a picture of what you want and gives the High Self energy to make it happen."

"You mean it's the subconscious mind that sends the prayer through, along with the energy the High Self needs to fulfill it? That's the ultimate secret?"

Kat sank back in the sofa, as if absorbing a punch from an invisible heavyweight boxer.

"That's the secret, Kat. The three selves comprise a unique relay system, when you think about it. Think of a human being like a house with three levels. One floor, below ground, is a basement with no windows where the low self lives. There's a phone line from the basement to the floor above. This floor is on ground level, and it's where the middle self lives. The middle self can see out, although the view is blocked by doors and windows, and it phones down to the low self in the basement and communicates all that it experiences. The low self is like a computer, storing all the information it receives for future use. Emotions and images get filed together with related subjects. Are you with me so far?"

"So far, yes." Kat's quick mind was tracking pretty well, but she was still blown away by the newness of it all.

"Okay. Now the third level of the house is an attic made completely of glass. The High Self resides there and can see everything clearly. Unlike the middle self, there are no obstacles to block its view. This attic has a phone line, too, but the line only goes through to the low self in the basement. In other words, the middle self is not the part of the person that ultimately speaks to the divine. It's the low self that has the final word with the High Self during a prayer request."

"Well, that explains why most of my prayers never got answered," Kat muttered. "I used to be a Catholic. All those rosaries and litanies—all coming from my middle self and certainly not with any emotion."

Liana smiled serenely. "Well, the kahuna would say you were praying without breath. Do you know the word that Hawaiians use to describe the white man?"

"Yes. Kalani told me they call us *haoles*."

"That's right. Haole. The word *ha* means breath. *Ole* means without. When you put them together, it means 'without breath'—which is how the Hawaiians thought the missionaries prayed. They prayed with their middle selves, their logical, conscience minds, thinking that that was how a prayer got heard. But the kahuna prayed by gathering lots of breath and getting very emotional. They prayed with their low selves. They stored up energy by breathing hard and created pictures and words in their minds so that the low self could send them on to the High Self. I hope you won't act like a haole next time you pray," Liana teased.

63

"Me, too."

"The most important thing to remember, Kat, is that the low self only talks to the High Self when it feels worthy. If it feels any shame or guilt for having done something wrong, it won't speak to the High Self on behalf of the middle self."

"Why wouldn't it feel worthy?"

"Think back on your own childhood. Think of all the things that your parents and teachers told you were sins when you were growing up."

"Oh, wow, all kinds of things. Everything in the Ten Commandments, you know, the standard stuff. No lying, cheating, stealing, killing. In school we were told not to hit each other, cuss or smoke. That type of thing."

Liana leaned forward, touching Kat's hand. "What else? Think back," she prodded.

"Hmm. What else was I told was bad to do? Most definitely alcohol. Oh, and sex. My parents always preached to me about how it was wrong to consume alcohol until you were of age, and how sex was wrong unless you were married."

"Right. I've even heard people say that dancing is sinful or that eating chocolate is bad for you."

"You mean it isn't?" Kat shot Liana a look of mock dismay.

Liana laughed. "Apply the Huna motto. Only if it hurts someone." She drained off the last of her iced tea.

"All right," she said, snuggling into the sofa. "Back to your low self. Some of the things it was told were sinful to do, you have done anyway as an adult. Let's say you consume alcohol, use profanity, and have sex even though you were not married. Naturally your low self, which takes every rule literally, is going to feel ashamed whenever you do these things. Remember how stubborn it is. It hangs on to whatever it was once told like a dog gloms onto a bone."

"That's so true, Liana," Kat said. "Just the other day I was thinking about what a fool I was during the years right after I divorced my husband, Mark." Kat's voice lowered hoping Kalani wouldn't hear this self-confession. "I was so angry at him for rejecting me that I threw myself at any man who looked half-way interested. Just for the ego-boost. When I finally realized how much I'd been on "self-destruct," I was so ashamed of myself. I vowed to stop tripping and turn my life around. Now I'm very cautious about whom I let into my life, but I still regret all those years of self-loathing."

Kat wrung her hands and looked away for a moment. "And I don't know how to stop feeling so guilty about it. It's such a hard tape to erase."

"It is." Liana's voice was soothing and reassuring. "Because these tapes become guilt complexes that are secretly harbored by the low self. Just think of all the many complexes that can build up in someone's lifetime."

"I know I have a ton of complexes, Liana. Besides the big things, I still feel guilty about lots of little things, like eating chocolate, or not wanting to visit my mother because I can't stand to see how Alzheimer's has destroyed her, or cussing out God for short-changing human beings in intelligence. These are all middle self choices that somehow my low self feels bad about it because it's been told they're sins, right?"

"Exactly. Now, if we know that only the low self can send a prayer up to the High Self, and it's filled with guilt and complexes, what are the chances that it's going to want to show its little face, so to speak, to the big Aumakua and deliver a message?"

"Like a snowball's chance in hell," Kat quipped.

"So, the only way to make the low self feel worthy enough to talk to the High Self is to get rid of the guilt complexes and sins. How do you let go of all that guilt, especially if you have intentionally hurt someone, which is the only sin the kahuna acknowledge?"

"Personally, I would try to forgive myself and make amends in some way." Kat sank back comfortably into the sofa's soft pillows.

"Right. You forgive yourself and you forgive others, and you determine to get back on the right path. Sometimes you do good deeds to make up for the things you are ashamed of. You'll make a donation to charity or volunteer some time in a shelter. You do whatever it takes for the low self to feel good about itself again so it will send the prayer through to the High Self. It's like untangling a knot in a phone extension cord to improve communication."

Liana wiped the beads of perspiration breaking out on her forehead as she talked excitedly to Kat. "Basically, that's how the kahuna got their prayers heard. Before they asked the High Self for something, they performed rituals and chants to convince the low self that its sins had been forgiven. Now, it turns out that the low self needs physical stimulation, not just words. Think about the sacraments like baptism. Water is poured on the forehead so the low

66

self can feel the sensation of being cleansed while the priest or minister recites special words to impress it as well."

"I get it," Kat said, bolting up again. "The water and the words work together to persuade the low self into believing that the sin is literally and figuratively washed away."

"Mind-boggling, isn't it, Ms. R.?" Kalani observed, coming in to curl at her grandmother's feet.

"And then some, Kalani." Kat shook her head. The fog still hadn't quite dissipated from her mind. "But the kahuna perspective on things puts everything into focus for me. It explains what I've been trying to understand all my life."

"Sorry to interrupt. Where were you, Grandma?" Kalani asked.

Liana stroked Kalani's hair and smiled. "We were talking about how the subconscious mind needs physical stimulation when you're trying to get its attention. Like in baptism. It needs to physically feel the water as the middle self talks about its sins being washed away."

Liana looked at Kat intently. "That's why it's best to create your energy shield in the shower, Kat. The ritual involves cleansing the energy around you of all negativity and washing it away. The low self will respond better if you can help it visualize all the bad vibes going down the drain, while, at the same time, you're actually watching water go down the drain. It's simple, really," Liana said, as Kat rolled her eyes.

"It's really easy, Ms. R.," Kalani coaxed gently. "I've been doing this since I was seven."

The next hour sped by as Liana and Kalani taught Kat how to rid her aura of any negativity she might have accrued and install a protective shield around her. She envisioned aka cords all around her, like a fishing net, bogging her down. She imagined herself pulling the webs off of her body, casting them down on the ground, to be absorbed into the earth. Then she breathed in air, feeling her lungs expand and contract, aware of the added energy or mana she was pulling into her body. She pictured white light all around her, going in and through her. This beacon of light created the shield she needed to protect her from evil and negativity that might come her way. She felt safe, uplifted, and sacred—all at the same time.

Later that night, on the way home, Kat pulled into a Shell gas station. Leaning dreamily on the car while gasoline gushed into the tank, she replayed scenes from the evening, going over every word until she was satisfied she'd locked them in her memory banks forever.

Kat recalled the faces of Liana and Kalani, so animated and open. *What a chance they took, opening up to me like that. I mean, I'm practically a stranger, and they're telling me age-old secrets. Which I guess aren't secret anymore. Why me? What if I thought they were Loony Tunes? What if I'd pooh-poohed it all?*

They knew! Somehow they knew I would accept them. But how did they know? The kahuna were great psychologists with a few insiders' tricks up their sleeves. And if what they do can be duplicated, if anyone can be taught to get the same results, then their system works. How else can you explain fire-

walking and floating sticks? Still it's gotta be hard to do or everyone would be doing it.

Something's going on here. Something that I've got to know more about. It's almost as if my life depends on it. Silly. I've only been connected to this stuff for a few hours, and yet I feel as if I've been preparing for it all my life. I mean, I know I can't be a kahuna like Liana or Kalani. But I feel bound to them in some way I can't explain. I just know it.

Just then the lights from the gas station went off, allowing Kat to take in the spectacular canopy of stars that filled the night sky.

"What exactly are you trying to tell me?" she asked.

When the stars didn't answer, she got back in her car and drove home with an unfamiliar, smoldering fire in her heart.

Chapter 7

It was already a muggy sixty-five degrees at seven-fifteen a.m. when Kat pulled up to her marked space in the faculty parking lot on Tuesday morning. She secured her sun reflector against the windshield and rolled each car window down an inch for ventilation.

Andrea Chan pulled into an adjacent stall and waved at Kat. As the school district's sole nurse, Andrea had to really stretch her time to cover six schools. To get the job done right, she put herself on a fast-paced schedule and set her body on double-time. She talked fast, thought fast and generally sped around like a jackrabbit.

"Hey, Andrea, you're supposed to visit us on Wednesdays. What brings you here a day ahead of schedule?" Kat asked, grinning at her friend.

"Gas leak." Andrea smiled back, her unruly curly hair springing out from a crumbled sun hat she wore.

"Nothing serious, I hope."

Andrea smirked and shook her head. "Got an email from Dan Hargrove, one of your science teachers. Says he can smell natural gas leaking in the classroom. Gotta check it out. Want to come with me?"

Andrea and Kat hurried to Hargrove's classroom, hoping to beat the bell before class began. The distinct odor of natural gas hit them as soon as they entered. Hargrove was hunched in front of his computer, typing up a storm, and didn't notice either of them come and go. Kat suggested a visit to the building contractor might be in order.

At Andrea's usual fast pace, the two women headed toward the back of the campus where the construction crews were headquartered. On the way, Kat picked Andrea's brain on gossip from the district office where Andrea had a cubicle. Andrea loved gossip, just as much as Denise did, but on the scale of importance, Andrea's was considered much more valuable since it involved the elusive central administrative staff. She had dirt on everyone from the superintendent who was a closet alcoholic, to the substitute file clerk who was having an affair with the married night custodian. No one in the district office escaped her wagging tongue.

"What do you know about this construction company?" Kat asked.

"Not much. Except that your principal, Gabe, was gung-ho for the district to contract with them," Andrea replied.

Kat and Andrea bounded up the steps two at a time to the small, white portable which served as the headquarters for the construction company. Owen Snelson, the general contractor, was going over blueprints with Wes Holden, the owner of the company which had secured the contract to install the new pool at Anthony High. After introductions, Holden snapped up his plans, excused himself and scooted out the door. Then Andrea told Snelson about the smell of natural gas in Hargrove's classroom.

"This is the first I've heard of a possible gas leak, Andrea," Snelson said, "but I'll send someone to check it out. Want me to call you or Kat?"

"You can call me," Kat said. "Andrea's not on campus every day, and it'll be easier for me to follow up with Hargrove." She handed him her business card on the way out.

Back in her office, Kat emailed Hargrove to tell him about Snelson's promise to investigate his complaint. The phone rang a minute later. It was Dawn Silva finally getting back to her.

"Hi, Kat. Got the scoop on Rudy Baker."

"Good. I'm all ears."

"Well, if Rudy were an ice cream flavor, he'd be called Rocky Road. He was born to an unwed teenage crack addict, but not adopted by the Baker family until the age of six. He was a difficult child, threw temper tantrums, beat up smaller kids, was cruel to animals. Really had his adopted parents up against the wall. Finally, a biological uncle took him in when he was about twelve. Became his custodial guardian. But Rudy's behavior got worse. He got into drugs, joined the Crips, then invited his fellow gang-bangers to steal the stereo and hubcaps off his uncle's Cadillac when the poor guy had gone with a neighbor on a bus trip to Reno."

"Oh, God...." Kat's heart sank.

"So, the uncle turned him in to the juvenile authorities. He spent some time in Juvenile Hall and earned even more time when he beat up a room mate who looked at him funny."

"Probably mean-mugged him."

72

"Right. Now he's at the foster home with Don Bass, but I don't think for long. Seems that your principal's been seeking to become Rudy's foster father. That's a little like chasing after a man-eating crocodile in your birthday suit. Dumb and dumber, you know?"

"That's Gabe for you. He thinks he's going to save this kid single-handedly."

"Well, I don't know what he's been smoking, but Rudy's a time bomb just waiting for the right time and place to go off."

"I agree, Dawn. I've never believed in throw-away kids, but there are some kids hell-bent on self-destruction, and they're not going to change their ways."

"You got it. Anyway, Kat, keep your radar out for him. Let me know if I can help you with anything else."

Kat hung up the phone, pursing her lips in thought as she pulled up the computer screen to log in Dawn's report on Rudy. For a moment she thought about sending a copy to Gabe, but decided against it.

No sense in antagonizing my boss, she thought. *There will come a time when, out of the blue, Rudy will shove somebody out into traffic just to see how high he'll bounce, and then what will Gabe say? It's just a phase the poor kid's going through?*

This is no kid's phase, Kat thought glumly.

Chapter 8

At the start of sixth period, Kalani walked into Kat's office, carrying a package wrapped in bright birthday paper. "This is for you, Ms. R.," she said shyly, placing the gift on the corner of Kat's desk.

"But my birthday was last month," Kat said.

"Well, now that you are learning more about the Huna way of things, you're a brand new version of yourself, right? So in a way, it's your re-birthday." Kalani batted her eyes playfully, grinning like a Cheshire cat.

"Now, that's putting the kahuna spin on things. Shall I open it now?"

"Why not?"

When Kat opened the box, she was surprised to see a clay replica of a terra cotta soldier, like those that had been excavated in China in 1976. The slate gray statue stood over ten inches tall and depicted a warrior wearing armor, which draped over his shoulders and covered his chest. His hair was pulled back on the top right side of his head in a fat bun. Arched eyebrows and a Fu Manchu mustache created a foreboding expression that promised any transgressor an immediate ticket to hell.

"A terra cotta soldier! I absolutely love it, Kalani. I've always dreamed of going to Xi'an to see the real ones they found there."

"We knew you'd like him, Ms. R. He's a warrior, just like, er…anyway, Grandma thought you'd like to

74

practice putting mana into him. You know, store it up in case you need some extra energy."

"What a great idea, Kalani. Thanks. I'll do that—if I still can remember how."

"I know how. I'll give you pointers any time you need them."

"And any free time you have while you're working in the office here, just come in and charge it up for me. We'll both work on it, okay?"

"Sounds like a plan, Ms. R."

Kalani started to leave, but Kat was concerned about the sadness she felt in the girl.

"So, how was your visit with your mom last weekend?" she asked.

Kalani sank slowly in one of Kat's chairs and looked at her feet. "She just doesn't seem like her usual self," she answered finally. "I mean, I know she's trying to recover from the breakdown, but it's like she's in a trance or something. I know that sounds weird, but..." Kalani's voice faltered. Her eyes brimmed with tears.

"Don't worry, honey," Kat assured her. "She'll be all right. It takes time to heal from that kind of ordeal, you know?" But deep down, she, too, worried about Leilani Kingston.

Kat picked up a stack of papers from her in-basket and handed them to Kalani. "Why don't you file these detention slips for Mrs. Longer. That'll keep your mind off of things for a while."

Kalani nodded and went over to Mazie's outer office to file.

Kat put her new statue next to the cactus and stared down at both of them on the windowsill.

Here are my two warriors, she thought, *on a mission to keep the negativity down in the VP office at Anthony High. Keep up the good work, guys. And send some good energy out to my Kalani, okay?*

At home that night, Kat stacked the last of the plates and silverware in the dishwasher. She'd been sterilizing all of her utensils and dinnerware before storing them for the first time in the cupboards. She turned on her recessed patio lights and looked out the bay window into her side yard at the vibrant azaleas and quiet camellias that graced the area.

Caesar rubbed against her leg with his ear.

"For once you're not begging for food," Kat said. "Just marking your territory. You think I belong to you, huh?"

Suddenly the hair went up on the back of Kat's neck. She was overcome by the strange sensation that someone outside was watching her. She ran from window to window looking out, unable to shake the feeling.

"Why do I feel like someone's beady eyes are looking at me? Come on, Attack Cat. Let's go check out the yard."

Kat turned on all the backyard lights, grabbed a flashlight and a cell phone for reinforcement and stormed out the door, making as much noise as possible to scare the intruder off.

"I'm calling 911 right now, so whoever's out here better scram," Kat yelled. She went around the left side of the yard, Caesar charging out just ahead of her. To her left, a gray satellite dish stood proudly between beds of rosemary and the garbage can. Next to the dish, three fruit trees, nectarine, apricot and peach, huddling in collusion, filled the corner of the yard. Pyracanthus bushes lined the entire back fence and at the right corner sat a three-tiered fountain, its basins overrun with algae that had taken advantage of the months when the house was vacant and the pump had been turned off. Gardenias, roses and wisteria vines ran along the right side of the fence.

Kat listened intently, but the only sounds came from neighboring yards. Croaking frogs. Backyard chimes playing on the breeze. The yip of a little dog. Canned laughter from a television blaring through an open screen door.

Kat stood up on her toes, trying to look over the top of the fence. Nothing. She checked out the lawn for footprints. Nil. She closed her eyes, internally assessing the danger. Zilch.

Whoever it was is gone. I could have sworn someone was looking at me. Hmmph. You may have eluded me this time, whoever you are, but don't think I won't catch you next time because I will.

"Caesar! Come here," Kat called.

They retreated to the house. Kat was disappointed to have been proven wrong and yet relieved that no one had actually surfaced. Then, just to be sure, she opened her front door to check the porch for signs of a trespasser. Sure enough, someone had been there to drop off what Kat assumed were two housewarming gifts. One, a delicate, lavender and white orchid plant, had an attached note from Liana, wishing Kat well in her new house. The other was a large conch shell.

Liana is so sweet. Maybe the floral deliveryman delivered this late, and it was his presence I sensed.

Kat put the conch shell in the center of a bed of pansies, which bordered the driveway, then clutched the orchid to her chest and carried it inside so she could introduce it to Caesar.

"Let's see. What shall we name this baby, Caesar? You know, things last longer when they have a name."

Caesar looked at her inquisitively but decided these mutterings had nothing to do with food. He walked away with his tail up in the air.

"Okay, be that way, Brat Cat," Kat said. "I'll name this little guy myself. It should be something Hawaiian, like that singer that Kalani once told my class about for a "show and tell" report. Iz. That's it. Iz it is."

She put the plant on a corner coffee table where the right amount of filtered light would reach the fragile plant. "I hope you're happy with us here, Iz," she said.

Before she went to bed, Kat spent an hour experimenting with Caesar, mentally sending him messages from another room, testing to see which worked better, words or pictures. Silently calling him didn't work as well as when she closed her eyes and visualized a can of cat food being opened. She imagined the whrrrr of the opener and the sucking sound as the lid was pried off. She smelled the reek of fish and tin and could see Caesar bounding into the room. That visualization really worked because she opened her eyes just in time to see Caesar leaping up on the counter top where the opener was.

"Good cat! You read my mind!" Kat crowed. "But bad cat, you're not allowed to jump up on the counters."

Kat lifted him off the counter, put him on the floor and ran her hand over his coat, scratching him on the back in front of his tail. Caesar waited patiently as Kat rewarded him with a small can of tuna. She found the whole experiment terribly amusing and was still giggling as she turned off the lights and headed off to bed.

Kat had no idea she had just opened the long locked gate to mastering the ancient Hawaiian arts. She had boldly stepped out on the path toward her life's destiny as the next Huna Warrior.

Chapter 9

It was Spirit Week, a hectic time on campus packed with rallies and fund-raising activities. Kat had very little time for office work, so when a few minutes opened up in her schedule, she grabbed the stack of incoming mail and hurriedly combed through it. A large, manila envelope addressed to the Registrar from the Placer County Office of Education caught her attention. On a hunch she opened it.

It's Rudy's cume file, she thought to herself, feeling justified in snooping through someone else's mail. She took the envelope back to her office and quietly shut the door for privacy.

Kat opened up the back cover of the folder first. Photos of Rudy from the first to the eighth grades were carefully pasted next to his teachers' hand-written descriptions and comments. Except for his first grade teacher, all of Rudy's teachers thought he was a bright, but deviant, kid who could not manage his aggression and anger. *Rudy is very much a loner and resists correction.... Cute kid but needs to learn acceptable ways to vent rather than punch his classmates.... Has great ability, but does the least to get by.*

Suddenly the eighth grade teacher's remarks jumped off the page. *Several students have complained that Rudy has stolen money, Sony Walkman players, and Air Jordans from them. All items were eventually returned, except for the money, but with no remorse on Rudy's part. His guardian (uncle) says at home, Rudy terrorizes the neighborhood,*

throwing rocks through windows and torturing cats. I
recommend that the family seek counseling for him.

"No remorse," Kat said aloud, looking out her office window to the teeming student quad. In her mind, Kat saw Rudy as an eighth grader, brazenly grabbing someone's tennis shoes in the locker room and threatening to deck him if he squealed or asking to "borrow" a Walkman and promptly forgetting to return it. Rudy operated from a misguided sense of entitlement. When he wanted something, he felt it should be his, and if he had to take it away from someone, so what? He had learned that life wasn't going to give it to him any other way.

So, Kat thought, staring again at the photos of Rudy, *I've been right about Rudy all along. He has absolutely no feelings for anyone or anything. It's a good thing Caesar wasn't around during the move last weekend. Rudy probably would have torched him.*

God, Rudy, what happened to the sweet-looking first-grader you once were? How did life manage to morph you into the budding criminal you are now?

Sighing, she slowly closed the folder and put it back in the manila envelope. *Do I tell Gabe now and face another chewing out, or do I just keep a closer watch on Rudy? I know. I'll take this to Sean. He majored in psychology. He'll know what to make of this profile.*

Kat took the envelope and walked down the hall to give it to Lorena Smythe, the secretary for both the counselors and the registrar who shared a suite of offices. She popped her head in to Sean's cubicle where he was going over a class change with a student.

81

"Sorry to interrupt, Mr. Matthews, but I wanted to let you know the cume file we've been waiting for is in. Lorena has it. You really need to go over it before she puts it in the vault."

"Right. Thanks, Ms. Romero. I'll be sure to do that." Sean smiled up at Kat as she quietly shut his door.

Toward the end of the school day, Tony Navarro, the head custodian, radioed Kat and asked her to meet with him in the cafeteria. Since Kalani was her aide that period, Kat asked her to accompany her on the walk across campus so they could talk.

"Kalani, do me a favor," Kat asked. "I'll send Liana a thank-you note, but please thank her for me for the beautiful orchid plant she sent me as a housewarming gift. I've never grown orchids before so it's going to be a new experience, but I'm going to research how to take care of it so it'll last a while. I named it Iz."

"Great name, after a great singer."

"And thank her for the conch shell, too. I put it in my front yard."

"Okay, I'll tell her." Kalani looked at Kat a bit puzzled, but said nothing.

As they stepped into the air-conditioned cafeteria, Tony Navarro waved them over to a corner table. He was leafing through a blue-ringed binder lying open in front of him.

"This binder was left here after second lunch," Tony said. "I was going through it to find out who it belonged to and came across some things I think you should see, Ms. Romero." Tony looked over at Kalani and added, "Uh, it's really for your eyes only, if you know what I mean."

Kat turned to Kalani. "I'm going to be here a while. Why don't you go back to the office and see if Mrs. Longer has something for you to do."

Kalani nodded and walked back out through the cafeteria doors.

Tony flipped the pages toward the back of the binder. "Go to this section, Kat. That's the part that got me."

Kat was horrified to see page after page filled with drawings of violence and gore. Knives dripping with blood. A woman hanging from a noose, her tongue swollen and distended. A man's eye being gouged with a knife. Next to the side of this drawing, in small printing Kat could barely read, was another ghastly entry: *I want to disembowel someone and know what it's like for their guts to slither across my hands when I pull them out and throw them on the ground. I want to see their face as they take their last look at life. Their last thought is about me killing them. And I have the power! The power!*

"Oh, my God," Kat gasped. She turned to the front of the binder, looking for homework papers that would reveal a name. A bolt of terror shot through her when she read the words she knew she'd find: Rudy Baker.

"I don't know this kid," Tony said, "and I'm no shrink. But I'd say he's a bit wacko if you ask me."

"As Mazie would say, you ain't never lied," Kat replied, shutting the binder quickly, her stomach slightly queasy from its graphic content. "I'll see if I can get the district psychologist's read on this. Thanks for alerting me to this, Tony."

Kat returned to her office still reeling from the shock of finding Rudy's binder. She motioned for Mazie to follow her into her office where she shut the door and showed the binder to her.

"Jesus, Lord. This kid's a nut case," blurted Mazie, her mahogany face breaking out in a sweat.

"That's what I've thought all along, Maze. As if the violence depicted weren't enough, take a look at the tiny handwriting. That's usually an indication of low self-esteem. I've had a bad feeling about Rudy all along, but now that I've seen this, not to mention his cume file, I think I've got to get him transferred to a different setting where he's least likely to hurt somebody. But I know Gabe will fight me on this because he thinks his guidance is the only thing Rudy really needs to turn his life around."

"The devil has Rudy and ain't gonna let go, Gabe or no Gabe," Mazie said. "I've seen kids like him all my life. Even in the Marines. They'd join up thinking the rules and regs would keep 'em on the straight and narrow, but, most of the time, they just ended up in trouble anyway."

"The district psychologist, Marianne Crenshaw, needs to see this. See if you can get her here—pronto. She'll know how to explain it all to Gabe without him going ballistic."

"Amen, sister," Mazie said, waving her hands above her head.

After yard supervision at the end of the day, Kat changed into jeans and tennis shoes for the Homecoming football game that night. Thoughts of bloody knives and gouged eyeballs kept surfacing in her mind. Her stomach churned, and she knew she had to find some kind of distraction. She decided to go over to the entrance ramps of the stadium where the kids were decorating their floats. Hanging out with students always cheered her up and reminded her why she got into education in the first place.

Chapter 10

As the crowd drifted in to the stadium for the game that night, the mood was light and happy. High schools usually planned their Homecoming game when they'd be playing a team they were pretty sure they could beat, and SBSBAHS was no exception. The Anthony High Cougars were tangling with the Rio Ventura Vikings, who, despite their tough-sounding name, were a scraggly, disjointed team with the worst record in the league.

Kat was stationed at the entrance to the football stadium, just inside the gate, close to the booster's club snack bar. She and Becky Farnsworth had volunteered to sell PTSA memberships to interested parents, who were few and far between and probably worn out by going to school activities and had forsworn minimal involvement once their kids got into high school.

The provocative smell of popcorn and hot dogs lured Kat to the snack bar. She bought hot dogs and cokes for herself and Becky.

"Why, thank you, Ms. Romero, I appreciate this," accepting the paper tray Kat held out. Becky gobbled the hot dog down in two bites.

"You're welcome. Please call me Kat," Kat said through a mouthful of food.

Becky slurped her soda loudly through her straw. "I can't wait for the half-time show when they crown the King and Queen of Homecoming. Mike's up for King, you know."

Kat stifled a laugh. "Yes, I'd heard that." *If he wins, how will they find a crown big enough for his head?* she thought perversely.

Kat craned her neck, squinting in the direction of the back entrance to the stadium where floats and cars were lining up. *What an endless drag this is,* she thought. She hated football with a passion, the result of being forced to watch it at home with her ex-husband Mark or when he played in the annual charity football game between the law enforcement "Guns" and the fire department "Hogs." No matter who was playing, Kat thought watching the game was the most under-rated method of human torture known to man. *I'd rather chew razor blades,* she mused.

When the horn blasted to signal the end of the first half, she and Becky folded up their PTSA table and carried it over to the ticket booth for safekeeping. Then they went over to the side gate to make sure both teams exited the field safely as they headed for the locker rooms.

Kat took the stadium steps two at a time to the announcer's booth for a better view of the half-time show, while Becky joined the spectators in the stands. One of the teachers, Richard Stevens, headphones on and fingers tapping, brightened when he saw Kat come through the door.

"Hi, Kat. Good to see you."

"Likewise. You look right at home as an announcer, Rich. Were you ever a DJ?"

"Yep. At the radio station on my college campus," he said, swiveling back to the console as he heard his cue.

As Rich flicked on switches and twisted dials, music blared out of amplifiers and the rear gates of the stadium swung open. Nine Corvette convertibles, topped with royalty candidates and in varying degrees of age and ostentation, made their way around the front of the home team bleachers where they were received with whistles, hoots and hollers of appreciation. As each one pulled up to the temporary stage set up for the royalty court, two candidates from each class extricated themselves as gracefully as possible from the car and walked to their designated spot on the riser. Even Mike Farnsworth managed not to trip over his size 16 shoes.

To everyone's surprise, riding in the last car, a sleekly polished 1993 black beauty, was Gabe Minelli, accompanied by his wife, daughter, and "son," Rudy Baker. Richard announced that the principal and his family had arrived, and they waved at the crowd with the practiced ease of heads of state.

Gabe swept a hand-held microphone off a nearby stand and, with his Mr. Show Biz inflection, introduced the royalty candidates to the screaming crowd. When Mike Farnsworth's name was called out, Becky jumped up and down, waving silver and pink pompoms in the air. Even from inside the enclosed announcer's booth, Kat could hear her shrieking, "Mikey! Mikey!" Several people near her put their hands over their ears, scrunching their faces like they had acid reflux disease. Oblivious to the low opinion Mike's peers held of him, Becky was stunned when Robert Ostler won and her son didn't. She wailed about the contest being rigged, but no one paid attention and the cheering went on for several minutes and the winning couple smiled and waved to the cameras.

When the second half started up, Kat found Becky in the snack bar line, blotting her tears with a tissue.

"I'm so sorry Mike didn't make it, Becky," Kat sympathized. "I know how much you wanted him to win, but it's still an honor just to get nominated." She patted Becky's shoulder and gave her a sideways hug.

"Thanks, Kat," Becky sniffed. "There's always next year, I guess." She stepped up to the snack bar counter and turned to Kat. "What would you like? I'm buying this time."

"A small popcorn will do the trick. Thanks."

The two took their food to a table near the entrance. Since the chairs had already been stowed away, they sat directly on the table.

Becky drank her soda with a straw and arched one eyebrow at Kat. "I don't know about you, but I was appalled to see Gabe with that hoodlum in his car."

Kat looked at Becky whose face was pinched with anger. She knew better than to get drawn into a discussion about students with a parent, but her curiosity made her ask anyway. "What have you heard about Rudy Baker from the kids?"

"Mike told me Rudy's a gang banger from San Francisco."

"Really?" Kat tried to sound as if this was a total surprise to her. She flicked back a wisp of hair that had blown into her eyes and studied Becky's face.

Becky frowned and pursed her lips. "None of the kids can understand why the principal is so friendly with Rudy. I mean, putting him in the same car with him

89

tonight and announcing him as family." Becky shuddered, unable to hide her disgust.

"That surprised me, too," Kat admitted. "He must see something in him that we don't, I guess." Kat realized she was getting deeper into dangerous territory in this exchange. She had to walk the fine line between agreeing with Becky and betraying Gabe.

"Well, you can pass the word on to Mr. Minelli the parents in PTSA do not approve of his behavior with that...that criminal," Becky huffed. "The whole school knows about the fight he had with Mikey. When the principal goes overboard like he did tonight, being nice to a thug, it's sending the wrong message out to the rest of the kids. Like getting in a fight means you'll end up being the principal's best friend."

Just then one of the cheerleaders ran up to Kat to enlist her help to suppress a few rowdy students in the stands. Kat sat among the students for the rest of the game, glad to be away from Becky Farnsworth, but worried about what to do about Rudy. There were no instant options, and Kat sensed she was running out of time.

Kat stumbled out her front door Sunday morning, bleary-eyed and in need of a caffeine fix. As she bent over to pick up the newspaper, she glanced over at the flowerbed where she'd put Liana's conch shell. Some sort of primordial ooze seemed to be puddling at the base of the shell and had spread to most of the pansies, smothering them with a rust-colored slime Kat couldn't identify.

"What in the world is that? It looks like vulture phlegm. I'll have to tell Liana about this."

She took the classified ad section from the paper, carefully wrapped the shell in it, then walked around to the other side of the yard and tossed it in the garbage can. Just as she was circling back to the house, the phone rang. It was Liana.

"Hi, Kat. I hope I'm not disturbing you, but I need to talk to you about the shell you told Kalani about."

"Wow, great timing, Liana. I was just thinking about you. Don't think me ungrateful, but I just had to throw it away. There was some kind of sticky stuff leaking from it. Don't know what it is, but it's killed all the plants in the flowerbed. Got any idea what could have been in it?"

"That's just it, dear. I only sent you the orchid. Not the shell."

"Oh, sorry. When I saw your note on the orchid, I just assumed they were both from you."

"I have a bad feeling about that shell, so if it's all right with you, I'd like to come over with Kalani tonight to look at it and see what needs to be done."

"But I've already thrown it away, Liana."

"Depending on what we find, we may have to detoxify it and do a blessing in case any of it contaminated your new house. My sense is it's pretty dangerous, Kat. We're visiting Leilani this afternoon, but we could stop by your place around seven tonight."

"I'm visiting my mother in Stockton today, but I should be back by then." Kat gave Liana directions to her house before she hung up the phone. She was always

91

amazed at Liana's sense of timing. Like the first day of school when Liana had known Kat was desperately in need of a massage. And now when she was worried about the orange slime that had already ruined her new flowerbed.

Once on the freeway to Stockton, Kat passed the time listening to a CD by Keali'i Reichel, on loan from sweet Kalani. It was his *Kawaipunahele* album that had been playing in the background when she'd had dinner with Kalani and Liana weeks before.

Funny how life is, she thought. *A month ago, I would never have listened to this guy. Didn't even know he existed. Now I can't get enough of him.*

One hour later, the bluish gray walls of the Stockton Alzheimer Center came into view as Kat drove in to the visitor parking lot. The building was ell-shaped, with one wing for the severely afflicted and one for those in the beginning phases of the disease. Kat's mother, Maxine, was in the advanced stages and had resided in her wing for nearly a year.

Kat was happy to see her father, Henry, in the room, putting some flowers in a vase on her mother's nightstand. She kissed him and hugged him tight. "Hi, Dad. I was hoping to see you here."

She turned to her mother and kissed her on the cheek. "Hi, Mom. It's me, Kat."

Her mother looked at her blankly at first and then smiled in slow recognition of her daughter. She had lost the ability to talk coherently. All that came out was gibberish which Kat kindly pretended made sense. She clasped her mother's hand and sighed, looking desperately in her eyes for some glimpse of the personality that used to be inside.

Kat sat on her mother's bed. She stroked Maxine's head gently, smoothing out her disheveled hair.

"Guess what, Mom? I'm now a high school vice-principal. The school is so new, it's still being built. And there are two of us VP's there to handle the large number of students. But I'm having fun with them, just like I did when I was little."

Henry grabbed Maxine's other hand and patted it softly. "Years ago we owned an apartment complex, Maxine. You'd baby-sit for our tenants' children, and when Kat got home from school, you'd set up a little school in the corner so Kat could play teacher with them. You'd borrow butcher paper from a nearby grocery store so Kat could teach her kids how to print their ABC's."

Trying her best to respond, Maxine muttered incomprehensibly.

During Henry's recollection of Kat's early attempts at teaching, Kat had remembered her mother's proud smile of approval at her first efforts at teaching. *My mother was always supportive of me,* Kat thought. *Always encouraged me to try anything I wanted to. Made me feel invincible.*

Kat looked at the babbling stranger beside her and screamed to herself. *Oh, God, I want my mother back! She was always a loving, good-hearted human being. Why her, God? She doesn't deserve this miserable existence.*

Kat snapped out of her resentment and gave her father a forced smile. "So, Dad, how are you? How's your back doing?"

"The back's fine, Kathrine. I'm still going to the chiropractor once a week, and they keep assembling all my pieces back together. I'm just one big jigsaw puzzle they work on all the time."

Henry Romero smiled at his daughter and pulled up a chair for her to sit near him. When Kat was in her teens, he'd fallen off the roof of their apartment house and had hit the ground, landing flat on his back. Since then, he'd routinely go to the chiropractor to "straighten out the kinks," as he liked to say.

He ran his hand over his bald head like he was smoothing out the hair that used to be on it. "So, how's the new house coming along, Kat?"

"Oh, Dad, I'm just thrilled. You know how long I've waited to own my own home. Forever, it seems," Kat sighed happily. She fished in her purse for an envelope. "Here, I brought some photos of moving day to show you and Mom."

Henry poured over each of Kat's photographs, especially those which showed the house's landscaping. Having worked at Nakashima's Nursery for over thirty years, he knew the scientific and popular names of every flower, shrub and tree indigenous to California and the Pacific Northwest. During the years when Kat lived with him and Maxine in an apartment complex he owned and managed, his garden was a profusion of olfactory delight with roses, lilacs, sweet peas, carnations, lavender and pink lilies adjacent to a bountiful vegetable patch—all thriving under his loving touch. Even now that he had moved to a mobile home park, he still managed to coax a small plot of dirt into yielding his favorite vegetables and flowers in abundance.

"Any room in your backyard for a vegetable garden?" Henry asked after he finished looking at the photos. "Just think of the zucchini, onions, garlic and tomatoes you could grow."

"So I could drive my neighbors crazy like you did? They always wondered who the phantom Veggie Man was, dropping off grocery bags of produce on their porches in the middle of the night."

"Yes, but think of all the tasty zucchini bread we'd get. Or the canned jars of stewed tomatoes." Henry licked his lips recalling his neighbors' reciprocity.

"I haven't met any of my neighbors yet," Kat said, "but I hope they're as nice as the ones we had when I was little."

"When you were little and we owned the apartment complex, I used to screen all my prospective tenants very carefully. Especially when it came to you. If they acted like you were a nuisance to be tolerated, I wouldn't rent to them. Your happiness and safety always came first." Henry bobbed his head to punctuate his words.

"You and Mom always put me first, Dad. Which might have been my downfall when it came to marrying Mark."

"How so, Kat?" Henry asked.

"All my life I was surrounded by people who were really nice to me. I became conditioned to think that most people were just as nice as could be. Maybe that's why I fell so hard for Mark. I had never before experienced such betrayal, so I never suspected it, either. Until it was too late." Kat looked over at her mother who was watching her with an apprehensive expression on her face.

"But let's not talk about my marriage," she said. "Let's talk about happier things, like your marriage. Tell me again, Dad, when you first met Mom in your high school chemistry class."

Henry was glad to oblige Kat's request. "We were lab partners, Kat. And let me tell you, the sparks in the Bunsen burner weren't the only ones flying when we had to solve for our unknown substance."

Kat laughed, encouraging Henry's pleasant recollection of the past as the afternoon shadows fell.

Chapter 11

When Kat arrived home, she found Liana and Kalani in the driveway, waiting for her. Liana was flicking water from a bowl onto the flowerbed, chanting in Hawaiian.

"Hi, you two," Kat chirped, glad to see her friends again. "I hope you haven't been waiting long. I've been visiting with my parents." She clicked on the garage door opener and parked the car in the garage.

"We've only been here a few minutes, dear. I have some charged water to bless your house and garden with," Liana said with a slight tremor in her voice that Kat had never heard before.

"We need to get the shell, Ms. R. The one you thought Grandma sent," Kalani said, nervously chewing on the edge of a fingernail. Their obvious fear suddenly registered with Kat.

"Come with me," she said. "I threw it in the garbage can." She led them around the side of the garage to a gate which opened into the backyard. The deep green plastic can was facing the fence. Kat opened the lid and started to retrieve the newspaper wad containing the shell.

"Wait, Kat," Liana warned. "Don't touch it. I've said a special prayer of protection. I'll get it." She plucked out the package and gingerly carried it to her car, holding her breath the whole way. Kalani popped open the trunk where Liana placed it in a box and sealed it with duct tape brought from home.

"Wow, that sucker must be pretty poisonous. What is that stuff, anyway? Agent Orange?"

Liana smiled grimly. "Pretty close. It's definitely got some kind of poison seeping out. It's a good thing you didn't take it in the house. No telling what kind of damage it would have done there." Liana slowly exhaled in relief.

"But why would someone send me something so hideous?" Kat gasped. "I don't have an enemy in the world, not even my ex-husband. I can't think of anyone who'd want to hurt me."

"I'm going to take the shell to my house and neutralize its negative energy. Then I'll do some special prayers to see if I can trace it back to whoever sent it to you." Liana's voice was firm and confident.

"Which reminds me," Liana continued. "When you make the shield of protection in the shower, try asking your low self to show you the picture of who's been sending you negativity. The person's face will appear in your mind's eye."

"I didn't know you could do that," Kat said. "Well, come on in and see the house. I'll introduce you to Caesar." She quickly unlocked the front door.

Caesar bounded out like he'd been trapped in a jack-in-the-box. First he sniffed Kalani, then Liana. Kat's eyes widened as he immediately rubbed his head against Liana. Then, to her continued amazement, he stretched both paws up as high as he could on Liana's right leg, begging to be picked up, which Liana did to his instant delight. He purred loudly and rubbed his face against her chin.

Kat was stunned. "I've never seen him do that to anyone but me," said Kat, chagrined at Caesar's overtures which up until now had been saved for her alone.

"So this is your ferocious Attack Cat, Ms. R.," Kalani teased. "Hi, Caesar, you sweet thing, you." She chucked Caesar under the chin, as he tried to rub against her hand, making sure he'd earmarked his territory.

"You two definitely pass his inspection," Kat remarked. "He's been known to bite strangers."

"Well, this just goes to show you. We're not strangers. We're friends," Kalani said brightly.

"So, come on in, my friends. Welcome to Caesar's palace." Kat ushered them in for a brief visit spent talking about flowers, waterfalls, and the mysterious ways of cats.

Chapter 12

Monday morning found Kat searching through her wardrobe to find a black outfit that wouldn't make her sweat in the ninety-degree heat forecasted for that day. Later, as she entered the administration building, she was grateful the air conditioner was taking care of business.

Walking down the darkened hallway, she saw a lone figure waiting in the vice-principal suite of offices. It was Kalani, eyes closed as if in prayer, tears streaming down her face.

"Kalani, what's wrong?" Kat hurried to open her door and led the stricken girl into her private office. Kat had never seen Kalani so distraught.

"My God, Kalani, did something happen to Liana?" she asked, swallowing hard. Kalani slowly shook her head.

"It's your mother, then, isn't it?" Kat's throat felt constricted.

Kalani nodded, unable to transcend the misery and grief that engulfed her. Kat knew not to press her. She'd open up when she was ready. Instead, she scooted her chair close to Kalani's so their knees were touching, then placed her hands on Kalani's and visualized pink light around them.

For years, Kat had been reading metaphysical books, particularly those dealing with energy fields, chakras and auras. She had learned certain colors represented powerful forces which people often called upon to aid in healing others. Green, for example, was the basic color of physical healing. White light signified divine protection and wisdom. The color, pink, Kat recalled, resonated with the vibration of love. *Love, so profound and forceful,* Kat thought, imagining Kalani surrounded in a shimmering, pink light. *Love to soften Kalani's despair. Love because that's all I have to offer.*

Finally, Kalani looked up at Kat. "My mom is dead," she said softly. Her words thundered in Kat's ears.

"Oh, no. Kalani. I'm so sorry," Kat said, her voice catching with emotion. "I can't believe it. You just saw her yesterday and she was fine, right? What happened?"

"When we got home, someone from the hospital had left us a note to call them, so we used Mrs. Eagen's phone. They said Mom committed suicide. She slit her wrists."

Kat was stunned. "But she was in a psychiatric hospital, for God's sake. Where would she get a knife? Why wouldn't they watch her?"

"After we left, she'd been locked in her room, alone. When a nurse went in at midnight to check on her, she was dead." Kalani covered her face in her hands.

"Two things had to have happened here, Kalani. First, she had to have had access to a knife, either from another patient, a hospital employee or a visitor. And, second, she had to have been very despondent to have ended her life. How'd she appear to you when you saw her Saturday?"

Kalani slowly looked up at Kat. "She still seemed dazed, like she'd been hypnotized or something. We'll know more when the police talk to us today. I just wanted you to know why I won't be at school the rest of the week."

Kat cradled Kalani in her arms for a while. "Come on," she said firmly. "I'm taking you home. Liana needs you with her now."

"Okay, Ms. R. Thanks." Kalani forced a smile, her muscles tense with grief.

Kat locked up her office, just as Mazie was coming in. She whispered to Mazie where she was going and headed out to her car, Kalani leading the way.

During the short drive to Kalani's apartment complex, Kat played a number of scenarios over in her head. Kat tried to see the logic in each one, but nothing was making any sense.

Always go to motive and opportunity, she thought in her detective mode. *What was Leilani's reason for doing herself in? She had a family that was supportive of her. She had a beautiful daughter who needed her. So what if she'd been acting strangely lately? That's what people who've had nervous breakdowns do. But to be so disturbed that you'd do yourself in? And to just happen to have a weapon to do it with? How could a knife go undetected in a psychiatric ward? Don't these places have security measures in place to detect weapons and other harmful devices? Don't they carefully screen their employees? What about visitors? Could someone have come in with a knife and passed it off to Leilani? And if they could, why? She didn't pose a threat to anyone. She didn't have money. She wasn't into drugs. She was a fragile woman who found life simply overwhelming. So what? We all do at times. Besides, she was getting help to cope, wasn't she? Isn't that what they do in hospitals? Provide therapeutic talks and medication? Maybe she*

102

had the wrong meds, but how could meds induce her to take her own life? None of this makes any sense.

Kat followed Kalani up the apartment stairs and met Liana who had heard the car and was in the open doorway expecting them. Sobbing uncontrollably, Kalani rushed into her bedroom as Kat hugged Liana for a long time. Finally, she pulled away, her hands on Liana's shoulders, and gazed into her sorrowful face.

"Liana, if I could take this pain away from you, I would," Kat began, "but I don't know how. All I can say is I'm here for you. I'm so sorry about Leilani. I understand how someone can be in such despair that they give up on life, but not Leilani. She had everything to live for. She had you. She had Kalani. I don't understand." Kat shook her head, perplexed.

Liana wiped away the tears that had run down her face. "I never saw this coming for Leilani," she said. "I thought she was getting stronger, but everything affected her so much, poor thing. How could this be her final choice, Kat? How could she come to such an ugly end? She's the daughter of a kahuna. I should have been able to protect her more, but I just didn't see this coming. Not for Leilani." Liana buried her face in her hands and wept.

"I don't understand it, either, Liana," Kat whispered, "but if there's anything you want me to do for you, to make it right, tell me. I'll do it." Kat slid her hands down the sides of Liana's arms and grabbed her hands, still studying her doleful expression.

Liana nodded. "Kat, there *is* something you can do for me. Go to a nursery and buy a kava plant, as big as you can find it. If the local nurseries don't have it, go to the

103

health food store and buy some fresh kava root. Come back here when school is out. I'm going to teach you how to do divination so we can get to the bottom of all this, and I need the kava to do it right. But I can't leave the apartment today because I don't want to miss the police. Can you do this for me, dear?"

"Anything for you, Liana," Kat replied. "And when the police get here, be sure to ask them to give you a complete report from the hospital staff. Ask if they have copies of any visitor sign-in sheets or if they have tapes of everyone who comes and goes. They've got to find out how she got hold of a knife. Also, find out what meds she was on. Maybe there's some kind of link there that would explain some of it. In the meantime, I'll talk to my ex-husband, Mark. He's a cop and might be able to find out more than what they're willing to share."

"All right, Kat. And thanks for bringing Kalani home. We'll see you after school." Kat could feel Liana trembling as she gave her another hug and left the apartment.

Chapter 13

When Kat entered the now familiar apartment, she was surprised to see the dining room table had been transformed into a shrine for Leilani. Draped in tapa cloth, the table held an altar of floral, scented candles surrounding her photographs from childhood through the present. A large, carved staff was propped against the table as if it was bowing in homage to her memory.

Kat smiled at Liana and Kalani, who were draping wreaths of ti leaves around the largest portrait of Leilani. She held out the bag of kava root to Liana.

"None of the nurseries around here carry the kava plant. All I could get was the root," Kat apologized. She followed Liana and Kalani into the kitchen.

Liana pried open the plastic bag containing the kava roots. "Let me show you how we make kava. Have you ever tried it, Kat?"

"Can't say that I have, Liana."

"It's definitely an acquired taste, Ms. R.," Kalani said, "So you may find it strange at first."

Kat watched carefully as Liana chopped the kava root into small pieces which she then ground up and placed in the center of a dish towel. Next, she placed the kava root within the cloth into a calabash bowl filled with water. She kneaded the root with fingers and fists, until the water took on the color of coffee with cream and had a slightly foamy surface. Finally, the process was complete, but Kat was still confused as to its purpose, hoping an explanation would be forthcoming.

Liana poured the mixture into three coconut cups as Kat and Kalani took their seats at the kitchen table. "Kalani and I are used to kava, Kat, but you might want to sweeten yours with honey or maple syrup."

"Honey will be fine, thanks."

Kalani scooted her chair out to search the pantry for honey and brought it to the table for Kat. Holding her cup with both hands, Kat first sniffed at it, then made a face as though she had just smelled turpentine. She heaped a few tablespoons of honey into the bowl and stirred rapidly before sipping again and making another sour face.

"What do you think, Ms. R?" asked Kalani, the start of a smile on her face.

"It's different," Kat conceded, trying to be tactful. "But I'm willing to keep trying to acquire a taste for it. What's it supposed to do?"

"It'll help us with spiritual insight," Liana replied, taking a big swallow of kava. "It opens things up for me, and I use it to get in touch with my low self. It might work the same way for you, Kat. Don't sip it. Slug it down. And don't drink all of it. When it's half gone, swirl the remainder around and study it, like this." Liana swirled her kava and stared at the liquid as it settled in her bowl.

"My mouth feels numb, Liana."

Liana smiled. "Don't worry. That's normal. Just relax and ask your low self to bring you back information about Leilani's last few days on earth. Pictures will come up in your mind's eye. Don't try to make sense of them, just let them come and go as they please."

"Okay, here goes." Kat closed her eyes and waited. Nothing. *Oops,* she thought, *I forgot to ask my low self to help me out. Dear low self, I need your help. I need you to go out to the hospital where Leilani was a patient and scurry around for any information you can find about why and how she did herself in. Ask our High Self for guidance in this request. Thank you, little buddy, for coming through for me.*

Kat took a deep breath and sat back. Suddenly a swimming pool came into view in her mind's eye. She clearly saw a muscular male with long black hair jumping on a diving board in a competition of some kind. He executed a difficult maneuver known as a periwinkle, hitting the water with barely an entry splash, as all the judges held up cards with 10's printed on them.

When this image faded and nothing else appeared, Kat opened her eyes and looked sheepishly at Liana and Kalani.

"I'm not sure I'm doing this right, you guys. I don't quite know what to make of the image I got." Kat smiled weakly at them.

"Come on, Ms. R. Tell us what you saw."

"Well, I saw a tall, tanned man up on a diving board in some kind of diving competition. I didn't see his face because the view I got was looking at his back. But he had long dark hair, and he apparently did well because all the judges gave him 10s." Kat shrugged and stared at the kava roots at the bottom of her coconut cup. "Your guess is as good as mine what any of it means."

"What about you, Grandma? What'd you see?" Kalani's eyes were lined with worry.

Liana rubbed her eyes and sighed. Finally, she answered, "I saw someone opening a briefcase which had a knife hidden inside in a false bottom. My sense is that the person with the briefcase was a man, but I wasn't shown his face. Very unusual because I rarely miss it." Liana folded her arms across her chest. "The briefcase might just represent the way the knife got in there—you know, sneaky, like."

"Well," Kalani's voice quivered, "I saw the same man Ms. R. saw. Tall with long black hair tied back in a pony tail."

"And?" Kat and Liana asked at the same time.

"And I recognized him," Kalani hesitated, then admitted, "It…, it was my father." She covered her face and sobbed. Liana and Kat looked at one another in grim silence.

A wave of anxiety swept over Kat as she grabbed Liana's arm. "Liana, they've been divorced for years. Why would he want to kill Leilani?"

"I don't know, Kat."

"Is there any record of him coming to visit her?"

"They said no one except Kalani and me had signed in to see her. She went out into the grounds for a walk, but no one recalls anyone unusual talking to her." Liana closed her eyes to concentrate on receiving more psychic input.

"I'm feeling nervous about this guy, though. I mean, your father, Kalani. My gut feeling is he's involved, only I can't prove it."

"Let me work on it a while, Kat. Just drop it for now, and if you get any inkling about it later, let us know. Maybe we'll get more information after the autopsy comes out," Liana said, choking back tears. Even saying the word "autopsy" was hard for her.

Kat stayed a while, until she could give nothing more in terms of comfort or insight, then left for home.

The rest of Kat's week was deluged with the usual fare from a vice-principal's menu. Two kids had a sprawling fight in the cafeteria at lunchtime, prompting their audience to stand on the tables and chairs and shout the first name of a popular television talk show host known for encouraging similar antics. Another group of kids was caught gambling with dice after school under the stadium seats. Lots of students were late to class, no-shows at detention, and remiss at bringing their books. The hours flew by as she filled out detention slips and suspension forms, and entered accounts of student events into her computer.

On Thursday afternoon, Marianne Crenshaw met with Kat and Sean in the counseling office's conference room. Sean laid Rudy's cume file on the table, alongside Rudy's binder which Kat had brought in. Marianne, the district's psychologist for the past six years, was in her sixties, spoke with a slow southern drawl, and was the kindest-looking woman Kat had ever seen. Her hazel eyes sparkled, and the crow's feet at the corner of her eyes deepened with every smile—which she did quite often.

However, as she thumbed through Rudy's file and binder, she clucked her tongue in disapproval.

"A loner...bully. Violent and explosive personality. What else do you know about this kid, Kat?"

"When I think of Rudy, a big danger sign usually flashes up in my mind. He got into a fight the first day of school which didn't exactly endear him to me. On the other hand, he was good enough to help me move during Labor Day weekend," Kat said.

"I helped Kat move that day, too," Sean added, "and Rudy showed off his gunshot wounds to us at the pizza parlor that night. Seems to me if he's getting shot at, more than likely he's done his share of shooting back."

Kat looked at Sean with new appreciation. "You're right. Why didn't I think of that?"

"Well, that'd be about what to expect from a former gang member, right?" Marianne reasoned. She flipped through the drawings in the binder again.

"I'd like to do a complete psychological evaluation on this student. It sounds like he might be severely emotionally disturbed and may need placement somewhere else. Anthony High doesn't have a program for SED kids, but the county does."

"Works for me," Kat said, relieved that someone else would corroborate her take on Rudy. "Can you do me one favor, though?" she asked Marianne. "Can you tell Gabe about this before you test Rudy? Gabe's been making plans to become his foster dad, and he should know what he's getting into, don't you think?" Kat crossed her fingers under the table, fervently hoping that someone else, besides her, would stand in Gabe's line of fire over Rudy.

"I'd be happy to, Kat. I'll stop by to talk to him right now if he's available." Marianne smiled broadly. "I'll try to schedule testing for the week after next. The sooner the better, right?"

Kat and Sean nodded their approval. Kat took the cume to put it in the vault, while Sean took the binder to return it to Rudy.

Later that afternoon, Kat got a call from Gabe's secretary, Denise, requesting an immediate meeting in the vault.

A few minutes later, safely ensconced on their cardboard boxes, Denise described Marianne's visit to Gabe.

"I didn't even have to put my ear to the wall, Kat. Gabe was so furious, the windows were rattling. He shouted something about Rudy not having conduct disorder and told Marianne she didn't know what she was talking about. Can you imagine that? Marianne, of all people. He told her not to mess with Rudy and said he's already hired a private psychologist who will start seeing Rudy in a group setting once a week. Which you and I both know is bull."

"Didn't he find those drawings just a tad grotesque?"

"That's the kicker. He refused to even look at them. He told her it was a healthy sign that showed Rudy was venting his anger in an acceptable way."

Kat was appalled. "What an idiot! How'd Marianne handle his little tantrum?"

"You know how calm and sweet she is. I couldn't hear a word she said, but I think she's just going to go

111

ahead and test him. Gabe knows better than to interfere with her job."

"You'd think he'd *want* Rudy tested so he'd get the right kind of help he needs, though." Kat frowned in disgust. She wanted to hit something, but nothing in the vault was expendable.

"No way. Gabe thinks *he's* the right help. I called Angela to let her know what's up. She's met Rudy, but he's acted like an angel around her, so now she doesn't know what to think."

"He hasn't shown her his ugly side. But he will."

Kat returned to her office where she spent the rest of the afternoon interviewing candidates to supervise the Refocus Room where teachers could send unruly or uncooperative kids for a time-out. *We need a place for unruly and uncooperative adults, too,* Kat thought, as the last interviewee left. *Like Gabe, for instance. He needs to get his act together and stop using kids to fill his empty life.*

She looked at the terra cotta soldier, standing forlornly on her windowsill. *Time for a little energy infusion, kiddo, before I go home for the day.*

Chapter 14

Friday morning rolled around with Kat still in bed at seven-fifteen. She awoke with a start, Caesar licking her cheek.

"Good God! I should be at work right now! Damn alarm didn't go off!"

Adrenalin racing, she threw back the covers and dashed to the bathroom.

Ten minutes later, dressed and with a minimum of makeup, Kat heard the doorbell ring. She looked out the peephole and saw a tall, gray haired, distinguished-looking man standing on the front porch. He was wearing jeans and a short-sleeved shirt, but looked like he belonged in an expensive suit. Calling Caesar to her, she cautiously opened the door just enough to show her face.

"Hi. I'm Alex Burkette, your neighbor." As he pointed to the yellow house with white trim directly across from Kat's, she opened the door a bit more.

"Hi. I'm Kat Romero. What can I do for you?" Kat smiled her friendliest smile.

Alex pointed to her front lawn where her sprinklers had soaked for so long, the excess water had formed a small canal which coursed down the street toward a big drainage pipe.

"I'm usually up around five or so each morning, and I noticed your sprinklers have been on since then. It's a shame to flood the gutters like that. Maybe something's wrong with the timer on your system?"

Alex's tact didn't escape Kat's notice. "Well, I just moved in a few weeks ago, and, to tell you the truth, I haven't spent enough time around here to check the sprinklers. I appreciate your telling me, though, Alex. I hate wasting water," Kat said sheepishly.

"If you'd like, I can take a look at your timer. Unless there's someone else to do it for you, or you'd rather do it yourself." He shyly diverted his blue eyes away.

"No, there's just me. I'd like you to take care of it now, if you have the time. It's in the garage. Let me pop the door up."

She went back in the house, then scooted out to the laundry room which led into the garage. She hit the garage door opener, then opened the storage cabinet where the sprinkling system was installed. Alex walked into the garage, slowly taking inventory of its contents.

"Here it is. Do you need any tools or anything?"

"I brought my reading glasses. Just need a flashlight." Alex pulled out the pair of glasses he had tucked into his shirt pocket.

"Hang on just a sec, and I'll get one." Kat raced to her bedroom to retrieve the huge flashlight she kept under her bed and trotted back to the garage.

"Okay, here you go." She put it in his palm, feeling a little like she was playing nurse to his doctor. She tried not to sound breathless from all the dashing around she'd been doing.

I've got to get in better shape, she thought. *I can't believe a short run like this has me panting. Unless it's him I'm reacting to. Hmm. He is a hunk.*

114

Alex looked over the dials and settings and went to work. As he fine-tuned the timer, he explained to Kat how the system worked so she could adjust it whenever the seasons dictated a change.

He was finished in a few minutes. Kat thanked him profusely for coming to the rescue.

"I'd offer you a cup of coffee for all your efforts, Alex, but I'm late for work. I'm one of the VP's at Anthony High, and I'm supposed to get there before the kids do." She laughed, nervously wondering why she found Alex so disconcerting.

"I understand. I'm a writer, and I work out of my home, so whenever you have time, we can chat. Glad to have been of help, Kat." Alex sauntered back to his house as Kat jumped into her car to drive away.

Nice guy, she thought. *I'd like to get to know him better. Something tells me I'm going to like what I find.*

At the administrators' meeting later that day, Kat noticed a distinct chill in Gabe's voice as he asked her to oversee the administration of the CBEDS report, an annual survey taken by all schools in October which gave demographics on their students and faculty. While Kat was glad that, by giving her this assignment, he'd recognized she could get the job done right, she could see it was a struggle for Gabe to be civil to her. She decided to broach the subject at the end of the meeting when Serge left, but Gabe beat her to the punch.

"Kat, could you stay for just a minute?" he asked frostily. "There's something I want to discuss with you."

Kat nodded compliantly and stayed seated. She opened her planner so she could take notes to disguise her discomfort.

Gabe shut the door to the conference room, then returned to his chair at the head of the table. "You probably can tell I'm upset with you, and you probably know why, right?" Gabe said, drumming his fingers on his desk.

Kat looked him directly in the eye. "My guess is you disagree with Marianne's decision to test Rudy for placement elsewhere."

Gabe nodded. "And whose decision was it to ask Marianne over here?"

"Mine."

"On what basis?" Gabe's eyes smoldered with rage.

"Tony found Rudy's binder in the cafeteria. We were both appalled by what we found inside. Have you seen it?"

"No, I haven't." Gabe's face started to register mild alarm, but he caught himself.

Kat grimaced. "Pictures of a woman hanging from a tree, another person gouging someone's eyes out, knives and blood dripping everywhere and dialogue about how great all this would feel if he could be the last face that someone saw before he killed them. I wanted Marianne to take a look and see if I'm off base here in thinking something's wrong with Rudy. Apparently, she agrees with me."

"Well, I don't. I think drawing is an expression that's healthy. All he's doing is venting his anger in an acceptable way to get it out of his system," Gabe snarled.

"But what if he's not venting? What if it's an indication of the things he'd truly do, given the opportunity?" Kat said tightly, almost holding her breath.

Gabe's face flushed with anger. "Look, Kat, you and I will never see eye-to-eye when it comes to Rudy. So from now on, I just want you to leave him alone. Do not get him tested. Do not pass go. Do not collect $200. Do I make myself clear?"

"Okay, I'll leave him alone," Kat said wearily. "But the testing is Marianne's call."

"I've already turned in the paperwork for him to become my foster son, and I won't grant her permission to test him," Gabe snapped.

Kat frowned at her boss. "Testing or not, the kid's a volcano that's showing all the signs of an impending eruption. He needs a shrink, some coping skills, and a smaller setting," Kat pleaded, knowing her words fell on deaf ears.

"He needs a family," Gabe said, stonily, "and some TLC. I mean it, Kat. Leave him alone. I'll be responsible for Rudy. If he gets in trouble on campus, send him to me, and I'll take care of it. Got it?"

Gabe pushed himself away from the table and stood up, looming over Kat. Frustrated with Gabe's arrogance, Kat stood up ramrod straight and bayoneted him with her eyes.

"Have it your way," Kat said. "But don't say I didn't try to warn you when Rudy's halo falls off." She grabbed her Franklin planner, shoved her chair back in place and swaggered out of the room just to let Gabe know he hadn't gotten to her. Her shaking hands betrayed the look of confidence she flashed as she exited the room.

Great, she thought in dismay as the door shut behind her. *Now I've really done it. I just made an enemy of Gabe. How bright was that? He's my boss! He can make my life a living hell. How can it get any worse?*

Then another thought struck her. *Rudy! That little psycho knows where I live. What if he breaks in? What if he sets Caesar on fire? And there's no telling what he'd do if he turned on me.*

Sweat beads formed on her forehead with another realization. *Rudy didn't turn in those gang bangers who shot at him like he said at the restaurant. He hunted them down and killed them.*

Kat hurried back to her office, cold chills running down her spine. *Oh, my God! What will he do next?*

Chapter 15

Saturday morning Kat slept in late—well, as late as Caesar would permit. His need for food always took priority over her need for sleep, so he pawed at her face until she woke up.

In the shower, she did her usual prayer for protection, putting up a shield of light around her. This time, though, she put up a mirror shield so the negativity that might be sent her way would bounce off the shield and return to the person who sent it.

No use in me sending any hate, she reasoned. *If someone sends me bad vibes, they just return right back to the sender. Gives new meaning to the sayings, "what goes around comes around," and "as ye sow, so shall ye reap," now doesn't it?*

When she asked to be shown the person who was sending her negative thoughts, Rudy's leering face flashed in her mind's eye.

No surprise there. He probably blames me for upsetting Gabe with his bad-news past. Oh, well. C'est la vie, Rudy. Get over it.

After a breakfast of almond butter and banana slices on toast, washed down with orange juice and a handful of vitamins, Kat decided it was a perfect day to replace the ooze-covered pansies in her front yard. She called her father who, when he picked up the phone, said he had just started getting up "in sections" as he liked to joke.

119

"I need your expertise, Dad. I've decided to replant the flowerbed in my front yard. The one near the driveway that had pansies in it. But I want to get something other than pansies. Got any suggestions?"

"How about some bright orange marigolds?" Henry muffled his laughter by putting his hand over the receiver while Kat stewed silently. "I'm just kidding. I know you hate marigolds. Let me think. I'm trying to remember the layout of the yard from the pictures you showed me. All right. How about hemerocalis or Rudbeckia Goldsturm? Lavendula stoechas Otto Quast might be nice, too."

"Dad, Dad, speak English."

"Okay, okay. How about daylilies, black-eyed Susans, or Spanish lavender? Any of those would look fine, Kathrine."

"Sounds like a plan," Kat said, making a list as he spoke.

"That reminds me. I'm still working on plans for my combination birthday and retirement party. Are you, Sean, and Chelsea still coming?"

"We wouldn't miss it. I love you, Dad, even if I don't say it often enough."

"I love you, too, Kathrine."

"I'll talk to you soon," she said, then hung up in a hurry to get to the nursery.

Pulling out of the driveway, she looked across the street just in time to see Alex driving into his garage. He got out and waved at her as a female got out of the passenger seat. The woman looked to be in her mid-thirties, her long copper-colored hair swept up on the sides

120

and held with a barrette. Kat waved back and felt a twinge of disappointment.

I should have known Alex would have a significant other, she thought. *I should have asked, but he never mentioned a wife or girlfriend, and I didn't see any ring on his finger. Go figure. Geesh. Why am I acting like a scorned lover? I barely know the man. Stop it, Kat. Just stop it. He's just your helpful neighbor, nothing more. He acted interested in me, and then shows up with another woman. That's something my ex would do. Well, I'm staying away from this guy. Who needs the grief?*

Kat drove off to the nursery, soon busying herself with the selection of flowers, potting soil, fertilizers and a slew of gardening tools she'd probably never use, but felt that, as a bona fide homeowner, she should have "just in case."

In the afternoon, tired of working and needing a break, she called Dawn Silva to see if she wanted to catch a movie. They met at the Tower Theater, an older movie house in Sacramento, which showed all the esoteric and European features that the standard theaters didn't. Kat, who had majored in English and minored in drama, fancied herself a movie buff and was very particular on what she spent her hard-earned money to see. She always read multiple reviews before making her final choice. Sometimes she'd rent videos to see at home, but she loved the escape that two hours in a darkened theater provided. It was so comforting to be cocooned without a worry or a care in a refuge that fed her senses and her soul.

Not to mention her appetite. Luckily, Dawn was as indulgent as she was in the munchies department. They pigged out on chocolate-covered raisins, popcorn, nachos

121

and sodas. A quiet aura of satisfaction and entitlement settled over the two of them for the rest of the evening.

Chapter 16

A celebration of Leilani Kingston's life was held at Cooper's Mortuary in Sacramento, Sunday night at seven o'clock. As Kat signed her name in the guest book at a small table just inside the mortuary door, she could hear strains of Hawaiian music drift into the lobby. After Kalani greeted her with a lei and a hug, Kat went in to say hello to Liana who was sitting in a side room with family and friends. A framed photograph of Leilani rested on top of the closed casket and was encircled by a dozen plumeria leis, flown in by Leilani's Hawaiian relatives.

Kat recognized some of the teaching staff from the junior high and was chatting with them when she noticed a uniformed police man, beckoning her to come out to the lobby. As soon she scanned his profile, Kat knew it was her ex-husband, Mark Matthews. She excused herself from her colleagues and slipped quickly out of the pew.

"Hi, Kat," Mark said briskly when she approached him. "I read about this service in the paper and figured you'd be here. Listen, I talked to the detective in charge of the investigation, and so far they're stumped as to how the knife got through their security at the hospital, especially in a room that's under watch like hers. The preliminary autopsy indicates suicide. She slit her wrists lengthwise and bled to death. Every indication is that she was alone in a locked room at the time. No one knows how she got the knife." Mark shrugged his shoulders and grimly returned Kat's gaze.

"Any record of any visitors within the last month or so, Mark?"

"Just sign-in sheets with only her mother's and daughter's names on them. No video camera."

"How about a machine or a wand to scan purses or briefcases?"

"No. Sorry."

"How long do you think this investigation will have top priority?"

Mark cleared his throat uneasily and swallowed. "To be honest with you, Kat, it doesn't have top priority now. She was a patient in a mental facility and had access to a weapon which she used to end her life. It's not likely any more staff will be put on this case. We're short-handed enough as it is with murders and robberies. My guess is it'll be dropped by next week."

Kat nodded and bit her lip so she wouldn't give way to tears. She could feel a slow rage building inside. "What you're saying is, Leilani isn't important enough or rich enough to waste anyone's precious time," Kat snapped. "What a sad commentary on our society when a human life is so devalued."

Mark looked away, embarrassed. "I'm sorry, Kat. What with cutbacks and lack of staff, it's just the way things are."

Kat took a deep breath and exhaled slowly. "I know. I just wish...." The words caught in her throat as she once again fought back tears.

"Look, I've got to go," Mark said, backing away from her. "If I find out anything else, I'll call you. Are you going to be okay?"

"I'll be fine. Thanks for looking into it for me."

Mark nodded and headed for his car. Kat blew her nose into some tissue and tried to compose herself before walking back in for the rest of the service.

Monday morning brought its usual ritual with Kat dressed in black. She was running off an agenda for the after-school faculty meeting when Mazie came in the copier room pushing a heavy cart loaded with toner cartridges. She greeted Kat as she searched the cabinets for space to store the supplies.

"How're you doing, boss?" Mazie said, panting from exertion.

"I'm okay, but how about you? You sound a bit out of breath."

Mazie's face strained as she lifted the last of the cartridges to an overhead cabinet. "My asthma's acting up again. I can't seem to get it under control. It's the reason why I left the service, you know. Handling all those weapons and marching all the time plumb wore me out."

"Why didn't you tell me that before?" Kat scolded. "Next time, I'll arrange for Tony to put these away for you. You shouldn't have to worry about lifting heavy stuff, Mazie."

"No big thing. I have my inhaler in my desk. I'll just take a hit and in a few seconds, I'm AOK."

"Well, that's good to know," Kat sighed, smiling at Mazie. "I want you to be healthy so you can help me with the kids."

"You mean breathe fire on 'em, like the mean ol' dragon lady that I am?"

"Exactly. Or mow 'em over like in that movie, *Code 3*, when the good guy counts to three then slams the bad guy upside the head with a door. But only as a last resort." Kat winked at Mazie.

"Gotcha, boss." Mazie chuckled.

Kat and Mazie closed up the supply room and walked back to their office suite.

"I gotta ask you something, Kat," Mazie said, holding the door open for Kat. "How come you always wear black on Mondays?"

"Wow," Kat exclaimed, unlocking the door to her office. "You're the first one to notice in the shortest time ever. It's my uniform. I'm a member of the Church of our Lady of Perpetual Mourning for Weekends. I wear black every Monday in protest of having to give up the freedom of weekends."

Mazie shook her head and grinned. "Girl, you are something else. I thought maybe someone died in your family on a Monday, and you were honoring their memory."

Kat snorted. "Nope. Nothing that deep. I just live for the weekends, and I hate to give them up."

"Me, too." Mazie reached for the inhaler in her desk drawer. She gave herself two squirts and sucked down the spray with a look of reverence on her face. Once she had her breathing under control, her eyes focused on the surveillance monitors behind her desk.

"Check this out, Kat," Mazie said, pointing to one of the screens. "Isn't that Blaze Amaro trying to sneak off campus?" Screen five showed a student racing toward the back gate which Tony Navarro was in the process of chaining shut.

Kat grabbed her phone and paged Tony. She could see him on the screen answering her call. "Tony, Blaze Amaro is heading your way. Don't let him out. He's been cutting lately. I'll have one of the campus monitors escort him up here. Gonzo, did you copy that? Tony's chaining up the back gate by the stadium."

"Copy. I'm on my way." Gonzo's earsplitting voice made Kat jump, and she quickly adjusted the volume button on her phone.

Kat had printed out Blaze's attendance record and was studying it when Gonzo led Blaze into her office.

"Hi, Ms. R. Long time no see."

"Good to see you again, Blaze, but I'm not too happy to see this." Kat held the printout for him to see.

"What's that?" He tried to project a look of innocence which Kat saw right through.

"It's your attendance sheet, kiddo. I can't believe you've cut so much. Look at this. There's only about four days where you went to every class." Kat's forehead wrinkled as she stared at Blaze.

Clearly in discomfort, Blaze stammered, "Yeah, well, I just can't sit through all those boring lectures and stuff, you know? Sometimes I need a break."

"Does your foster dad know that you've been taking these, uh, let's see, twenty-two breaks?" Kat increased her penetrating stare.

"I don't think so. He hasn't said anything to me if he does know." Blaze shifted in his chair and drummed his hand on his thigh carelessly.

"Knock it off, Blaze. This is serious. You can't possibly be passing any of your classes when you've missed so much. Especially periods one and six, which you cut more often than any of the other ones."

Kat slid the printout across her desk and leaned back in her chair. "So, where do you go when you leave campus? What do you do?" Kat asked, knowing she wasn't going to get a truthful answer.

"I go to the donut shop or hang out at the park." Blaze maintained the feigned look of innocence on his face.

"I see. And who else goes with you?"

"No one. Just me." Blaze smiled weakly at Kat.

She pondered these words for a while, then eyed him, like a soldier trying to deciding whether to go into enemy territory.

"You know what, Blaze? I'm not buying ten cents worth of that baloney. But I'll make a deal with you. Tell me what you know about your housemate, Rudy Baker, and, in exchange, I promise not to call your foster dad about your cutting. But you have to promise to straighten out your act and get to class. Deal?"

"You got it, Ms. R. But you gotta promise not to tell anyone else what I tell you about Rudy. Man, if he finds out I ratted him out, I'm history."

Kat could see the fear in Blaze's eyes. "Okay. Whatever you say, stays in this room. Now, tell me, has Rudy ever shot anybody?" Kat half stood, reaching over to shut her door. It was a good thirty-five minutes before she opened it again.

The next morning Kat got to school early to log on to her computer and make notes on her conversation with Blaze. *I promised not to tell anybody, Blaze, but that doesn't mean I can't input this info into the Events data base,* she thought.

After her entry on Blaze, an e-mail message from the librarian caught her eye. During the night someone had broken into the television studio which was located in a back room of the library and was temporarily being used for new computer storage. Since workers had not yet finished connecting the library alarm system, and the school district was too cheap to spring for night security, it had been relatively easy for burglars to take two computers and monitors.

Kat got on her phone and reminded the custodians and the campus monitors to double-check the locks everywhere on campus before they left for the night and to put chains on the television studio doors until the library's burglar alarm could be installed. She also notified the district office about the theft.

Kat checked the rest of her e-mail messages and found that Dan Hargrove was still complaining about the smell of natural gas in his classroom. Worse, he threatened to file a grievance with the teachers' union since nothing had been done about his complaint.

Remembering she never heard from Owen Snelson, she placed the call. When he answered, Kat reminded him of the complaint he had promised to investigate.

"I apologize for not getting back to you, Kat," Owen began. "We've had some snags come up with the swimming pool and delays in getting the alarm system installed. But, hey, just to assure you and Mr. Hargrove, the kids are not in any danger. It turns out the intake air pipes were built too close to the outgoing air valves, and it's not actual gas they're smelling. It's just a residue odor of gas."

"Owen, help me here. The gas they're smelling is not really gas, it's just the odor of gas—is that what you're telling me? Because if it is, I'm confused." Kat tried to keep the sarcasm out of her tone. *It's a good thing we're not on a video conference call,* she thought, *because the eyes rolling in the back of my head would be a dead giveaway.*

"That's right, Kat. The vent that sucks the smell of natural gas out of the building was built too close to the one that sucks fresh air out of the area and into the building. But basically, there's no problem with student safety. The little amount they're detecting is not going to hurt them."

"That's about the lamest thing I ever heard, and I know how Mr. Hargrove is going to react to this. He's threatening to go to the teachers' union."

"I'll be happy to call him and explain it to him directly, if that'll help," Owen offered with forced cheer in his voice.

Kat gave him Hargrove's phone number just as Owen's cell phone lost its signal and the call was terminated. *I'll never understand why construction jobs go to the lowest bidder,* Kat thought, hanging up her phone. *Everything suffers because they have to cut corners and later make weak excuses for their faulty construction plans.*

Mazie broke her reverie with a referral on Rosalind Jacarro for wearing indecent clothes to school.

Rosalind, a petite sophomore with spiked hair dyed black streaked with purple highlights, clunked haughtily into Kat's office. She sported thick black boots, black net nylons with conspicuous gaps like potholes on a highway, a postage-stamp short skirt, and a see-through blouse revealing a black bra. She plopped down in the chair farthest from Kat's and blew bubbles with a big wad of blue gum.

"Here, Rosalind." Kat held out the wastebasket. Rosalind threw her gum in the basket without moving out of her chair.

"Great. That's a three-pointer from here." Kat smiled at the hostile girl hoping to soften her. "Do you know why you were sent to see me?"

"Yeah. I've been told my clothes aren't exactly appropriate."

Wow, she's a four-syllable girl. My kind of kid, Kat thought.

"*Correctamundo.* The see-through blouse is a no-no. Your skirt isn't long enough to cover a gnat, and those fishnet nylons with all the holes have got to go. Too suggestive and distracting. You've read the student-parent handbook, haven't you?" Kat reached up to a bookcase to get Rosalind a copy of the rulebook.

"I don't need a copy. I've got one at home." Rosalind crossed her arms, kicked one leg over the other and began tapping one foot in the air.

"Great. So, at this point, you have two choices. I can send you home to change or I can loan you a sweat suit that was left in gym class last year, and you can wear that all day. Which would you prefer?" Kat called up Rosalind's personal information screen on her computer as she spoke.

"If you send me home to change, you have to call my parents, right?" Rosalind began picking the green polish off her fingernails.

"Right. Unless you go with the sweats. Then I won't call them because you won't be leaving campus." Kat looked at Rosalind expectantly.

"All right. In that case, I'll take the sweats. I don't need to be hassled by my parents any more than I already am." Rosalind threw her nail pickings in the wastebasket.

"So, what's going on at home? Kat asked sympathetically.

"Just the usual teenage crap. I want to be me, and they want me to be them. They're just getting on my last nerve." Rosalind's voice quavered as she fought off tears.

Kat looked into the computer screen that showed Rosalind's yearbook picture from the previous year. Rosalind's countenance—short blond hair, light lipstick and very little make-up—had gone from preppy to Gothic in a few short months.

"Looks like you've made some big changes since last year, you know? Maybe your parents are having a hard time accepting the *new* you."

132

Rosalind scoffed, "That's the understatement of the year. They just don't understand me. At all. We're on totally different wave lengths, you know?" Her bones clacked into place as she rotated her shoulders to relieve the tension that had settled in them.

"Sounds like you're way too stressed," Kat winced, empathetically.

"And my stress level wasn't helped coming to school this morning, either. You need to tell those hard hats to stop whistling at us."

"What? The construction crew's whistling at you?" Kat's mothering instinct kicked into gear.

"Yeah, me and Joanie Rasmussen. Just about every morning we have to walk past those creeps. They stare, flap their tongues at us, whistle, pull their zippers up and down—you name it." Rosalind got more animated with every phrase.

"Are they the guys working on the library, by any chance?"

"The very same. They make me sick."

"Me, too, kiddo. Believe me, I'll put a stop to that. You have the right to walk to school without being harassed. Now, let's get you those sweats and get you back to class, okay? And see if you can go a little easy on your parents. They're doing the best they can, even if their tolerance level might not be what you'd like to see, you know?"

"I know. Thanks, Ms. Romero. You're okay." Rosalind stood up to follow Kat out.

"So are you, Rosalind. So are you."

Rosalind followed Kat to the health assistant's office where the lost and found box was stashed. She left the girl there busily tossing clothes around, looking for something in her size.

Just after lunch, Gabe, Serge and Kat met for an administrators meeting in the conference room next to Gabe's office. They took turns laying out problems and complaints that had cropped up since their last meeting. Kat was addressing the issue of how to handle the uncouth construction workers when the district superintendent walked in.

Robert Purcell was a white-haired, bulbous-nosed man, with a non-stop Alfred E. Newman smile. Originally from Oklahoma, Purcell had a dichotomous sense of style evincing both a cowboy and an Indian look. He'd wear cowboy boots, Stetson hats and bolo ties to complete his John Wayne western motif. Then to show equanimity for the Native American, he'd wear turquoise in every way known to man. Bolo ties with a turquoise center. Turquoise inlays on his watchband, wedding ring and i.d. bracelet. A feather in his turquoise-colored hatband. Kat thought if there was a way to drill turquoise into one of his front teeth, he'd have done it. She knew from Andrea Chan's gossip his own staff mocked his wardrobe and other than among his immediate cabinet members, he was widely despised in the district as a pseudo-educator who hated people but loved the power of the superintendency.

"Sorry to barge in like this, but I wanted to let you know the latest on the swimming pool," Purcell said, his penetrating eyes sweeping the room, quickly assessing the impact of his sudden visit. He loved it when he could

134

interrupt a meeting, so everyone would have to drop their agenda and focus on him.

"What a nice surprise. Have a seat, Dr. Purcell," Gabe gushed in his phony DJ voice.

Purcell pulled a chair out and placed his hat on the table, hands folded prayer-like in front of him.

"I won't stay long," he drawled. "I just thought you should know that we're now in negotiations with the city's Parks and Recreation department to share the maintenance costs of the pool during the summer when they use it. We're hoping that they'll pick up a portion of the insurance on it as well."

Purcell grinned like he'd just won a jackpot at the nearest casino. At heart he hated spending money, whether it was the district's or his own, and he nearly wiggled with pleasure over getting the city of Folsom to share the enormous costs of a pool insurance policy.

"Well, our swim team has been practicing at the Y and can't wait until the pool is officially up and running," Kat said, amiably.

"When's the pool scheduled to be finished?" Serge asked.

"We're hoping it'll be completed some time in January. Just depends on weather and politics—like most things, I guess." Purcell stroked his mustache and grinned.

"Oh, that's rich." Gabe guffawed a tad too loudly.

Purcell's smile immediately died as he looked at Gabe derisively. He studied Gabe to see if he was reading him right. "Well, I'll let you three get back to your meeting," he said, rising with Stetson in hand.

135

Kat caught a glimpse of turquoise shaped points at the tip of his boots. She pretended to yawn to suffocate the laugh that threatened to escape.

"Okay, thanks for stopping by." Gabe's smile lasted only as long as it took to shut the door.

Kat and Serge glanced at each other, silently confirming their suspicions that Gabe was an insecure brown-noser.

"Now let's see, where were we before our esteemed superintendent dropped by?" Gabe put on a serious face once more.

Kat raised her hand half way. "I was talking about the complaint that some of the hard hats working at the library are wolf-whistling at our girls in the morning. How about if I go talk to Owen Snelson? Maybe he can get his subcontractors to lay the law down on their crews."

"Good idea. Let us know how that goes, okay? Now, Serge, I think it's your turn," Gabe prodded, cutting Kat's response out of the conversation.

"Well, my news is not good," Serge began. "Last night about eight o'clock, one of our ninth-graders, Jasmine Richardson, got hit by a car and was taken to the hospital with a broken right leg, a broken arm and several teeth knocked out."

"Oh my God," Kat cried, "how'd that happen?"

"She and Rudy Baker had just left the public library and were crossing Blue Ravine. From what the kids say, the light isn't long enough for them to cross safely through, and it turned red before they'd gotten across the street," Serge said.

"Did anything happen to Rudy?" Gabe's voice went cold with alarm.

"You know how Rudy's always playing catch with a ball? Seems he dropped one as they started through the intersection and went back to the curb to get it. Jasmine was waiting for him in the middle of the crosswalk when the signal changed, and the car came roaring through on the green light."

Serge shook his head in dismay. "So, to answer your question, Gabe, Rudy's fine, just shook up about seeing his girlfriend get hit by a car. The kids said he tried to punch the driver who stopped after the impact, but some other bystanders got involved and held Rudy back. You might want to talk to him, though, Gabe. He's pretty upset, as you may well imagine."

"I'll see if he's in class today and take him to the hospital to see how Jasmine's doing," Gabe responded, his eyes tight with worry.

"You might want to check with her family to see if she wants visitors, Gabe. You know how teenage girls are about their looks. Jasmine might be worried about Rudy's reaction to her sudden lack of teeth," Kat suggested.

"Another good idea. Thanks, Kat. I'll do that." Gabe stood up to signal the end of their meeting. Kat and Serge barely had time to gather their belongings before he was on his computer looking up Jasmine's parents' phone number.

Back in the VP suite, Kat greeted Kalani with a hug and led her into her office. She shut the door quietly, then perched on the edge of her chair.

"Kalani, have you by any chance heard about Jasmine Robinson's accident?"

"I more than heard, Ms. R. I was there when it happened."

"You were there?"

"Grandma and I were coming back from the grocery store, driving on Blue Ravine, and the car that hit Jasmine was just three cars ahead of us. We all slammed on our brakes to avoid crashing into each other. Grandma pulled over to see if we could help, and we had to pull Rudy off the driver who hit Jasmine. He had him by the throat and was choking him, but Grandma threw some white light on Rudy to calm him down, and we led him back to Jasmine's side so he could hold her hand until the ambulance came."

"Who called the ambulance?"

"The man who hit Jasmine had a cell phone, and he called it in. He felt terrible because the light was green, and he didn't see Jasmine in the intersection until it was too late."

"Have you heard how Jasmine's doing?"

"No, I haven't heard a thing, but there's something else that happened that night I think you should know about. It's about Enrique Gavaldon." Kalani lowered her voice despite the fact that Kat's door was shut.

"Is Enrique the kid whose mom is really heavy and lies on the couch with the door open all day?" Kat asked, vaguely remembering the student from his middle school years.

"That's him," Kalani said. "I used to feel sorry for him because his mother was so helpless, but Enrique's got a mouth on him, you know?"

"Yes," Kat agreed, "I remember him from Horace Mann. Always blurting out something inappropriate."

"Well, he was there at the accident and laughed the entire time. I tried to get him to shut up, but he kept it up." Kalani was embarrassed just recalling the incident. If Enrique didn't have enough sense to be ashamed of his own behavior, then she'd be ashamed for him.

"What on earth would possess him to laugh at a time like that?" Kat was repulsed at the boy's reaction.

"Beats me. He kept saying stupid things like: 'You shoulda seen her when she hit the windshield. It was so funny!' Then he'd laugh like a hyena."

"How did Rudy react to him?"

"I don't know if he even heard Enrique. Rudy stayed by Jasmine's side until she was put into the ambulance. He was really upset, so Grandma tried to calm him down."

"Well, I'll keep an eye on Rudy," Kat said. "Not that I'm supposed to. Just between you and me, I've been ordered by Mr. Minelli to stay away from Rudy, and if he's involved in anything, I have to let him handle it." Kat sighed in frustration.

"I'll let you know if I hear anything from any of the other kids, Ms. R." Kalani got up to go into the outer office.

"Kalani? Thanks for filling me about Enrique."

"We're a team, Ms. R. We're a team." Kalani beamed from ear to ear, then went to see what work was waiting for her on Mazie's "to do" list.

139

Kat sat in her office, reviewing everything she had learned about Rudy from his cume folder, his binder and Dawn Silva's report. Then she ran through her own personal observations. *This is his final exam,* she thought. *He'll either pass it by letting Enrique go, or he'll blow it—big time.*

Low self, Kat asked silently, *how would you assess Rudy? Is he as dangerous as I think he is?* The sinking feeling in the pit of her stomach gave her the answer she wanted to know.

Chapter 17

Kat was tired when she dragged herself into the house that night. It had been an emotionally draining day. She walked down to her mailbox and retrieved a mound of catalogs and bills.

I must remember to get the mail everyday, she thought. *It piles up way too fast.*

She combed through the stack, quickly pulling out a post card that was sandwiched between two bills. It was from Conner O'Sullivan, her old high school boyfriend. He planned to be at this year's reunion and wondered if she was planning to go because he'd love to see her.

Ooh, what was that? Kat thought. *My heart skipped a beat. Noooo. I can't be hung up over Conner after all these years. But wait. He's bringing his wife. Cripes. How can I gracefully get out of this? I've already sent my money in. I want my money back. But then again, I'm curious to see how his taste in wives runs. Of course, if Conner's bringing his wife, I can't show up empty-armed. Too bad Alex's dating that red head. I'd be tempted to ask him to go with me, but I'd never get involved with a man who's already attached to someone else.*

Just then Caesar entered through his cat door and put his front paws on her legs, begging to be picked up.

"Want to be my date to my class reunion?" Kat asked, scooping him up and holding him like a baby. Caesar squirmed out of her arms and jumped to the floor near his empty cat dish. "I take it that's a no," Kat said, reaching for the cat food.

141

Later that night, as she was turning down the sheets getting ready for bed, Kat wondered how different her life might have turned out if she had married Connor instead of Mark. She fell asleep with a grin on her face, fantasizing about Connor, but the dream she had that night told her everything she wanted to know. She dreamed she was a contestant on The Price Is Right and every time she picked a prize door, it opened up onto a flat wall, obviously a metaphor for a dead end road. She got the message.

The next day thunderclouds gathered in the October sky as Kat tugged at the hood of her windbreaker. She was in the middle of the quad, hustling stragglers to get to class on time. Lunch was over, and the late bell had already rung, but Kat couldn't return to the warmth of her office until all the students were back in class. Along with the campus monitors, Kat, Serge, and Gabe each covered pre-assigned sections of the campus every day to get tardy students into class. Just as the four administrators converged in the middle of the quad and were about to congratulate themselves on a job well done, the fire alarm went off.

"Oh no, not again," Gabe groaned. He used the radio on his phone to alert the listening staff to report to their usual fire drill stations.

"That's the eighth one since school started," Serge griped, running with Kat and Gabe back to the main office.

"I bet it's the construction workers sneaking cigarettes again," Kat said. *Damn, I have got to get in better shape*, she thought, as she huffed and puffed to keep up with her colleagues.

Once in the building, all three darted to the hallway where the main panel was blinking to indicate where the alarm had originated. The word *Theater* was lit up in red on the grid.

Gabe called Tony Navarro to check out the theater while Kat went outside to wait for the fire crew to show up. *I bet we get fined this time*, she thought. The fire chief, she knew, was getting irritated with the many false alarms generated at the new school. The first few times he was tolerant, but during the last episode, he was downright nasty, threatening to impose a $500 fine on the school for any future false alarms. There were plans in the works to install more video cameras near the fire sensors around campus in the hopes of catching the vandals, but until that happened, the kids all knew it was a free-for-all for them to pull the alarms in obscure sectors on campus or to light matches under the ceiling fire detectors in the bathrooms and run.

Tony radioed back to say he had found two sheepish-looking hard hats who "forgot" they weren't allowed to smoke on campus. Serge had called the alarm company to stop the fire crew from coming out for another false alarm, but it was too late. The fire truck's distant wail could already be heard. The administrators braced themselves for the wrath of the fire captain.

Suddenly, Kat heard her name on the radio speaker. It was Andrea Chan, advising her that a student had been seriously injured during the fire drill and to meet her in the health clinic right away. Kat took off like a shot, adrenaline kicking in to speed her progress. By the time she bolted into the health room, a crowd of student looky-

143

loos had gathered. She parted her way through them to discover Enrique Gavaldon on a cot, moaning in pain. She turned to the students who were craning their necks trying to get a look.

"Look, you guys have to get back to class," Kat said, motioning the students to leave. "The show's over. Now. Let's go."

The group reluctantly dispersed, and Kat asked Janet Crane, the health assistant, how Enrique got hurt.

"I can tell you that, Kat," piped up Lily Boone.

Lily was a tall, lanky math teacher, in her forties. Despite her popularity with the students, she had a demeanor about her that implied she was always worried about something. Her brows were permanently knit together, as though the direst catastrophe was about to happen any minute. Today's event, however, seemed to justify her usual countenance.

"When the fire alarm went off, I dismissed the class and told them to walk over to their designated section of the blacktop. I was about to lock my door when I heard Enrique saying, 'Help me. I can't walk.' I found him crawling on the floor in the back of the room. I ran back outside and called for someone to help me. Rudy Baker came back and helped me carry Enrique out of the room and onto the lawn until Janet could bring the wheelchair."

Lily took a swig from a water bottle, her gloomy face perspiring from this brief accounting. "I've asked him to tell me how it all happened, but he hasn't been able to tell me."

Kat nodded, then bent down to speak to Enrique who was lying on the cot with his eyes closed.

144

"Enrique, this is Ms. Romero. Can you tell me what happened?"

"Oooh, my back," he groaned. "Did you call my mom?"

Janet answered for Kat. "Yes, we talked to her, Enrique, and she authorized us to send for an ambulance. It's on the way."

Enrique grunted, sweat forming on his face. He was clearly in pain.

"Listen, Enrique, you have to tell us what happened to you," Kat said.

Before he could reply, Andrea Chan, the district nurse, burst into the room, breathing hard from running. Kat filled her in on what little she knew. Andrea hurriedly called Gabe to alert him an ambulance would be arriving any minute on campus and he should direct the EMT's to the health office. Then she took Enrique's vital signs and started her report. She, too, asked Enrique what happened to him, but got no answer, just more cries of pain.

After Enrique had been taken to the hospital, Kat visited Lily Boone's classroom. She stood quietly at the front of the room until the students settled down.

"I want you all to take out a piece of paper and a pen or a pencil," she said.

One by one the students rattled their backpacks and popped open their binders. Kat noticed they were unusually subdued and compliant, considering the disruption they'd just gone through with the bogus fire alarm.

"Now, I want you to write as legibly as possible what you saw and heard from the moment you heard the

145

alarm go off until you returned to the classroom here. Write down specifically anything you've heard and seen, who said what to whom—that type of thing. Raise your hand when you're finished and I'll collect your papers. Any questions?"

Mitchell Davis, a gawky sophomore in the back of the room, put his hand up to get Kat's attention. "I have one, Ms. Romero. What does legibly mean?"

"It means so I can read it. No chicken scratch or hieroglyphics, okay? You can print if your handwriting is too scribbly."

Kat circled the room until all the students had turned in their responses. She thanked Lily for her help in collecting the papers, secured them with a paper clip, then returned to her office.

She locked herself in her office to discourage interruptions while she kicked her speed-reading skills into gear. It took only five minutes to scan the stack. She put two of them aside, mulling over what to do about them. Two students had fingered Rudy Baker as the person who had injured Enrique. When the students were vacating the room for the fire drill, Rudy had thrown Enrique to the floor, muttered something like "This is what you get for laughing at my girlfriend," and stomped on his spine with the heel of his boot as hard as he possibly could.

So Rudy had heard Enrique laughing when Jasmine had gotten hit by a car, Kat thought. *He just waited until the opportunity arose to get even.*

Kat was horrified and fascinated at the same time. *How could a kid cave in another kid's back, then return to the scene of the crime and play the good Samaritan by helping the student he injured to the health clinic? The kid's a budding psychopath.*

Kat immediately put in a call to her ex-husband. She was surprised to have gotten through on the third ring, just as he was surprised to hear from her.

"Mark, since you're assigned to Anthony High, I need you to investigate something for me. About a half hour ago, one of our students, Enrique Gavaldon, was seriously injured by another student. He's being taken to Kaiser Hospital. Any chance you can stop by there and get him to identify the person who assaulted him?" Kat crossed her fingers and waited for Mark's reply.

"I'm just finishing up a report here, Kat," Mark said. "Should be done in a few minutes. Got to check with my boss first, then I'll swing over to see this kid. What's his name again?"

"Enrique Gavaldon. Two students have already pinpointed a kid named Rudy Baker as the one who did it, but I need Enrique to verify the name before we suspend Rudy and press charges."

"Okay, got it. I'll call you when I know something," Mark said amiably.

"Thanks, Mark. Appreciate it."

Kat hung up and sank back into her chair, grateful that Mark would step in to help. After their divorce he had mellowed toward her, often wanting to do her favors, like fix dripping faucets or tune up Sean's car. It was his way of saying he was sorry, Kat knew.

Now with her eyes closed, she visualized how Gabe would react to Rudy's impending arrest. *Oh, God,* she thought, *there isn't enough pink light in the universe to soften the blow. Gabe will be outraged.*

Chapter 18

Caesar was unusually friendly when Kat came home that night from school. He purred and rubbed against her like he was earning points for a Boy Scouts badge. Kat would have scooped him up for a hug if the phone hadn't been ringing when she walked in the door. She threw her purse and keys on the dryer and scurried to answer it. It was Mark.

"Hey, Kat, I got a chance to talk to Enrique. It took a lot of convincing, and at first he wouldn't admit it was Rudy. But when I told him two students were willing to serve as witnesses, he finally agreed to file a complaint. Turns out that Enrique made fun of Rudy's girlfriend when she got hit by a car not too long ago, so he figures Rudy was paying him back for being mean."

"What's Enrique's prognosis?"

"MRI shows two ruptured discs. He's being prepped right now for surgery. The doctor said he'll insert grafting hardware, rods and a cage. Says the kid'll be lucky to walk again."

"Wow, that's pretty serious. What are you going to do about Rudy?"

"I'll send somebody over to the school to get statements from your two witnesses, then my partner and I will arrest Rudy first thing tomorrow morning. What do you think—at home or at school?"

"Definitely at school. Why don't you come at 8:30 so we can time his arrest with the end of first period. I want the other kids to see him being hauled away in a cop car, you know? It'll send a loud and clear message that we won't tolerate that kind of behavior."

"Okay. I'll see you in your office tomorrow morning." Mark started to hang up, but Kat had one more bit of information to share.

"And Mark? Be really careful with Rudy. He's a former Crip. Rumor has it that he shot two people as part of his initiation into the gang. I made the mistake of listening to Gabe Minelli, our principal, and hired Rudy to help me move to my new house. Now that I know him better, it's dawned on me that he was getting ready to steal my sapphire and diamond necklace when I walked in on him in my bedroom closet. Watch him like a hawk, Mark. He can be very charming and manipulate the pants off you."

Mark snickered. "He even thinks about it, he's buzzard bait."

"Gotcha. See you in the a.m. Thanks."

Kat hung up the phone, turned, and gasped. In the hallway, two red glowing eyes stared at her, eyes which were suspended in space, eerie and penetrating. Her throat constricted with fear, and for a moment she was so stunned, she didn't know how to respond. Then, her fear erupted into anger as she screamed, "Get away from me!"

The eyes held fast, their menacing gaze boring through Kat's. She held up her left hand, palm up, and her right hand, palm out, and mentally commanded mana to flow out and push the eyes away. She glared back at the

150

eyes and again demanded them to get away from her. "Now!" she roared. She directed more energy streams toward the eyes, until they gradually retreated and faded away.

Trembling from the effort, Kat sank on her couch to calm herself until her knees could stop shaking. Her heart beat so loudly she thought for sure her neighbors could hear it.

What on earth was that, she thought. *God, I wish I could talk to Liana right now. Maybe the eyes belong to the same person who sent the conch shell. If they do, then somebody's really out to get me. But who...Wait a minute! I know what I can do. Why didn't I think of that before?*

She went to the shower and turned the water on full force, stripped off her clothes and quickly stepped in. She did her forgiveness prayer, reinstated her force field, and put a mirror shield of protection around her body.

All right, low self, little buddy. Show me the face of the person who's sending me hate. Show me the person whose eyes came to visit tonight.

Like a photo developing in a dark room, an image began to form in her mind's eye. It was an older male with flowing gray hair, a grimace of pain on his face.

Who is that? And what does he want with me? I swear, Liana, I'm going to buy you a phone!

Still troubled and frustrated, Kat turned off the shower and toweled dry. Even though it was fairly early, she was emotionally spent. She put on her pajamas, readied for bed, and allowed Caesar to share her bed with her—a rare treat for him-- with orders to wake her up if any more demonic-looking apparitions emerged while she

151

slept. Caesar took these requests in stride, gracefully licking his paws and washing his face before settling down with Kat for the night.

Chapter 19

Kat got to school an hour earlier than usual, sprinting from her car to the administration building to dodge the continuous downpour that was saturating the Sacramento valley since midnight. Once inside her office, she got on-line to key in Rudy's assault on Enrique. She also filled out the paperwork for a five-day suspension for Rudy as well as a request for a pre-expulsion hearing. This involved printing out Rudy's transcript, attendance record and referrals to the office all year. Kat had also put in a call to the school Rudy attended before coming to Anthony High, leaving a message on the VP answering machine for someone to call her with information on any suspensions Rudy may have gotten during the previous school year.

Oh, God, give me the courage to deal with Gabe once he learns Rudy's been arrested, Kat prayed, her eyebrows furrowed with worry.

Kat decided to dial Dawn for moral support, but it was too early for the start of work, and Dawn's answering machine picked up. Kat left her a message, briefly describing Rudy's impending arrest and asked her to call when she could.

Mazie soon came bustling in, surprised to see Kat with so much paperwork done so early in the morning. As Kat filled her in about Rudy's assault of Enrique and Mark's scheduled visit to arrest him, Mazie clucked and harrumphed disapprovingly.

"That kid's psycho," she said, shaking her head. "Well, I had that lunatic pegged from the get go. Where's Mark gonna do his thing?"

"I'm going to have Rudy meet me, Gabe and Mark in the big conference room by Gabe's office. I'm hoping to wrap everything up by the end of first period. That way when Mark takes Rudy away in handcuffs, it'll be during the passing period, and all the kids will be out and about to see the big show."

"I bet you anything that Rudy will act the fool for the crowd, too," Mazie sighed smugly. "I'm gonna set one of the cameras on our main door so I can watch from here." She fiddled with some dials on the console and adjusted one of the cameras to give her a wide view of the front of the administration building.

Just before eight thirty, Mark and his partner, Darren Riley, arrived in full uniform, their guns holstered, their chests puffed out. Four students, all on referral in the VP suite, stared at them wide-eyed with fear.

Nodding at Mazie, Mark walked directly in to Kat's office while Riley sat next to a rangy male student whose Adam's apple bobbed up and down as he swallowed nervously. Darren smiled at the teenager who obviously didn't appreciate an up-close-and-personal visit by the police.

"You're here early," Kat said. "All set?"

Mark shrugged. "Almost. I thought I'd drop by to say hi to Sean first. Since I'm here."

"Come on, I'll show you where he is," Kat offered.

When she and Mark left together, the students on referral let out a collective sigh of relief except for the boy

154

adjacent to Darren who was now sprouting beads of perspiration to accompany his active Adam's apple.

Mazie turned her head to cover up her smirk at his discomfort. *Serves you right, you little heathen,* she thought. *That's exactly what you'll have waiting for you if you stay on the road you're walking down.*

As they approached the counseling office, Kat asked Mark to keep it secret that she and Sean were mother and son.

Surprised by this request, Mark agreed, but with one caveat. "I hope you don't expect me to play the same game, Kat."

"Oh, no," Kat replied. "We just don't want the kids or faculty playing us off against each other or using our relationship to get to either one of us, you know?"

Mark nodded in reassurance and knocked on Sean's door.

Sean opened the door and beamed at his father, delighted at the surprise visit. "Hi, Dad. What brings you here?"

"I'm here on business, but wanted to say hi." Mark looked around Sean's office and acknowledged the student sitting near Sean's desk. "I can see you're busy, so I won't stay. Nice office, Sean. It's good to see you. It's been a while."

"Good to see you, too, Dad. Thanks for stopping by. I'll call you so we can get together, okay?" Mark nodded, and Sean closed the door slowly, watching his parents wistfully as they headed for the principal's office.

Mark signaled to his partner to join them as they headed for the principal's office. Mazie called the campus monitors to have them bring Rudy to the main office.

Denise buzzed Kat and the two officers into Gabe's office. The startled look on Gabe's face told them he'd been caught unaware of the situation.

"Officers," Gabe said, standing up to shake hands with Mark and Darren. "What brings you here this fine morning? Have a seat. Please."

Gabe pointed to the chairs nearest him, but they pulled two out that were closest to the door and sat down. Gabe quickly scanned his suit for wrinkles and smoothed both arms down nervously.

"Ms. Romero called me to investigate an assault and battery that occurred here yesterday during the fire drill," Mark began. Kat could feel Gabe's beady eyes drilling into the side of her head, but she remained focused on Mark.

"One of your students, Enrique Gavaldon, was seriously injured and taken to the hospital by ambulance," Mark continued, his matter-of-fact tone squelching any questions.

"That much I heard about," Gabe interjected. "He had some sort of back injury. Had trouble walking." Gabe's wide eyes were dry and twitched nervously as he tried to catch Kat's attention. She ignored him and stayed glued to Mark's every word.

"Right. Well, I interviewed Enrique for two hours at the hospital before he'd talk to me. He was scared to death that his assailant would retaliate against him and his family. It was only after I promised to keep the perpetrator permanently away from him that he was willing to tell me who assaulted him."

Mark looked at Kat as if asking permission to tell all. Kat's nod to go forward was infinitesimal so that only someone who knew her well could read her body language.

"Ms. Romero also spent time investigating the incident and was able to find two witnesses who were willing to verify the identity of the assailant. Before I tell you who he named, let me tell you that Enrique sustained two ruptured disks and underwent laser surgery."

Mark heard a quiet rap on the door and got up to answer it. "And here he is now."

The door swung open, and Rudy, escorted by the two campus monitors, Gonzo and Sabrina, shuffled into the room.

First Gabe's eyes popped out and his mouth hung open in amazement. Then he glared at Kat viciously, biting his tongue so he wouldn't release the venom he wanted to spew all over her.

"Rudy, please have a seat over here," Mark commanded, pointing to the chair farthest away from the door. *Guess he knows Rudy would try to run if he could,* Kat thought.

Mark got up to shut the door, then turned to address Rudy whose eyes were darting angrily back and forth from the officers to Gabe.

"Rudy Baker, I have a warrant for your arrest for assaulting Enrique Gavaldon yesterday in Mrs. Boone's classroom at the start of the fire drill."

157

Rudy stared at the policeman defiantly but said nothing.

Darren read Rudy his Miranda Rights, but Rudy continued to sulk in silence while Gabe seemed to deflate right before everyone's eyes.

"Rudy, did you do this to Enrique?" Gabe shivered at the thought.

Rudy shoved his chair away from the table. "No, Dad, I didn't. I'm being framed. Whoever those snitches were just don't like me. I didn't do it!" Rudy latched on to Gabe's arm and shook it hard to convince him of his sincerity.

Mark sneered in contempt at the boy. "Just like you didn't shoot two rival gang members to get into the Crips."

Rudy's head swiveled instantly toward the cop, searching his face questioningly. Kat stared at the table, determined not to give herself away.

"And just what are you insinuating, officer? That Rudy's guilty of attempted murder?" demanded Gabe.

Oh boy. He better come up with something good, Kat thought.

"After I left the hospital yesterday," Mark said coldly, "I did some research on Rudy's background. I talked to his uncle and his sister. His sister said Rudy popped two Bloods as part of his initiation to get into the Crips."

Gabe's breath caught in his throat, and he sputtered, "Rudy, is that true?" He peered closely into Rudy's face.

158

"No, Dad, it's not true. My sister's got a great imagination, that's all." Rudy tugged on Gabe's arm. "Please! You gotta believe me. I never killed anybody."

"I never said killed, Rudy. I said popped, meaning shot," Mark said testily.

Gabe looked at Rudy and, despite his initial reservations, caved in to Rudy's pleas for support. "If you said it isn't true, then I believe you, son," he half-whispered.

Mark shot a quick look at Kat for confirmation, then assumed his command of the conference.

"For now, we're going to give you the benefit of the doubt on that charge, Rudy. It's only hearsay. But for this current violation, you're under arrest. Stand up and face the wall. Put both hands up high and place them against the wall." Mark frisked Rudy as Darren slapped handcuffs on him before leading him out of the office.

Just as Kat had hoped, the bell had rung to dismiss class and students were pouring out of their classrooms into the quad and hallways. A group of them, gawking and pointing, saw Rudy being led away in handcuffs to the patrol car.

Kat followed the officers out the front door and mouthed thanks to Mark as he pushed Rudy's head down and placed him into the back seat of his squad car. She waved at the video camera which she was sure Mazie was watching, then skewed up her courage and walked back to Gabe's office.

Gabe, both hands propping up his stony face, sat trance-like at his desk. Kat shut the door and returned to her seat, waiting for Gabe to compose himself.

Finally, he turned to her, his icy stare penetrating right through her. "I thought you were going to turn any Rudy incidents over to me first, Kat. Did you or did you not say that to me?" The veins in his neck were throbbing noticeably.

"There wasn't any time, Gabe," Kat insisted. "When I got the kids to turn in their incident reports and discovered they were saying Rudy did it, you were at the district office at the principals' meeting. You gave me standing orders not to disturb you at those meetings. Besides, I didn't find out for sure until late last night when Mark, I mean, Officer Matthews, called me at home."

"So, why didn't you call me at home when you found out?" Gabe asked, pointedly. "For that matter, why didn't you have Officer Matthews arrest Rudy at home, instead of embarrassing both of us by doing it here?"

"I didn't call you at home because, frankly, I didn't want you to tip Rudy off. He'd have probably run away, you know? Besides, the warrant wasn't issued until this morning. Everything depended on silence and timing," Kat replied earnestly.

Gabe thought about what Kat had said, all the while working his facial muscles and biting the sides of his mouth.

"Look Gabe," Kat reasoned, "if we didn't move fast on this, Enrique's mother would sue us for negligence in letting her son's attacker off the hook. And what if Rudy had run away? Who knows what other consequences would have happened here? I had no choice." Kat swallowed hard, hoping Gabe wouldn't notice her nervousness.

160

Finally, after what seemed like hours, Gabe softened. "I guess you didn't," he mumbled, tugging on his coat sleeves which had ridden up his arms.

Kat handed him a set of papers. "Since you're now his guardian, I'm giving you a copy of his five-day suspension notice. Because of the severity of Enrique's injuries, I'm going for an expulsion as well. Again, I have no choice here, Gabe. I have to follow administrative protocol. I'm sorry. I really am."

Gabe said nothing, and Kat went back to her office, shaking like a leaf, emotionally spent.

She locked the door, pulled the blinds shut, and sat in the darkened room with the terra cotta soldier in her hands, praying for the energy that had been stored in the little statue to charge into her body. She visualized the energy flowing to her like a water trough, gushing, bubbling, and saturating her body through and through. After a few minutes, she felt rejuvenated.

Later that afternoon, when Kalani reported for work in the office, Kat suddenly remembered the glowing red eyes from the night before. She pulled Kalani into her office and closed the door.

"I've got to tell you about something that happened last night. I'd have called you, but you still don't have a phone, right?"

Kalani nodded, eyes wide.

"Did you hear about Rudy getting arrested this morning?"

Kalani nodded again.

"Well, last night I'd been on the phone talking to Officer Matthews about arranging for Rudy's arrest. Just as

I hung up the phone, I saw a pair of red glowing eyes in the hallway."

"Oh my God." Kalani shuttered, searching Kat's face for signs of distress.

"The odd thing was, it was just a pair of eyes, no face, no person, just demonic eyes suspended in the air."

"I screamed at them to go away and held my hands out like this," Kat continued, gesturing to Kalani. "Then I visualized mana pushing the eyes away and erasing them like on a white board. They eventually disappeared, but the whole thing was terrifying. When I couldn't call you or Liana, I got the idea to do the protective shield ritual and asked to be shown the face of my enemy."

"Let me guess," Kalani suggested in her quiet voice. "It was a thin male, with long gray hair and bony shoulders, right?"

"Yeah, I only saw his face, but how did you know?" Kat's mouth hung open in bewilderment.

"Because he's the same one that sent the conch shell. Grandma told me she did a little prayer ceremony to find out who sent you the shell, and his image popped up."

I'm not going crazy after all, Kat thought.

"Funny. Before I did the mirror shield, I thought it was a younger guy out to get me next. But now, this old guy showed up. I've never seen him before in my whole life. Who is he and why is he after me?"

"I don't know, Ms. R. Sometimes you don't have to do anything to have people be threatened by you. It's just who you are that bothers him."

"Who I am? But I'm nobody. I'm just a teacher and a vice-principal. I'm not a movie star, a pro athlete, or an elected official. And I'm certainly not rich and famous. What could he possibly want with someone as innocuous as me?"

"But you had the power to make the eyes disappear, didn't you?" Kalani prodded. "Think about that. No one told you how to do it or what to say, but you automatically knew how to direct your energy to protect yourself and make him go, right?"

Kat was stunned. "I, uh, I never thought about it that way. About me having any kind of special power, I mean. But you're right. It just came naturally to me. Do you think my so-called power threatens this person somehow? Could that be what it's all about, Kalani?"

"I think so and so does Grandma. You need to come over to see her so she can explain it all to you, Ms. R.," Kalani said gently, skirting the worry in Kat's eyes.

Kat scrutinized Kalani's face. "Why do I have the feeling you know more than you're telling me, Kalani?" She smiled at the brown-eyed beauty who only grinned enigmatically.

"Okay, when can I come over? I can't tonight. I've got to supervise the football game. Tell you what. Have Liana call me tomorrow at home and maybe we can get together this weekend."

"Okay. I'll have her call you. But I'm going to give you Mrs. Eagan's number. She's lives right next door and lets us use her phone anytime we want. She also takes our messages in case you need to get in touch with us." Kalani dug in her backpack for a pencil and ripped a page out of her notebook, quickly scribbling the number for Kat.

Kat took the note and breathed a sigh of relief. "Thanks, Kalani. I wish I knew what this is all about, but I'll wait—impatiently, I might add—to hear from Liana, so I can get closure on all of this."

"I hate to disappoint you, Ms. R., but it's not going to be closure that you'll get. It's really the start of something big, something so…well, I'm sworn to secrecy. You need to talk to Grandma." Kalani waited for these words to sink into Kat's mind.

Squinting her eyes skeptically, Kat simply nodded, as Kalani went out to help Mazie file student referrals and attendance reports.

Oh my God, she thought. *Now what? The start of something big? Why can't my life be normal and dull? I don't recall writing a script where I starred as the crisis queen.*

Kat listened patiently for an answer, but all she heard was the sound of students outside her door waiting to be dealt with for misbehaving in class.

When school was finally out, Kat helped Mazie sort and pack the CBEDS surveys to return them on time to the California Department of Education. As they stacked the heavy return boxes in the mailroom for pick up, Kat noticed Mazie wheezing.

"Hey, Maze, would you like for me to get your inhaler?"

Mazie sat on some nearby cartons to rest. "I don't have an inhaler with me today, Kat." Mazie sucked air in laboriously and tried to calm herself.

164

"But you really need it, especially now." Kat shot a look of concern at her, as Mazie sighed and rolled her shoulders, stalling to give herself time to decide whether to confide in Kat or not. She decided to take the chance.

"I'm on a real tight budget right now, Kat," Mazie admitted. "Been sending money home to my mom. She's behind in taxes and needs my help, so I skimp on meds, and I'm out of inhalers until payday. Now, don't get me wrong. I'm not telling you this for sympathy or a handout, and I wouldn't take anything from you even if you offered. Anyway, don't worry about me. I'll make it. It's only temporary."

Kat covered Mazie in green light to bring in healing energy for her asthma before speaking. "Okay, Mazie, if you won't take any cash from me, how about you and I doing a prayer for money? I just learned a new way of praying that's pretty powerful. Want to try it?"

"I'm game. Prayer certainly can't hurt," Mazie answered with a smile.

Kat led Mazie into her office where she shut the door, gave her a quick review of the Huna philosophy, and performed the *ha* ritual on Mazie's behalf. Mazie sat still, her breathing coming easier now.

When Kat was done, she opened her eyes, bright with promise. "That's it, Mazie. We have launched our prayer to get you some money. Now it's up to the universe to find a way to make it happen. Notice we didn't specify how or when it will happen. We just need to trust that it will, okay?"

"Girl, you are too much. I don't know how you did it, but I'm breathing a bit easier all the way 'round.

Thanks, honey," Mazie said, putting her arms around Kat and squeezing hard.

"You're welcome," Kat said, wincing from Mazie's powerful grip.

"I owe you, girlfriend," Mazie said, wagging her finger at Kat.

"No, you don't," Kat countered.

"No matter what happens, even if the prayer gets answered, and the answer is no, you still cared enough to try. For that, I got your back. And I'm not taking no for an answer on that, got me?"

"Gotcha," Kat said. Then she stood up and saluted. "I mean, yes, Ma'am, Sergeant Longer."

"All right, then." Mazie saluted back. "Let's get this stupid stuff over with." With that, she and Kat went back to packing CBEDS surveys, this time with renewed energy and a deeper bond of friendship.

Chapter 20

Something tells me I should pay a little surprise visit to Alex today, Kat thought, blinking at the bright sunshine penetrating the gaps in her bedroom drapes. It was Sunday morning, and she'd slept in until almost nine, which was late for her. She looked over at Caesar, asleep in his bed in the corner of her bedroom.

"Wake up, Attack Cat!" she shouted, delighted that she got a chance to wake him up first for a change.

Caesar yawned and stretched, then rubbed his ears and washed his paws.

"What? No head rubs? No purrs for me?"

Caesar continued his grooming in an aura of aloofness.

"Are you jealous because I've decided to talk to Alex today? Well, not to worry, Caesar. No one will ever replace you in my heart. Anyway, I think Alex already has a girlfriend. However, just in case I'm wrong about that, I do need a date for my class reunion."

She reached over to pet Caesar, and suddenly he came alive, purring, licking her face, kneading his paws on her arm.

"Wow, if I didn't know better, I'd think you and I were telepathic," she said, making one last swipe down his back and over his tail. He stared up at her, slowly tilting his head.

"Let me try something with you, Caesar," Kat said, with sudden inspiration. "Remember that little catnip

167

mouse you like to play with? Show me where you put it. Take me to your mouse."

Kat watched in amazement as Caesar stepped around her and headed toward the laundry room. She followed him, watching as he clawed at an object stuck between the washer and dryer. First a little black nose emerged and then the tell-tale chewed ears.

"It's your mouse! Oh, Caesar, I'm not just imagining it. You do understand me!"

Caesar rubbed against Kat's leg and purred. She picked him up and tousled his head.

"I'll talk to you later, Caesar. I promise. But for now, I need you to go outside so I can get some cleaning done." She set him down and watched in wonder as he disappeared through the cat door.

By ten o'clock she'd brewed coffee, threw a coffee cake in the oven, and squeezed fresh oranges for two small glasses of juice. Then, as casually and confidently as possible, she crossed the street and rang Alex's doorbell. No answer. She tried one more time and was starting to walk back home when Alex appeared in a bathrobe at the front door.

"Hi, Alex. I hope I didn't wake you. I can't believe it's been over a month since I promised you coffee, so I thought I'd make good on my promise. Unless today's not a good day for you?" She swallowed back the nervous lump in her throat.

Kat could count on one hand the number of times she'd ventured first to seek out a man's company and felt jittery about her boldness. *Of course, this wouldn't constitute an actual date,* she reasoned. *It's just a little neighborly chat inside a house instead of over a fence.*

Alex put his hand over his mouth to hide a yawn and adjusted his glasses. "I apologize for yawning, Kat. I'd love to have coffee with you. Let me just wake up a bit, and I'll be right over."

"Okay. See you soon." Kat stumbled backwards, stepping right onto his Sunday newspaper. "Oops, sorry about that," she said, handing him the mangled mound of paper, the front page tattered from her tennis shoe.

"No problem. Don't worry about it," he answered, grinning. "I mess it up almost every day myself when I come out here without my glasses."

"Thanks for saying that, Alex, even though I feel like a clumsy oaf. See you."

Kat turned and crossed the street, pausing to see how the newly planted daylilies were doing. She glimpsed back at Alex's door and was surprised to see him still looking at her. Caught staring, he shut his door really fast. Kat walked back in her house, a smile of satisfaction on her face.

Oh no! The coffee cake! She flew inside and banged open the oven door. *Whew!* She breathed a sigh of relief. It hadn't burned to a crisp. *Man, I'm not used to being domestic any more. At least not enough to feed another human being other than myself.*

Kat arranged some freshly picked daisies in a vase for the center of the table and put the warmed coffee cake on a trivet. She noticed Caesar was standing expectantly at the front door when Alex rang the doorbell.

"Hi Alex," Kat said. "Come in. Don't worry about Caesar. I'm sure you'll pass his inspection."

Alex stooped to pet Caesar who offered an ear to be scratched. "Hail, Caesar," he said. "You're sure a long way from Rome."

"How do you take your coffee, Alex?" Kat asked, once he'd been seated at the kitchen table.

"Black's fine, thanks," he replied, looking around the room at the variety of plants, ivies, ferns and silk flowers that shared her living space. "You must really like plants," he commented, "but more than that, they appear to like you. I bet you have a green thumb."

"Not really. Well, maybe. You should see my Dad's house. He's getting ready to retire after nearly thirty years of working in a nursery. He knows the scientific name of every plant you can think of. He's got a peace lily so huge, he's named it Audrey, like in The Little Shop of Horrors. When you walk by it, you think it's going to reach out and devour you."

"Feed me, Seymour," Alex recited in a high-pitched voice.

"That was good." Kat laughed. She sliced the coffee cake and placed a healthy portion on a plate for Alex.

"So how are things at Anthony High going? Are they finished with the construction yet? I drive by there once in a while, and it seems there's always some kind of building going on," Alex said, polishing off his orange juice in two gulps.

"Nope, they're still working on the library and the swimming pool. Should be completed early next year. Want more orange juice?"

170

"No, thanks, I'm fine for now." With his coffee mug clutched in one hand, Alex leaned back in his chair and glanced out the window, taking in the view of the backyard. "Nice landscaping back there," he commented. "The landscaping at your high school is really great, too."

"Yes, it is. I think it makes the kids act better when they're in a beautiful setting. It wasn't like that for me when I went to high school," Kat said wistfully.

"Not for me, either. It's been a long time since I was in high school. All I have are fading memories of being self-conscious and worried all the time. Is it still like that for most kids?"

"Pretty much. It doesn't matter what size or shape they are, just about all teenagers are insecure. They're just trying to find their way in life. Looking for that 'one thing' they can be proud of or be known for."

"I understand." Alex smiled knowingly.

"They also try to test the limits on how much they can get away with. That's part of my job—to draw the line and keep them from crossing it. I'm still too new at administration to get used to the negative vibes, though. I was pretty popular as a teacher, but now that I'm a disciplinarian, most of the kids and some of the teachers automatically see me as the enemy. I guess I need to grow thicker skin so my feelings won't get hurt so much when I get cussed at or criticized. The problem is I don't want to lose the sensitivity that made me a good teacher to begin with, at the expense of growing that thicker skin. I just have to find a balance."

171

Kat looked down at the coffee cake on her plate, untouched. "I'm talking too much. Tell me about you. What kind of writing do you do?"

"I'm more of a teacher of writing, than a writer, really. I teach at Sierra River College. The Writing for Publication classes. I've been getting up early during the week to work on my first novel, but it's only in the outline stage at this point." Alex ran his hand through his wavy gray hair.

"I used to teach English and Language Arts before I became an administrator. I always thought some day I'd write the great American novel. So, in a way, you're living my dream, Alex."

"I used to be a journalist. I wrote the sports column for the *Napa Sun*. Then I found my way to Sacramento and started teaching students how to get into print. Actually, I take that back. I don't teach them so much as coach them through the process. I encourage them to believe in themselves first and never give up on their dreams of becoming writers."

"That's a lot like how I work with my students," Kat said. "When they wind up in my office, they're usually in trouble and just about every time, they're angry about something from home or something that happened when they were younger. I know that anger is a secondary reaction to fear. So I try to cut to the heart of the conflict and find out what they're afraid of. Then I try to help them see all the other ways they could have solved the problem without resorting to threats, name-calling, and fights. They just need to be encouraged to take a deep look at themselves and try liking what they see. So many of our kids just don't like themselves."

"That's true of adults, too," Alex said. "The average age of my students is forty-two. For the first month of class, I work hard on improving their self-esteem just to get them to give themselves permission to write. So many of them are perfectionists. They don't think they'll measure up to their own high expectations. Or they fear failure. They think they'll miss the mark and be ashamed. Once they're more confident to start writing, they turn out the most amazing work I've ever seen. But it takes a lot of encouragement to unleash the power that's in them, you know?"

"Yes, I do," Kat answered agreeably. She started to clear the dishes from the table. "So what's your novel about?"

"It's a mystery to me," he said, laughing. "No, just kidding. It truly is a mystery. Since I left the newspaper, I've thought a lot about putting my experience with sports to good use. So, I'm writing a mystery about a professional athlete who finds himself recruited as a spy for the CIA. I've got the characters down pretty much. I just need to tighten up the plot a bit."

"Sounds intriguing. I'd love to read it when you're finished."

"You're on. I haven't worked on it in weeks. My father passed away, and I've been too busy with funeral arrangements and family visits to get back to writing. Remember when I waved to you a few weeks back? I'd just picked my sister up from the airport. She and I had to organize the funeral and write funeral notices and

173

eulogies. So now that all of that's over, I can get back on schedule with my book." Alex cleared his throat, struggling to keep his emotions in check.

Kat felt jubilant upon hearing that the mysterious redhead in Alex's life was his sister, but realized that now was not the appropriate time to react with glee.

"I'm sorry to hear about the loss of your father, Alex. My parents are both living, but my mother's not doing too well. She has Alzheimer's and has been hospitalized for a while in Stockton. My dad sees her once a week, and she still recognizes him, but she can't communicate much anymore. It's sad." Kat looked wistfully away.

"That's rough, Kat," Alex sympathized. "You and I are at that age, though, when the roles reverse, and we, children, end up taking care of our parents, aren't we?"

"Uh huh. Speaking of age, Alex, I need to ask you something." Kat watched his face carefully, anticipating his reaction.

"I have my thirtieth-year high school class reunion coming up next month, and I was wondering if you'd like to go with me. It's a dinner at a restaurant at Jack London Square in Oakland. I've only been to one reunion, so I haven't seen anyone in years, but for some reason, I want to go to this one. And I'd rather not go alone. Of course, if you're involved with someone, I'd understand if you said no."

"I'd love to go, Kat. I went to high school in Colorado, and I've never been back to any of my reunions. My thirtieth won't be coming up until next year."

174

"So I'm one year older than you, hmm?" Kat teased.

"Probably two. I skipped a grade in elementary school."

"Skipped it because you were away or skipped it because you were smart?"

"Which do you think?"

"Smart."

"You got it."

Suddenly the phone rang, breaking up their repartee. Kat excused herself to answer it. It was Liana.

"I really need to see you, Kat," she said. "Can you come over this afternoon?"

"Sure, I'd love to see you," Kat said. "I've got company right now, but how about if I stop by around one?"

"Thanks, dear. I'll see you then. Bye." Liana hung up.

Alex looked at Kat uncomfortably, like he'd intruded on an intimate call.

"That was one of my students. Well, actually her grandmother. I'm going over to see them this afternoon," Kat said, noticing that Alex looked relieved.

"Oh, I thought it might be your boyfriend or something," he joked.

"No, no boyfriend. I'm like you. Unattached."

"Which is not the same as detached, I hope."

"I've been both, and I prefer to be unattached, at least right now."

"Me, too. I've never been married. Not for lack of interest, but I think the universe has conspired against me in that regard," Alex said stoically.

"What do you mean?" Kat asked, filling her coffee mug again. She could feel her muscles relax now that the one item on her agenda had been taken care of.

Alex stroked his head and peered off in the distance. "I was really close to someone I'd met at the newspaper, and she died in a car accident caused by a drunk driver. Then my next girlfriend--the love of my life, really—died from melanoma at the age of 31."

Alex cupped his chin in his hands and sighed. "I know it sounds dumb, but I almost feel like I'm putting someone's life in jeopardy just by being close to them."

"Sounds like you've gone through a lot of pain, Alex. I've been married once and have a son, but divorce isn't the same as the losses you've faced. Except maybe in just one way—our hopes and dreams got dashed on the rocks and were lost forever. The philosophers will tell us that tragedies steel you somehow and make you grateful for surviving, but I don't often feel grateful. My spiritual teachers told me that we learn through dualism and the contrast of opposites, but I've always felt that whoever created us made the ultimate cosmic joke by giving us free will and only double helixes, you know? I wish life came with a manual to figure it all out."

Kat reached over to put one stray daisy back in the bunch. *I hope I didn't offend him by being so blunt,* she thought. But when she looked up, Alex was smiling.

"You're right, Kat," he said, "on both counts. I'm glad to have come through the fire, and I agree with you

176

on the Creator being a stand-up comedian. It explains a lot about the world, don't you think?"

Alex wiped his mouth with a napkin, then pushed back from the table and looked at his watch. "Well, I hate to eat and run, but I've got a golf game to get ready for. A couple friends of mine from the college get together every Sunday, weather permitting, to tee it up over at Rancho Murieta Golf Course," he said, putting the napkin down on the table. "Breakfast was great, Kat. I'm so glad we got a chance to get to know each other better. Oh, while I'm thinking of it, here's my phone number."

He pulled a business card from his wallet and wrote his home phone number on it with a pen he had clipped to his shirt pocket. "Call me about the reunion so I can put it on my calendar at home." He gave her the card and started for the door.

Kat read the card and beamed a smile at him. "Thanks for coming over, Alex. It's been fun. I'll call you."

She watched him as he sauntered across the street. Then he paused and looked back to see if she was watching him.

She smiled widely, but did not wave. Slowly, she closed the door. She didn't see Alex smiling all the way back to his house.

Chapter 21

When Kat knocked on Liana's door later that day, Kalani answered it sporting a black eye. Kat instantly snapped into her mother mode. "What happened, kiddo? Are you all right?"

"What do you mean?" Kalani checked herself out in the hall mirror. "I don't see anything."

"Good one, Kalani. You mean to tell me you can't see that black eye?" Kat stood shoulder to shoulder with Kalani and looked into the mirror with her.

Kalani broke out in a mischievous grin. "Fooled you, didn't I, Ms. R." Kalani took out a tissue she'd put in the pocket of her sweater and wiped the black eye off her face.

"I'm in charge of make-up for the school play, and I took the make-up kit home with me to practice a few things this weekend. Looked real, didn't it?"

"I'll say. For a second, I thought maybe our Hawaiian boogieman might have gotten to you." Kat breathed a sigh of relief. She followed Kalani into the kitchen where Liana was brewing a fresh pot of jasmine tea.

"Hi, Kat." Liana put the teapot down to give Kat a hug. "I thought we'd talk in here where it's warm and cozy. Want some tea?"

"I'd love some, Liana." Kat sat down in what was now becoming her special spot in the kitchen. She looked at the African violets growing on the windowsill, the tapa cloth table mats, the aquarium of angelfish in the corner of the room—all so cozy and inviting. She felt at home here.

Liana's tawny hands, spotted with age, patted Kat's back as the three of them pulled chairs out to sit in the tiny kitchen. The apartment, located in the middle of the second floor of an apartment complex, overlooked the communal swimming pool which stood empty in the October sun. Kat looked out the kitchen window at the pool, gathering her thoughts on where to begin, but Liana broke the silence for her.

"Kalani told me about your experience with the glowing eyes, how you instinctively knew how to protect yourself and get rid of it. You know, Kat, the same person who sent you the eyes also sent you the poisonous shell."

"That's what Kalani said, Liana. I'm just at a loss to explain why anybody would want to scare me like this. Why anybody would be after me. Kalani said it had something to do with my innate power being a threat to someone."

"It's a warning, Kat. A cease and desist letter, as an attorney might say. This person is more or less checking you out, measuring the depth of your power, seeing who his enemy is."

"But I'm not anybody's enemy, except maybe Rudy's right now. He's not behind this, is he?"

"No, he's not. As far as I can tell, it's someone in Maui. I've been looking into the calabash bowl to get glimpses of where he is, and I saw the crater Haleakala, so for sure it's Maui. But he's been putting up barriers so I won't discern who he is."

"Liana, what kind of threat would I pose to a stranger in Maui? It just doesn't make sense." Kat crossed her arms and leaned them on the table. "But I'm pretty sure you two can explain it to me, right?" She looked first at Liana and then Kalani and they looked lovingly back at her.

"We'll try, dear," Liana said sweetly. "Let me start by telling you about an old Hawaiian legend that exists only among the kahuna who practice the ancient magic." Liana got up to pour hot tea into three mugs, then settled into her chair at the head of the table.

"Long ago, the Hawaiian islands were first settled by travelers from Bora Bora," Liana began softly. "A member of this first landing party, Tupuna, was a *kahuna po'o*, an expert in all arts. It fell to him to begin the process of selecting who would become the next generation's *kahuna po'o* in this new land of theirs. Since these first Tahitian settlers were all adults and Tupuna had no son of his own to pass the knowledge on to, he had to wait until a second expedition could bring children to the islands or when the little *keikis*, the children of the first settlers, grew old enough to start the intensive training it took to become a kahuna.

"In Bora Bora it had been customary for the head kahuna to select one child to train in all the aspects of the ancient ways—to become a *kahuna po'o*, like Tupuna. However, once he landed in Hawaii, knowing he only had a few years left to live, Tupuna received permission from the chief to breech protocol by teaching many children one specialty each. For example, one *keiki* learned to be a *kahuna aloha*, an expert in love magic. Another *keiki* became

180

a *kahuna ha'iha'iwi*, a master bone-setter. Yet another, a *kahuna kalai*, an expert carver or a *kahuna kuhikuhi pu'uone*, an architect. In this way all of the arts, from healing to divination and even to the death prayer, were eventually covered. Then all of the kahuna would single out the individual in their group who they felt had enough mana and intelligence to learn all the arts. One by one, each kahuna would pass their specialized training on to this exalted individual who would become a great *kahuna po'o*—a master of all the arts involved in the ancient magic.

"A major rift occurred centuries later when one of the *kahuna 'ana 'ana* refused to share his knowledge of the death prayer with the individual who was chosen to become the *kahuna po'o*. This renegade kahuna wished to reserve that special power all to himself and to his lineage. He passed on the knowledge of the *'ana 'ana* to his children as they did to theirs. Today we think there are at least three individuals who specialize in the practice of the *'ana 'ana* and who seek to dominate the rest of us who have no knowledge of this death prayer. Are you with me so far?"

Kat nodded and poured herself more tea. Kalani opened a package of oatmeal cookies, loaded them up on a plate and brought them back to the table.

"Now, before he died, Tupuna told his fledgling group of kahuna that, once he began living in the afterworld, he would continue to be with them in spirit and guide them and their successors from The Other Side. He told them that when the time came for them to cross over, they would be expected to team up with him to become the *aumakuas* for all future kahuna. To prevent the philosophy from becoming corroded or corrupted by

181

kahuna who might use their knowledge for evil purposes, Tupuna promised to send a Huna Warrior, an omnipotent keeper of the "secret," who would conquer the evil kahuna and safeguard the sacred traditions. This Huna Warrior would appear whenever the ancient magic was being misused or defamed or in danger of disappearing. No books would include any mention of this invincible person's existence because all of the ancient knowledge was passed on exclusively by word of mouth to initiates who were sworn to secrecy never to reveal a word about the Huna warrior.

"Tupuna and the ancestral kahuna who now reside on The Other Side of the rainbow, what we term heaven, bestow their special powers to the Huna Warrior when the time is right. Often this person is unaware of his or her true destiny until other kahuna, who recognize the special powers within, can enlighten the individual about the path he or she is on. The renegade kahuna of the world know that at present there is one Huna Warrior on earth who has the potential to use all the powers of a *kahuna po'o* and can stop their abuse of the ancient magic. So they seek to destroy the Huna Warrior as well as those who help this person grow in awareness of her powers."

"*Her* powers?" Kat's throat tightened, and she could barely get the words out.

"Yes, Kat," Liana replied, studying her intensely. "And deep down, you know who it is."

Kat listened in disbelief at first, then looked alternatively perplexed, suspicious, self-conscious and finally aghast. She put her mug of tea down and wiped her face with her hands, as she finally comprehended the full import of Liana's story.

She stared at Liana, then at Kalani, her body tingling with a newfound sense of strength and energy as if telling her about her destiny suddenly allowed her to feel the power she'd been denying was there. Tears stung her eyes and ran down her face.

"*I'm* the Huna Warrior?" Kat gasped. "But that can't be. There must be some mistake. I'm not a kahuna. I'm not even Hawaiian. I can't be the Huna warrior! It's not possible."

"Kat, remember when I first met you at Kalani's Back to School Night last year? We shook hands, and I thought I felt some of your strength back then. Then on the first day of school when you came over, and I gave you the lomi lomi massage? I could feel your soaring power. I am a *kahuna lomi lomi,* and I specialize in body energy. I feel your light and energy growing in intensity every time I see you."

"And remember Ms. R. when you guessed that both grandma and I are kahuna? You knew right away. You recognized us in the same way that we recognized you," Kalani said, her face glowing with excitement.

"Kat, think back in your childhood. Weren't there times when you knew with absolute certainty that you were going to win something at the raffle, and you did? Did you ever guess ahead of time who was on the phone before you picked it up, and nine times out of ten, it was who you thought it'd be? You've been clairvoyant all your life, but never thought much about it because it was normal for you, right?"

"Or when you're disciplining kids in your office, Ms. R.," Kalani added. "I can see auras and the color of energy. I've seen how you throw light around the kids who are arguing to make them calm down. You do it spontaneously. You always use your knowledge to help others. That's what a Huna Warrior does."

"I've told you about my ancestors being kahuna, Kat. I'm in constant contact with them. They also confirm that this is your destiny." Liana smiled at Kat's skeptical expression.

Kat shook her head and stared at the table. "I still find it too hard to believe. I'm just barely learning about kahuna magic. And knowing about it isn't exactly the same as being able to actually do it, you know?" Kat knitted her eyebrows in agitation. She was clearly distraught at hearing about this sudden designation. *Huna Warrior? Me? No way,* she thought. *They must be out of their minds.*

"Don't worry, dear. We're here to help you learn," Liana said, patting Kat's hand. "We'll teach you everything we know and get the other kahuna to teach you whatever we don't. While you sleep, the *po'e aumakua* will be teaching you on the other side. Night and day you will be learning, whether you are conscious of it or not. They will infuse you with the mana you need to be the strongest Huna Warrior ever."

Kat sat in silence, still trying to get over her shock. Finally, she looked up at Liana, then Kalani. "I..., I don't know what to say," she stammered. "This has just knocked me for a loop. I mean, you'd think, if this were true, if I am the Huna Warrior, I'd have had an inkling, some iota, of my destiny by now. This has completely blind-sided me."

Liana clucked sympathetically. "Great people grow into an awareness and then a gradual acceptance of their destiny," she said, peering into Kat's searching eyes. "It doesn't happen overnight. You've had no time to get used to the idea because we've just now made you aware of it. But, in time, you'll look back on your life and see how everything you ever experienced has prepared you for this moment."

"I guess I should feel honored," she admitted, "but being the Huna Warrior makes me a target, and that's a scary thought. It also brings a tremendous amount of responsibility, and I'm petrified I won't measure up somehow. I mean, can't I do an apprenticeship first so I can have a trial run at it?" Kat asked, gulping tea nervously. "I don't have a clue about how to be the Huna Warrior. I don't even know where to start. And you're sure you've got the right person?"

"We're sure, Ms. R. We're your kahuna family," said Kalani, circling around Kat and hugging her shoulders. "We're all in this together."

"Kat, we need you, but, more importantly, the world needs you. We suspect whoever is after you is after me and Kalani and probably all the existing kahuna on the planet. The kahuna in Hawaii are rapidly dying off. When you become the Huna Warrior, you'll not only help the Huna magic, but you'll be saving the remaining kahuna. Think of it as helping out an endangered species."

Kat still could not believe her ears. The words reverberated in her head, but she was still too stunned to

185

grasp their total meaning. She stared at her two friends across the table. "But I'm afraid," she admitted.

"That's a natural reaction, Kat. But listen to me. You're not in this by yourself. We're with you, Kalani and I. We'll never leave you. Never. Not on this side and not on the other."

Kat sighed heavily and gazed at the fish zipping through the bubbles in the aquarium. "I wish I believed in myself as strongly as you two do. I guess only time will tell if I'm up to the challenge of becoming the Huna Warrior. In the meantime, I'll train, I'll study, and I'll be open to learning whatever you think I need. But, at the same time, you need to know the skeptic in me will be scouring the universe for signs of confirmation what you're saying is true because I still think you've got the wrong person."

Kat walked over to the kitchen window and looked out at the pool, then faced Liana and Kalani resolutely.

"I do know this, though," Kat said, weighing her words carefully. "Whatever is destined for me will come about even if I don't understand it all just yet. If it's in the stars, then it's just a matter of acceptance, time, and courage."

Kat walked back to the table and snatched up a cookie, crunching into it like a bear tearing into a freshly caught salmon. Unaccustomed strength seemed to be permeating her body.

"Okay, let's get serious. Show me how you neutralized the poison in the conch shell, Liana. And Kalani? How'd you learn to see auras?"

Liana laughed and clasped her hands together. She rose and walked to the stove, added more water to the teakettle, and put the burner on high. "I can see it's going to be a long night," she said, eyes twinkling. "Better make some more tea."

Chapter 22

Later that night, Kat snuggled into her robe and slippers by eight o'clock, exhausted from the soles of her feet to the roots of her hair. Her head reeled. Her knees trembled. She curled up on the sofa with Caesar and tried to explain to him that she was about to become the Huna Warrior, made all the more difficult because she still wasn't clear what it meant exactly or what she was supposed to do in this new capacity. All she knew was she'd promised to meet with Kalani daily and with Liana on weekends, schedule permitting, to learn some new aspect of Huna magic and the kahuna who had passed away to the other side would be teaching her while she slept at night.

"As a magician, my bag of tricks is pretty empty right now," she said with a laugh. "All I know is how to put up a shield, store energy in a statue, and make glowing eyes disappear. Big whoop. The hardest part is I'm sworn to secrecy—at least for now—and I've never kept anything from Sean. How will I ever keep my big mouth shut about this? I mean, this is big."

When the doorbell rang, Kat nearly jumped out of her skin. She looked through the peephole and to her immense relief and delight, it was Sean and Chelsea.

"Come on in, you two. I wasn't expecting company tonight, so I hope you'll overlook the outfit." Kat giggled, lifting her robe to reveal her bunny slippers, floppy ears and all. She hugged Sean first, then Chelsea, and guided them into the living room where they sat in matching recliners while Kat sprawled out on her sofa. Then she thought better of it. "Hey, you two lovebirds take the couch so you can sit closer together. I'll take the recliner."

Sean and Chelsea held hands as they cozied up on the couch. He settled down on the seat Kat had been occupying. "Thanks for warming up the couch for me, Mom," he said, appreciatively.

"You're welcome. Now, to what do I owe this fine surprise?" Kat noticed the gleam in Sean's eyes.

"Well, we've got some great news to tell you, and we wanted to tell you together. Can you guess?"

"Hmm. You just found out that Donald Trump died and left you in his will?"

"No, better than that," Chelsea hinted, all aglow and giddy. Kat had already noticed Chelsea was hiding her left hand ring finger, but she continued to play along.

"You won the lottery?"

"Not even close." Sean knew his mother was on to them, but wanted to keep the suspense going. "Come on, Mom. You're usually quick at guessing something this important. We don't pop over your house on a Sunday night just for any old reason. Think. Think!" His ear-to-ear grin was a dead giveaway.

"Well, there's got to be a good reason why Chelsea's covering her left hand, so my guess is you two are engaged!" Kat cried, holding out her arms like an emcee announcing the next star.

"Yes! You guessed it!" Chelsea shouted.

"You're going to fit right in to this family," Kat told Chelsea.

"I'm so happy for you two!" Kat exclaimed, sincerely this time. " Just deliriously happy for you. Let's celebrate! I think I even have some champagne!" She hurried to the kitchen and opened the refrigerator, hoping that a champagne bottle would miraculously appear on the mostly empty shelves. *What good is it to be the Huna Warrior,* she thought wryly, *when you can't even make champagne appear out of thin air?*

In desperation, she rifled through the kitchen pantry and discovered a bottle of Chardonnay that someone on her faculty had given to her as a housewarming gift. *Yes!* She snagged three wine goblets off her hanging glass rack, grabbed an opener and the bottle, and dashed back to the living room, her slippers clumping all the way.

Sean uncorked the wine while Chelsea showed off her sparkling diamond engagement ring. Kat oohed and aahed over the beautiful platinum setting as Chelsea flashed her new adornment in every conceivable angle.

"It's too big," Chelsea twirled the ring around her finger. "But I'm taking it in to the jewelers tomorrow to get it sized."

"Let me offer the first toast to my darling son Sean and to my dear Chelsea, soon to be my daughter-in-law. Congratulations on your engagement!" Kat lifted her glass and clinked it against theirs before sipping her wine. "Now I want to hear every detail about how you proposed, Sean."

"Well, we were at PF Chang's restaurant last night, and I had worked it out with the waiters to serve a fortune cookie to Chelsea which I'd already written my own fortune on. It read: Will you marry me? Good plan, huh?"

"Very clever. I expected no less from my wonderful son."

Chelsea was laughing so much she barely got her next words out. "The trouble was, they mixed up the cookies and ended up serving the one Sean had stuffed to an old lady next to us. She had forgotten her reading glasses and couldn't read the tiny print. So she had her date read it out loud. Which he did—loud enough for us to hear. She immediately jumped up and shouted, "Yes, I'll marry you." He got really red in the face and said he had no intention of marrying her. He accused her of putting the waiter up to it. He was snorting water out of his nose by the time he finished telling her off."

Chelsea and Sean doubled over with laughter.

"Everyone in the restaurant was staring at them, including us," Sean continued. "And then I just grabbed Chelsea's hand and said, 'That cookie was meant for you, Chelsea. Will you marry me?'"

"Oh, how sweet." Kat was touched by the scene playing in her mind.

"And, of course, I said yes." Chelsea flung her left hand in the air to look at her ring. "Oh, no! My ring's gone!

"Let's look for it. It's got to be around here some place." Kat hastily dropped to her knees.

The three searched everywhere, frantically lifting pillows and upending knick-knacks as they covered the living room inch by inch.

After a futile first effort, Kat thought, *Wait a minute. What would the Huna Warrior do to find something that's lost? Simple. She'd send out an aka cord to locate it.*

"Hold it, you two," Kat announced suddenly. "I'm going to try something. It's a long story, but one of my students, Kalani Kingston, and her grandmother, Liana, have been teaching me the Hawaiian way to pray. Let me try it and see if I can pray to find the ring. I'm new at this prayer method, so humor me, okay?"

Kat sat back and took a deep breath to relax. Then she closed her eyes and prayed out loud. *Low self, little buddy, I need your help to find Chelsea's ring. It flew off her hand and landed somewhere in the living room. Stretch out your little finger and bring me back the picture of where the ring is, please. Use the energy I'm sending you to find the ring.*

Kat took in four breaths, picturing a fountain filling up and spouting inside her. Then she offered the energy from the four breaths to her low self to use in its search of the missing ring.

A few moments later, a smile grew on her face. She could see where the ring was in her mind's eye. "Aha! I know where it is!" Kat crowed. She snatched up her orchid, Iz, and there was the ring, nestled in the dirt at the base of the plant.

"Wow, how'd you do that?" Chelsea gushed, happy to have the ring back on her finger.

Kat told them a little about the Huna philosophy of three selves in one body and how the kahuna way of praying involved gathering mana or energy for the low self to send to the High Self to get a prayer delivered. She steered clear of any mention of being the Huna Warrior.

Sean and Chelsea listened intently. Then Sean summed it all up with his own spin, calling it a mix between Polynesian Psychology 101 and Pacific Positive Thinking.

"As a psychology major and a philosophy minor," he began, "I've come across the same concept of energy in a few of my classes, Mom. The Hawaiians may call it *mana*, but the East Indians call it *prana*, the Greeks call it *pneuma*, the Asians call it *chi*, and the Iroquois Indians call it *orenda*."

"Not to mention," Chelsea added, "the nineteenth century German physicist Baron Karl von Reichenbach called it *odic force*, and the twentieth century psychoanalyst Dr. Wilhelm Reich called it *orgone* energy."

"And a partridge in a pear tree," Kat sang out, and everyone laughed. "Hey, not to change the subject," she said, "but let's change the subject. Let's talk wedding plans!"

"Can't tonight, Mom. We're heading over to see Dad and tell him our good news in person, but maybe the three of us can talk more about it on the way to Grandpa's retirement party. That's only two weeks away."

"Great idea, Sean. We'll do it then."

After Kat saw them to the door, she began visualizing a perfect wedding and talking to Caesar about it into the wee hours of the night.

Chapter 23

Ten days later, Kat was the school's representative at the district's pre-expulsion hearing. Gabe, now officially Rudy's foster father, accompanied Rudy who had recently been released from Juvenile Hall and was still on an extended suspension from Anthony High.

Nick Threadkill, the district's Child Welfare coordinator, conducted the hearing which was the first legal step to determine if an expulsionable offense had been committed by a student. Using a tape recorder to capture the entire proceedings, Threadkill, a former basketball coach with a style similar to Bobby Knight, read his formal statements in a gruff, scratchy baritone. Kat, too, read her written statement and submitted several witness statements as evidence to support her case. Throughout the hearing, Rudy stared down at his lap, his arms crossed in silent protest. When Threadkill asked if there were any questions, Gabe had one.

"As you may or may not know," he began, his face directed at Threadkill to deliberately obliterate his vision of Kat, "I recently became Rudy's foster father. Since I live in Davis, I was hoping to take Rudy out of Anthony High and place him at Davis High. If I did so, would you still continue with the expulsion hearing?"

Nick Threadkill glared at Gabe, answering in obvious disdain for the nature of the question. "You're an administrator. You know it's in the best interests of the district to hold the expulsion hearing even if you pull

194

Rudy out of our high school. Once you enter him in the Davis district, by law you'd have to disclose that he left our district to escape expulsion proceedings. In short, you gain nothing by pulling him out now, Gabe."

Gabe blinked languidly, trying to maintain an air of nonchalance. "I just asked a simple question, Nick," he said in a huff.

"I hope I've answered your question, then," Threadwell snapped. "We'll send paperwork out to give you official notice that the expulsion hearing is set for this coming Friday at nine in the morning. Please have Rudy attend along with any legal representation you deem necessary. Kat, be sure to bring any witnesses with you that will support the school's side."

"I don't think it'll be necessary for any attorneys to be here. I can pretty much guess what the outcome will be," Gabe answered sarcastically, glowering at Kat.

"What's that supposed to mean?" Threadkill growled, half-standing with his hands spread out before him on the table. He glared menacingly at Gabe who coldly stared back at him.

"Ask Kat. She's had it in for Rudy since the first day of school." Gabe's lips tightened with anger.

"Excuse me, Gabe, but this isn't about my behavior. This is about Rudy and his behavior." Kat turned to Threadkill. "I'll bring witnesses and all the proof I need for Friday, Nick. Don't worry about that."

She gathered her paperwork and left the room with Gabe slowly following, his body language giving way to the rage he was trying to suppress. The veins in his neck pulsed with anger, along with the deep scowl on his face and his clenched fists all painted a picture of a ferocious temper about to explode. Fortunately, she didn't have to see him the rest of the day because she would be supervising a girls' basketball game at a competing district's high school.

If I didn't know better, Kat thought, *I'd think it was Gabe's red glowing eyes I saw in my hallway. He's really mad at me.*

At home that night, she busied herself by decorating the inside of the house for Halloween, one of her favorite holidays. She'd already put Jack-o-lanterns on the front porch and hung a scary witch doorknocker which cackled with glee whenever someone came near it.

I hope I have enough candy this year, she thought, hanging fake cobwebs and plastic spiders in her doorway. *Last year I ran out and had to dig in my purse for coins to toss in the kids' bags. Hmm. That gives me an idea.* She grabbed the phone, and Alex answered with a mouthful of food.

"Hi, neighbor, this is Kat. I didn't catch you at dinner, did I?"

"Nope, just trying out the Halloween candy I bought," he answered, smacking his lips into the phone.

"What a coincidence. I was just going to invite you to help me give out treats on Friday. You can vacate your house, bring your candy over and mix it with mine. I don't want to run out again like I did last year, and it might be fun to get to know each other a little better before we go to the reunion. What do you think?"

"Hmm. Tough choice, Kat. Answering the door all night by myself or taking turns with you. Do I have to wear a costume?"

"Nope."

"Good. I was hoping you'd say that. What time should I be over?

"The ghosts and goblins usually start arriving by six o'clock, so I'd say be here no later than 5:45, okay? See you then."

Kat hung up, pleased with Alex's response to her proposal.

On the morning of Rudy's expulsion hearing, Kat took an extra long time in the shower, carefully installing her wall of protection. She visualized a thick energy shield in the form of a reflective mirror that would deflect anyone's negative energy. She thought about reversing the energy flow and sending it back to its source, but decided against it. *There's too much hate in the world already,* she thought, *to be sending it back to them. Liana tells me Mother Earth has the power to absorb all the negativity and transmute it into positive energy, so I'm just going to send it either into the earth or to any place else where it would do the most good. And to add icing on the cake, I'll do a zip up courtesy of the Donna Eden DVD I watched the other night. The zip up exercise will keep all my energy in tact for lasting self-protection.*

The expulsion hearing was held in the district office's conference room where a magnificently crafted oak table filled most of the room. Three microphones had been placed across the center of the table, their cords all attached to Nick Threadkill's tape recorder. Three voluntary administrators, one principal and two vice-principals from other schools in the district, sat on one side of the table. They were the panel of jurors who would listen to the testimony presented by the school and ask questions of Rudy and the witnesses.

In previous years, Kat had represented the district's side in expulsion hearings a half a dozen times, so she knew her role and the process well. Basically, the hearing was a miniature trial, and Kat was the prosecuting attorney. She could summon witnesses who would bring credibility and support for the school's side—namely, that a student had committed an offense which warranted an expulsion from the district. She would also read to the panel the principal's recommendation for the length of the expulsion, which was usually the rest of the current semester and the one following. Gabe had signed the recommendation with great reluctance, but deep down he knew his allegiance had to be on behalf of all of the other students at Anthony High whose safety would be compromised if Rudy were allowed to stay. He also knew his loyalty had to be with the district, not with Rudy, if he were ever to be considered for a central office position.

Enrique's' mother, Dolores Gavaldon, was the last to enter the room. Since Enrique was still recovering from his spinal injuries, Mrs. Gavaldon represented her son. She was a huge woman, made even more imposing wearing a green plaid poncho and hair piled up in a beehive style. Looking over the rims of her black-framed bifocals, she spotted an open chair sturdy enough to support her bulk and sank into it, a disgusted look on her face.

Nick Threadkill welcomed Mrs. Gavaldon to the proceedings and placed a microphone in front of her.

Then, in a booming voice, he read the regulations and procedures for the meeting. Introductions were made around the table, and the actual "trial" part of the hearing began.

Kat read formal statements written by herself, Lily Boone and Andrea Chan about the events that had transpired the day that Enrique got hurt. She submitted police and hospital records as well as the students' statements, including Enrique's, which named Rudy as the perpetrator of Enrique's injuries. Kat explained to the panel that she could not identify the names of the two student witnesses because of confidentiality and their fear of Rudy's retaliation, but she assured them that they were reliable witnesses. On the one occasion when she peeked at Gabe and Rudy, their confidence and bluster seemed to be waning. *And I'm just feeling stronger with every minute, guys,* Kat thought. *You can't hurt me.* She suppressed a grin.

At first Rudy tried feebly to protest his innocence, but one of the panel members badgered him with a series of questions until he came unglued.

"He deserved what he got!" Rudy snapped, his face flushed with rage. "That'll teach him to laugh at my girlfriend. Jesus Christ! She got hit by a car, and he thought it was funny!"

Audible gasps erupted all around the room, as Mrs. Galvadon half-rose in her chair.

"Listen, you little *gusano!*" she said, pounding the table in anger. "Enrique doesn't act right all the time, okay? He walked in on his father who had hung himself in the garage. Now suicide is not anything to laugh at, but he laughed at that, too. It's not real laughter. He just does it out of nervousness."

Dolores looked sharply around at the faces in the room and calmed down a bit, but continued to command everyone's attention.

"I've taken Enrique to doctors, and they tell me that sometimes people do laugh at the wrong time or at the wrong things. Why couldn't you have just understood that some people make mistakes? No, you had to hurt him, and now he can barely walk. He doesn't want to go back to school, either, because he's afraid that you'll be there or that other kids will make fun of him, too. You told my boy not to tell anyone what you did, or you would hurt me and his father. Well, his father's dead and that leaves just me. So you better understand something, you *serpiente*. You even come close to my door, and it'll be your last day on earth. You understand me, boy?"

Rudy pushed his chair back and stood up, leaning over the table and staring boldly at Mrs. Galvadon. "I'm not your boy," he snarled, "and if I had a chance to do it all again, I'd kill that stupid freak."

Mrs. Galvadon broke out into a loud cussing streak in Spanish, jabbing her finger in the air at Rudy while Gabe forced Rudy back into his seat and gave him a reproving look.

"That's enough, Rudy," Gabe said sternly. "Don't make things any worse than they already are."

Gabe glanced at the three panel members whose shocked faces and sudden whispers to each other revealed to him what their verdict would invariably be.

"All right, everyone just simmer down," Nick Threadkill barked into his microphone. The room grew silent.

"Does the panel have enough information to make a judgment?" he asked. Each member said yes, and Threadkill officially closed the hearing. Rudy's admission, coupled with his blatant refusal to show any kind of remorse and his continued threats against Enrique, made the panel's job an easy one.

The decision wouldn't be announced that day, though. Threadkill told both parties that they'd be receiving the panel's decision in the mail in the next few days.

When the hearing was concluded, Kat walked over to Andrea Chan's office to say hi, but Andrea wasn't in. She was trying to stall for time so she wouldn't be in the parking lot at the same time as Gabe and Rudy. There was something about those two together that made her shudder. She hoped that Gabe would come to his senses and transfer Rudy out of Anthony High right away. Then Rudy would be out of her hair, and she could work on patching things up with Gabe. Setting things right between them meant a lot to Kat—mainly, keeping her job and not losing her house. *Boy, that's a real mission impossible,* she thought, *Huna Warrior or no Huna Warrior.*

Returning to her office, Kat found Kalani and Mazie working madly to get a mailer out to parents. *Good,* she thought. *There's no one in the office with a referral. Busy work. Just what I need to get my mind off of Gabe.*

Expulsion hearings always got to Kat. They always felt like she'd just starred in a play which left her feeling self-conscious and ill at ease for some reason. Without saying a word, she pulled up a chair, grabbed a pile of envelopes and started stuffing the pre-folded mailers. Mazie's favorite light jazz station was playing softly on the boom box under her desk.

"How'd the expulsion hearing go?" Mazie asked. She looked at Kalani, then spoke again to Kat. "You can tell us. Our lips will be sealed, right, Kalani?"

Kalani gave a big nod, so Kat began to relate what happened at the hearing. Just as she ended her description of Rudy's exchange with Mrs. Gavaldon, Kalani blurted out, "Mrs. Longer, I just heard your name on the radio. Listen."

Mazie turned up the volume and heard her name, too, followed by "You have five minutes to call the station to claim WIFM's weekly $1,000 grand prize. If you're one of our faithful Friday listeners, Mazie Longer, give us a call right now."

Mazie's eyes bugged out. "Oh, shoot! I don't know the station's phone number!" she said in a panic. But Kalani was already looking it up in the phone book and read off the numbers as Mazie shakily punched them in on her desk phone. Kat and Kalani listened to the one-sided conversation.

"Hi, there. I just heard my name being called for your Faithful Friday jackpot. Yes...I'm Mazie Longer. I work at Anthony High School. Oh, thank you!...I can't believe it! I've entered your contest every year for years on end, but this is the first time I've ever won. Uh huh. What's that again? On the corner of Madison and Hemlock? Okay,

I'll come by on Monday for the check. And thank you so much! Bye now!"

Mazie put the phone down and screamed triumphantly, "I just won $1,000!" She flew into Kat and Kalani's open arms for a group hug which was accompanied by lots of whooping and cheering and jumping up and down. Denise Dutra, who had been walking down the hallway to the counselor's office, heard the commotion and opened the door.

"Hey, what's going on in here? You guys are way too happy, even if it is a Friday," she teased.

"Mrs. Longer just won $1,000 from a radio station," Kalani cried out with an ear-to-ear grin.

"Wow, that's terrific, Mazie! I'll go tell everybody," Denise said, retreating into the hallway. Within minutes counselors, teachers, and para-educators poured into the office to voice their amazement and congratulations over Mazie's good news.

When school was out and quiet had descended upon them once more, Mazie looked at Kat and in a low voice said, "It worked, Kat. Your prayer? It really worked."

Kat grinned widely. "Yes, it did. Cool, huh?"

"Girl, it's unreal. That Huna stuff really works, doesn't it? Instant results guaranteed." Mazie's gazed at Kat in admiration and awe. "How'd you learn about it?"

"That's a long story. Someday I'll tell you, but it's Halloween, and right now I've got to beat the heavy traffic in time to greet the trick-or-treaters." Kat grabbed her purse out of her locked file cabinet and started to shut the lights in her office when Mazie suddenly appeared in her doorway.

"Look, before you go, I want you to know something," Mazie said, her eyes misting. She put her large hands on Kat's shoulders. "I will *never* forget what you've done for me, Kat. That money I won today changes everything. Not only will I breathe easier—literally—but I'll be able to have the best Thanksgiving and Christmas ever. I can't thank you enough, but I'm gonna keep on trying, you hear? Whatever you need, just say it. I've got your back."

Mazie and Kat hugged each other in a long embrace. When she broke free, Kat looked deeply into Mazie's eyes.

"You don't have to thank me. I'll always be here for you," she said, getting a bit teary-eyed herself. "But I've got to admit it feels really good to know someone like you has my back. I've got a feeling there's going to be plenty of opportunities for payback."

"Whatever it takes, I'm behind you all the way. Hold on a sec, and I'll go out with you."

Mazie turned off the monitors and radios and secured the office. Then she and Kat hurried to the darkened parking lot, both anticipating the excitement of Halloween.

Before starting the engine, Kat pretended to look for her keys so Mazie would leave the lot before she did. She wanted to pray.

"Dear low self and my precious High Self," she whispered, "thank you for delivering my prayer, for hearing it, and for coming through with my request on behalf of Mazie. We are both so grateful to you."

A quiet sense of fulfillment and serenity filled Kat's heart. *This must be the upside of being the Huna Warrior,* she thought to herself. *The satisfaction of helping someone in need. Maybe I was meant to do this after all.*

Chapter 24

Kat drove through the heavy commute, unable to stop brooding about Gabe and hoping she'd arrive home with enough time to spare before the hordes of trick-or-treaters deluged her neighborhood. Just as she pulled into her garage, Alex sprinted across the street with a half full bag of Snickers miniatures and a full one of Reeses pieces.

"Hi, Alex." Kat got out of her car. "Sorry I'm so late. Traffic." She unlocked the front door of the house and threw her purse in the hall closet.

"That's okay, Kat," Alex replied cheerfully. "It gave me more time to sample these." He held up the Snickers bag. "I can't believe how addictive they are."

"Which is why I stashed mine in the garage when I bought them last week and tried to forget they were there. Let me get a package out of there to start with, and when we run low, I'll get some more. If I brought them all out at once, I'll eat 'em faster than you can say oink."

Kat went to the garage and retrieved a large bag of Hershey's Kisses. When she came back into the kitchen, she threw a matchbook at Alex who instantly caught it.

"Good catch. If you light all the candles, I'll set up my boom box near the entryway. I've got a tape we can play that has all kinds of Halloween sounds—cats screeching, doors creaking, ghosts howling. I just love Halloween!"

Alex laughed, snatched one more piece of candy for fortification, and started lighting candles. "I used to love it as a kid, but it's definitely lost its mystique for me, I must confess. You probably like it because of the drama it brings, right?"

"Yeah, I like seeing the costumes, people's ingenuity. And the little ones look so serious—like they're participating in a sacred ritual. I like rituals. Must have been my Catholic upbringing."

Kat threw the switch on her CD player to start the Halloween tape. Screams and haunting refrains filled the air. Alex rolled his eyes and kept lighting candles.

The first youngster rang the doorbell.

"Oh, look at you. And what are you supposed to be?" Kat asked the tiny tot, whose father stood proudly in the shadows.

"I'm PungeBob SquaohPants."

"Really?" said Kat, totally opaque about the name.

The boy's father piped up, "He's SpongeBob SquarePants."

"Oh, how cute," Kat replied, still clueless. "Well, here you go, SpongeBob." She threw four Hershey's Kisses into the plastic pumpkin that the little boy held out.

The father prompted the child, "Now what do you say, Nathan?"

SpongeBob replied, "Ank you," and jumped up and down with glee as he held his father's hand to seek more treats at another house.

"I bet *you* know who SpongeBob is, don't you, Alex?"

"Yep. He's this cartoon character that lives under the sea," Alex answered, happy that his unrestricted television viewing had finally impressed someone.

"Is this a show you watch on a regular basis?"

"Nope, I only watch it once in a while. I usually opt for a smattering of everything now days. You never know where you're going to get the next idea for a story or an article, you know?"

"I gotcha. It's like fishing. You have to keep your line in the water because you never know if you might catch the big one."

"Hmm. Fishing. Do you ever do it?" Before Kat could answer, Alex was interrupted by the next trick-or-treater and the next and the next. The steady barrage kept Kat going back to the cabinet in the garage to refill the candy bowl by the door. Within an hour, the candy bowl was nearly empty.

"You get the next kid, Alex," Kat said, "and I'll run down to the mini-mart and pick up some more candy. It shouldn't take long."

"Okay, Kat, but make it quick. I'd hate to disappoint any of the kids. Especially the older ones. Last year our stingy neighbor to the right of me turned off his lights and pretended he wasn't home and got his windows soaped. The cuss words were not only insulting, they were misspelled."

"I'll hurry," she yelled, scrambling to her car.

She'd been gone about a minute when the doorbell rang. *Five pieces of candy left,* Alex thought. *I hope it isn't a mob of kids.*

Squinting into the peephole, he saw a tall creature in a black flowing robe. *Good,* he thought. *It's only one person so I won't run out of candy.*

He opened the door to a male with a hooded cowl which covered much of his face. His leathered fingers poked out like spines from beneath a long black cape. An eerie green fog seemed to trail him, enveloping his feet and hiding his shoes.

Alex nearly gagged from the foul odor, fetid and feral, which hit his nostrils in offensive waves as he waited for the familiar "trick or treat."

The stranger seemed surprised to see him, but remained silent, X-raying Alex from head to toe. The hair on the back of Alex's neck stood up, and he sensed immediate danger. Which, for Alex, meant going into his tough guy stance.

"Wait a minute, fella," challenged Alex. "Aren't you a bit old to be trick-or-treating?" He stood tall and stuck out his chest, eyes piercing, determined not to blink first.

The man said nothing, just stared back into Alex's eyes like a zombie. "Where is she?" he finally uttered, a macabre smile on his thin lips.

Alex decided to play dumb. "Where's who?"

"The woman who lives here." The man's steady gaze was beginning to unnerve him, and Alex didn't rattle easily.

"I don't know what you're talking about," he lied. "You must be mistaken. I'm the only one who lives here."

The man stretched out a bony finger that seemed to elongate by itself. "Don't lie to me! I know she lives here."

Suddenly, a car slowly drove up to Kat's house and parked in her driveway. Annoyed by this intrusion, the stranger stared at the car, then turned back to glare fearlessly at Alex, his red eyes glowing like hot coals.

Alex fluttered his eyes in mock fright and smiled tightly. He threw a Hershey's Kiss at the stranger. "Hit the road, Jack."

"You don't know who you're dealing with, do you?" He laughed a hollow laugh, and for the first time Alex became aware of an insidious dread in the pit of his stomach.

The lights on the car outside flashed on and off, catching the stranger's attention again.

"You haven't seen the last of me," he shrieked, mimicking Kat's Halloween tape's shrieks. Twirling his cape around his face, he disappeared into the green mist circling his feet, leaving Alex gaping in disbelief. The mysterious car backed out of the driveway, its left tail light out, and roared down the street.

"Good one," Alex yelled out into the blackness of the night. "Good trick with that finger extension. Nice make-up job, too. But you're still too old to trick-or-treat."

Alex shut the door and slowly slid his back down the door until he was sitting on the floor, his heart pumping furiously. "All right, Alex, what the hell was that? Think, man, think."

He calmed himself with some deep breaths and tried to make sense of what he'd just experienced. "Logic tells me it was a kid from the high school playing a trick on Kat," he reasoned aloud. "And the smell from hell must be something he dredged up in chemistry class just for the occasion."

Alex searched in the kitchen and found a can of Lysol. He was spraying the entry way when Kat returned from the store.

"Geezus, Alex, who died in here? What's that horrible smell?"

"Kat, you just missed it. Right after you left, some older kid showed up in a grim reaper's costume, asking for you. He looked a little off, so I played stupid and told him you didn't live here. He disappeared in a cloud of green smoke, but not before promising to come back. And not before he polluted this place with a stink bomb that can best be described as putrefied meat and rotten eggs topped off with a huge helping of sulfur." Alex emptied the can of Lysol and threw it in the garbage can under the kitchen sink.

"You do have a way with words, Alex. Your description of that God-awful stench is right on." Kat held her breath long enough to open up the windows above her sink.

"So what did this guy look like?" She tried to keep the fear from rising in her throat. *Could it be Rudy pulling one of his scare tactics? He knows where I live, doesn't he?*

"I couldn't see his face. He wore a hood and a long cape. His hands were wrinkled and spotted. Great make-up job, I think," Alex recalled, wiping his brow with the back of his hand. "A very talented guy, disappearing like that. I still can't figure out how he made his eyes glow red. Special Hollywood effects, I guess. Very clever."

211

Kat's heart thundered in her chest. "Red glowing eyes?"

"Yeah. Blood red."

"And what exactly did he say?" she prodded, biting her bottom lip nervously.

"He told me I didn't know who I was dealing with and he'd be back. Presumably for you. I mean, he knew I was lying about you not living here." Alex exhaled loudly. "Listen, I could stay here for a while if you think he's going to come back tonight and bother you."

"No, that's okay. I appreciate the offer, but I'll be all right. It's probably Rudy, a kid from school we expelled today. He helped me move so he knows I live here. I'll lock myself in and put the burglar alarm on. Not to worry."

Alex opened the front door and looked up and down the street. "Seems we didn't extra candy after all, Kat. The street's empty now."

Kat forced a smile and followed him outside. "You're right. Another Halloween night is over. Before the grim reaper showed up, though, we were having a good time, huh? And who knows what would have happened if I'd been here by myself?"

Her skin crawled with the mere thought of an unknown, relentless enemy out there somewhere lurking, waiting for her.

"Yeah, Kat. If someone wants to get you, what better time to come than on Halloween when everyone opens their door to complete strangers?" Alex said, trying to make light of the situation.

Kat knew Alex had been shaken up, but decided to follow his lead and play down the incident.

"Right. Which is why next year, I'm closing up my house. We'll do Halloween at yours. That'll really confuse whoever that was. Deal?"

"Deal, Kat." Alex gave her a quick hug. "It was fun tonight. Thanks." He walked across the street, pausing in the doorway to wave before disappearing into his house.

Kat locked all the windows and doors, then searched around for Caesar who was hiding under her bed. She tried to coax him out, but he wouldn't budge.

Who could blame him, Kat thought, *when a real goblin shows up at your door on Halloween night? Tonight I'm putting a huge energy shield around the entire house so that no evil entity can hurt us, Caesar.*

Kat lay awake that night for hours on heightened alert, her ears amplifying every little sound. The wind through the trees sounded like the beckoning whistle of a banshee. A scrawny branch scraping against her bedroom shutter became the scratching of a demon trying to get into her room. Sleep would not come easily.

Chapter 25

"The house is growing!" Kat gasped.

She stood in her driveway staring at her house which was pulsing and contracting like a human heart, expanding five to six inches with every beat. Dumbfounded, Kat watched helplessly and shook with fright. Her jaw dropped as the window blinds blinked on and off like glowing eyes on the face of a monster which seemed to be looking right at her. She screamed, but no sound came out. She tried to run, but her feet were cemented to the driveway. The glowing windows suddenly burst into flames which threatened to ignite the entire structure. From a distance Kat could hear the sirens of a fire engine coming to her rescue. *Help me. Oh, please help me,* she prayed, squeezing her eyes tight. As the engine neared, its high pitched sirens transformed into human voices. "Where are you, Kat? Where are you?" they wailed. "I'm right here!" she shouted.

The sound of Kat's own voice woke her up. She sat up in bed and turned on the lamp next to her bed. She quickly scanned her bedroom, her heart pounding in her chest. Caesar jumped up on the bed to see what the commotion was about.

"It was only a dream, Caesar. Only a hideous dream."

She clutched him tightly to her chest and sank back into bed, but images of her house, blinking and growing like a creature from a science fiction movie, kept surfacing.

I wonder what it all means, she thought, trying to recall what she'd read in her dream interpretation books about houses and what they symbolized. *A house represents where one lives or a person's life style. So my house, meaning my way of life, is expanding. That's true because of my role now as the Huna Warrior. But I'm afraid of the change. It's so unexpected and still so strange to me. Let's see, the windows acting like eyes means there's a new awareness from within, and the fire from the eyes could represent the growing passion I'll have for it all. Still, my feelings of terror and my sense of danger won't subside. Why?* Kat continued to try to make more sense of her dream until sleep overtook her at last.

When the radio alarm went off, the early morning sun had pushed its way through the crack in Kat's bedroom drapes and settled on her face. Her hair was matted from sweat and her right cheek was creased from lying on a wrinkled pillowcase. Half-awake, she struggled to tune in to the radio announcer who was talking about the weather: *While parts of the Midwest and the East are experiencing the full brunt of autumn with falling leaves and descending temperatures, northern California is bright and clear. It's Indian summer, folks, and the balmy weather is calling you out to the golf course, lake or....*

Kat turned the radio off and sighed, still rallying from the terror of Halloween and the haunting dreams that followed. Normally, the cure would have been to follow the suggestion of the disk jockey and head outside to clear one's head in the seasonal sunshine. A drive to Daffodil Hill, or maybe a picnic in the wine country of St. Helena or Napa would be in order. But not today. Today she suddenly missed her father—tremendously. It was his

215

seventieth birthday and retirement party, and Kat wanted to be near him. Perhaps psychologically she needed to feel protected, as she had been when she was a little girl, and her father was younger and stronger. Maybe she could forget the horror of last night once she was clustered with her family and their love.

On the way to pick up Sean and Chelsea, Kat stopped by a liquor mart to buy a bottle of anisette, her father's favorite liqueur. Once a week, usually on a Saturday night, Henry would pour himself a double shot, contort his face like he'd just swallowed gasoline, then settle back in his easy chair with a satisfied grin. That was the extent of his liquor intake. It wasn't much really, but it was a ritual he never skipped.

Kat positioned the anisette in a well in the trunk to prevent the bottle from rolling into her father's other gift—a framed copy of the origin of the Romero family name, along with details on the family crest—which she'd found in her usual perusal of mail order catalogs. She'd covered it with bright red wrapping paper left over from Christmas—frugality was much appreciated in her family—and tucked pillows around it so it wouldn't slide around too much during the two-hour drive to her father's house.

Looking in her rear view mirror, Kat saw Chelsea in her car right behind her as she pulled into Sean's apartment complex. Kat waited for her so they could walk up the stairs together to Sean's place.

"Good timing, Chelsea," Kat said, hugging her.

"That's me. Miss Punctuality."

Chelsea knocked on Sean's door, and when he didn't answer, she used the spare key he'd given her to let herself in.

"Sean?" she called out as she walked into the apartment.

No answer.

Chelsea searched hurriedly through the apartment and found Sean still in bed. She shook his shoulder to wake him up.

"Come on, sleepy head, wake up," she said snickering. Sean's eyes only fluttered, but he remained motionless.

Suddenly Chelsea realized something was wrong. Very wrong. She panicked.

"Kat, come here. Something's wrong with Sean!"

Kat rushed to Sean's side, and the two women struggled to prop him up with pillows. Kat held his left hand, sending a jolt of mana hoping to revive him.

"Come on, Sean! Wake up, honey."

"Is he all right, Kat? Should we call an ambulance?" Chelsea felt Sean's wrist and relaxed a bit when she felt his strong, steady pulse at her fingertips.

"I think he's coming to." Kat anxiously studied Sean's face.

Sean moaned and shook his head like a swimmer trying to clear water out of his ears.

"Mom?" Sean mumbled groggily. He tried to focus but could not. Finally, he saw his mother.

"Sweetheart, are you okay?" Kat put her hand on Sean's forehead, but felt no sign of fever.

Chelsea kissed Sean lightly on the lips. "You scared me. Us. What happened to you? I hope it was only that you ate too much Halloween candy"

"The neighborhood kids made sure I had none left," he laughed hoarsely. "I had a weird dream last night, though. Dracula came to suck my blood, and I tried to fight him off, but I ran out of strength. Check out my neck, Chelsea. Any fang marks?"

Chelsea inspected his neck. "Wait, what's this?" She bent down for a closer look, pretending to bit him. Sean pulled her on top of him and they kissed and bear-hugged each other.

"Okay you two, no more of this hanky-panky. We've got to get our show on the road. We don't want to be late today."

Chelsea made coffee while Sean showered and dressed. Kat had brought the Sunday paper with her and pretended to work on the New York Times crossword puzzle, but inside she was seething with anger. It was bad enough some unknown enemy showed up on her doorstep last night making threats, but the thought someone would actually attack her son during the night sent her into a rage. A rage she fought to control since she didn't want to set off any alarms. Her earlier fear had given way to sheer determination to put an end to this adversary.

Whoever he is, she thought, *doesn't know who he's dealing with. He doesn't know it, but he's just launched the Huna Warrior into the world. No one threatens my family. No one.*

Later, in the car, Kat steered the conversation to the subject of wedding ceremonies, hoping to distract herself

218

during the two-hour drive to Henry's house. Sean, an outdoor lover and non-traditionalist, wanted a casual wedding, without the restrictions of a tux, a church, and a limo. Chelsea, though, wanted a romantic setting where she could be surrounded by family and friends. They discussed all kinds of possibilities—wedding chapels, national parks, even backyard settings.

Finally, Kat suggested they get married on a beach in Hawaii. That would provide the romantic ambience Chelsea wanted as well as the outdoor, relaxed atmosphere Sean preferred.

"Mom, you're a genius," Sean gushed. "Chelsea, when I graduated from high school, Mom took me to Hawaii for two weeks. It was so cool. We went to four islands, Oahu, Kauai, Maui and the big island of Hawaii. The problem is they are all so beautiful, I don't know which one to choose for the wedding."

"I've been to Waikiki when I was ten and loved it," Chelsea said, "but it might be a bit too crowded with vacationers in August."

"All the islands are crawling with tourists in the summer," Kat noted. "So let's look at it another way. Sean, think back. Which of the islands did you feel some kind of affinity to? Which one made you feel like home?"

"When you put it that way, Mom, I liked Maui best. That's where I learned to scuba dive. Remember our trip to Hana and the seven sacred pools? And the luau at the hotel where I tried poi for the first time? Yeah, now that I think about it, Maui was my favorite spot."

"Then Maui it is! Let's talk to a travel agent first thing tomorrow. I hope we're not too late to set something up. We only have nine months to make it happen."

"Don't worry, Chelsea. If it's meant to happen, the universe will conspire to make it so," Kat said wisely, realizing her words were meant for her own ears as well. If *I'm meant to be the Huna Warrior,* she thought, *the universe will conspire to make it happen.*

Once Kat reached her father's home, she suppressed her fears about death threats and mysterious assassins that kept threatening to surface. Henry's home in the Manor Mobile Home Park for Seniors in San Leandro was packed with his neighbors, co-workers and relatives, including his favorite cousin, Madeline, who was Kat's godmother. A long sheet of butcher paper hung across Henry's carport which read "Happy 70th Birthday and Happy Retirement, Henry."

Kat noticed that one corner of the sign had pulled away from the masking tape which held it in place and was flapping in the breeze. She pounded the paper against the tape before entering the house with Sean and Chelsea trailing behind her.

Henry's face lit up when he saw them. "My daughter's here," he announced to the happy throng of well-wishers. He hugged Kat, then turned to the crowd. "And this is my grandson, Sean, and his girlfriend, Chelsea."

"Correction, Dad. This is Sean's fiancée, Chelsea."

The partiers erupted in cheers and applause. Henry hugged and congratulated Sean who laughed and waved at them while Chelsea turned beet-red with embarrassment.

Henry's dining room table was crammed with hors d'oeuvres, fruit trays, meat and cheese platters, casseroles and fresh pies that everyone had brought for the pot luck.

Kat scanned the display hungrily. *It's amazing how, when people are left to unassigned, random choices, most of the food groups get covered, anyway,* she observed.

"All right, everybody. Let's dig in," Henry said, grabbing a plate off the stack at one end of the table.

Kat followed suit, snapping up a strawberry here, spearing a meatball there, until she had sampled a little bit from each dish on the table. She steered her mound of food over to her godmother, Madeline, otherwise known as Maddy, who was grumpily nibbling on some celery sticks and carrots.

"How are you, Maddy?" Kat asked, wiggling into the seat on the couch next to her.

"I'm okay, Kat. It's awful being on a diet at a party, is all," she complained, glancing longingly at Kat's dish. She adjusted her glasses that were slipping down her nose.

"I'll fix that. This is party time. Sometimes you have to bend the rules a bit and have some fun. Let me see what I can do."

Kat put her dish down on the couch to save her seat, then got a fresh plate and filled it with a taste of everything, just like her own, and brought it back to Maddy who was shooing Henry's pet pot-bellied pig away from Kat's plate.

"Don't let Zenobia eat anything, Maddy. We don't want her to think she's a pig, now, do we?" Maddy giggled as she pushed the persistent pig away.

Kat handed Maddy her plate. "Here's a sample of everything. Eat whatever you want, say a prayer to yourself that today's calories will burn up tens times faster than normal, and tomorrow will take care of itself. All we're guaranteed is today, Maddy. Enjoy it now. I seriously doubt on your death bed you're going to say, 'I wish I'd eaten more carrot sticks,' do you?"

Maddy happily accepted the food, and the two caught each other up on all the family news, each of them holding their plates up high, out of Zenobia's reach.

Sean and Chelsea sat on either side of Henry, relating all their wedding plans, while Henry's neighbors, many of whom already knew each other, mingled and chatted easily with his friends from the nursery.

When his guests had stuffed themselves, Henry stood up to thank everyone for coming and began to unwrap his gifts. He had just opened a card from his co-workers at the nursery who had enclosed a check for five hundred dollars, his eyes bugging out in astonishment, when the doorbell rang.

Kat went to answer it and was stunned to see a policewoman in a blue uniform from the San Leandro police department.

"Is there a Henry Romero living here?"

"Yes, he's my dad," Kat answered.

"May I come in to talk to him?"

Kat showed the officer in and pointed Henry out. The policewoman pulled out her badge and stepped up to Henry, flashing it quickly.

"Can I help you with something, officer?"

"You're under arrest for speeding, sir," she said with a twinkle in her eye.

"Speeding? But my old Ford can barely reach the speed limit," Henry protested. He looked at his friends for help, but they were all snickering and grinning.

"Sorry, sir, but our cameras caught you speeding and snapped a photo of your license plate as your car went through the intersection of East 14th and 143rd Avenue." The policewoman grabbed her handcuffs and, finally catching on to the joke, Henry put his hands out in front of him. She snapped on the cuffs and read his citation.

"This is to certify that you, Henry Romero, have been arrested for speeding through an intersection. You have the right to remain silent..." Henry pretended to look on in shock until the officer cracked a smile. She continued to read.

"Anything you say can and will be used against you by all your friends and family. You have a right to garden, morning, noon and night, if you want to. You can fish to your heart's content—even if you never catch anything bigger than a minnow—and feel free to exaggerate about its size. You have the right to challenge all your friends at the Manor to a daily game of Aggravation. And lastly, you have the right to retaliate in kind to your cousin Madeline who wants to wish you a very Happy 70th Birthday!"

Then the officer belted out an Ethel Merman rendition of "Happy Birthday" while Kat and others snapped pictures. Henry howled with glee at his pseudo-arrest. Once the cuffs were off, he shook his finger at his cousin.

"You just wait until you're seventy, Maddy. I'll get you," he threatened playfully.

"Yeah, yeah, Henry," Maddy replied, her big arms jiggling like gelatin as she clapped her hands in a round of applause. She was delighted to have pulled this surprise off for Henry and pushed herself off the couch to personally thank the police officer impersonator, an employee of Silly Singing Telegrams, before she left.

"Well done, Maddy," Kat said. "He broke out in a sweat before he realized it was all in fun."

"I got him, didn't I, Kat? I just hope he doesn't go overboard getting even with me." Maddy sighed, knowing her cousin's love for practical jokes.

"I wouldn't worry about it till you turn sixty-five—which is?"

"I may be fat, but I'm not stupid. I'm not telling anyone in this family when I turn 65," Maddy harrumphed.

By six o'clock, when the party fervor had ebbed away and all the guests had gone home, Kat, Sean and Chelsea helped Henry put leftovers away and load up the dishwasher.

Then Henry dragged out his favorite board game, Aggravation.

"This is your basic introduction into the Romero family, Chelsea," Henry said. "You have to learn to play

224

Aggie, as we call it. Plus, you'll have to go fishing with us sometime. I'll teach you how to 'tickle' the trout and make them bite your hook. And I'll show you how to grow the biggest, best-smelling roses in the world."

"I think I'm going to love being in the Romero family," Chelsea replied, squeezing Sean's hand.

Henry set up the game board, well-worn from years of use, and explained the simple rules of Aggravation. "The main thing to remember is if you roll sixes, you get another turn. When you get all four of your pieces in the center, you win."

Three hours later, exasperated that Henry had won most of the games, Kat's competitive nature got the better of her. She decided to try to influence the dice to turn up more sixes—a strategy she noticed Henry used to generate more moves on the board. Liana had told her that thoughts could be transmitted on the tiny streams of energy called aka cords. Now she experimented to see if her thoughts, sent via the aka cords, could affect the roll of the dice. To her delight, she began to throw more sixes which helped her win the next five games.

So that's how Dad's managed to win so often over the years, she thought. *He's been willing those dice to turn up mostly sixes. But how does he know about aka cords?*

It took considerable focus for Kat to secretly gather extra energy as she breathed, then send it to influence the turn of the dice. The strong concentration soon tired her out. Upon her suggestion, everyone agreed to call it a night and go to bed.

Rather than drive back to Sacramento that night, Kat had planned to spend the night at Henry's. His extra

225

bedroom had two small twin beds which she and Chelsea claimed. Sean grabbed a pillow and a handmade quilt that Maxine had made and went out to sleep on the couch.

Before she went to sleep, Kat said a prayer for protection around the house and everyone in it. She had misgivings for not having included Sean and the rest of her family and friends in her previous night's prayer, but, until today, she hadn't fully realized the extent to which they were all in danger. She listened and waited in the dark for what seemed an eternity, and when she sensed everything was safe, she fell into a deep, peaceful sleep.

Sunday morning at Henry's house was a unique experience for Kat. Even though it wasn't in her childhood home, waking up in her home town still brought back so many memories—lazy days of summer playing gin rummy with her best friend, Patricia, winning the library contest for reading and reporting on the most books in a two-week period, walking to the movies with thirty cents in her pocket and feeling like the richest person on earth. Henry's pot-bellied pig, Zenobia, ruined Kat's daydream by nosing her pillow, snorting and grunting for food.

"Stop it, Zenobia. God, you never change. I take that back. You get chubbier every year, your royal porkness," Kat said sweetly.

Zenobia, her heavy black belly dragging on the floor, ran around the bed to get Kat's attention. "Why can't my dad have a normal pet, like a bird or a cat?" Kat grumbled, getting up and putting her robe and slippers on. "Why is he attracted to a pet that weighs more than he does?"

226

Kat knew perfectly well why Henry loved Zenobia. He had read somewhere that every year hundreds of pot-bellied pigs ended up abandoned by households all over America after their cuteness wore off, or their potty training failed, or their owners became overwhelmed by their destructiveness when left alone all day. Henry had located a pig shelter, or sanctuary home as they liked to call themselves, and brought home the first pig that came running up to him like a long-lost friend. He had named her after the street he lived on, Zenobia Court, and found that she was smart, friendly and good company, filling his lonely hours now that Maxine was confined to the Alzheimer's' Center.

Zenobia followed Kat out to the kitchen and waited expectantly for her to open the refrigerator. Kat found a piece of raw pumpkin and held it out to the pig who squealed and gobbled it on the spot, then hoofed it to one of the back bedrooms to a pile of blankets that Henry had put there for her to root and scuffle in.

Kat walked down the hall to the guest bathroom and performed her usual morning rituals while everyone else slept in. Later, as the coffee perked, she worked the Sunday *New York Times'* crossword puzzle which was her favorite because the answers were on another page.

Everyone helped make breakfast. Henry fried a pound of turkey bacon and scrambled eggs while Kat and Chelsea buttered toast, and Sean poured orange juice.

"So, Dad," Kat said later after finishing her eggs, "how does it feel to have made it to this milestone in life? What do you have to say for yourself as you face your leisure years?"

227

Henry thought his answer over a long slurp of orange juice. "Well," he said at last, "I figure whatever years I have left will be spent in the 4F Club—enjoying my family, friends, flowers and fortune."

"Fantastic," Kat chirped.

"Far out," Sean added.

"Fortuitous," Chelsea chimed in.

Henry eyed Chelsea up and down with approval. "Yep, you're going to fit in this family just fine," he said emphasizing the "f" in fit, family and fine.

They all laughed and tossed their napkins at him.

"No fair," he continued.

"Father!" yelled Kat, rolling her eyes.

"Okay, okay, that's my f-f-final answer," he said, grabbing his plate and glass and heading for the sink.

Kat turned to Chelsea. "Are you sure you know what you're doing marrying into this family?" she asked.

"I take the f-f-fifth on that question," Chelsea retorted, and this time everybody's eyes rolled.

On the way back home, with Henry following her in his car, Kat made her way to Stockton to visit her mother. Henry took in a huge bouquet of daisies from his garden, and Kat brought some candy she'd bought at the grocery store.

Maxine had gotten worse, Kat noticed, since her last visit. When one of the nurses came in to change the towels in the bathroom, Kat asked her if she was aware of a change in her mother's condition. The nurse informed her that her mother had fainted a few days before, but a visiting doctor had checked her out, and nothing was broken.

228

"Could the fainting episode have happened on Friday night, by any chance?" Kat asked, a worried scowl on her face.

The nurse checked the notes on a clipboard that was chained to the foot of the bed. "Why, yes it did. Are you asking for any particular reason?"

"No, just curious, that's all." Kat tried to mask the terror that shot through her. *Oh my God,* she thought, *first me, then Sean, now my mother! Someone's menacing me and my family, and I can't for the life of me figure out why.*

Heading back home later that afternoon with Sean and Chelsea, Kat brought up the coincidence of her mother's fainting happening the same night as the grim reaper's visit and Sean's dream about Dracula.

She told them about what Liana had said about an evil kahuna wanting to challenge Kat. But she couldn't bring herself to say that she was being groomed as the next Huna warrior.

Sean asked, "But why would a renegade kahuna be after you, Mom? You're one of the nicest people in the world. I don't get it."

"Neither do I, honey. But I suppose I'll eventually find out." Kat looked at her speedometer and realized she was going ninety miles per hour. Her focus was not on her driving, but on the deep fear and vulnerability she felt in being stalked by an unknown practitioner of the ancient magic. She sensed the range of power this man had if he were a powerful kahuna seeking world dominance. He'd stop at nothing to get his way. If he could kill off other kahuna, killing Kat should be a snap. But he had gotten to Sean and her mother. Kat was alive and well, so, she reasoned, his motive must be just to show off his skills to scare her away. For a moment she even entertained the idea that she might be under his control right now, and he might be pressing her foot to the gas pedal.

Kat also tried to suppress the strong feelings of guilt which accompanied her worry about having endangered the lives of her family. Being the Huna Warrior brought a heavy responsibility because everyone she was connected with, from family to friends and colleagues at work, could now become targets of the Hawaiian assassin. She vowed to put up energy shields of protection every day for them, but waves of fear and feelings of powerlessness continued to shoot through her long after she'd dropped Sean and Chelsea off and had returned home.

When will he strike again? Is Henry his next target? How far will he go? Kat's questioning mind kept asserting itself into another troubled night of sleeplessness.

Chapter 26

The old Hawaiian's son paced the floor, waiting for his father to recover from his exhaustive ventures of the past few days.

"I used to be able to do so much more when I was young like you," Kahili uttered weakly.

His son ignored his whiny tone and kept slicing a ripe pineapple on a small wooden table.

"How'd you make that `ena `ena pilau?" Hukui asked non-chalantly.

"The smell? That's my signature mark. It lets them know who did the sorcery, and they never forget it," the old man replied. He looked with alarm at his son and wiped away the perspiration that had formed above his upper lip.

"How long did it take you to perfect it?"

"About fifteen years."

"I'll have to think of a different sign so they'll always recognize my work. Or maybe I'll keep the smell in, and people will think it's your work, not mine. Then when they retaliate, they'll direct all their vengeance on you." Hukui laughed hollowly, malice written all over his face.

"You can't learn it overnight," the old man stressed, hoping to deter Hukui's threat.

"We'll see about that." He slapped and rubbed his hands together, then reached out for his father's shoulders. The old man cringed and backed up against the wall.

231

"Relax, father. I'm not going to strangle you." The son began to massage Kahili's shoulders which trembled from weakness and fear.

"Here, I'll give you *lomi lomi* and make you stronger. Today you will finish your instruction as a *kahuna ho'opi'opi'o*. Tomorrow I will practice until I get it right."

"You mean until someone else dies." The old man arched one eyebrow, glaring at his son whose shark eyes stared off into the distance. "There will be repercussions, Hukui. There are people elsewhere in the world whose power is more potent than yours. Don't you ever wonder what consequences will occur when you wreak havoc upon innocent people?"

"Why should I? As long as you're my teacher, I'm learning from the best. I figure you'll teach me a way to dodge any threat that may come my way."

Hukui picked up a piece of pineapple and stuffed it greedily in his mouth. He looked at Kahili for a while, suspicion growing in his mind.

Suddenly he snatched the old man by the collar and pulled him close, nose to nose. "Is there something you're seeing that I should know about?" he asked Kahili. "Are you hiding something from me, father?"

"No, son," Hukui said calmly. "No, I don't foresee any harm or danger for you." He stared back at his son, a look of sincerity planted on his face.

"There is only one person you and I know of, and she's no threat." Hukui snorted contemptuously. "She'll never defeat me. Never. Not unless she wants her whole family dead."

232

Kahili stared out the window, unable to shake the deep fear that gnawed at him and wouldn't let go.

Chapter 27

Monday morning, Mazie and Kat pulled into the staff parking lot next to each other. Before she'd barely gotten out of her car, Mazie smiled broadly and handed Kat a huge bouquet of flowers.

"These are for you, Kat. I came to your house on Friday night to surprise you, but didn't stay because I saw some guy in your doorway dealing with the trick-or-treaters. Maybe I copied the house address number down wrong."

"Oh, phooey. I'm sorry I missed you. You probably had the right number, but you must have stopped by when I ran out of candy. My neighbor, Alex, was helping me out so I could dash to the store for reinforcements."

Kat shoved her nose into the flowers and inhaled deeply. "These are beautiful, but you didn't have to...."

"Uh, uh, uh," Mazie said, shaking her finger at Kat. "I told you. These are for you for praying for me. And don't say no, I shouldn't have. I don't take no for an answer."

"Thanks, Sarge." She and Mazie walked into the administration building. "Now, let's see where we can scrounge up a vase."

At the PTSA meeting later that evening, Kat reported on school activities, speaking in place of Gabe who had stayed in Davis for the day, enrolling Rudy in a continuation school near his home. She always thought it was best to be honest with the parents, so she revealed all the details about the gas smells, leering hard hats, and false fire alarms that had plagued the school for the past few months. For balance, she made sure she divulged the action the school had taken to solve all of the problems which the parents seemed to have appreciated. Kat left the meeting feeling good about the dialogue which had followed her report, and many of the parents thanked her for speaking at the meeting.

Two days later, Kat's pleasure was short-lived, though, when Becky Farnsworth got up at a school board meeting and blasted the superintendent and the board for hiring incompetent workers who couldn't construct a simple air vent, much less keep their mouths shut when the girls walked on campus.

District Superintendent Robert Purcell turned red with embarrassment as the board president pounded the gavel.

"Mrs. Farnsworth, let me reassure you that the construction contractors we have hired are all very reputable. But we will certainly investigate the behavior of the work crews on campus with regard to how they interact with the female students. Was it something you personally observed?" Purcell asked.

"No, but I became aware of the problem when one of the vice-principals, Ms. Romero, gave a report at our last PTSA meeting on activities at the school."

"Thank you, Mrs. Farnsworth. We'll look into this," Purcell said curtly. Putting his hand over the microphone, he whispered to the board chairman, "Ms. Romero shouldn't be giving the parents inside information which should have been addressed internally first. She's really overstepping her bounds. I'll speak to Gabe about it."

Kat wasn't present at the board meeting, but she heard about it the next day when Gabe called her into his office.

"Kat, the next time I ask you to fill in for me at the PTSA meetings, I'd appreciate it if you wouldn't air our dirty laundry in public. At the board meeting last night, Mrs. Farnsworth chewed out the board and superintendent for the incompetent and sleazy contractors we've hired. She wouldn't have known anything about this if you hadn't spoken of it. You are ill-advised to talk to any parents about our problems, got that? Just tell them mundane things, like our football team winning the last game or invite them to supervise the next dance. Those kinds of things, okay?" Gabe practically spit his words at Kat.

"Well, then, next time you want me to report on the school for you, Gabe, you should give me specific guidelines about what is politically correct to say. The only message I got from you was, 'Cover for me at the meeting tonight. I won't be able to attend.'" Kat sighed in frustration.

"Don't worry. There won't be a next time." Gabe huffed, got up from his chair, and sat on the corner of his desk, trying to calm down. "You know, Kat, I understand you are new to the administrative game, but it's all about politics. The superintendent doesn't want you stirring up the troops. He wants them to think everything's going fine, even if it isn't, got it?" He tapped his finger on his desk impatiently, waiting for Kat's reply.

"You know what, Gabe? I didn't go into education for its politics. I went into it to help the kids. If informing the parents about the problems we're solving on a daily basis to make it easier for their kids to learn is wrong, then I must be in the wrong profession." Kat stood her ground, jaw tight, not budging and not apologizing.

"Well, maybe you are, Kat. Maybe you should go back to the classroom if you don't have what it takes to make it as an administrator," Gabe uttered snidely, his mouth twisted in an expression of contempt.

"Maybe I will. It sure beats being second guessed and undermined all the time." Kat turned on her heels, went down the hallway, and locked herself in the vault to pray that her High Self would help her keep her job, get Gabe off her back, and find a way to thwart her enemy. She couldn't get rid of a deep-seated feeling of unease. She had no clue how to attack monsters she could not see.

Chapter 28

Getting ready for her class reunion, Kat was ambiguous about the event. On the one hand, she looked forward to seeing how her high school friends had weathered the past thirty years of life. *Odd, she thought, it sounded like a prison sentence. But, hey, we can drink and drown our sorrow, commiserate with one another, and compare the bruises and bumps we've all endured along the road of life. It'll be like a catharsis—an 'I'll show you my scars if you show me yours,' type of experience. Fun!*

Kat looked into the mirror to put on her earrings and thought back at the hurtful memories she had of the girls in her class. She remembered all too well the jealous glances and stinging barbs from the girls she'd thought had been her friends. She had known betrayal and not just from Mark. She also was none too happy with the idea of enduring the shallow cocktail talk at reunions of people who really didn't know each other as teenagers, and certainly didn't take the time to know each other now.

We have these great non-relationships, Kat thought. We were bonded at one time in a forced marriage of sorts, and, although I only really kept in touch with two or three of them throughout the years, I'm still feeling connected to them. I wonder why. Curiosity? Self-righteousness? It certainly isn't small talk. Maybe there are aka cords which are still attached to the past and are bringing me back to visit the people who shared the past with me. A reunion doesn't have to be a negative thing, so why am I putting such a bad spin on it? After all, when the

238

invitation came, I could have just thrown it away. Maybe I just jumped at the invitation out of loneliness. Which in turn forced me out of my shell to ask Alex to accompany me. Which is maybe what my unihipili knew I needed all along. And, hey, Alex is a good judge of character and an observer of human nature. It'll be fun to dissect the whole event with him. So I'm going to change my attitude and have a good time and not get hung up on the past. After all, people do change. I know I have over the years.

Alex rang her doorbell at four o'clock sharp, looking natty in a gray pin-striped suit.

"Alex, you look wonderful," Kat gushed, when she saw him.

"Thanks, Kat. You look wonderful yourself," he said with a grin.

Kat wore her standard black dress, spruced up with a black sequined jacket. Alex eyed her appreciatively as he held his car door open for her. They drove in his blue Chevy Blazer which accommodated his 6'2" frame and long legs. Kat had brought her senior yearbook along to help jog her memory of fun-filled anecdotes from her high school years. She chatted happily, engrossed in the past, during the drive to the bay area.

Even though Kat had gone to school in San Leandro, the reunion committee had decided to host their dinner in Jack London Square in Oakland. Scott's Seafood restaurant offered a spectacular view of the bay, with yachts and sailboats criss-crossing in front of San Francisco's majestic skyline.

Alex put his car in a nearby parking garage and strolled hand in hand with Kat to the edge of the square. They breathed in the sea air and marveled at the port of

Oakland, which, with its gigantic shipping cranes looming everywhere in view, looked eerily like the movie set of a science fiction film.

As they walked up to the restaurant, Kat heard a familiar voice from the past.

"Kat, is that you?"

Connor O'Sullivan, Kat's high school flame, stepped out of the shadows to shake her hand. He introduced his wife, Sheryl, to Kat, and Kat introduced them to Alex. *I can't believe he married a mouse,* Kat thought, sizing up Sheryl in a glance.

"You still look terrific, Kat," Connor gushed, holding her hand a second too long. "The years have been kinder to you than they have to me."

"I wouldn't say that, Connor. You're still that energetic person I will never forget. What are you doing now? Where do you live?" Kat asked politely, trying not to notice how much Connor had aged since she last saw him.

"We live in Omaha, Nebraska. I'm in charge of security at Creighton University. Sheryl's a loan officer at one of our local banks," Connor said, stretching his neck to stand taller. "And how about you? I thought I'd see you on the silver screen by now," he bubbled. "She starred in all the school plays," he said to Alex.

Kat tried to laugh congenially, but the only thing that came out sounded like she was clearing her throat. "No, I never made it to Hollywood, Alex. I'm a high school vice-principal," Kat said, pride gleaming in her eyes. "I live in Folsom. My son, Sean, is a counselor at the same high school I work in."

"Really? Our daughter Kathy works in a high school, too. She's a speech therapist."

Kathy? He couldn't have named his daughter after me. Could he? Kat thought to herself, surprise riveting through her.

"And Alex? What is it you do?" Connor asked, eyeing his rival with an obvious and ridiculous competitive spirit that almost made Kat laugh out loud.

Alex looked around him, then whispered, "I work for the CIA, but it's classified." He motioned zipping his lips and loved it when Connor's mouth dropped open.

"Oh, wow, sure, okay," Connor stammered.

He bought that? He's blushing. I can't believe he's been my secret fantasy all these years. I've been so wrong. Kat bit the corner of her mouth to keep from laughing.

"I think we better go in now," Sheryl suggested meekly, shivering in the cool night air. "It was nice to meet you two."

"Same here," said Kat and Alex together. They looked at each other and laughed. "You know how it is with us old couples. After a while we say the same things at the same time," Alex joked.

The two couples entered the restaurant, and, for the rest of the evening, Kat and Alex made a concerted effort to dodge any more Connor sightings. She and Alex sat with Patti O'Hare, Kat's lab partner in chemistry class, and enjoyed talking to her and her husband during dinner. Former classmates drifted by their table, amicably greeting them and showing off photos of their children.

While registering for a souvenir booklet covering the reunion, Kat and Alex signed their names Superman and Wonder Woman and could barely stop laughing long enough for the camera to snap their picture. Alex's irreverent sense of humor and quick wit were intoxicating to Kat. He kept her in stitches the whole way home until they arrived at her door—at which point she began to babble nervously about what a good sport he had been to go with her to the reunion.

Alex stopped her cold by grabbing her shoulders and looking her squarely in the face.

"You don't have to thank me, Kat. I should be thanking you for sharing a glimpse of your past with me. If you're half as attracted to me as I am to you, you know what my next move should be. But I think you and I are too discerning about each other's needs right now. You and I both need to take it slow and see what develops, all right?"

Alex's words soothed Kat's soul. When she realized she'd been holding her breath during his little speech, she slowly let it out and gazed into his eyes for a long time before speaking.

"Alex, you're a dream come true. You're funny, intelligent, and sensitive—everything I want in a man. I'm sure you can tell I'm a little gun shy in the romance department, but I'm not going to run away from someone who makes me feel like you make me feel. So, yes, let's take our sweet time with this relationship. It'll be like slowly peeling the paper off a special gift—with great anticipation of the certainty that we're going to like what we find."

"I know I like what I've found so far," Alex said, taking Kat in his arms.

"Me, too," Kat said, her eyes moving down Alex's face to his waiting lips. They kissed gently, their mouths in a sweet caress.

Kat's heart was racing as their bodies embraced. She could feel Alex muscular body throb as if he were infusing his emotions into her body so she'd understand kinesthetically all he was feeling.

Reluctant to let her go, Alex held Kat tight for a while, then whispered, "Good night, Kat. This is just the beginning of what I hope will be many more great times together."

"I hope so, too. Good night, Alex," Kat said. She watched him get back in his car, drive across the street and park before waving at him and closing her front door. Once inside, she leaned against the door and closed her eyes, still reeling from Alex's touch.

Wow, she thought. *I've wanted someone like him in my life for a long time. Thank you, God, for sending Alex to me. I feel like a little girl who has blown out the candles on her birthday cake, and her wish was instantly granted. Happy birthday to me!*

Chapter 29

Ten days later Kat held a Thanksgiving dinner at her house. It'd been three years since she last hosted the holiday dinner, so she was a little rusty at timing all the various dishes—or all forty-eight food groups, as her son liked to say. Sean and Chelsea were spending the holidays with Chelsea's parents in Denver while Alex was joining his sister in Colorado Springs. So Kat had invited her father, Henry, Kalani, and Liana to share the day with her.

Liana brought some candied yams, sprinkled with macadamia nuts and brown sugar, and Henry brought two pies, one pumpkin and one chocolate cream. Kat had placed the turkey in the oven in the morning so it would be ready for their three o'clock meal. She planned it for the mid-afternoon to give Henry enough time to visit Maxine on his way back home.

Liana and Henry sat next to each other at the dining room table, and as they talked animatedly to one another, it suddenly struck Kat how much alike they were. It wasn't just their gestures or skin tone. It was the shape of their faces, their eyebrows, the silhouette of their heads in the back lighting provided by the winter sun.

I can't believe how much they look the same, Kat thought. *Even their voices seem to match in tone and expression.*

"Where are you from, Liana?" Henry inquired pleasantly.

"I was born in Honolulu and lived there until I was twenty-six, then moved here to California," Liana replied.

"I was born in Honolulu, too!" Henry exclaimed. "In 1933."

"That's the year I was born!" Liana said. "What day? And don't say November first."

"But I have to because I was born November first as well! I can't believe it. It'd be a hoot if we were both born in the same hospital."

"When did you come to California?" Liana asked, peering closely at Henry as if she were memorizing his face.

"My parents immigrated from Spain to Hawaii. They spent some time working on the Ewa Mill plantation, harvesting pineapples, before coming to San Leandro. That's where I grew up. And I'm still there," Henry chuckled.

"Well, if I didn't know you were Spanish, I'd have guessed you were Hawaiian," Liana admitted. "You have that deep tan and brown eyes that many of us have."

Kat broke in excitedly. "She's right, Dad. Just looking at you two side by side is uncanny. I never realized the resemblance before, but you two really look alike."

The oven timer went off, sending everyone into a flurry of activities. Henry carved the turkey while Liana made gravy. Kat and Kalani set the table, and Caesar rubbed his ears against each of them, shamelessly hustling for a treat or two.

After everyone loaded their plates and took their seats at the table, Liana started the round of thanks.

"My great-grandfather always said *O ka maluhia no me oe*—which means peace be with you. That is my wish for each of you today and always," Liana said, stopping her eyes at each face around the table as she spoke.

Kalani was next. "I just wanted to say to Ms. R., thanks for inviting us to this special Thanksgiving Day, the first of many, I hope."

"I hope so, too," Kat said, glowing with gratitude. "I'm thankful to each and every one of you who have so graciously shared your lives and your wisdom with me. How lucky I am to know you and love you. For that I give thanks."

"I guess it's my turn," Henry said shyly. "I'm happy to be in Kat's first house, celebrating Thanksgiving with her and her friends, who are now my friends. I know she's wanted her own place for a long time."

He tilted his head, eyes twinkling at Kat. "The place looks good, even without marigolds," he teased. "Happy Thanksgiving, everyone. Now let's eat."

Toward the end of the meal, Liana brought up the subject of food preferences between the low and middle selves, which necessitated a brief explanation to Henry about the Huna philosophy of three selves in the human body. Then she returned to her original topic.

"Have you ever thought that your low and middle selves might have totally different preferences toward food?" she asked Kat.

"You mean like when my low self craves chocolate even though my middle self knows it's not good for me?"

"Or when I eat cheese puffs," Kalani said. "I once ate a big bag all by myself and got so sick, I still can't put a

246

cheese puff in my mouth without thinking about that awful day. I used to love them, but now my low self says they're a big no-no." Kalani's face puckered up remembering her cheese puff pig out.

"We may not realize it," Liana continued, "but we all have lots of conflicts between the two lower selves. However, one of the best ways of finding out what the low self likes or dislikes is to ask it by way of a pendulum."

"Is it like the pendulum on a grandfather clock?" wondered Henry aloud.

"Same principle," Liana replied. "Have you ever heard of dowsing?"

"Sure. I've seen movies where people used limbs from a tree to dowse for water so they'd know where to put their well," Henry replied. "They'd hold the branch out in front of them and start walking, and it would start twitching when they found water. It was the darndest thing. The branch would bob up and down like it had a mind of its own."

"It did have a mind of its own. It was showing the unihipili's mind," Kalani said.

Liana smiled at Kalani, clearly proud of her granddaughter's contribution to the conversation. "The interest in dowsing goes way back to many cultures and traditions, and it's really popular here in the United States, especially with farmers. There are thousands of people who have joined the American Society of Dowsers to master dowsing techniques and even help developing countries find water for their people. Sometimes they use divining rods and sometimes pendulums. But all of them are interested in getting to know their low selves better.

247

And it's such a great way to tap into the genius of their higher selves by way of their subconscious minds."

"So, what do we need to get started?" Kat asked excitedly.

"You need a light string or a chain with a weight of some kind. Something with a pointed end would be best, but it can be just about anything, like a heavy pendant."

"I've got just the thing. Kat sprinted to the jewelry box in her bedroom closet. She came back with her sapphire and diamond pendant dangling on a gold chain.

Good thing I didn't give Rudy a chance to steal this, or I wouldn't have it to use as a pendulum today, she thought.

"Will this work?" She handed it to Liana who nodded in agreement. Liana held the pendant two inches above the tabletop and waited until it was motionless. Suddenly, the necklace started swinging vertically, then slowly came to a stop. After a few moments, it stopped for a bit, then began swinging horizontally to her body.

"Yes, it will do," Liana pronounced solemnly. "I just asked my low self if it wanted to talk to me and to show me a yes and a no. The yes answer is like making a plus sign and the no answer is like a minus sign. That's how my low self prefers to talk to me."

"Mine's different, Ms. R," Kalani said. "I've trained my low self to make the pendulum swing clockwise for a yes and then counterclockwise for a no."

"Hmm," Kat said, intrigued by the mystery of it all. "I think I'll do the plus and minus signs. May I try it?"

Liana laughed, handing her the necklace. "Of course you can, dear. It's your turn."

"All right. What do I say first?" Kat felt a bit self-conscious using her necklace as a communication device.

"Well, you can start by training your low self how to talk to you. If you want it to answer a yes as a swinging motion up and down, then show it this motion and tell it that it means yes. Then show it how to answer no. Last, ask it if it is ready to talk to you and train it to swing at an angle, between a yes and a no answer. It's as simple as that," Liana said. "Trust me, it'll love talking to you. All you have to do is have the willingness to do it."

"The hardest part," Kalani said, "is making sure you only ask questions that can be answered by either a yes or a no. And try not to ask it about the future because it doesn't always know what's going to happen and will sometimes try telling you anything you want to hear just to make you happy."

"Okay, little buddy," Kat began, holding the necklace as still as possible to start with. "I really want to talk to you, and I'm hoping you'll want to talk to me. If you do, here's how to tell me yes." She swung the pendant back and forth a few times, away from her body and back again. Then she moved the pendant so that it swung on a horizontal plane. "Here's how to say no, and here's how you can show me you're ready for the question." She swung the pendant at a 45-degree angle and waited until it stopped. "Do you want to talk to me?"

Everyone watched as the sapphire and diamond pendant began swinging by itself at a 45-degree angle. They all seemed to let out a collective breath at once.

Kat snorted in amusement, pleased that her low self wanted to talk to her. She waited until the pendant became still again before asking her question.

"Okay, let's see. Are there some foods the middle self likes that you don't?" The answer was yes.

"Is one of the foods you like chocolate?" Yes.

"I thought so!"

"Ask it if it likes cow's milk," Henry interjected.

"Do you like cow's milk?" The pendant started to swing in a negative mode.

Kat looked over at Henry quizzically.

"When you were a baby, Kat, you were allergic to cow's milk. Couldn't keep it down. We fed you goat's milk instead."

"Oh, that explains my lactose intolerance. Okay, Dad, here you go." She handed the necklace to Henry. "Your turn."

Henry went through the initial steps to train his low self to answer him. Then, he surprised everyone with his first question.

"Low self, Liana and I were both born on the same day in the same year in the same city. Kat thinks we even look alike. Are we related in some way?"

The necklace swung wildly in a positive response. Yes. Kat gasped. Liana's eyes teared. Kalani's eyes got big as a doe's in a forest.

"Is she a close relative?" Henry asked. Yes.

"Is she my cousin?" No.

"Is she my sister?" Yes.

"My twin sister?" Yes.

250

"How can that be?" Henry sputtered. The pendant became motionless.

"That's not a yes or no question, Mr. Romero," Kalani reminded him.

Henry put the pendulum down and looked at Liana. "I don't know why, but from the first moment I met you, I felt like I've known you all my life. I don't understand how this whole pendulum thing works, though. Maybe it's telling me what I want to hear, to confirm my inner feeling. I just don't know. What do you think?"

"Henry, I felt the same way when we met. It was an instant recognition. I think it can't all be just a coincidence. I believe there are no accidents. But if your parents were Spaniards and mine were Hawaiians, how can we be related?"

"Maybe you were related in another lifetime, and it's a bleed-through memory of some kind," Kat suggested.

"No, I get the feeling it's this lifetime, but how can that be? The next time I can get back to the islands, I'll do some research on my family tree. Maybe something will turn up to explain it," Liana promised.

"Do you have a copy of your birth certificate, Liana? I could dig around to find mine, and maybe we could compare them. See if there's any clue to back up our suspicions."

"Good idea, Dad," Kat said. "I could ask Chelsea to do some research on the Internet for us, too. Maybe look up the newspaper announcements when you two were born to see if there's something in them that would explain any of this."

"Well, it turns out we have more to be thankful for this Thanksgiving than we ever thought possible," Kalani said with a sly grin. "We could all be related."

"Could be, Kalani. Could be," murmured Henry. "Now the true test of family genetics will be to see how you handle Aggravation." He got up to get the game which he'd stored on one of Kat's book shelves.

"Oh, Dad, you're not going to torture them with that stupid game, are you?" Kat teased.

"Why not? I've tortured you all your life. Why should you have all the fun? How about it, Kalani? Liana?"

"I'm willing, but only if we take it slow, Henry. I've never played this game before," Liana pleaded.

"And show some mercy to a first timer, Dad," Kat begged. "He's ruthless with those dice, always throwing sixes."

"I've played this before, Grandma. It's easy," Kalani said, getting in the spirit.

The next few hours were whiled pleasantly away, with lots of pie eating and dice throwing. It was a carefree, relaxing afternoon. Kat remembered to snap some photos for her album. A friend had once told her, "You know when you're in a moment of greatness." Something told her that in later years, when she looked back at her life, this would be one of those moments.

Chapter 30

At the administrators' meeting late Monday afternoon, Kat asked Gabe how Rudy was doing. He'd been on her mind lately, and now she was genuinely interested in hearing some good news about him. Gabe was vague in his reply to her, muttering something about Rudy being a tough nut to crack. Then he quickly changed the subject to a discussion about the upcoming Winter Ball. At the end of their meeting, Gabe asked Serge if he would cover for him for the next few days while he was away on personal necessity.

For once, when I want to talk about Rudy, Gabe dismisses the subject, Kat thought. *Something's up.*

She had been thinking about an earlier conversation that morning with Dawn Silva about new research coming out which indicated the teen brain was a work in progress and continued to develop into the early twenties.

The logical extension, Kat mused, *is that I might have written Rudy off too soon. His brain probably needs to mature some more so that he can curb his temper and at-risk behavior. Maybe I shouldn't have given up on him. Maybe he can mature and change for the better.*

On the way out of the conference room, Kat motioned for Denise to follow her in to the vault where they took their usual positions once they were behind closed doors.

"What's the deal with Gabe being out the next few days? And why do I have a feeling it has to do with Rudy?"

Denise's eyes sparkled with glee. "You hit it right on the head. It *is* Rudy. Again. Seems he's been punching Brittany, trying to get her to tell him the code to Gabe's wall safe. How's that for nerve? He was already caught sneaking money out of Gabe's wallet, but strong-arming his daughter? No way will Angela put up with that crap."

"Who would?" Kat shook her head. "You know, it's funny. I was just thinking about Rudy this morning. That maybe I'd jumped the gun by thinking he was incorrigible. My friend Dawn told me about a new book that claims the teenage brain doesn't get fully developed until the early twenties, so I was thinking maybe Rudy just needed a chance to mature. But now my sense is, at the rate he's going, he won't live long enough to see his twenties."

Denise nodded in agreement. "Right now, he's killing the goose that laid the golden egg. Not too smart."

"His low self is running his body," Kat blurted.

"His low self?"

"His subconscious mind. It's in charge of Rudy's emotions, and it's clearly in charge of Rudy. He's not using any logical thinking. I think he just gets his kicks with deviant behavior, and right now he's just doing what makes him feel good."

"Well, if he can't straighten up his act, Angela wants him gone. So Gabe's taking him for a few days to some kind of intensive therapy. It better work because Angela's even using the "d" word."

"The "d" word?"

"Yeah, divorce."

"Wow, she is serious. Well, let me know how it goes. Gabe bristles whenever I ask about Rudy, like I'm trying to jam him, you know? But you and Angela are tight, and she'll open up to you."

"I'll keep you up to speed, Kat." Denise opened the vault door, then turned back to Kat. "By the way, I gotta tell you, whatever make-up you're using is really great. You look positively glowing. It's either that, or you're seeing someone new. Which is it?"

"Well, I haven't changed my makeup, so it must be Alex, one of my new neighbors. We're just good friends, though."

"For now," Denise shot back, suspicion registering on her face. "Anyway, there's something different about you that I can't put my finger on just yet. But give me time. I'll get it."

The Winter Ball, a formal affair, was traditionally the last dance of the calendar year. Student committees had worked diligently to transform the multi-purpose room into a showy spectacle carrying out the theme "It's in the Stars." Silver and gold stars made of glitter, poster board, and Styrofoam hung from the ceilings and walls. A disco ball twirled at the center of the ceiling, sending little rays of light dancing across the star-speckled room. White Christmas tree lights flashed and swirled around the entrance doors where the excited students were queued, waiting impatiently in the cold for the doors to open.

While the deejay, a twenty-something personality from one of the local radio stations, readied the students' pre-selected music in one corner of the room, an effete photographer and his assistant set up their portrait backdrops and lights in the opposite corner.

Before they admitted the students, Kat and the other administrators met with the group of parents and teachers who'd volunteered to be chaperones. Kat passed out a list of the rules while Gabe coached the parents on how to break up any couples dirty dancing.

"I'm giving each of you parents a flashlight," he announced in a theatrical voice which resonated throughout the room. "If you can't see any light between bodies, and it's obvious they're grinding into each other, they need to be separated. After you've warned them once, and they continue to defy you, make them sit out in the lobby for fifteen minutes before you let them back in the dance. Third strike and they're out. Bring them to me or one of the other administrators, and we'll call their parents to come get them."

Serge spoke up at that point. "Also, if you smell any liquor on them, or if you suspect they're acting a little strange, bring them to one of us. We can usually detect if they're on something."

"One last thing," Kat added, feeling a bit like she was an army sergeant talking to new recruits. "Once they leave the dance, they are not allowed back in. For any reason. If they need to use the phone, but have no money, we'll let them use our cell phones."

"Any questions?" Gabe asked, his eyes scanning the group from left to right.

Becky Farnsworth raised her hand. "Just one. The kids are supposed to be formally dressed for this dance. What if they show up in jeans? Do we let them in anyway? I mean, what if jeans are the best they have?"

"When the kids bought their tickets, they were told exactly what was acceptable and what was not. They were specifically told no jeans allowed. So tonight, if they show up at the door in jeans, we'll have to call their parents to see if they can either bring them something more suitable to change into or take them home. Believe me, we want them dressed up. They act better when they're all dressed up, and they're less prone to fight in expensive clothes."

"That's good," Becky sighed loudly, "because I certainly don't want my Mikey messing up that nice suit I bought him for tonight."

The parents and teachers took their assigned stations as Gabe unlocked the lobby doors to let the shivering students in. Kat checked student ID's and guest passes while Serge collected pre-sold tickets and sold tickets at the door. Some of the teachers helped staff the snack bar in the lobby; others checked in students' purses and coats. After testing their flashlights, the parents stationed themselves in their posts in the darkened dance room.

It took more than an hour for the outside line to drop down to a trickle. Kat was pleased to see Kalani walk in with her date, Bobby Parrington, a lanky junior who had befriended Kalani in her beginning drama class. *She's drop-dead gorgeous*, Kat thought, admiring the royal blue chiffon dress she'd splurged on for Kalani when she'd heard she'd been invited to the dance.

257

Kalani, who never wore makeup, had made an exception for tonight, and her hair, usually in a braid or hanging straight, was done in a swept-up coiffure that dramatically highlighted the delicate beauty of her smooth bronze face. Bobby seemed enchanted with Kalani's transformation, Kat noticed.

Be nice to her, Bobby, or you'll answer to me, she thought, eyeing Bobby suspiciously.

Suddenly Kat was aware of eyes boring a hole through the back of her head. She swiveled around in her high-backed stool to discover Rudy, wearing his ever-permanent sneer, walking in with Jasmine Robinson.

"Hi, Rudy, how's it going?" Kat asked nonchalantly, accepting Rudy's guest pass from Jasmine.

"It's going great, now that I don't have to see you every day," he snipped, loosening his tie a bit.

Kat rolled her eyes, restraining herself from any come-back that would lower herself to his level.

Rudy smirked, grabbed Jasmine's hand and bolted for the dance floor.

The next two hours dragged by at a snail's pace for the chaperones, all of whom complained at some point in the evening about the nasty lyrics, the loud, thumping bass, and the sorry selection of music provided by the jumping deejay, who did his best to surpass the number of decibels of an incoming jet at the Sacramento International Airport. Their feet hurt, their energy had flagged, and, one by one, they turned into die-hard clock watchers.

By eleven o'clock, one could almost hear a collective *Hallelujah*. Kat and the other adults hustled the kids out as fast as they could, quickly handling their claim checks and practically pushing them out the door. When all the students had finally gone home, Kat, Serge, and Gabe walked back to the administration building together to count money and store the ticket boxes and flashlights in the vault for future use.

"Well, this turned out to be a relatively easy night," Serge said, chaining the gate just outside of the multipurpose room.

"That's because it's too cold for the kids to hang out afterwards." Kat pulled her wool jacket tightly around her chest.

"True. I've stayed as late as one in the morning waiting for kids to go home," Gabe agreed.

"I don't see your Jaguar out here, Gabe." Kat pointed to the cars in the administrators' parking spaces.

"I let Rudy drive it tonight. I want him to feel that I trust him. It'll improve his self-esteem. I'm driving Angela's car tonight," Gabe said sheepishly, embarrassed to admit he'd been reduced to driving a measly Geo Metro.

"I didn't think I'd ever see you in anything less than a Beamer," Serge teased.

"No telling what we'll sacrifice for family," Gabe said, one eyebrow arched dramatically. Then, in an uncharacteristic move of generosity, he told Serge and Kat to go home. He'd be wrapping things up himself so they could start their weekend early.

Grateful and relieved, Kat immediately jumped in her car, warming it up for a few minutes to defrost the windows. *My feet thank you, Gabe,* she thought, as she kicked off her dress shoes and wiggled into flats she'd stashed in the back seat.

Arriving home twenty minutes later, she was greeted by Caesar who seemed to chastise her for being late by meowing non-stop until she picked him up and fussed over him. Alex had left a message on her phone to call him in the morning, but other than that, the house was just as she left it, with one major exception. Caesar had killed a bird and had brought it in through the cat door to show it off to Kat. He stood proudly by his trophy as she fought a gagging reflex.

"So that's what you're meowing about," Kat said. "You are such a good killer, but could you take the bird outside, please? I really don't want to have to clean up guts and feathers all over the house tomorrow—not to mention having to pick up a dismembered beak and two feet."

Caesar just looked at her quizzically until she closed her eyes and visualized him picking up the bird and exiting through the kitty door to the backyard. Once she sent him that picture, he got the message and did exactly what she'd hoped he'd do.

"If I can command my cat with my mind without trying, then what could an equally powerful enemy do to me?" she mused.

Clearly, her powers as the Huna Warrior were growing exponentially. She'd need them sooner than she thought.

Chapter 31

After a cozy morning spent in bed reading the paper and working the crossword puzzle, Kat returned Alex's call.

"Hey, Alex, it's Kat. I got your call. What's up?"

"Nothing much. I didn't know if you had plans for New Year's Eve and thought maybe you and I could get together."

"Gee, I'm sorry, Alex. I've got plans to see the fireworks at Lake Tahoe with my friend, Dawn Silva. I might have mentioned her to you. She and I go there every year on New Year's Eve. We hate the drinking scene, and the lake is so beautiful at night. It's been a standing date for us for four years now."

"I understand." Alex couldn't keep the disappointment out of his voice.

"But I'll tell you what. We have a faculty Christmas party coming up next Friday night. Want to go with me to that? It won't have the same kind of pizzazz as New Year's Eve, but you'd certainly liven up the party for me. What do you say?"

"Well, I can't say I'm not bummed about New Year's Eve, but next weekend sounds fine. I won't have to wear a suit, will I?"

"You're off the hook on that one, Alex. I'd say just slacks and a jacket. Definitely no tie. Teachers never wear ties, anyway—just the administrators."

"Good. Ties always make me feel like I'm getting ready to be lynched. What time do I pick you up for this?"

"The party is at seven-thirty at our principal's house in Davis. Six forty-five would be perfect. Are you writing this on your calendar?"

"Yes, how'd you know?"

"Because you seem like an orderly kind of guy who's responsible and doesn't forget unless there's a good reason to."

"You are one observant woman, Kat."

"Yeah, that's why they pay me the big bucks. I think I'm up to two-fifty an hour now."

"I'm impressed," Alex deadpanned.

"Okay, see you soon." Kat hung up and frowned. The thought had occurred to her that she could have invited Alex to join her and Dawn in Tahoe, or she could have cancelled on Dawn all together and spent the evening with Alex. But she'd already learned what it was like to be the third wheel or to be dumped by a girlfriend, who opted for a last minute date with a male. She'd made a promise never to mistreat any of her friends like that.

A "Thank God, it's Friday" atmosphere prevailed on the Friday before the winter break began. At the Minelli's that night, the house was ablaze with lights, and everyone was in the mood to let their hair down. Kat and Alex arrived before the majority of the faculty in time for Angela to give them and a few other early birds a personal tour of Gabe's house.

At the entry way was a winding staircase that led to the second floor. One room housed enough exercise equipment to furnish a professional gym and another showcased a handsome pool table, its polished cherry wood gleaming and pristine, bordering its deep-green felt covering. A balcony just off the master bedroom afforded a spectacular view of the backyard pool with its dramatic backlighting and waterfalls.

"I bet Rudy loves the pool," Kat said to Angela as they gazed at the backyard from the balcony.

"Actually, Rudy won't get near it. He can't swim," Angela replied uneasily.

"Oh, that's too bad." Kat led the small group down the hallway and stopped to look at a framed photograph on the wall.

"That's a family photo when we all took a cruise to the Mexican Riviera last summer," Angela said. She pointed at the people in the picture. "That's my sister, Gina, and her fiancé. They're getting married New Year's Eve."

"He looks familiar," Kat said. Where do I know him from?"

"You've probably seen him on campus. He owns the pool construction company that's putting in the pool at Anthony High," Angela answered proudly.

"Oh, yes, Wes Holden. I met him once at the little trailer in the back of the school," Kat said.

"And you say he and your sister are getting married soon?" Felicia Davenport, the Assistant Superintendent of Educational Services, stepped forward from the midst of the group to peer closer at the photograph.

"Yes, we're all going to Las Vegas for their wedding on New Year's Eve."

263

"I'm sure it'll be lovely." Felicia smiled snidely, checking her recently polished nails for flaws as she headed for the stairway.

Once downstairs the intimate group broke up to either tour the first floor on their own or mingle with the rest of the staff who had been arriving in a steady stream.

Kat took Alex to meet Serge and his wife Olivia, but after a few minutes, Serge excused himself to chat with Felicia Davenport who had come to the party by herself, claiming her husband, a tax attorney, was home working on an important case.

Felicia nursed a tall gin and tonic while she tinkered out a melody on Gabe's baby grand piano. After a few more drinks, Felicia was coaxed into playing Christmas songs while everyone gathered around the piano for a sing-along. Kat felt sorry for Olivia who had retreated into the Minelli library and was sitting in an overstuffed chair, reading a magazine.

Wonder what that's all about, Kat thought. She noticed Serge hovered around Felicia the rest of the evening, bringing her drinks and laughing at her mistakes on the ivory keys while Olivia sulked in the library.

When Sean and Chelsea finally arrived, Kat introduced them to Alex.

"Great to finally meet you, Sean," Alex said. "Your mom's told me a lot about you."

"If it was good, then it's all true," Sean said, extending his hand to Alex's. "This is my fiancée, Chelsea." Sean put his arm around Chelsea's shoulder, proudly showing her off.

"It's nice to meet you, Chelsea. From what I've seen so far, you're marrying into a great family."

Chelsea grinned and shook hands with Alex. "Why, thank you. I couldn't agree with you more."

The four of them piled their plates high, grabbed iced drinks, and sat outside in the patio near the outdoor heaters. Mazie Longer, Richard Stevens, Denise Dutra, and Tony Navarro joined them around a rectangular glass table, talking and joking comfortably into the late hours of the night.

On the way home, Kat asked Alex if he'd had a good time.

"I had an exceptionally good time, Kat. Thanks for inviting me. I'd repay the favor, but since I work for myself, there are no company parties I can invite you to."

"You can throw your own party, Alex. And you don't need a special occasion. Just make something up."

"Good idea. I may just do that. Of course, I wouldn't want you to think it's a date," he kidded.

"No, I would never think of it as a date. Just a party thrown by a company of one."

At Kat's front door, Alex leaned into her and kissed Kat, gently at first, then gradually with more and more passion. Kat opened her front door, and they backed into the foyer in a mutual embrace. As Alex's tongue explored her mouth, a wave of insecurity swept through Kat, and she pulled away. Alex looked at her quizzically.

"Hold on, Alex. I'm not ready for this next step." Kat gulped nervously.

"What's the matter, Kat? I like you. I think you like me. We're two unencumbered adults, healthy and normal in every way, right?" Alex gazed hopefully into Kat's eyes.

"Right, except for the normal part," Kat mumbled to herself. *How can I tell him about being the Huna Warrior? If I still find the idea scary, I can imagine how he'll react. I don't want to scare him away so soon in our relationship.*

Kat looked up at Alex, a thin smile on her face. "There's something about me that you need to know, and I can't tell you about it just yet. I'm still getting used to it myself."

Alex's face paled with alarm. "Don't tell me you're sick. I couldn't take another...." Alex grabbed her shoulders, peering into her face for answers.

"No, Alex, I'm not sick. I...I have a new responsibility...um...a new job that could get in the way of you and me being together in the way I think we'd both like to be, if you know what I mean."

"No, I don't know what you mean. What new job?"

"That's just it. I can't tell you until I find out more about it and go through a lot more training. I just don't want us to get our hopes up there'll be a lot more time for us to be together. I don't know how it's going to go. It's complicated."

"Kat," Alex said with a sigh of relief, "Whatever this new job of yours entails doesn't mean I won't keep trying to see you or be with you. I'm a very patient man. I've got all the time in the world."

Kat nodded as Alex's hands cupped her face and kissed her on the nose. "Don't worry. I'll be here for you. And whenever you want to tell me about this 'complication,' just let me know. Goodnight, sweet Kat. Tonight was great."

"Good night, sweet Alex. I'll talk to you soon."

They both waved at each other before going into their respective houses.

Kat sat on the couch in the living room and sent out a golden thread to Alex, trying to get a sense of what his reaction would be when she told him she was the next Huna Warrior. The sinking sensation in the pit of her stomach told her what she wanted to know.

Chapter 32

Kat left Folsom early Christmas morning to meet Henry at the Stockton Health Care Center and open gifts with Maxine. Fog filled the valley floor, slowing the holiday traffic to a snail's pace.

Henry's pensive face turned into all smiles once Kat bounded into the room, presents piled high in her arms.

"I was worried about you coming all that way in the fog," he reluctantly confessed to Kat. She hugged him first, then went to her mother who was sitting in bed, a red blanket dotted with Christmas trees and teddy bears covering her feet.

"See the holiday blanket I got for your mother?" Henry beamed with quiet pride.

"It's nice, Dad. Very cheery." Kat handed her parents their presents. "Merry Christmas, Mom and Dad."

Kat helped her mother open the smallest of the three gifts she'd brought for her. It was a framed photo of Chelsea and Sean celebrating their engagement. Maxine smiled, excited at opening the present, but puzzled as to who the strangers in the photo were.

"That's your grandson, Sean, and his new fiancée, Chelsea," Kat said, pointing them out to her mother. "I'll put this on your night stand so you can see it any time you want to, okay?" She shoved aside a vase holding flowers from her father's last visit to make room for the new frame.

Henry pulled a burgundy sweat suit out of its box to show Maxine. "Look what I got from Kat."

"I got a matching one for Mom, too, Dad," Kat said, opening the box for her mother and laying the outfit on top of her. Maxine babbled her approval toward a grinning Kat and Henry.

From Sean, Henry received a bottle of his favorite cologne which, before her incapacity, Maxine had traditionally bought him. For Maxine, Sean had wrapped a toy lion, which clapped its hands and cheered when the light sensor set him off. While Kat installed batteries in the lion, Henry doused himself with his new cologne and leaned his neck over for his two favorite women to smell.

"You reek, Dad, but it's a nice reek," Kat teased. Maxine blinked both eyes at the same time.

"How's Mom doing, Dad? Did you talk to any of the nurses?"

"They're not saying much, Kat, but I see her slowly going downhill. It's like the lights in a city going out one at a time."

"I know, Dad. I don't see her as often as you do, so the difference seems pretty radical to me when I do." Kat picked up her mother's hand and kissed it.

Henry's eyes glistened. Kat's simple gesture of love for her mother had touched his heart. He loved it when the three of them were together again, just like old times. Not wanting to open the floodgate of anguish he felt watching his beloved wife steadily drift away, he'd quickly changed the subject. "Kat, I've got presents here for you and Sean. Why don't you open yours?"

269

Reaching behind the curtain that separated Maxine's space from her roommate's, Henry dragged out a huge unadorned cardboard box.

"Sorry I didn't wrap it, but once you see it, you'll know why I didn't," Henry hinted mischievously.

"It better not be a bunch of marigolds, Dad. That's all I can say," Kat snickered. She used her car keys to zip through the tape wrapped in layers around the box. "Geeze, Dad, you must have used the whole roll of tape on this."

The box flaps finally pried open, Kat carefully reached in to extract a living three-foot tall, Douglas fir tree which Henry had decorated with Kat's favorite childhood Christmas ornaments. An angel, robed in creamy satin and lace, sat atop the tree, arms open wide, presumably bestowing peace on earth and good will to men.

"Our family ornaments! I thought they were lost to me forever. I've missed them so much because they remind me of past Christmases with you and Mom. Thank you, Dad. I'll treasure them forever."

Now it was Kat's turn to cry. She put the tree back in its box for the moment and sat in her father's lap, arms draped around his neck as she had done in her younger years. He hugged her tightly, stroking her head in silent comfort. After a moment, she wiped her tears and returned to her tree, lifting it so her mother could see it.

"How did you know I didn't have a tree up this year, Dad?"

"How'd Sean know I ran out of cologne?"

"I'm not telling any secrets."

270

"Mum's the word. Anyway, I'm glad you like the tree, Kat. You can plant it in your yard and enjoy a living Christmas tree all year long."

"You're right, Dad. I know just the spot, too. And thanks for the ornaments. I can hang them on the gold garland I have around my fireplace mantle."

Henry handed Kat an envelope. "And this is for Sean from his grandpa," Henry said, eyes twinkling. "I got him a gift certificate so he can splurge on something nice."

"Thanks, Dad. You know how low we educators are on the totem pole of monetary compensation."

"Not as low as retired nursery workers."

Suddenly, an orderly pushed a cart into the room and freshened Maxine's bedside glass with chilled water. "Maxine is scheduled for her shower now. Would you like to wait here for her or in the lobby?" he asked politely.

"We're going to get a bite to eat, and my Dad will probably return," Kat replied, taking Henry's hand and pulling him up.

Kat drove with Henry to a restaurant she'd taken Maxine to when her mother was still able to walk. She and Henry sat in an upholstered booth facing out toward the street. They watched the heavy traffic ebb and flow, sipping hot drinks, coffee for Henry, cocoa for Kat, until their lunch orders came.

During Kat's childhood years, whenever the family had gone out to dinner, they would each order something different so they could share their meals and sample all the unique tastes in one another's orders. Kat and Henry fell into this same routine today as he dished out some of his lasagna in her plate, and she scooped some breaded

271

shrimp from her dish into his. They did this automatically without asking, glad they could sustain some semblance of family tradition despite Maxine's absence.

Henry waited until their desserts arrived—dark chocolate mousses sprinkled with coconut flakes—to ask Kat if she'd learned anything new about the coincidence of him sharing a birthday with Liana and the possibility they were twins.

"I called Chelsea about it the day after Thanksgiving, and she promised she'd get to it during winter break which started less than a week ago. I'll see her tonight at Sean's and ask her if she's made any progress. Chelsea's parents flew in to have Christmas with her, and her twin brother's also flying in. I can't wait to meet them."

Kat rolled up her sweater sleeves and dug into her dessert. Henry hadn't touched his yet.

"You know, Kat, I just can't get Liana out of my mind," he said, his head tilted in reverie. "Don't get me wrong. It's certainly not a romantic attraction at all. I just feel protective of her somehow, like a brother would of a sister. I've got to know, that's all. It can't be just coincidence that we were born in the same city on the same day and year and look so much alike. But beyond the outward appearance, I feel connected to her inside, you know? I wish I understood it all better, that's all."

Henry got serious about his dessert and within seconds it had disappeared, leaving him smug with satisfaction.

"That's exactly how I feel about Liana and Kalani, Dad," Kat confided. "I can't tell you how much I'm drawn to them. Both are working with me on a, uh, a project that I can't tell you about just yet, but they are two of the sweetest, wisest, most honorable people I know. Besides you and Mom, I trust them implicitly." Kat pushed her empty dessert dish away and wiped her mouth with a napkin.

"I sensed that about them, Kathrine. I hope Liana has some luck in her research, unless Chelsea turns up something first," Henry said, a dreamy look in his eyes as if he were trying to replay Thanksgiving Day over in his mind, minute by minute, dissecting every bit for verification of his feelings.

"Me, too, Dad. Me, too." Kat asked the waitress to bring her the ticket. As they waited, father and daughter stared out the window at the busy traffic and the lifting fog, wondering what surprises awaited them in the coming year.

Chapter 33

Later that night, having first stopped by home to change into a red velvet pantsuit, Kat knocked on Chelsea's door and was instantly embraced by Sean who helped her carry several gifts in. He walked her into the living room to meet Chelsea's parents, Sheila and Jamison "Jamie" Scott, while Chelsea, mitts on hands, waved hello before pulling a prime rib roast out of the oven.

A blend of sophistication and earthiness, Sheila looked young enough to be Chelsea's older sister rather than her mother. She wore an ivory wool suit with gold piping, accented by large gold loops on her ears and a matching necklace.

Sheila took Kat's extended hand and pumped it firmly. "It's so wonderful to finally meet you, Kat. Chelsea's told us so much about you."

"All of it good," her husband interjected jovially. Jamie, too, looked "well-preserved." Clad in a crisp tweed jacket and gray slacks, he was a handsome man, confident and charismatic. He shook Kat's hand, white gleaming teeth revealed in a charming smile.

Kat beamed back at Chelsea's parents. "I'm so happy to meet you both. We've got a lot to look forward to now that Chelsea and Sean are engaged, don't we?"

Kat studied their faces intently, then blurted, "Wow, I can see how Chelsea is a blend of both of you. She's got your dazzling smile, Jamie, and your beautiful grace, Sheila. What a wonderful combination. I just love Chelsea."

That said, Sheila, who owned and operated an interior design company, and Jamie, an attorney specializing in contract law, instantly bonded with high school vice-principal Kat whose income might be on the diminutive side, but whose perspicuity was honest and, more importantly, endearing.

Chelsea's twin brother, Charlie, arrived a few minutes later, returning from the store because Chelsea had run out of butter. He wasn't an identical twin, but no one could deny the sibling similarity. Same profile, mannerisms, even laugh patterns.

Just like Liana and Henry, Kat thought. *Twins.*

Charlie gave Kat a warm hug. "Chelsea never stops talking about you, Kat, so I feel like we've known each other forever," he said, putting the butter in Chelsea's waiting hand.

"I've heard a lot about you, too, Charlie," Kat laughed. "All of it good," she added, smiling coyly at Jamie. "How's your graphics design business going?"

"Great. I just picked up another client-- a new creamery that's opening in Santa Barbara. It's a small family business, starting from scratch, so I'll be the first to design their logo and print ads, pick out the dominant colors and shapes in their outdoor signage as well as their indoor displays like signs and napkins. Creating all that is so cool."

"I've read twins are opposite in some respects. Often one of them is left-handed, while the other is right-handed. Is this true of you and Chelsea?"

"We're both right-handed," Charlie said, "but I'm much more right-brain dominant and have more of an artistic bent, while Chelsea, our budding lawyer here, appears to be more left-brain dominant."

"Yeah, and together we kick butt," Chelsea said, punching Charlie playfully on the arm. "Dinner's ready now. Please sit wherever you'd like."

Kat sat in between Chelsea and Sheila, enjoying their personalities—Chelsea, being outgoing and bubbly in contrast to Sheila who was more introspective and deliberate. She could see how Sean's more reserved nature toned Chelsea down a bit and how her bubbly personality lifted him up out of his natural reticence. It was a nice balance.

When dinner was over, Kat caught Chelsea alone in the kitchen and asked if she'd made any progress on solving the mystery of their "Hawaiian connection," Kat's code words for research on a relationship between Liana and Henry.

"I've been swamped, Kat. Sorry. I'll work on it tomorrow, I promise," Chelsea whispered.

"No, not tomorrow," Kat said, shaking her head. "Tomorrow, you're hitting all the after-Christmas sales with me, remember? I mean, you can't pass up a chance to lunatic shop. It's the test of a true believer. After four hours of power shoving, underhand thrusts, and over the shoulder grabs, I guarantee you a spot in the NFL. The day after Christmas sales require nerves of steel and the contortion ability of a Chinese acrobat, though. You sure you're up to it?"

Chelsea laughed. "I'm sure. I'll come by your house at eight, and we'll head for the mall. I'll research the Hawaiian connection after I recover from our shopping expedition. If I'm not suffering too much from battle fatigue."

"That's a deal. Let's go open gifts, shall we?"

She and Chelsea joined the others in the living room, enacting a scene that was occurring in millions of other homes around the world. None of the gifts were costly, just thoughtful. None of the sentiments were gushy, just real. And all of the moments were those that Kat silently stored in her heart for reserves to call upon when the future, with its unknown perils and pitfalls, required some semblance of calm and normalcy.

I don't know about this Huna Warrior life, she thought. *I've never wanted to place myself in this kind of danger. The older I get, the smaller I've wanted my life to be. I've just wanted to be safe and live to a ripe old age. All I wanted was to take my grandchildren out for ice cream cones and movies once in a while.*

Besides, what if I can't do this, whatever this *is? And what if I'd be putting other people in my life, like Alex, in danger? He's an innocent bystander who could get seriously hurt by just spending time with me.*

Kat got up, poured herself a glass of eggnog, and returned to the festivities, determined to put her worry aside and enjoy the moment. *Maybe that's why they call it the* present. *All I have is now and it's a gift. Yesterday is gone and tomorrow will take care of itself.*

At that same moment, across town, Kalani stood before the mirror in her bathroom, experimenting with

277

make-up from the kit she'd managed to borrow once again from her drama teacher. She studied the face she'd created in the mirror, then compared it with the photograph of her mother that she held up to the light. With a little nose putty, the right shade of face makeup, a smudge of charcoal eyeliner and a dab of rouge, she looked so uncannily like Leilani that tears sprang in her eyes.

"I really miss you, Mom," she said to the mirror, closing her eyes to wipe away the tears.

"I miss you, too, Kalani." It was Leilani's voice, loud and clear, reverberating inside Kalani's head.

Kalani looked around, her heart jumping, but saw nothing except her own reflection in the mirror. She shut her eyes to concentrate on hearing her mother's voice once more.

"I'm always with you, Kalani," Leilani said. "Always watching over you. Just think of me as being in the other room. I'm here to help you and Grandma. All of us are here. Just say the word, and we'll be there for you. Always, Kalani. Always." Leilani's voice trailed into silence.

Kalani opened her eyes and looked again in the mirror. This time she saw Liana, standing in the doorway smiling through her tears.

"Grandma!" Kalani cried. "I heard my mother from the other side!"

"Yes, dear," Liana said. "I've been sending her mana every day so she would eventually have the strength to talk to you. She's slowly building up her power so she can join the others who help us in any way they can."

"Oh, Grandma, you knew a visit from Mom would be the best gift I could ever have gotten today, didn't you?" Kalani hugged Liana so hard, they almost tipped over together.

"*Mele Kalikimaka*, Kalani dear," Liana said, deeply moved by Kalani's joy.

"*Mele Kalikimaka*, Grandma. You've made it the merriest of Christmases for me now. Thank you, thank you, thank you!" Kalani punctuated each thank you with a kiss on Liana's cheek. Liana laughed and pulled Kalani into the kitchen where their Christmas dinner awaited them.

Chapter 34

New Year's Eve afternoon evolved into a kaleidoscope of activities. Kat and Dawn checked in to their hotel in Lake Tahoe. Sean and Chelsea helped to organize a Monte Carlo night fund-raiser for Big Brothers/Big Sisters. Kalani and Liana cooked for a potluck dinner which the second floor residents of the apartment complex were throwing for themselves.

Later on into the evening, Gabe and Angela toasted Wes Holden and his bride at their wedding reception in Las Vegas.

At midnight, Alex, with Caesar on his lap for company, watched the television countdown show originating in Times Square. Then, hearing the commotion in the middle of the block, Alex pushed Caesar through the cat door at Kat's house and went outside to join the other neighbors who had set up their own fireworks show in the street.

At the same time, miles of ocean away, Hukui gazed out into the star-studded heavens above Maui. His face, illumined by the moon, crumpled into a menacing sneer as an ineffable fireball rocketed across the sky.

"Fly, *akualele*," he prayed. Spirit away into the night to bring destruction to my enemies. Soon their lives will be sputtering flames, dying, dying, and then, poof! They will vanish into oblivion while my light shines brighter than the sun. May the new year bring the fulfillment of all my desires."

The lonely surf beat mournfully on the rocks below, as his father, Kahili, cowering in the shadows, silently prayed to be rescued from the nightmare that was now his life. A few days before, remembering the traditions he'd heard as a boy, he had shot a golden cord of aka out of the dark corner. In his mind's eye, he had watched as it threaded its way into the crumbling stones that comprised the temple floor.

"Bring me back the mana that has been secretly stored in the stones by the Aumakua of old," he had prayed. And the prayer had, indeed, taken flight. His former strength had come back to him.

Now, in front of his son, the old man feigned weakness, moaning pathetically from the dark corner, convincing his son of his continued subservience. But inwardly his hopes soared as the familiar energy returned stronger than ever. The old man mulled over a plan of escape and hid the smile that threatened to burst through his pretense of despair. Hope, at last, glimmered in his eyes.

Liana, he cried out silently, *save me!*

Chapter 35

On the first Friday of the New Year, Alex took Kat skiing for the day. He noticed skis hanging from the rafters in her garage when he first fixed her sprinklers back in September and thought it would be fun if he could treat her for a change. He'd been thinking a lot about her lately, remembering their last kiss and how warm she had felt in his arms. He missed her.

During the two-hour trip to the mountains, Kat filled him in on her possible Hawaiian connection. She was thrilled her father might be the twin of her favorite student's grandmother. Alex was simply fascinated by the serendipity of it all.

"What are the odds that they *are* twins and have found each other after all this time?"

"Astronomical." Alex shook his head in awe.

"True, and yet it's no accident. The universe doesn't work that way. It conspired to help them find each other."

"So it was fate that they'd meet?"

"I believe so." Kat smiled, happy to be in on one of the universe's secrets.

"Then it must have been fate as well when you moved in across the street from me." Alex pulled Kat gently toward him to kiss her.

"Could be, Alex," Kat said, her beaming smile sending a glow to Alex's heart. She, too, felt the magic between them. Her body tingled with his touch. *I've got to tell him about me. I want him to know, but maybe not just yet. I don't want to spoil this beautiful day.*

"It's a perfect day for skiing," Kat said, as they pulled into the Heavenly Ski Resort in Lake Tahoe.

Light snow flurries were forecast for the afternoon, but the morning made good on its promise to be cold, crisp and, well, heavenly. Since she'd only learned to ski a few years before, Kat planned to take a refresher lesson when she arrived. "I don't want to wind up a Huna warrior in a body cast!" she mused as she watched Alex head for the black diamond run. The plan was for them to ski at their own levels and meet at noon for lunch at the resort's cafeteria.

After her lesson and a few hours of runs on the intermediate slope, Kat was worn out. She decided to rest and wait for Alex by a grove of trees that lined the entry way to the lodge's restaurant. She popped off her skis and propped them on one of the racks along with dozens of other pairs, then searched for a comfortable place to sit. Spotting a majestic Ponderosa pine tree, looming over one hundred and twenty feet tall, she flopped on the ground at its base and leaned against its strong cinnamon bark.

She gazed up into the branches, silently marveling at their symmetry and simple elegance. The thought of "symmetry" triggered the memory of a William Blake poem which began, "Tiger! Tiger! burning bright in the forests of the night, what immortal hand or eye could frame thy fearful symmetry." And that in turn, reminded her of the first line of Sara Teasdale's poem, Barter, "Life has loveliness to sell."

283

When she got to the line about the scent of pine trees in the rain, she breathed in the smell of the Ponderosa pine she'd been leaning against. "You smell so delightful, tree," she said aloud. "Just like vanilla."

"Why, thank you, ma'am," the tree replied.

Startled, Kat looked around, but no one was there.

"Did the tree just talk to me?" she asked softly.

"Yes, I did. It's so rare when someone hears me."

The tree's voice was low, flowing through Kat's consciousness like the wind.

"Omigod, I can hear you, tree! I've never had a tree talk to me before. Thank you!"

She stood up and stretched her arms around the tree, its rough bark layered like the interlocking pieces of a puzzle, and hugged it.

The tree's reply swished through Kat's inner ears. "You are most welcome, ma'am. You are rare, indeed."

"Since I don't believe in coincidences, I know there's something special I need to hear, or we wouldn't be talking together like this, right?"

"Right. I'm here to remind you that all plant life has knowledge to impart—if only humans would pay attention. We're always ready to communicate with you because we are part of you, just as you are part of us. Your very life depends on us for nourishment and comfort. In turn, we gladly give ourselves to you. Together we have forged a sacred, ancient bond. It is part of the Creator's plan to have this flow of love and energy from one living organism to another."

"Yes, it is. Since the essence of God is love, and God lives in us, through us and as us, then it follows it is

God's love and energy flowing through each of us you and I exchange," Kat said. "It may be manifest in varying degrees, but it's all the same thing. We're all one with one another."

"Well said," replied the tree. "The soul of Father/Mother God is the soul in all of us. So, yes, we are all of the same essence."

"Thanks for the reminder, friend," Kat said, massaging her aching limbs. "I have an enemy who's been a real challenge to me lately, and sometimes I forget, down deep, he's just like me."

"I hope I have been of help to you today. If there is anything more I can do, please ask."

"Actually, I do have one request. Skiing today has really taken a toll on my stamina. Can you give me a boost of energy and maybe take the pain away from my sore muscles? That is, if you have any energy to spare. I wouldn't want to deplete you in any way."

"I would be happy to pull up energy from the earth for you," the tree offered, its voice a powerful force whispering in the cold air. "Mother Earth is a living, vibrant being whom you can always depend on for help in healing."

"I know," Kat exclaimed. "I love to sit on the ground and soak up the positive vibes I feel coming from the earth. I'll pretend to be gardening, but I'm really communing with Mother Earth."

Kat looked around furtively and then asked, "About my request. What do I do next?"

"Please stand and put your arms around me like you did before. Ask the Mother to fill your being with her healing light. I will do the same. See if you can feel our vibrations merging and becoming one."

Kat stood tall and put her arms around the tree trunk as far as they could stretch. Then she opened the chakras in her body, particularly in the palms of her hands and the soles of her feet. She pictured her heart chakra as a tiny sun growing in brightness, shining from the center of her solar plexus and lighting every pore in her body so that she became a star of light. Her feet seemed to sink deep into the ground, like the roots of the tree she embraced. She could feel the earth's energy work its way from the bottom of her feet to the top of her head. Within seconds she felt buoyant and free of pain. She took a few steps away from the tree to test the flexibility in her body, then scanned its criss-cross trunk and thick branches.

"I'm back to normal, dear tree. Thank you so much. I will never forget you for this. You are a marvel to behold."

"It's been my pleasure, ma'am. Feel free to call upon us any time."

"Us?"

"Me and others like me. And, of course, Mother Earth. In times of trouble, think of us."

"I will. I promise."

Kat looked at her watch and realized she needed to hurry if she were to meet Alex on time. Taking one last, luxurious breath of mountain air, she headed for the lift lines and soon saw him sitting on an old log. He stared at her sternly as she plodded over to him.

"I've been watching you for about five minutes, Kat. Tell me you weren't talking to that tree," Alex said, frowning, but trying to force a smile.

"Well, yeah, I was," Kat admitted, chagrined. "I talk to flowers, too, but up until now, I've never had a two-way conversation with any of them."

"So you're telling me this tree talked to you?" Alex asked, holding back a laugh.

"Yeah. He said he rarely had anyone talk to him. In fact, he said I was rare. Must have liked the word 'rare,' I guess."

"Humph!" Alex snorted playfully. "Rare as in one-of-a-kind or rare as in a bit eccentric?"

"Alex, I think the more you get to know me, the more you'll see I'm a little bit of both."

Kat looked around disconcertedly. The snowfall which had started a half hour earlier was heavier now.

"The weather looks like it's getting worse, Alex," Kat said. "Let's call it a day and have lunch at a great Chinese restaurant I know on the way back home."

As they trekked off to the resort parking lot, Kat decided the time had come to broach the subject of Huna with Alex. *If I lose him now,* Kat thought, *I never really had him anyway.*

At the restaurant, Kat waited until after they had ordered and Alex had excused himself to go to the rest room to rehearse her explanation. Engrossed in thought, she fiddled with wooden chopsticks absentmindedly, then decided for some quirky reason to try to send enough energy into the chopsticks to float them across the table in reminiscence of Liana's great-grandfather. It was a test of

287

her Huna powers, but the timing couldn't have been worse. Alex returned to the table just as the two floating chopsticks settled silently onto his napkin. The look on his face told her she had just blown it and was in for an uphill battle.

"What in the hell is going on here, Kat? Did I just see these chopsticks drop by themselves on my side of the table, or was I seeing things?"

"I floated them over to your napkin," Kat admitted reluctantly.

"First you talk to trees and now you're floating objects through the air. This is beginning to really freak me out, Kat."

As their food arrived, she decided to go for broke. She told him everything, including the Halloween night visit of her enemy, Leilani's murder, and the role she was being asked to take on as the Huna Warrior. Alex listened attentively, but the look on his face changed from objectivity to suspicion and then to worry and dismay.

"Look, Kat," Alex said after nearly a minute of silence when she had finished talking. "When I first met you, I thought we had a lot in common, especially since both of us were in the field of education. It was great going to your reunion and faculty party, and I've enjoyed being with you. You're funny and bright and beautiful." He took a swig of beer before continuing.

"But I don't pretend to understand this Huna malarkey. Frankly, it sounds a bit crazy. It's too bizarre. I mean, can't you just tell them no? Maybe they can get somebody else to be the Huna Warrior." Alex pushed himself back from the table and stared at Kat.

288

"You know what, Alex?" Kat answered slowly, "I've been thinking the very same thing. I know I'm in for trouble, and I have no idea of knowing exactly what I'm going to have to face. I'm already in danger. My friends and family are in danger. But it's something I just have to do. I wanted you to know before you and I ratcheted this relationship up a notch. You need to decide if it's even worth the risk." Kat watched Alex's face as he struggled with his emotions.

"Kat, I don't know quite how to say this," Alex said, draining his beer mug. "I know it was difficult for you to open up and share with me. I appreciate knowing what makes you tick. But it sounds like a voodoo cocktail. When you add in the twist of real danger, it's a drink I just can't swallow. Besides, you know my personal history—all of the loss. It's been so hard on me. I knew when I first met you the two of us could develop into a couple. My heart told me this, and I always listen to my heart. I really want you in my life, Kat. But it sounds like this Huna Warrior moniker means you're a magnet for danger. I don't want to lose you. I'm not sure I can go through that again." Alex looked down at his half-eaten lunch and slowly pushed the plate away.

"I'm sorry. So very sorry. I don't want to hurt you. You've already been through too much." Kat gently pressed his hand until he returned her gaze. "Can we still be friends, Alex? I don't know what's in store for me. God obviously wants more from me than most people. And all I've ever wanted is to be 'most people.' I don't want to be eccentric...and I'm tired of being alone. I need you to stay

289

in my life, as a friend, until I can resume a normal life or until you can risk becoming closer to me."

She looked wistfully up at Alex's handsome face and smiled. Alex smiled back. "Oh, Kat. If only…" he gently placed his hand over Kat's. "Okay, no conditions. Friends it is. And you promise, if the coast is ever clear…I'll be the first to know?"

"I promise."

Later that night, long after Kat and Alex had returned home, Kat thought about the tree and how talking to it was so natural. She knew it must be part of her Huna training. Surrendering to her destiny, she was finally ready. She prayed aloud.

"Thank you, up there, all of you *Aumakua* who are aiding me while I sleep. I'd never have guessed talking to trees would be part of the training for the Huna warrior, but I suppose it'll come in handy someday, right? Even though I'm still not convinced I'm any kind of warrior, let alone the Huna Warrior. Anyway, it's confirmation you're with me at night, like Liana said, infusing me with knowledge of the secret ways. Thank you, each one of you who are helping me on The Other Side. I am eternally grateful.

"Thanks, too, for giving me the courage to talk to Alex," she continued. "This Huna Warrior lifestyle is complicated enough for me right now without involving and endangering someone as sweet and wonderful as Alex. It's more than either one of us could handle.

"Lastly, I humbly ask you to give me the strength and courage to face this enemy…this evil I don't understand. I feel his menacing presence bearing down on me. Help me, please. Help me prevail."

Chapter 36

The next day, Kat scanned her email on her home computer and noticed one from Chelsea, flagged red. Excitement crept up her spine in shivering tingles as she clicked to open the message. Chelsea had gotten a copy of the *Honolulu Advertiser* from November 3, 1933, which had been stored in microfiche at the Hawaii State Library. In its birth announcements, there was an entry which stated that a set of twins, Akani and Liana, had been born to Hui and Mary Maniuki at the Kapiolani Medical Center on November 1, 1933 at 3:19 a.m.

Chelsea added a footnote to her message in bold print: ***Could your father have been Akani? Have Henry check his birth certificate for the exact time and place of birth.***

Kat hit Henry's number on her phone's speed dial and quickly read Chelsea's e-mail to him.

"Call me when you find your birth certificate, Dad. Oh, isn't this exciting? You might be Liana's twin! That would make her my aunt! Wouldn't it be something? Maybe the Romero's adopted you and never told you about it."

"You know, I've never told you this before," Henry admitted, "but I never felt I really fit in with the Romero family. I never thought too much about it, though. I thought it was just me. It was just the way things were. But if I were adopted, why wouldn't my parents have told me?"

"Good question. Maybe someone in the Romero family knows the truth. Try Maddy first. She could convince a Carmelite nun to break her vow of silence. If anybody knows anything, Maddy will pry it out of them," Kat said, remembering her godmother's unrelenting knack of persuasion. "I'll have Liana contact her relatives in Hawaii, too. She might find out the real lowdown from them as well, right?"

"Right as rain. I'll call around, and let you know what I find out. Keep me in touch. I love you, Katherine."

"I love you, too, Dad."

She hung up.

"I can't wait to tell Kalani and Liana about this. They've got so much power, they're bound to figure it out."

Kat had gotten halfway through the lobby of the administration building on Monday morning when Denise intercepted her and pulled her into the vault.

"Oh, boy, this is going to be good," Kat laughed, sitting on her usual stack of boxes. Denise's worried face, though, punctured her elation.

"No, actually, it's not, Kat. Gabe's going through a nervous breakdown of sorts. He's blaming you for a lot of his troubles."

"Me? Why?" Kat felt like a wrecking ball had just been swung into her stomach.

"Over the break, Rudy went joy riding in Gabe's Jag with three of his buddies. He got in a big accident, and the car was totaled. Two kids are still in the hospital. Gabe

293

had to turn Rudy in to Juvenile Hall. He cancelled the adoption plans. Otherwise, he'd have to personally answer the lawsuit from the parents of the injured kids. My guess? It could have cost him two million bucks."

Kat let out a whistle of surprise. "Okay, so how am I to blame for Rudy stealing the car? It's not like I hypnotized him or forced him into it."

"Well, he thinks you hurt Rudy's self-esteem by getting him expelled from here in the first place. He resents the fact that you had Rudy pegged from the get-go."

"So I'm to blame because I couldn't get him to open his eyes?"

"That's only part of it," Denise rattled on. "The superintendent's asked him to resign or be fired, and Gabe thinks you're behind it all."

"What? How?" Kat pounded her fist into the box she was sitting on, angry with the direction this conversation was taking.

"Remember the faculty Christmas party? The tour of Gabe's house? You were looking at a family photo in the hallway and recognized Wes Holden? Angela explained Wes was going to marry her sister on New Year's Eve, right? Turns out the minute they got married, Gabe was in violation of a 1090 Government Code which says you can't direct a contract to a relative. By marrying the owner of the pool company, Gina became a part owner of the company which got the contract to install the pool here. So now the school board claims Gabe directed the pool contract to a relative, and he's guilty of a felony."

"But that doesn't make sense. The contract was enacted when Wes was no relation to Gabe. And Gabe never benefited from the deal, did he? I seriously doubt he got any kickbacks from Wes—he makes a lot as a high school principal. I mean, he's whacky when it comes to rescuing wayward boys, but I've never gotten the impression he was greedy to the point of doing anything illegal."

"Right. He's too ambitious. He wants to be a superintendent. He's not about to do anything risky. If he did break the law, he didn't do it intentionally."

"I'm not so sure they're right about that government code. I'll have a friend who knows contract law check it out." Kat sighed, letting out a long breath.

"You know who else is pissed? Wes Holden. The district is refusing to pay for the work he did on the pool. He's out thousands of dollars. They claim they don't have to pay him because, with a 1090 violation, the contract becomes null and void."

Denise nervously spun one of her rings around her finger. "Anyway, Gabe thinks you're the one who spilled the beans to the superintendent about the 1090 violation. And he's writing up a bad evaluation to put in your file."

"What? He can't do that!" Kat protested. "It's illegal to downgrade me in an evaluation for something that's not related to my job description. Besides, until today, I've never even heard of a Government Code 1090. And I've never ratted on Gabe to anyone. All I've ever tried to do was warn him about Rudy."

"The 1090 thing is probably just an excuse to get rid of him, Kat. Let's face it. Rudy's accident? It's all over the papers in Davis. Guess where Dr. Purcell lives? Davis. He sees Gabe's parental relationship with Rudy as an embarrassment to the district."

"The question is," Kat said, swallowing her fear, "who told Purcell the way to get Gabe was through a 1090? That's his real enemy."

"Hmm. Everybody at the DO is thick as thieves, right? So who can get the skinny? The dirt? The low down?" Denise asked mischievously.

She and Kat chanted together, "Andrea Chan."

"I'll call her right now," Kat said, scrambling to get up off the crates. "And Denise? Thanks for the heads up. It means a lot to me not to be ambushed by Gabe, you know? I like staying one jump ahead of him."

"Any time, Kat." Denise smiled assuredly as she locked the vault door. "Happy to help."

Kat hurried to her office to call Andrea for the inside scoop on Gabe's forced resignation. When Andrea answered on the first ring, Kat related all she'd heard from Denise.

"As you know, my office is next to Felicia's secretary, Jill," Andrea said, her words spoken in quiet tones. "She and I are good buddies. She says Felicia's got the hots for Serge. Serge has the hots for Gabe's position, and Felicia found a way to get rid of Gabe. You know Felicia. She'd screw a snake if someone held it down for her, so she got her husband, that Caspar Milquetoast who's an attorney, to see if they could charge Gabe with something. At first they were going to try to smear him with accusations of being a pedophile. His history of helping boys is legendary, and Felicia thought she could

296

make more of it than is actually there. But when she found out Gabe's sister had married Wes Holden, she forgot about the false pedophile charges and nailed him on the Government Code 1090 violation."

"Andrea, you're a lifesaver," Kat said. "Let me know if you find out anything else. They think I was the one who tipped off the superintendent."

"That's Felicia's style, Kat. She always covers up her dirty work by framing an innocent person. It's probably one of her sleazy personalities. You know everyone calls her Eve."

"Eve?"

"Yeah, as in Three Faces of," Andrea cackled. "You never know from day to day which personality will surface with Felicia. Anyway, I'll keep you posted, Kat. Hang in there."

Kat went into the administration meeting wearing the biggest energy shield she could muster. Just as Denise had revealed earlier, Gabe was in the foulest of moods. The veins in his neck looked like thick, blue cords throbbing from his ears to his Adam's apple. Kat threw pink light over the entire room and mentally uttered the words, "Calm down."

I feel sorry for Gabe, she thought. *He's a victim of school politics. Any one of us could be next. Father/Mother God, please help Gabe get through this trying time.*

As Kat sent waves of healing energy to encircle Gabe, she noticed his body softening and his tension dissipating.

Gabe began the meeting by telling Serge and Kat about the letter of resignation he'd be tendering effective at the end of the semester.

"I want to spend more time with my family," he said unconvincingly.

Serge and Kat sat passively as Gabe rattled on, oblivious to his colleagues' skepticism.

"I've given it some thought, and I've decided not to adopt Rudy after all. He wasn't adjusting to our normal family life and will probably be better off in a group home of some sort where he can get the daily guidance he needs."

Gabe avoided eye contact with Kat when he said this, knowing he was parroting her own advice to him.

"In the meantime, I'm going to work on putting my own family back together. Rudy's presence has been a bit divisive, and we need to regroup around each other again."

"Who's going to take your place here in the interim?" Serge asked.

"You are," Gabe replied curtly. "Felicia Davenport will be calling you to set up a meeting with the two of us so you start as interim principal next semester."

"That's only three weeks away," Kat said, thumbing through her Franklin planner. "We'll have to double up on game supervision, unless the athletic director can step up to the plate and cover some of them."

"I'll ask him, but you know he'll want to be paid for extra duty work" said Serge.

"No doubt," replied Gabe, picking at a loose thread on his jacket. "These teachers won't help us out of the generosity of their hearts."

When the meeting was over, Kat walked back to her office, glad Gabe hadn't asked her to stay so he could chew her out again. She didn't know if the light she sent him would heal his heart or change his mind. She had to be prepared he just might still spring that awful evaluation on her. If he did, she could be demoted back to the classroom with her salary cut in half. She could lose her house. She decided to pray.

"Help me, dear *Aumakua*. Help me surmount this." Liana's face suddenly loomed in Kat's mind. "Yes. Thank you. I'll talk to Liana about this."

Chapter 37

Once most of the students had left campus after school, Kat drove Kalani home.

As was their habit by now, Kat, Kalani and Liana gathered around the kitchen table, where Kat quickly ran down the latest news about Gabe and Rudy.

"I don't know if there's anything I can do about Gabe sending in a poor evaluation of me. But if I have to go back into the classroom, I won't make enough money to keep my house." Kat's face was etched with worry.

"I don't see that happening, Ms. R." Kalani said quietly.

Liana agreed. "My sense about Gabe is that the foundation he's built his life around is crumbling, and he's grasping at straws to try to make sense of it." She held out a plate of ginger snaps to Kat.

Kat took a cookie and nervously nibbled on it. "Something occurred to me when I was talking to Denise about all this, though," she said. "I remember saying something like, 'I didn't hypnotize Rudy and make him go joyriding.' Now I'm wondering if this could have been my low self telling me about your father, Kalani. Could Hukui have hypnotized your mother into killing herself? Could he have worked on her subconscious mind from afar? Maybe he came to visit her weeks before, left the knife hidden on the hospital grounds somewhere and then planted in her mind the suggestion to do herself in, weeks after he'd gone."

"I've thought of that, Kat. And yes, there are those capable of influencing others from a remote location. Like you, I believe Hukui caused Leilani's death. There's something else you need to know. Something I haven't told you," Liana said, hesitation in her voice.

"For a while now, I've been getting telepathic messages from an old friend in Maui who's been in grave danger. He thinks I can save him."

"Who is he?"

"Kahili Kingston, Hukui's father."

"He's also a powerful kahuna, Ms. R.," Kalani said.

"Well, if he's a kahuna, can't he protect himself from danger?"

"Apparently not, Kat. I need to help him."

"But Liana, why would you put yourself out like that? You could get hurt. Besides, where are you going to find the money for a trip to Hawaii when you can't even afford a phone?"

"I can afford a phone. What I can't afford is Hukui tracking us down through a phone number. He's tried to take Kalani back to Hawaii with him before. Besides, all I need is a plane ticket. Once I get there, I can stay with my cousins in Maui."

"Which reminds me," Kat said. "Chelsea found your birth announcement in the *Honolulu Advertiser*. It said twins, Akani and Liana, were born to Hui and Mary Maniuki. Those were your parents, right?"

Liana nodded, blinking away the sudden tears which filled her eyes.

"Do you have your birth certificate here? I need to check it against the newspaper account."

While Liana went to get her birth certificate, Kalani smiled shyly at Kat. "Ms. R., when grandma goes to Hawaii, could I stay with you?"

"Absolutely. For all I know, you're my second cousin, kiddo. I'm partial to relatives," Kat replied, playfully slapping at Kalani's shoulder. "When is she planning to go?"

"Next week sometime."

"Here it is," Liana said, hustling back to the table. She handed her birth certificate to Kat. It was identical to the newspaper account except in one category.

"I don't get it, Liana. This says you were a single birth. Why, then, did the newspaper say twins?"

"I have no idea," Liana said, shaking her head. "But I'll hound my relatives when I get back home. Someone's bound to know something." She crossed her fingers and smiled with excitement.

"Speaking of knowing something, I'll phone Chelsea. She's a whiz kid on the Internet and could probably find you the cheapest fare to Maui. We need to solve this 'twin' mystery, Liana, because it's driving me nuts."

A week flew by and Liana arrived safely at the airport in Kahului, while back in Folsom, Kat was in her guest bedroom, helping Kalani unpack her clothes. Kalani didn't have a huge wardrobe to put away, but Caesar wasn't helping matters jumping into the suitcase, kneading the clothes, and purring while rubbing against

302

Kalani. She caught him in her arms and gave him a kiss on the top of his head.

"All right, Caesar. I'm glad to see you again, too," Kalani cooed. "But please don't shred my clothes, okay? I need them for school."

Kalani put him down, and he sauntered to a corner to relax and lick his paws. Kat was astonished at this sudden transformation. Caesar actually obeyed a request of a relatively new person in his world. Not only did he respect her, but he understood her every word.

"Kalani, why didn't you tell me you could talk to animals?" Kat blurted.

"I don't know. I guess it never came up." Kalani locked the empty suitcase and stashed it in the clothes closet.

"Have you always been able to do it?"

"Ever since I was five. Grandma taught me."

"Did I tell you I can talk to trees now? I know the *po'e Aumakua* are steadily working on me, but it's always a surprise when I'm able to do something I've never done before. It feels natural."

"I know exactly what you mean, Ms. R. It feels like home."

"Which reminds me, Kalani. I want you to feel at home here. I have a spare key in case you need it when I'm away supervising a game at school or something. Come on. I'll show you the alarm system."

"You mean Caesar isn't the only alarm system you have?" Kalani teased. "He told me all about his duties as guardian of the house."

"Oh, he did, did he?" Kat said, pretending to glare at Caesar. "I always call him 'attack cat,' but so far the only things he's attacked are the birds outside."

"Yeah, I know. He says he's sorry for the mess, but so proud of himself he just had to show you."

"He's a braggart—just like his namesake. I hope that's the only time he takes after Julius Caesar. Did you know the real one once cut off the hands of four thousand Gauls?"

Kalani grimaced in disgust. "Anyway, he likes when you send mind pictures to him, and he told me to tell you...."

Most biology experiments at Anthony High didn't get as thoroughly dissected as Caesar did by Kat and Kalani for the rest of the night.

Chapter 38

A week and a half flew by. Saturday morning, a tulle fog day in the Sacramento valley, found Kat and Kalani ensconced in the living room while a fire crackled in the fireplace. Steaming mugs of hot chocolate on hand while they were selecting a CD to listen to when the phone rang.

It was Liana, just in from Maui and needing to be picked up from the Sacramento airport. She had called Kat the night before to say she was on standby and wasn't sure which flight she'd make, but would call as soon as she got in.

Kat and Kalani raced around the house to close it up and headed for the airport, excited to have Liana safely back home and eager to hear all about her trip. Liana wanted to wait until she was settled back in the apartment to tell them about her adventures, and Kat's feet danced underneath the kitchen table as she waited impatiently for Liana to brew some tea.

"Where should I begin? There's so much to tell you," Liana said, an enigmatic smile on her lips. "First of all, Kat, you need to know Henry is truly the lost Akani, dear. You are my niece after all."

"Yes!" Kat shouted, pumping her fist in the air. She flew into Liana's waiting arms and hugged her tight. "I knew it!" she screamed. "How'd you find out?"

"Illegally, I'm afraid. My cousin, Luly, has a grandson who works at the Bureau of Vital Statistics in Honolulu. He got into some confidential adoption files. It seems your father Henry was given away to the Romero family to settle some gambling debts my father had."

"He must have owed a fairly hefty amount if he was forced to hand over his son. What little I know about the Hawaiian culture, I do know they revere their children. It must have been pretty traumatic for your parents to give one of their children away."

"It was, Kat. When my father was a teenager, he got in with a group of kids who liked to play a game called fan-tan. It works like this. One person grabs a handful of bean-like pebbles which are counted out in groups of four. Everyone places a bet on whether the remainders are going to one, two, three or four, with the dealer betting on four. For a budding kahuna like my father, it was a way to test his psychic abilities—which turned out to be very under-developed when used for gambling. By the time my mother was getting ready to deliver us, the debt was huge, and there were a lot of threats being made on both his life and my mother's unless he paid up. When they began terrorizing his family with home invasions, he was at the end of his rope. He knew a go-between who found the Romero's. Money was exchanged, the debt was paid, and birth certificates were altered to account for the adoption. Henry's new parents left for California, and I grew up without a brother."

"Oh, Dad is going to be so happy to know for sure he has a sister, Liana. He told me how he felt he's known you forever, and how he never felt he quite fit in with the Romero family." Kat beamed at her aunt.

"Hey, Ms. R., that means we're for real cousins," Kalani shouted, holding her arms out to hug Kat.

"That also means from now on, you can call me Kat, except at school, of course." Kat winked at Kalani. "So, *Aunt* Liana, did you ever find your friend who needed help?"

"I did, and I'm ashamed to say it was all a ruse to get me there to save him from you, Kat."

"Me? Why?" Kat put her teacup down and stared at Liana. The hair on the back of her neck stiffened with fear.

"I'll get to that, but first let me tell you about Kalani's grandfather, Kahili Kingston. Pour yourself more tea, my dear, it's a long story."

"When I was sixteen years old," Liana began, "my family moved from Honolulu to the fishing village of Lahaina on the island of Maui. At my new high school, I met two boys who immediately began to vie for my attention. Kahili Kingston, a handsome athlete, champion diver, exuding charm and confidence, and Keoni Kealoha, a good-looking, but shy, bookworm with a great sense of humor. Both boys poured on their charms to compete against each other for my attention. Their struggle was obvious to everyone but me, and I flirted openly with both of them.

"I was his only daughter, so my father, Hui, kept a watchful eye on me. When it was time for me to marry, he sought out a *kahuna aloha* to decide which boy would make the better mate for me. Everyone breathed a huge sigh of

307

relief when my engagement to Keoni was announced. We planned to wed after my high school graduation.

"It seemed everyone in Lahaina, but me, had become aware of the escalating hostility between the two boys over my hand. Kahili was known for his swagger and revengeful ways, but Keoni was not intimidated by him and stood his ground. It would have been only a matter of time before the two of them would have had a serious physical fight.

"Kahili was devastated at having lost me to what he considered a greatly inferior rival. He married the first girl who looked his way and moved down the coast to Kihei to get away from any reminder of his heart's greatest disappointment.

"A few months after we were married, Keoni joined the Air Force, and we eventually moved to Sacramento where he was stationed at McClellan Air Force Base. He worked in the telecommunications building on the base while I found a job working with a local catering company. Our first child was stillborn, and I still grieve over his loss. But then my Leilani was born and filled my heart with soaring joy and laughter. These happy years helped get me through the tough times when Keoni died in a car accident five years later.

"When he died, I sank into a deep depression. Although I received thousands of dollars in the accident settlement, I felt terribly lonely and isolated. I wrote letters to my parents pleading with them to come to California to stay with me and Leilani, at least until I could get back on my feet emotionally.

"Eventually my tear-stained letters persuaded my parents to come to Sacramento and stay for good. My father bought a two-bedroom house in Del Paso Heights where the four of us lived. Leilani and I shared a bedroom with twin beds."

Liana stopped her story at this point to assess its impact on her listeners, but they seemed entranced, so she continued.

"After Leilani graduated from high school, Hui and Mary took me and Leilani back to Maui for a reunion of the Maniuki family. Kahili Kingston had heard through the grapevine about the plans for our family get-together and showed up at the festivities at Kaanapali Beach with his youngest son, Hukui.

"Kahili's wife had died of cancer a few years before, and he was happy to see me, happier still to know my husband was dead. He begged me to stay with him at his house in Kihei, but I was repulsed by him. I saw flashes of red in his aura and sensed danger all around him. When I flatly refused to have anything to do with him, Kahili encouraged his son, Hukui, to make a play for Leilani. He was determined to stay connected to me any way he could.

"When the family reunion was over, and it was time to return to Sacramento, Leilani begged me to let her stay longer with my cousin, Luly. Weeks turned into months which turned into years. Leilani went to the University of Hawaii to study the hospitality industry and worked part-time at the Grand Wailea Hotel. Two weeks after graduation, she married Hukui at a small chapel on the grounds of the hotel.

"Naturally, my parents and I attended Leilani's wedding, and, although we kept our opinions to ourselves, each of us could foresee trouble ahead for her. Every time I was near Hukui or Kahili my skin crawled. Out of the corner of my eye, I could tell Kahili was watching my every move. I was polite as I could be, but made a point never to be alone with him during my entire stay. I turned down all of his invitations and refused to take his calls.

"My cousin Luly told me Kahili agonized about being rebuffed by me again. He told her he had dreamed about me for years, plotting and planning how to hold me in his arms and win my love—all for nothing. I was lost to him again.

"A year after Kalani was born, Leilani returned to Sacramento to live with me while her divorce from Hukui was pending. It seems that Hukui had changed a lot after they were married. He'd become possessive of Leilani, suspicious of every man who looked at her. When she'd return from shopping or work, he'd interrogate her like she'd just committed a crime. Who was she talking to? Why wasn't she home on time? Why hadn't she asked his permission before going to her friend's birthday party? Why did that guy look at her like that? Was she flirting with him?

"Questions soon led to arguments, which escalated into shoving matches, Leilani not giving an inch, but always getting the worst of it. Finally, she ran away to Luly's and filed for divorce, threatening to turn in the photos she'd taken of her bruises to the police if Hukui dared to contest the divorce. He didn't."

310

"Wait a sec. Let's go back to Kahili for a minute," Kat said, breaking into Liana's narration with burning curiosity. "If you've never liked Kahili, why would you go back to Maui to save him? Why didn't you just let him succumb to his own vices?"

"Because I wanted to confront him about Keoni, Kat. You see, before he died, my father had finally gained considerable skill in divination. He was shown that Kahili had caused my husband's car accident. I wanted to hear directly from Kahili how and why he did it, although I'm sure we can all guess why."

"Kahili's a *kahuna ho'opi'opi'po*, isn't he, Grandma?" Kalani whispered as Kat raised her eyebrows.

"Yes, he's an expert in causing sickness or distress. He sent the poisonous shell to you, Kat, and he visited your son at night, although Sean thought he was dreaming. He also went to your mother's hospital and frightened her so much, she fell out of bed trying to get away from him."

"He was at my house on Halloween, wasn't he?" Kat shuddered.

"In a way, yes, he was, Kat. You see, he's more than a mere *kahuna ho'opi'opi'po*. He's able to apport objects, dissolve them in one location and materialize them in another. He can also command spirits to do his bidding. The eyes in your hallway were those of someone who had passed away and were sent by him as a way of frightening you away. So was the spirit that showed up at Halloween."

"How did you find him?"

311

"My cousin, Luly, is a master dowser, so she used her pendulum over a map to find the general location, and then once outside she used divining rods to locate Kahili. He was chained to a wall in an abandoned temple, nearly starved to death and drawing whatever mana he could from the temple's sacred stones and from the air. I had envisioned him in chains, so I had Luly come with me and bring her bolt cutters. We took him back to her house to recover from his ordeal."

"Who chained him and why?" Kat looked around for something to nibble on. Kalani intuitively got up to get some crackers for her.

"Hukui. Who has it in his head that he wants to be the greatest living kahuna and has been forcing his father to teach him everything he knows." Liana shook her head, disgusted at the memory of pitiful Kahili, wallowing in filth, ribs protruding in his wrinkled torso.

She looked at Kat with concern. "It's Hukui who's after you, Kat. You're the Huna Warrior, and he's determined to kill you before you kill him and the other renegades. In fact, he tortured Kahili to reveal the names of some of the kahuna living in Hawaii, and he's working his way down the list. Luly's grandson researched the obituaries of everyone in the islands who passed away within the past two years. Three names jumped off the page at me. They were all friends of mine or my family. All kahuna. He's wiping us all out, one by one."

"I think I know how Mom died, Grandma," Kalani burst out suddenly. "Kahili taught my father how to send a message to her low self that she was weak and worthless and was better off dead. Or maybe he threatened to kill me

312

or you, unless she did what he said. Kahili must have taught him to apport a knife into my mother's room and then sent a message to her low self to slit her wrists. That's how it happened, isn't it, Grandma?"

"That's exactly what Kahili confessed to me once I forgave him for causing Keoni's accident."

"Tell me more about this accident, Liana," Kat urged, moving her finger in a circle like she was winding up invisible thread.

Liana nodded, sighed, and resumed her story. "One day, just for fun, Kahili decided to apport some bees into Keoni's car. At the time, apporting was new to him, just a game. He still had it in for my husband for being the one chosen over him, so when he decided to experiment with apporting living insects, he immediately sent them to Keoni, not knowing my husband was deathly allergic to bee stings. At any rate, the bees materialized in his car while he was driving on the freeway without his bee kit which was at home. He was stung over twenty times and lost control of the car, partly because he was swatting bees and partly because he couldn't breathe. He crashed into the divider and died in the hospital the following day."

"You're a more spiritually evolved person than I am, Liana, because I don't know if I could ever forgive such an atrocity," Kat said.

"Right now, Kahili is the key to all of us staying alive, Kat. He's our only hope because only he knows what Hukui is capable of and how best to defend ourselves. He truly doesn't want to be on the losing side. He doesn't want to kill anyone and, most of all, he doesn't want to cross you, the Huna Warrior."

313

"We need a plan," Kat insisted, hitting the table with the palm of her hand.

"We need to warn the others," Kalani interjected, biting her lip anxiously. "We need to find them before my father does."

Liana put her hand out to stop them. "You're both right, my dears, we need to do all of the above. But, for now, Kahili will stay in hiding at Luly's, and they'll work on finding out the names of the kahuna still living on the islands. This summer I'm hoping all of us can meet in Maui so, together, we can come up with a plan to stop Hukui, short of doing the death prayer on him."

"Hold it, Liana. The question is, does Kahili know the death prayer, and if he does, did he teach it to Hukui who could, in turn, use it on us?"

"Kahili knows the death prayer. That's how his wife died."

"He killed his own wife? Why, he is evil incarnate!" Kat was outraged that Liana would want to help a cold-blooded murderer like Kahili.

"Kat, you mustn't judge Kahili. His wife was in the hospital with pancreatic cancer. She was in terrible pain and had less than a few weeks to live anyway, and he wanted to spare her any more agony. So he chanted the 'ana 'ana and within three days, she was gone."

"The question is, did he teach it to Hukui?" Kat asked, concern showing in her furrowed brow.

"He's never taught anything to Hukui. You see, Kahili married Hukui's mother when she was already pregnant with him. So Hukui is not really his child, and he's always kept his distance from him. But Hukui's

314

bedroom was a thin wall away from the home shrine where Kahili prayed the 'ana 'ana. Kahili says Hukui may have heard him. But he never intentionally taught it to him, so even if he heard the words, he probably doesn't know what images to send and how to send them. You see, this particular ritual also involves having a dead person's unihipili at your disposal, an unihipili which has been separated from its middle self. Now, when Kahili was visiting his wife in the hospital, he knew her roommate was near death, so he coaxed this woman's unihipili out and directed it to take the life force out of his wife's body. So even if Hukui knows the words to the death chant, in order for it to work, he has to kill someone and force the unihipili of the dead person to do the killing for him. That's how the 'ana 'ana chant works."

A shiver ran down Kat's spine. "I hate to tell you this, but something tells me he already has."

Chapter 39

From his upper bunk in the dormitory, Rudy Baker looked out the barred windows of the DeWitt Center, the juvenile detention facility for Placer County, trying to figure out the best way to escape his hellhole. After his joy riding escapade and accident with Gabe's Jaguar, he had been sent back to juvenile hall where his case was re-evaluated. Given his repeat, escalating offenses, the probation department recommended an even tougher environment.

"DeWitt Center," the judge had decreed, "will provide an opportunity for personal growth, social development, accountability and responsibility for your behavior in the community."

What a bunch of crap, Rudy thought angrily. *How can you personally grow with over three hundred other guys who've done worse things than I did? Maybe learn to steal better or learn what to say to social workers to get them off your back. All I want to do is get out of here and get that bitch who turned Gabe and Angela against me.*

The bell rang to signal the start of Rudy's first class of the day—a county landscaping program where the students learn to maintain the grounds around the facility which was located in a remote rural area in the county. Rudy hoped he'd be picked to join the work crew that pulled the weeds just outside the gates that enclosed the facility. During his last phone call to Jasmine, she promised him she would bury a set of clothes for him in a

316

roadside ditch underneath the Ford dealership's billboard sign on Highway 49. If he could find a way to make a run for it to that sign and change his clothes, his luck might continue long enough to hitchhike into Folsom. Once he took care of business with that bitch vice-principal, he'd hightail it to Oregon to Gabe's vacation cabin.

He had made copies of all of Gabe's personal keys, car, house and cabin, as well as the master key to all the doors of Susan B. Anthony High School. He had friends who could duplicate the key to the President of the United State's personal john if they wanted to. He had to get back to Anthony High and dig up those keys. And the gun.

"Yeah, I'll get Kat Romero back if it's the last thing I do," Rudy vowed. "She's the real reason I'm here and not at Anthony High with Jasmine. She's the reason I'm here and not living at Gabe's. She made a special point of singling me out for punishment, so now it's payback time. And payback's a bitch. A dead bitch."

Rudy laughed until the voice inside his head began to laugh as well.

"Damn!" he yelled, rubbing at his ears. He thought he heard the voice again. Lately he thought he was going crazy. *Only crazy people heard voices in their heads, right? I wish it would just shut up. It shows up any time it wants to, like last night when I was in the middle of a great dream about me and Jasmine.* Kill Kat Romero, *it said. Don't worry, I'd like nothing more than to kill her. If I can only get out of this rat hole.*

Rudy stomped in frustration around his cell and caught his reflection in the steel post of his cot. An angry, brown-skinned man appeared to be standing in back of him. The hair on the back of his neck stood up.

"What the hell?" he mumbled.

He spun around to confront the stranger behind him, but there was no one there! He looked back at the post, but there was only his own face staring back at him.

Within minutes, Rudy's head began to throb as the voice in his head resumed its mantra: *If you want to get rid of me, you'll do what I say. Kill Kat Romero! Kill her now!*

Rudy staggered back to his bed and flopped onto the mattress, his ears plugged with his fingers.

"Okay, I will. Just shut up and help me get out of here!" he screamed.

Chapter 40

On the last day of the fall semester, at twelve fifteen, like a dam bursting, the students at Anthony High School bolted out of their classrooms and for once ran happily off campus without any prompting from Kat or the other administrators.

She ordered an extra large pepperoni pizza to be delivered to her office, so she, Mazie and Kalani could celebrate the occasion in their own small way. Most of the teaching staff were gone by one o'clock, but Kat planned to stay late to input last minute changes in student schedules and adjust the master schedule of classes for Monday, the first day of the spring semester.

At sunset the heavy Friday night traffic slowly threaded its way on the interstate highway which bordered the high school. The surface streets were equally as clogged as Kalani rode the city bus for home. She'd been helping the librarian check in returned books to earn a little spending money and was worried about the late hour she was getting home. Her backpack, only half-full of its usual contents, still weighed heavily on her weary shoulders. Now at her stop, she stepped off the bus, hitched the backpack into place and began the two-block walk to the apartment complex.

"Hello, Kalani," the Hawaiian said, stepping out of the shadows of a store awning. "Did you think you could hide from me forever?"

Kalani stood frozen in her tracks, her eyes wide with fear. "Dad! What are you doing here? I haven't seen you in five years!"

She could see the prevalent wisps of red in his aura and knew this visit was not friendly. She put up a mirror shield around her body and mentally called upon Leilani and the others for help.

"I heard about your mother passing away, and I thought you'd want to see me." Hukui stared at Kalani with a deadly calm.

Kalani could feel her heart pounding in her chest, but she was determined not to give herself away. She spoke in a hardened voice, her chin jutting out in defiance.

"You thought wrong, then. Why would I want to see you? You may not have done the *'ana 'ana* on her, but you killed my mother just the same. How did you find me, anyway? It couldn't have been the phone book because we've deliberately avoided having a phone knowing it was one more way for you to ferret us out."

Kalani threw her backpack down like she was throwing down the gauntlet, freeing her body to block any sudden moves her father was known for. She glared at him, keeping her face steely and unemotional, but silently screaming again for help from the *po'e Aumakua*.

"I have a friend at the airport who traced your grandmother's recent itinerary to Maui from here. A few phone calls to all the high schools in Folsom, and it was easy to find you, especially when the gullible students who answer the phone become quite chatty." Hukui grinned malevolently, mentally directing Kalani to yield to his superior guile and intellect.

320

Kalani raised her chin higher and gazed acidly at Hukui. "Okay, you've found me. Now what? Are you going to kill me like you did my mother?"

"Kalani, there are reasons for everything. Your mother was pregnant at the time she died. You didn't know, did you? She would have given birth to another kahuna, and that just couldn't happen, now could it? Not when I'm about to become the most powerful kahuna in the world."

Kalani drew a sharp breath, like she'd been slugged in the stomach. Hukui put his hands on her shoulders, but she looked down at his chest, refusing to maintain eye contact which she suddenly realized had been draining her energy.

Help me, Mom. Help me!

"I want you to come home with me, Kalani. I don't want you to be on my enemy list. I want my daughter back. Come home with me, Kalani. Please." Hukui tried to put his arms around the girl's shoulders, but she pushed him away and stepped away from him.

"There was once a time when I would have given anything to hear those words from you, Dad. I always dreamed about you coming back into my life because I missed you so much growing up. But when you threatened my mother all those years ago, we knew we had to hide from you if we wanted to live." Kalani shook her head and smiled tightly.

"You can't fool me, Dad. You claim you want me, Kalani Kingston, to be your loving daughter once again, but I know it's me, Kalani Kingston, in line to be one of the most powerful kahuna in the world, that you want to

321

control. You want to conquer all your competition, don't you, Dad? You think by scaring us away or killing us all off, you'll be number one, and that's all you want. It's always been all about you and your destiny. Well, guess what? I won't let you have it your way!"

Kalani listened to the words echoing inside her head and struggled to maintain her cool demeanor, all the while planning her getaway.

Suddenly, she heard her mother's voice, and it was strong.

Now, Kalani, now! Let your light shine!

A strong golden light suddenly shot out from every pore in Kalani's body. She could feel a burst of mana race through her like wildfire, sending out a light so bright, it was like a spotlight had been turned on from within, and Kalani had become a beacon shining in the darkness.

Hukui threw his arms up to shield his eyes from the burning light and groped forward, feeling blindly for Kalani who lithely jumped out of his grasp.

Kalani focused her breathing so she could generate more mana to create more light. She faced Hukui and took a few steps toward him. Hukui squinted, his arms crossed in front of his face.

"Kalani, stop it!" he yelled, walking backwards to escape the light's intensity. "I'm your father. I'm all you have left!"

"Oh, no, you're not!" Kalani screamed. "Show him, Mom!"

Instantly another light above Kalani's head shone forth. Her mother's voice boomed from the center of this light force. "Back off, Hukui. Leave her alone!"

"Leilani?" Hukui gasped.

Shuffling backwards, Hukui lost his balance and stumbled off the sidewalk into the path of a dark blue SUV which hurled him twenty feet into the air. He careened off a fire hydrant and lay in a crumpled heap on the sidewalk as the driver of the car and several bystanders rushed to his aid.

Kalani didn't see the accident. As soon as she'd heard her mother's voice, she turned around, ran full speed for home, and never looked back. Once back in the apartment, she let herself give in to her emotions and cried in Liana's embrace.

Tears of fury poured down her cheeks.

"How dare he try to take me with him! I'll die first," Kalani cried. "He doesn't scare me!"

"It's going to be all right, dear," Liana said in a soft, soothing voice. She wiped Kalani's face with her handkerchief. "You're safe now. He won't approach you again, at least not here."

Kalani was too wrapped up in rage to listen to Liana or calm down.

"Who does he think he is?" she fumed, pacing around the living room. "He's not the most powerful kahuna in the world and never will be!"

"No, he's not," Liana said quietly. "He's desperate for some kind of recognition. I know it sounds crazy, but at the heart of all his terrorizing is the need to be loved. No one loves Hukui, not even himself."

"How could anybody love him, Grandma? He's arrogant and evil and deserves to rot in hell."

Kalani threw herself into Liana's rocker and began rocking back and forth to calm herself down while Liana turned the water on for tea. On edge, she followed her grandmother into the kitchen.

"What did you mean earlier about him not approaching me here?"

"The kava leaves tell me he'll return to Maui," Liana said. "I'm not worried anymore about him trying to hurt us. We can take care of ourselves. It's Kat we've got to worry about."

Chapter 41

At sunset, the mercury lights, which were scattered throughout the campus, slowly amped up, casting an eerie glow over Anthony High School. Dark clouds covered the full moon as a cold northerly front blew into the Sacramento valley.

Alone in her office, Kat finished the last entry on her computer, turned the machine off, and rolled her pinched neck and aching shoulders. She got up to close her drapes and grabbed her Chinese warrior statue for a little energy boost. It tingled in her hands. She kept it cradled in her arms as she went through her routine of shutting down the office.

First, she returned her phone to its charging station, then she took one last look at the surveillance monitors behind Mazie's desk before turning them off.

Suddenly, one of the screens caught her attention. She placed the terra cotta soldier on top of the surveillance monitor and used the remote controlled camera to zoom in on the new pool area. The fuzzy images got sharper, and, even though the scene was poorly lit, it was enough for Kat to recognize a familiar face.

It was Mike Farnsworth and one of his girlfriends doing cannonballs in the pool. The pool had not yet been inspected, and since the school could be held responsible for any accidents, Kat was determined not to let any mishap occur during her watch.

"Mike Farnsworth," Kat said aloud, shaking her finger at the screen, "I'm coming to get you!"

"Like hell you will."

Kat spun around at the sound of Rudy Baker's voice. He was pointing a large handgun at her and laughed at the stunned expression on her face.

Kat's stomach lurched in fear. "Rudy! No!" she gasped, her mind racing.

Oh my God, he's going to kill me!

"Surprised to see me, Ms. R.?" Rudy drawled, a sardonic gleam in his eyes.

Kat's throat constricted. She stood mute, knees trembling.

Please, High Self, she prayed. *Save me!*

"It's payback time, bitch," Rudy sneered, his jaws clenched tightly. "It's time you know what it's like to be at someone's mercy. Tell me, what's it like to know your life is gonna end in a matter of seconds?"

Flashing across her mind, Kat saw Rudy's drawings from his binder. She realized he was about to act out his ghoulish fantasies. Kat's heart thundered in her chest. As she cringed in fear and backed up toward the surveillance monitor, Rudy's gun followed her in a dance of death.

"What's this all about, Rudy?" Kat sputtered. She threw an energy shield of protection around her shaking body.

"It's all about you!" he shrieked. His lips curled in derision. "*You* told Gabe not to give me a chance. *You* got me kicked out of here, so I didn't get to see Jasmine anymore. *You* turned Angela against me, too, so I had to

326

go back to juvenile hall and then lockup. *You're* gonna pay for all of it, you bitch!" The gun was only inches from Kat's face.

"I didn't paralyze Enrique. You did. I didn't punch Brittany and steal money out of Gabe's wallet. You did. I didn't go joyriding and wreck Gabe's car. You did all of those things, Rudy. That's why you got punished the way you did. And now you're making another poor choice. You're not going to get away with this, Rudy," Kat said with ragged breath. She tried to suppress the panic surging within her, but it continued to surface, and her hands shook violently in fear.

"Like hell I won't."

"Leave her alone, punk!" Mazie bellowed from the hallway, pounding on the glass with her fist.

Rudy twisted around and fired a shot off in cold rage at Mazie who dodged left and dropped and rolled on the floor. Shattered glass flew every where, but the bullet missed her and slammed into the wall where she'd been standing.

Kat snatched the terra cotta soldier off the console and hurled it at Rudy just as he spun around to shoot her. Another bullet blasted, this time through the file cabinet, missing Kat by inches. She screamed and bolted out the door. Peripherally she could see Rudy grimace, then slump in a stunned stupor to the floor. Kat caught up with Mazie who had run to the foyer, and the two women raced outside.

"To the pool, Mazie! Mike Farnsworth's there with someone and if Rudy sees him, he's a goner," Kat shouted as they sprinted toward the back of the school. Telepathically, Kat sent a prayer to Kalani and Liana.

Help! Rudy's trying to kill us. Send the police to the school!

Mazie started to wheeze, but gamely kept up with Kat's long strides until they rounded the corner to the pool area where she stopped to catch her breath.

It was so dark out that Mike Farnsworth didn't see Kat coming until she was just a few feet from him. He'd been posing on the high dive like a body-builder for Rosalind Jacarro who was toweling off and laughing at his stupidity.

"Oh, man, busted," Mike said, putting both hands up in the air when he saw Kat.

"Come here, you two, quick!" Kat demanded as she tried to catch her breath. Mazie hobbled up, wheezing like an accordion.

"Listen up, you guys." Kat's words were punctuated with hard panting. "We don't have much time. Rudy Baker's on campus, and he's got a gun. I think he stole the master key that will open every door except that one which is too new to have been put on the master key system." She pointed to the pump room. "Hurry! You've got to get in there and hide. Lock it from the inside, and don't open it until you hear my voice."

Mike and Rosalind scooped up their clothes and ran after Kat who unlocked the door and held it open for them.

"Don't come out unless you hear me or a cop say it's okay. I'm going to get some help." She herded the students inside, then noticed Mazie who had doubled over and was struggling for air. She leaned over Mazie and patted her back, directing a jolt of energy from her palm into Mazie's lungs. "You're going to be fine, Mazie. Stay in the pump room with the kids, and I'll try to find some help."

Mazie nodded. "When I drove in, I saw lights on in the trailer out back. Maybe someone there can call the cops."

"Good idea. I'll run over there. You okay?" Kat slipped her key lanyard back over her neck.

Mazie stood up and blew air out easily again. "Yeah, I'm okay. You be careful. I used to be a weapons expert in the Marines. That gun he's holding is a Glock. He's got a lot of bullets left if it was fully loaded to begin with." Mazie shut the door and turned the lock.

Kat tested the door handle to make sure it was locked, then took off in a flash, cutting through a corridor which led to an open field and the construction company's trailer. She could see the lights of a truck pulling out from behind the trailer, maneuvering its way to the exit at the end of the football stadium.

Straining every muscle in her body, Kat caught up to the truck and pounded on the passenger door. She recognized Wes Holden at the wheel as the truck skidded to a near-stop.

"Stop, Wes. I need your help. Stop!" Kat cried, sweat stinging her eyes. Holden glared, flipped her off, and sped away, covering her in a cloud of dust. She coughed and stopped to wipe the tears and dirt from her eyes.

Rudy watched the whole scene on the surveillance monitor in the VP office. He had come to, and the voice in his head was back, louder and more insistent than ever.

She's the enemy! Get her!

"You can run, but you can't hide, you bitch!" he screamed at the screen. He staggered out of the VP office and tore down the hallway, a wild beast on the hunt.

"Rudy's coming, Kat, run!"

"Kalani? What are you doing here?" Kat blinked to clear her dust-filled eyes and turned full circle. There was no one there. She heard Kalani's voice again, more urgent than before.

"Go to the pump room, Kat. But stay out of the pool! Hurry!"

Kat took off like a shot for the pump room.

Damn! she thought. *I should have just locked myself in with Mazie and the kids when I had a chance.*

Just as she entered the pool area, her left leg cramped and she stumbled forward, groaning in pain. She lurched into a dark hallway which opened into the pool area and peeked out. No sign of Rudy. She pulled her head back, leaned against the wall, and massaged the knot in her calf. Images raced through her mind as she tried to think of what to do.

Suddenly, she remembered the tree she had talked to in Tahoe. Call upon the Earth Mother for help, it had told her. Kat instantly closed her eyes and said a prayer for healing energy to come up from the earth and heal the crippling cramp in her leg. Within seconds, she could feel a power surge, warm and tingling, climbing from her heels and flowing through her body out the top of her head.

330

With renewed strength, she bolted toward the pump room. She yanked the lanyard off and squinted in the dim light to find the new key.

Suddenly, Rudy sprang out from the shadows, the gun firmly in his grip. "I got you now, bitch!" he shouted.

Kat's heart leapt in her throat. She knew she had just taken her last breath. She turned to face him. The hair on the back of her neck spiked in fear.

"Where are you going? To hide with the rest of the rats in there?" Rudy growled, his head tilting toward the pump room door. "Can't have witnesses. Let 'em out. You can watch each other die."

Kat's hand was shaking so badly she could barely find the keyhole. *I can't let him kill everyone. There's got to be a way to stop him...and I know just how to do it.*

"Did you ever see the movie *Code 3*?" she yelled facing the door, her voice hoarse and desperate.

"What are you talking about? Just open the damn door," Rudy snarled, nudging the gun into her ribs.

"On three. One, two, three!" Kat shouted the coded message to Mazie. Then she threw herself sideways as Mazie bulldozed through the door, slamming into Rudy like a linebacker, knocking him into the air and rolling him into the pool. From the safety of the pump room door, Mazie and Kat watched with horror as Rudy plunged into the deep end of the pool. They waited for what seemed like hours before he surfaced, choking and gagging, the gun still in his hand. He flailed and flapped like a bird with broken wings, then disappeared again under the water. The voice in his head exploded furiously as he sank. *No, you can't die! Kill her! Kill her!*

"Mazie, he can't swim! He's going to drown if we don't help him."

"That gun can shoot under water, Kat. I say, let the little prick die."

"I can't do that. I'm going after him. See if you can turn on some lights out here. I can barely see him." Kat kicked her shoes off and started to take her jacket off when she heard Kalani's voice again.

"Kat, stay out of the pool!"

"Okay, Kalani," Kat mumbled to herself. "Maybe I can help him without going in the water."

Just then Mazie turned on an outside hallway light illuminating a fiberglass pole and hook hanging on one of the walls. Kat ran over, grabbed the pole, and extended it to where she last saw Rudy go down. She swished it back and forth as lights continued to pop on in the area. A police car, siren wailing, barreled into the parking lot.

Kat felt the pole hit Rudy's body and braced herself to pull him up, the scene now lit brightly like a movie set. She worked the pole under his arms, now visible, and struggled to bring him to the surface.

Come on, Rudy. Don't die on me, Kat prayed.

Finally, Rudy's head appeared, hanging limply to the side, water pouring from his open mouth. Kat reached down to grab his jacket when his arm suddenly rose out of the water as if pulled by demonic strings.

The Glock was pointed at her heart!

"Rudy, no!" Kat screamed and dropped the pole. She threw herself on the ground and rolled away to escape the bullet that exploded behind her into the tile roof. Two police officers jumped out of their patrol car and charged up to the pool, their weapons in hand.

Kat ran up to them. It was Mark and his partner, Darren Riley.

"Mark! I've never been so glad to see you in my life. It's Rudy! He's trying to kill me." She pointed toward the pool as the underwater lights suddenly came on, and Rudy let out a blood-curdling scream. "He's...oh my God," Kat gasped.

Rudy, who had fallen back into the water, jerked wildly as electricity snaked through the pool. It coursed through Rudy's body, shaking him like a rattle. Hearing him scream, Mazie ran up to the edge of the pool, Mike and Rosalind at her heels. They watched in both horror and fascination as Rudy's body twitched and contorted underwater.

"Mazie, shut off the underwater pool lights. Quick! There's a short in the circuit." Mark stretched his arms out to hold the students back from the edge of the pool. "Everyone, get back," he ordered.

Mazie rushed back toward the light panel and flipped off the underwater pool lights. Then Mark used the pool hook to drag Rudy to the side where he and Darren could lift the body to the deck.

While Darren called for an ambulance, Mark knelt down and performed CPR on Rudy, thrusting on his chest, feeling for a pulse, looking for signs of life. After a few minutes, he looked up at Kat and shook his head. "He's gone."

Silence descended on the group as they stared helplessly at Rudy's lifeless body. Kat trembled in shock.

Rudy was dead. She looked over at Mazie and the two collapsed in a tearful embrace, relieved their ordeal was over.

Suddenly familiar arms wrapped themselves around Kat's shoulders.

Kalani!

Kat whipped around and hugged her as fiercely and tightly as she'd ever hugged anyone in her life. Tears flowed down her face as she whispered in Kalani's ear. "Kalani. I heard your warning loud and clear! You could see it happening ahead of time, couldn't you? Oh, Kalani. You saved us. Thank God for you," Kat cried, rocking Kalani in her arms.

"Thank God for you, too, cousin," Kalani whispered. "Thank God for you."

Kat pulled back from Kalani and saw Liana waiting patiently in the background. She held her arms open until Liana joined her little circle of comfort and support.

Chapter 42

Back at the administration building, after talking to the police, Kat changed into a sweat suit and tennis shoes which she'd kept in her file cabinet for emergencies. Then she joined Kalani and Liana in the staff lounge while Mazie gave her statement to officials in the VP suite of offices. They sipped hot chocolate from ceramic mugs, trying to make sense of the bizarre chain of events that had started on the very first day of school. Kalani broke the silence first.

"How do you think Rudy got electrocuted, Kat?"

"Faulty wiring in the underwater lights, maybe. Either shoddy work that hadn't been inspected yet or deliberate sabotage by Wes Holden. Maybe he was trying to get back at the district for not paying him for all the work he did on the pool. I saw him in his truck when I ran to look for help. He wouldn't stop. He was very angry. He just flipped me off and drove away. I'm sure the police will check it all out and arrest him for contributing to Rudy's demise."

Kat leaned back in her chair and rolled her stiff shoulders. "Speaking of the cops, I assumed *you* called them, right, Liana?" she asked, tossing her head around to loosen up her aching neck.

Liana nodded.

"How'd you know to send them to the pool?"

"We had a little help from The Other Side, Kat. Both of us were really frazzled by the time Rudy came to get you because Kalani's father showed up at the bus stop when she came home from school today." Liana pursed her lips in anger as her flushed cheeks belied her calm demeanor.

"Leilani helped cover Kalani in bright light that blinded Hukui long enough for Kalani to get away. When we sensed you were in trouble, we asked Leilani to tell us where you were, and she came through for us again. She could see you in the pool area, so that's where I sent the cops."

"And I sent you the warning not to go in the pool," Kalani said, proudly. She took a swig of chocolate like she was downing a shot in a bar.

Kat rubbed her hands over her face to mask the laugh that wanted to surface. "You two are something else," she said, shaking her head in admiration just as Mazie pushed the lounge door open and walked in.

"Girl, you ain't never lied," Mazie said. She pulled each one of them into a bone-breaking hug until they all begged for mercy. Then she grinned at Kalani like she'd just discovered a gold mine.

"Kat told me how you warned her not to go in the pool. I knew you were a gifted student, but I never dreamed you could do mental telepathy. Child, you are too much!"

Kalani blushed and squirmed self-consciously.

"I'm changing your office assistant grade to an A plus for that one, honey!" Mazie declared. "But then you probably already knew that, didn't you?"

Everyone laughed as Kalani smiled her best Mona Lisa smile.

"Speaking of A plus, you deserve one for picking up on my code, "on three," Kat said, patting Mazie's shoulder. "Good thing you saw that movie, too, because I was counting on you to come busting through that door. What made you come back to school anyway, Mazie? I thought you'd gone home for the day."

"I heard the news on the radio Rudy escaped from the Ranch. I had a gut feeling he'd come back here." Mazie tilted her head and shrugged her shoulders. "I told you before, I got your back."

"I probably wouldn't be here talking to you now if you hadn't shown up, Maze. I don't know how to thank you."

"That works both ways, honey," Mazie said, pounding Kat's back in a gesture of congratulations.

Kat noticed Kalani was wide-eyed and silent. Kat followed Kalani's startled eyes to the lounge doorway where Gabe Minelli, looking like a Mafia hit man in a disheveled suit and half-done tie, stood ready to pounce on Kat.

"I should have known I'd find you in here laughing, Kat Romero. It must amuse you to no end you've ruined two lives—mine and Rudy's. If you think you're not going to pay for this, you've got another think coming," Gabe roared, staggering around the table, his eyes bloodshot and teary.

"Hey, hey, hey, Mr. M.," Mazie said, standing up to block Gabe from getting nearer to Kat. "You're way out of line, sir. Rudy tried to kill me and Ms. R. She wanted to pull him out of the pool, but he kept shooting at her. The pool killed Rudy, Mr. M. Not Kat."

Gabe's face contorted in rage. "You stay out of this, Mazie! Kat's had it in for Rudy since he got here and never let up, never once gave him a break. She's had it in for me, too, and told the superintendent about Wes being my brother-in-law and getting all of us in trouble over the pool contract."

Panting, sweat pouring down his face, Gabe pounded on the table with both fists. "Why, Kat, why? I never pegged you for being so ruthless."

"Gabe, you need to talk to me about this one-on-one, but not here in front of everyone. Why don't we go into my office where you and I can have a private and polite conversation, okay?" Kat said sternly. She stood up, erect and sturdy like her terra cotta statue, and walked to the lounge door.

Gabe suddenly surfaced from his frenzy and realized she was right. He'd been making a fool of himself in front of staff, students and strangers. He followed her down the hallway to her office as Mazie called out, "If you're not out in five minutes, I'm coming to get you."

Kat motioned for Gabe to sit down as she settled into her desk chair and looked at him with innocent determination. She threw pink light around her grief-stricken colleague before she began.

"First of all, Gabe, I'm sorry about Rudy. I know he meant a lot to you. He had many fine qualities. He was bright and resourceful and had everything going for him when you took him under your wing. But Rudy continued to make bad choices. Choices that put him at death's door.

338

Choices you and I wouldn't have made for him, but which he made for himself.

"I know you tried to help him, but you did all the right things for all the wrong reasons. You were trying to make up for your own fatherless childhood by being the dad Rudy never had. But there were other people before you who had tried and failed with Rudy. His adopted dad. His uncle. Mr. Bass. None of them could turn him around because Rudy wouldn't let them."

Gabe hung his head and stared at his shoes. The sinking feeling in the pit of his stomach told him that everything Kat was saying was true.

"You can't blame yourself, Gabe," Kat continued "You did the best you could. I truly believe Rudy was happy with you and your family. As happy as he'd let himself be. Until he sabotaged it all. Deep down inside, he felt he didn't deserve such happiness, so he subconsciously set out to destroy it by stealing your car and forcing you to send him back to the county."

Gabe listened calmly to Kat's words, his hostility dissipating like air out of a balloon.

"I also want you to know that I had nothing to do with telling the D.O. about the 1090 violation. I asked around when I'd heard you thought it was me and found out it was Felicia Davenport's doing. She mentioned it to the superintendent who wanted any excuse to get you to resign. He must have been embarrassed by the negative press Rudy was generating, both by the injury he did to Enrique and the injuries to the kids on his joy-riding spree. He thought it cast aspersions on the district since you were planning to adopt Rudy, so he used the 1090 to force your resignation. He also used it to save the district from paying for the pool. You know as well as I do that he's known for killing two birds with one stone, if he can get away with it."

Gabe shot Kat a look of disgust, but said nothing.

"By the way," Kat said, "my future daughter-in-law is in law school, and I had her look up the Government Code 1090. It came into law when one of the state superintendents of education directed a huge contract to his wife. The bottom line here is the district lied. The 1090 doesn't apply to you. It only applies to husband and wife relationships or if there's a minor child in the home. It also only applies if you were getting a kickback from Wes, which I don't believe was the case, right?"

"Right, Kat. I'd never do anything like that. I only pressed for Wes' company because it had a quality reputation and would save the district money in the long run." Gabe sat back, his eyes unfocused and a frown on his face.

He looked up at Kat with a hurt expression. "You mean to tell me they tricked me into resigning? They must really hate me."

"It's worse than that, Gabe. They told you they'd file felony charges against you for the 1090 if you didn't resign, right? That in itself is a felony on their part. First of all, you didn't and couldn't commit the 1090 and, second, to coerce you into a resignation under threat of a felony which you didn't do means they've terminated you unlawfully. You might want to get an attorney to fight them and ask them to rescind your resignation. You deserve your job back."

Gabe visibly shrank at this suggestion. "But how can I work for a district that deceived me into resigning? If they'd resort to this kind of treachery to get rid of me now and I come back, they'll just find another way to attack me again. No, I can't work for them, Kat. I deserve better treatment than that." Gabe slumped in his chair, his hands under his chin.

"You know, Gabe," Kat said gently, "you once told me that maybe I shouldn't be an administrator. I took it to heart, what you said. I looked deep inside and asked myself why I got into education in the first place. I thought back to all the ups and downs I'd had in the classroom, and whether it was a true calling for me to work with kids for a living. And you know what? I realized, at heart, I truly am an educator, whether it's in the classroom as a teacher or in an office as an administrator. I'm passionate about kids, about their learning and about influencing them to be the best they can be. I'm in this for life. This is more than a career. This is my vocation. This is my calling."

"Well, to be honest with you, Kat, I only got into education because I wanted to have summers off with Angela. That's a pretty shallow reason, I know, but it's the truth. That and I liked to coach baseball. Of course, I've always been a competitor, and once I found success in education, I wanted to go to the top. Without paying my dues and without questioning my motives or understanding what drives me is my need to show off, to be accepted and admired."

Gabe shifted in his chair uneasily, then added in a rough whisper, "The time I've spent in education has never been focused on kids. It's been all about me. Me and my needs." A single tear fell from Gabe's eyes as he looked dejectedly at the floor.

"If you had to do it all over again, Gabe, what other career would you have chosen?"

"My mother owns a restaurant in Fresno, and I worked there as a kid. I could probably start one here, but I'd make it more like a dinner theater and bring in celebrities to talk to the crowd. Not sing or act, just talk and answer questions on stage. I bet a lot of stars—actors, sports figures, politicians—would like to have a forum to just talk about themselves and answer questions from the audience of diners. People could come in for dinner and when dessert was being served, the spotlight could turn on and *voila*."

Gabe sat up, inspired by his own words, and continued talking, his mind visualizing every detail. "I could call the restaurant The Hot Seat and build it in Sacramento. I used to be a sports announcer on radio, and I know how to contact professional athletes. I could start with them, then expand into bringing politicians on board. I mean, we're right next to Sacramento, the capitol of California, right? Best place to find plenty of politicians, and we all know how they like the spotlight," Gabe said excitedly. He pulled out a handkerchief and wiped the sweat and tears off his face.

"You know, I think you're on to something here," Kat said, catching his enthusiasm. "Not that I'm trying to steer you away from education, Gabe, but it sounds like The Hot Seat is something you'd be passionate about. I can hear it in your voice. It sounds right for you for all the

342

right reasons. I think you should follow your heart. That way you know you'll be happy." Kat nodded and smiled at Gabe who was looking at her as if he were seeing her for the very first time.

"You know, I've been wrong about you, Kat, and I apologize. I know you tried to warn me about Rudy, and I turned a blind eye and deaf ear to you. I also believe you when you say you didn't turn me in on the 1090. Not only that, but talking to you just now helped click into place what I really want to do with the rest of my life. If I could get as excited about opening up a restaurant as I have just now, I know that staying in education isn't going to cut it for me anymore. You're right. I have to follow my heart and pick a career that stimulates and fulfills me. It may or may not be the restaurant business, but it certainly isn't education," Gabe confessed, as Mazie slowly opened the office door and peeked in.

"Everything okay, boss?" she asked Kat. She looked over at Gabe. "Everything okay, Mr. M.?"

"Yes, Mazie," Gabe said. "Everything's okay now."

Kat grinned and arched her eyebrows in assurance. Mollified, Mazie shut the door.

Gabe put out his hand to shake Kat's. "I'm sorry for what I said earlier, Kat. And don't worry about the bad evaluation. Before I leave, I'll write you a good one. You don't deserve the one I wrote before."

"Thanks, Gabe." Kat cupped his hand with both of hers and sent him a bolt of healing energy. "I wish you the very best in whatever you decide to do. Keep in touch, all right?"

After Gabe had gone, Kat sank back into her chair and swiveled around to admire her cactus which was perched on the windowsill along side the little Chinese soldier which she'd thrown at Rudy.

Everything's back in its place, she thought. But only on the surface. Nothing, nothing, will ever be the same again.

Chapter 43

The next day, a windy Saturday morning, Kat slept the sleep of the dead. When she finally woke up at noon, she felt sluggish and depressed as she dragged her heavy body out of bed. After a lingering shower, she brewed coffee and sat at the kitchen table, staring out into her backyard at the bare fruit trees which seemed to shiver in the winter wind.

They look like I did yesterday, shaking in my boots, staring down the barrel of Rudy's gun. I'm still here, though. But just barely. If Mazie hadn't shown up to distract Rudy...God only knows.

Kat looked at her hands. She was still shaking. Terror filled her soul, and she didn't know how to overcome it.

If I am the Huna Warrior, why do I feel so helpless? And worse. Why do I feel so guilty? I know I didn't kill Rudy, but I played a part in his death. Can I expect more of the same as the Huna Warrior? And if this is the next big transformation in my life, am I the right one for the job? God, I wish there was someone I could talk to about this.

Kat shook her head to try to clear her muddled thoughts and let out a long, loud sigh. Caesar jumped up on her lap and pushed his head under her chin. She stroked him absentmindedly until she felt an overwhelming sense of someone calling to her. In her mind's eye, the image of her mother, Maxine, slowly took shape. She needed to talk to her mother. *Why Mom? She hasn't spoken an intelligible word in months. But I know better than not to follow my intuition.*

Kat grabbed her coat and purse and popped the garage door open. An hour later, struggling to open the door in the heavy wind, she entered the health care center's wing which housed her mother. Stepping around some stray leaves which had blown in with her, she signed in at the receptionist's desk and hurried down the hall to her mother's room.

Maxine was sitting near two glass doors which opened out into a small patio, watching a wren flitting around a bird feeder which Henry had previously installed on the patio wall.

Kat greeted her mother with a hug and pulled up a chair to sit next to her. As she took her hand, Maxine smiled brightly and pointed to the bird which was now pecking at a lever to release more seeds.

"Yes, I see the bird. Cute little thing, isn't it?" Kat tried to be cheerful, but it was forced and she knew it. So, she sat in silence with her mother watching as other birds swooped in, in competition with the wren for food. Kat held tightly to her mother's hand.

"Mom," Kat began with a trembling voice, "I'm troubled about something, and I need to talk to you. And even if you can't speak to me, I know what a good listener you've always been. Right now things are not so good. One of my students died yesterday, and I feel terrible about it. And my boss has been pretty mad at me. Even though we've worked things out, I still feel terrible about it. The worst thing is a man named Hukui who is out to get me. Turns out he's Kalani's father. She's one of my

346

students. I've just learned she's my cousin, but that's a story in and of itself. And if all this has totally confused you so far, I know exactly how you feel."

Noticing Maxine's rumpled hair, Kat took a brush from her purse and, standing behind her, began to brush her mother's hair.

"For a while things were good. I started my new job as the VP at the high school, bought my first house, Sean got engaged, and I finally met a guy I could get interested in. But then suddenly everything went wrong."

Following her mother's gaze, Kat looked up at the sky. A storm front was moving in as dark clouds strangled any sunshine that tried to peek through. Distant thunder boomed, scaring all the birds away, but Maxine's gaze remained straight ahead, her eyes glazed over, her mind adrift inside her head. Unfazed, Kat continued to pour her heart out to her mother.

"Now I have to defend myself against Hukui's scare tactics since he's bent on becoming the most powerful kahuna in the world and sees me as his greatest threat. And I've been asked to become the Huna Warrior, someone who's chosen to help protect the Huna magic and keep it alive. The bottom line is I feel like I did when I was a kid. Like a goldfish thrown into the ocean hoping to swim with the sharks. And I've put you, Dad, Sean, Mazie—everyone, really—in harm's way. I've lost the man I was hoping would be my new boyfriend over this, and almost lost my life yesterday. I know it's only going to get worse, and I don't know what to do, Mom. I feel stuck."

Kat put the brush down and looked keenly into her mother's face for any sign of recognition or acknowledgement that Maxine was even tracking what she was saying, but the expressionless face remained stoic and waxen. Kat leaned in to her mother conspiratorially.

"I don't know if Dad told you, but he just learned he has a sister named Liana. They're twins. Which makes Dad the great-grandson of a kahuna and me the great-great granddaughter of a kahuna. Liana's been catching me up on the secret kahuna teachings so I can become the Huna Warrior. But I don't know if I've got what it takes to succeed at the job. It's the biggest challenge I've ever faced. Should I do it? My heart tells me yes, but my head tells me to play it safe."

Kat started to cry in frustration. "Mom, I wish you could tell me what I should do." She dabbed her eyes with a tissue she'd pulled out of her purse and sighed again.

"Liana told me many of the kahuna pray every day for world peace, and for the spirit of aloha to encircle the earth. If all of their voices are extinguished, if their prayers go unsaid, I have no doubt the human race will be facing more war and destruction than ever before. Hukui's killing all the kahuna he can find, so I know if I don't help stop him, it'll be an incalculable loss to humanity. If I turn down being the Huna Warrior, I'll be letting a lot of people down. Including myself. But I'm so scared you or anyone else I care about can get hurt from all this, I'm paralyzed to move in any direction. And, I just can't let anything else happen to you. You've been through enough. But how can I protect you?"

Kat stroked her mother's cheek and pressed her hand into her mother's. Maxine continued to stare out at the darkening patio.

348

After a while, Kat tore out a page from a notebook she always carried to jot down a message to her father who would be visiting her mother later in the afternoon. Just as she started to write "Dear Dad," Maxine squeezed Kat's hand hard and looked her squarely in the face, eyes alert and penetrating. In a slow clear voice, she spoke for the first time in months.

"*Hilina'i kalele iho.*"

Kat gasped and stared at her mother, then came to her senses and quickly tried to write down what her mother had said.

"Uh, Mom, could you say that again?"

"*Hilina'i kalele iho.*"

Maxine reached out and touched Kat's heart with the palm of her hand and smiled. Maxine had been transformed right in front of Kat's eyes and was her old self again. The sparkle was back in her eyes, her communication to Kat deliberate and clear.

"Oh my God, Mom! You talked to me. And in Hawaiian, no less." Kat shook her head in amazement. "What a miracle you are. I have no idea what you meant, but I don't care. It's so nice to have you back."

As Kat grabbed her notebook to write the words down, Maxine slowly turned to stare at the bird feeder once more, the brief animation subsiding into her previously blank expression. Kat studied her mother's expression, hoping for another lucid connection, but, when none was forthcoming, a different realization spread through her and she grinned.

"Ooh, I got it. *They* spoke to me. Through you. Like magic."

Kat kissed her mother on the forehead, gathered her notebook, coat and purse and drove straight to Liana and Kalani's apartment.

When Liana answered the door, she was surprised to see Kat who immediately thrust the notebook sheet of paper out at her.

"Liana, hi!" Kat said excitedly. "I just got an unusual message from the Aumakua. I need you to translate this, please."

Kalani joined them in the kitchen as Kat told them about her reticence in becoming the Huna Warrior, and how, after pouring her heart out to her mother about all the bad things that had happened to her lately, Maxine had blurted out something in Hawaiian. Something she felt sure was a message from The Other Side.

Kalani brought her Hawaiian-English dictionary to the table while Liana put the kettle on for tea. A quiet peace descended upon Kat as she sat in the comfort of the kitchen, surrounded by her newfound family. She watched the angelfish zigzag in and out of the bubbles streaming in the aquarium and waited quietly for Kalani to finish the translation.

"What were you asking her when she spoke to you, Kat?" Kalani asked, flipping through the pages of the dictionary with lightning speed.

"I was asking her what I should do. About being the Huna Warrior. Why? What did she say?"

"Basically she said, 'Trust yourself, follow your heart.'"

Kat laughed. "Follow my heart, huh?"

"Well?" Liana asked, quietly, leaning in toward Kat.

"Well, my heart tells me the more I see of the dark side of life, the more I want to live in the light. My heart tells me to do everything I can to save the ancient Huna wisdom. My heart tells me I can count on you two and the po'e Aumakua because together we'll prevail."

At that instant, a jolt of energy blasted through Kat. The hair on the back of her neck stood up. She bolted upright, eyes widening as she watched the po'e Aumakua suddenly materialize in the kitchen. Arrayed in an assortment of colorful clothes, long capes and plumed hats, the Hawaiians, ancestors all, crowded into the small room, smiling and acknowledging Kat who tingled with their blessings.

"Can you see them?" she whispered without looking at Liana and Kalani who both nodded. Kalani brightened when she saw her mother, Leilani, appear near Kat's right shoulder.

Kat breathed a sigh of relief. She wasn't crazy after all. They were honoring her with their presence. They were confirming what she had been trying to deny for so long. She *was* the Huna Warrior, and they would protect her and her family as she traveled along this new path in her life.

Kat smiled back as individual members of the po'e Aumakua approached her, touching her shoulders, head and hands. Some kissed her cheek, some just nodded at her. Waves of love swept through her. Tears of joy welled in her eyes as the procession of visitors continued, profoundly touching her heart. She felt humbled and

351

overwhelmed with their outpouring of reverence and respect.

Gradually, the ancestors faded from sight, but Kat could still feel their energy in the room. When she returned her focus to Kalani and Liana, they looked jubilant and triumphant. A "we told you so" look on their faces.

"You were right," Kat said, reaching out to clasp their waiting hands. "I am the Huna Warrior. So bring it on. Let the magic begin."

Chapter 44

No sooner had Kat returned home from Liana's when she heard pounding on her front door. Looking through the peephole, Kat could see Alex, a sheepish yet worried look on his face. He held up the newspaper section of Sunday's paper. The front porch light illuminated the big headlines which splashed across the front page: "Student Gunman Drowns at Anthony High." She opened the door.

"Kat! Are you all right? I've been so worried about you!" Alex grabbed Kat in a deep embrace which startled her a bit at first. When she finally wriggled free, she invited him in to the living room where they plopped onto her overstuffed couch.

Over a glass of wine, Kat poured out all the grisly details Rudy's death. Alex listened, mesmerized by the drama of it all. When she finally finished, he clasped his hands over hers and shut his eyes for a moment, trying to hide the tears that threatened to surface.

"K...kat," he stammered, "I...I can't tell you how relieved I am that you came out of this alive and well. You're lucky, you know."

"Luck has nothing to do with it, Alex. I told you, I'm being protected. You don't ever have to worry about me, although it's sweet you did. It proves you care after all."

"Kat, about the other day, when I said Huna was voodoo. That was just the skeptic in me talking. When we got back home from skiing, the researcher in me got on the Internet and looked up everything I could find on Huna. I ran out of paper trying to download everything. I thought you said the word meant *secret*, but it's really not a secret any more."

"No, it isn't."

"Anyway, I just want to apologize for backing off from you so soon over something I was simply too ignorant to make a judgment about in the first place. I guess I was just over-reacting because...because I thought I might lose you."

Alex squeezed Kat's hands tighter, emotion catching in his voice. She straightened up and looked him warmly in the eyes.

"Alex, do you remember the play, *The Crucible,* about the witch trials in Salem? Remember the main character, John Proctor? He went to the gallows rather than sign a false confession and sully his integrity. The trial was a test for him, just as yesterday was a test for me."

"What do you mean, a test?"

"Well, let's look at it another way. What is a crucible? A cauldron, right? A melting pot for ores. It gets really hot so all the inferior particles clinging to a sample chunk are burned up, leaving the purest form of gold or silver or whatever fine metal is in it. The trial became Proctor's crucible. It tested his mettle, leaving him stripped to his core beliefs. So, when you think about it, I was put in a crucible yesterday and faced the fire. And now all my doubts, fears and insecurities have melted away. What's

354

left of me is the core me. I am the Huna Warrior, and if I'm put through another ordeal, I'll make it through again because now I know I have the right stuff within me—and the right connections on the other side—to triumph."

Alex nodded his head in understanding, as he gulped for air.

"So, I don't have to worry about you dying on me, right?"

"Right. I just have the feeling I've got time on my side. And if you know nothing else about me, you should know I trust my feelings."

"Speaking of feelings, Kat, you need to know mine. I'm crazy about you. What you went through yesterday—how easily you could have been killed—well, it makes me realize how precious our time is on this planet. Listen. I don't want to keep you at arms distance, or in our case, at house distance, any more. I want us to ratchet up our relationship."

"What does that mean, exactly?"

"You. Me. Together. We date, go out, see each other."

"Through thick and thin?"

"We've been through the thick. Let's try thin."

Kat let out a big sigh. "You know something, Alex?" she said, snuggling into his open arms. "This could be the start of something big." Then giving into her instincts, she reached over his shoulder and turned off the living room light.

Chapter 45

In a fire-lit cave in Maui, Hukui Kingston chanted in a strong voice, determined to master the deadliest of prayers. Smoke swirled through the small cave, past the ti leaves covering the remains of two corpses, the foul stench of rotting flesh seeping through the greenery piled to mask it.

"Rush upon them and enter. Enter and curl up. Curl up and straighten out," he intoned in a deep baritone. "Help me, Lono. Listen to my voice. I call upon you, too, Uli, to force my plan into reality."

The fire leapt, tongues of heat burning brightly into the stillness of the night. The flames reflected in the Hawaiian's determined eyes. He laughed, ready for the fight for supremacy he knew he must win.

Miles away on the island of Oahu, safely tucked into bed for the night at Luly's house, Kahili Kingston sat up in bed on alert. He could feel a dark and evil frequency threaten to permeate the room.

"It's time to sever the ties with Hukui," he said aloud.

He got up to fill his calabash with water, blessing it and filling it with mana as he returned to his room. He knelt on a tapa cloth before a small shrine he had created on a small table near his bed and placed the bowl of water near a ti wreath. A carved, wooden tiki stood in the middle of the wreath, showing the three selves, the top one having two faces to represent the female/male po'e Aumakua.

Kahili lit a scented candle and turned off the bedroom light, then breathed deeply to center himself. When he felt the old familiar peace settle in, he began to pray the Ho'oponopono, the prayer of forgiveness written by Morrnah Simeona and used by Huna practitioners around the world to cancel karmic debt and let people psychically disconnect from each other's lives through forgiveness. It was a re-enactment of sorts that allowed the person praying to take the part of the person responding to the prayer, acting in proxy so the actual person being released didn't have to be physically there.

After taking in several deep breaths, Kahili began: "Father-Mother-Son as One, if I, my family, relatives or ancestors have offended you, Hukui Kingston, your family, relatives, or ancestors, in thoughts, words, or actions from the beginning of our creation to the present, humbly, humbly I ask you all for forgiveness for all my errors, resentments, guilt, hatred, hurts, trauma, pain, offenses, and blocks which I have created and accumulated from the beginning to the present. Please forgive me!"

A single tear streamed down Kahili's face as he remembered the shattered expression on Hukui's face when he had described the anguish he'd felt during childhood. He mentally pictured his Hukui's response as if it were coming directly from his son's lips.

"Yes, we forgive you!"

Kahili dipped his fingers into the calabash bowl and sprinkled water over himself from head to toe.

"Let this water cleanse, purify, and release us, offender and offended, from spiritual, mental, material, financial, and karmic bondage. Pull out from our memory

357

bank or computer all the unwanted, negative memories and blocks that attach, knot, tie, and bind us together." He pulled invisible strands from around his body's energy field and flung them to the earth, picturing them seeping into the earth and being transformed into pure light.

Next, Kahili visualized thousands of aka cords going out from his solar plexus, his head and the rest of his body. He formed his fingers into scissors and made a cutting motion, counter-clockwise, as he prayed: "Sever, detach, untie, and release these unwanted memories and blocks. Transmute these unwanted energies into pure light!"

In his imagination, he sealed off the ends of the severed aka cords with blue light and let them snap back into his body. Then he began waving the palms of his hands over the outline of his body.

"Fill the spaces these energies occupied with divine light," he said, breathing deeply and out, putting his will and intention on the out-going breath.

Kahili waited patiently until he could discern a sense of completion and serenity, then said the last part of the prayer with force and clarity.

"Let divine order, light, love, peace, balance, understanding, joy, wisdom, and abundance be made manifest for us through the divine power of the divine Father, Creator of all life, Mother, Son, as One, in whom we abide, rest, and have our being...now and forever more. Amen."

Sitting back on his heels, Kahili suddenly felt flushed with energy as if a dam had broken and spread vitality to every part of his body and soul. Inspiration poured through him, as vivid pictures bombarded his peripheral vision, assaulting his consciousness and energizing his body.

"I'm back," he said softly to himself. "I've got the gift of seeing again!"

Kahili stared out into space looking at nothing but seeing everything. Visions of the future surfaced and submerged in his mind's eye. After a few minutes, he shook his head as if to shrug off the disturbing scenes and hurried to Luly's room to wake her up. He knocked on her door first, then shouted her name.

Luly woke with a start, her heart beating fast. "It's almost three in the morning," she mumbled, looking crossly at her digital clock. "What's the matter, Kahili?"

"I think I know a way to stop Hukui's path of destruction, but we need the help of all the other kahuna in Hawaii. How many have we found so far?"

"There's around thirty. We've found fourteen."

"We're running out of time. We've got to find them all. And it's not just about Hukui. It's about the end of the world as we know it."

Chapter 46

It was the first day of spring break—one week's reprieve from the madness of high school with its jammed schedules, exasperated parents, and wired teenagers. Kat nestled into her seat aboard a flight headed for Cancun. She and Alex had stepped up their relationship and were "going together," in an exclusive commitment to one another. Getting away from the pressures of work and needing a change of scenery, they planned a week's vacation in a beach resort where their phones wouldn't ring, and the mundane necessities of life wouldn't bog them down.

They felt like carefree children let loose in a playground with no one and nothing to answer to but the call of their inner wild. Visions of moonlit walks on the beach, tequila sunrise glasses clinking to the sounds of a nearby mariachi band, handheld dinners aboard a catamaran while watching the orange-drenched sunset, preoccupied their thoughts as the plane plunged through the clouds like a god personally delivering them on the palm of his hand.

On the way to pick up their luggage, Kat's elbow was tugged by a young man in his twenties, asking if she would like to get free gifts just for listening to a ninety-minute presentation on a time share his company was selling.

"But I'm in education," she said, gently detaching from the man's grip. "I'm sure I couldn't afford a time share here."

The man eyed Alex up and down. "Perhaps your husband would like to hear about this special opportunity."

"I'm her boyfriend," Alex said with a relaxed smile, "and believe her when she tells you she can't afford a time share."

"But neither of you has to buy one. All you need to do is listen to our presentation, and you'll get a free breakfast, two tickets to any tour in the area, a Mexican blanket, and bottles of kahlua and tequila. You can't go wrong. It's only an hour and a half at the most. We pick you up at your hotel, and, after our talk, we bring you back. The tour tickets alone are worth nearly two hundred American dollars."

Whether it was from the humidity or the exertion of his spiel, the young man began to sweat profusely. He pulled a handkerchief out of the breast pocket on his jacket and wiped his entire face.

Kat's heart went out to him. She remembered when she was young, having to sell candy bars door to door as a fundraiser for her school. She sensed the need in the young man to make a sale and felt her heart go out to him.

"Let me see the list of tours you have to offer," she said, taking the colorful brochure the young man instantly produced. She tried to repress the smile that wanted to pop up on her face when Alex looked at her as if she'd lost her mind.

361

"Look, Alex, we could go on a guided tour of Chichen Itza."

"Chi Chi Neetza? Sounds like a golfer I've heard about."

"No, silly. There's a Mayan pyramid at Chichen Itza. I've always wanted to see it. What the heck? It'll only cost us an hour and a half of our time, right?"

Alex shook his head. "And I thought I was an easy mark. Okay, you're on. You're such a softie, but if you want to go, let's do it."

After they had made arrangements to attend the presentation, they headed for a van that would take them to their hotel. The hotel strip in Cancun was ultra commercial and modern, lined with magnificent hotels each trying to outdo each other in grandeur and expense. The circular driveway to Kat and Alex's hotel was surrounded by a plethora of trees draped with white twinkling lights like fireflies in a forest.

Kat and Alex ascended a marble staircase where the doorman, dressed in a safari-type of uniform, shorts and all, opened the massive, ornately-carved doors for them and took their luggage. The foyer was richly appointed with statues of tourmaline and quartz, opulent bouquets of flowers arranged in hand-blown glass vases, and huge ceiling fans which had been specially treated to carry subtle wafts of perfume in the air. Their room was on the ground floor overlooking a series of cascading pools surrounded by lush, lacy ferns. Tiny birds darted over nearby steps which led to an outdoor cabana encircling an enormous swimming pool where children splashed happily under the watchful eyes of their parents who rested in nearby chaise lounges. Beyond the pool, the ocean beckoned with fingers of sea water tickling the shore.

"This is perfect, Alex. It's paradise. I can feel my tired body relaxing already. Let's unpack later. I'm ready for a walk on the beach."

"Sounds good to me." Alex quickly pulled off his tennis shoes and socks and changed into shorts and a t-shirt.

"I love walking barefoot," Kat murmured, wiggling her feet as she freed them from the bondage of her shoes. *I can't wait to get energy from Mother Earth through the soles of my feet. I'll show Alex how to do it.*

Kat grabbed her room key and held the door open for him. "Maybe we can find a restaurant near the beach after our walk. I'm starving!"

"Great idea," Alex answered. "Hold it. You aren't planning to levitate forks and knives, are you?" He flashed a broad, fake smile to let her know he was teasing, and she playfully hit him on the shoulder.

"Ain't gonna happen, pal. You know I've been sworn to secrecy about all that. No overt magic in public unless it's an absolute emergency."

Kat seemed to float out of her body as she and Alex walked out to the beach. She loved water and all of its many forms—lakes, rivers, rain, creeks, ponds, oceans, waterfalls, and puddles. Her ideal place to vacation was anywhere where water was present, but the ocean always held the strongest enticement for her. She could feel her spirit soar above the waves like a gull, then dive to skim the water's crest only to shoot upward toward a canopy of stars. All was calm and right as a sense of serenity and oneness with the universe filled her soul.

No wonder I was chosen to be the Huna Warrior, she thought. *The symbol for mana is water. Which I love and totally relate to.*

At the water's edge, Kat pulled Alex to her and whispered in his ear, "Want an energy boost, Alex?"

"Right here? In public?"

"Yes, goofy. Right here in public. But it's not from me. It's from the earth."

"Okay, I'll bite. What do I do?"

"Just ask Mother Earth to share some of her positive energy with you as you walk. There are openings or chakra points on the bottom of your feet. Imagine the flow of energy in the form of white light coming up out of the sand and slowly rising up through your body until it pours out of the top of your head. Like a fountain. Got it?"

"Gotcha."

"Only make sure you thank the earth for sharing her energy with you. She's a living, conscious entity, you know. Everybody wants a thank-you now and then, right?"

"Right."

Within minutes of walking barefoot on the sand, both Alex and Kat felt refreshed and invigorated. They spotted an outdoor restaurant on the grounds of a hotel next to theirs, popped in, and ordered dinner—soft shell crabs for her and stuffed calamari for him. Leaning back in giant wicker chairs with pillows at their feet and candle light dancing in their eyes, they shared a shrimp cocktail appetizer and watched as the sun dipped gracefully into the crimson sea, allowing their first glimpse of stars in the Mayan world.

When the waiter filled their glasses with crisp, white wine, Alex proposed a toast. "To our first vacation together," he said, tapping his glass against Kat's.

"May it be all we've been dreaming of."

"You've been dreaming about this?"

"Sure have. I've been envisioning this moment ever since we began planning to come here. Why do you think it's turned out so well?"

"I might have known you helped to create some of this," he said, waving his hand around to describe in gestures what he couldn't put in words. "Whatever you're doing, keep it up."

"Of course." Kat sighed contentedly.

Within minutes, their waiter served conch chowder soup in abalone shells. As the sky steadily darkened, they sipped soup and breathed in the cooler night air, mesmerized by the star-filled firmament above them. The salty breeze picked up, and the waves began pounding the shore with a primordial beat that stirred their blood. They felt suspended, like the stars, caught in an enigmatic struggle between their spiritual and physical natures.

"I don't think I've ever seen so many stars in the sky before," Alex said, taking Kat's hand, kissing it.

"Aren't they beautiful? Liana tells me the stars are alive, just like we are. They are constant reminders we're all connected in consciousness. We're all part of the same fabric, the same essence."

"The longer I live on this planet, the more I tend to see it that way, too. Although there are times that I wonder why more of us don't see it the same way."

"I know what you mean. I used to feel so angry at God for creating us with such limited brain power, not to mention a tendency for disease and dysfunctionality, topped off with a propensity toward violence and war. But Liana and my teachers on the Other Side have helped me realize what I've been struggling with all my life is the false idea we're separate from God. All my life I've had this profound sense of loss, abandonment and victimization because of it. I knew God existed, but I felt He/She was notably absent from my life. I felt angry and violated and blamed God for all my troubles—everything from my mother's Alzheimer's to my own loneliness. Now I've come to realize there is no separation from God. God is within me, acting through me, as me. Most importantly, I believe the God within me is the same as the God within you and everybody else. The idea of separation from God has all been an illusion."

"On an intellectual level, I agree with you, Kat. I just can't quite get it to stick emotionally. It's hard to feel the love of God when you don't always see it in action with your own eyes."

"True, and it's a lot easier to play a game of denial and separation than it is to play one of love and unity. It takes a shift in perspective. I used to beat myself up all the time over past indiscretions and poor choices I made. But now I don't review my past with such a critical eye anymore. I try to see my mistakes and backsliding as necessary lessons that have brought me to where I am

366

now. I also learned I used to love people only in my head. Now I feel the love deep inside my heart. It's what Liana calls the longest journey—the trip between the mind and the heart. Maintaining that love, never allowing it to waiver no matter what—that's the challenge, Alex."

"We just need to keep reminding ourselves we are all connected. That's why God gave us these magnificent stars, right?"

"Right. And if we think of existence as a game we're all playing, then we can give ourselves permission to have fun and feel exhilarating joy. Alan Watt put it best when he said life is just God playing hide and seek with Itself."

Alex nodded and smiled back at Kat, whose smile was brighter than the full moon which had suddenly slipped out from some lingering clouds and beamed its own ethereal smile down onto the couple.

After dinner, they ambled back to their hotel lounge where a trio of musicians played soft melodies. In the middle of their first slow dance together, Kat and Alex looked at each other with a sudden awareness they were in the wrong place to give full expression to their feelings for each other. They abandoned the dance floor and rushed to their room where they gave in to their desires with an ineffable mixture of delicate respect and wild abandon.

Early the next morning they dragged themselves to the hotel foyer, coffee in hand, and waited, eyes at half-mast, for the bus to pick them up and take them to the time share presentation. When the bus arrived a few minutes later, they lumbered aboard like turtles, still recovering from their exhaustive but intensely romantic interlude, before the caffeine had a chance to wake them up.

The bus circled the hotel strip, picking up other tourists in the area before dropping the group off thirty minutes later at the Yucatan Plaza Resort, a plush property which catered to golfers and family vacationers, located at the opposite end of the peninsula. They were immediately escorted to a lavish buffet breakfast which they ate in the company of Eduardo, the young man they'd met at the airport. He politely asked them questions about their backgrounds, obviously in preparation for the other salesmen to use in the hopes of signing them to purchase a share in one of their condos.

Five grueling hours later, Kat and Alex found themselves in line to receive their parting gifts, having successfully withstood the ever-mounting pressure by a relentless sales force Donald Trump would have hired in a New York minute.

How many times can you explain to people being here on vacation doesn't mean you've got all kinds of money to splurge on a timeshare? I shouldn't be so grumpy about it, though, Kat thought. *I should have known what we'd be up against, but they sure exaggerated about it taking only ninety minutes of our time.*

Back on the bus returning them to their hotel, Alex looked at Kat whose arms were loaded with their promised gifts of blankets, bottles, and tickets and rolled his eyes. "Chichen Itza better be worth all this," he said between clenched teeth.

"It will be, Alex. I promise," Kat said, smiling weakly.

Later that afternoon, after he got into one of the bottles of kahlua, Alex's mood brightened considerably. He called the concierge to recommend a local restaurant they might enjoy and finalized dinner plans for them to go to La Destileria, described in its brochure as "the only Mexican contemporary cuisine restaurant and museum of Tequila in Cancun."

Arriving at the restaurant a few hours later, Kat and Alex put the morning time-share fiasco behind them. They sat in an outdoor patio off of the main dining room where they quietly munched on chips and salsa, slurped giant margaritas, and admired the panoramic view of the city whose night lights were just beginning to shine.

For dinner they both decided to try the specialty of the house, Chiquihuite Maximiliano, a dish consisting of phylo dough wrapped around corn truffles, cream cheese and chicken breasts. Dessert was caramel crepes, filled with baked creamed bananas and walnuts, served over caramel and vanilla ice cream. At the end of the meal, when a photographer came by to take their pictures as a memento of the night, Kat wasn't sure she wanted to memorialize their gluttony in a photograph.

"I hope I don't look like the blimp I feel like," she moaned, trying to suck in her stomach.

"Good thing the table covers most of our newly acquired bulk." Alex held his breath—along with his abdominal muscles—while the photographer snapped away.

"We'll walk most of this off tomorrow."

"God, I hope so. The steps of the pyramid at Chichen Itza can't get here fast enough."

369

Espresso in paper cups worked its magic on them the next morning as the bus pulled in to pick them up for their tour to Chichen Itza. This time they hopped on and gingerly walked down the aisle to pick out seats where the windows would give them the best view.

Their guide, a short man in his fifties with etched, walnut skin and strong Mayan Indian features, announced on the intercom he would be their guide for the day. Like the day before, the bus circled the hotel strip, picking up other tourists until it was packed with more than fifty people, a mixture of Americans, two Australians, a small contingency of Canadians, and a family from Mexico City. Taking stock of the group, Manuel, who never announced his last name, spoke in excellent English to the group during the two-and-a-half hour trip.

Within minutes the lush, verdant landscape changed dramatically. Fields of impenetrable bamboo prevented a glimpse of some of its interior spaces, but once in a while dilapidated, wooden shacks with tin roofs could be seen from the highway. Barefoot children played outside, chasing nervous chickens around their yard. Soup simmered in black kettles hung over outside campfires where mothers in colorful shifts swept the dirt floors of their three-sided dwellings. The bus was moving too fast for anyone to get more than a cursory glimpse, but it was evident the area was pretty much made up of the haves and have-nots, with an obscure, mostly non-descript, middle class.

This is the part of the country they don't want the tourists to see, Kat thought. *The impoverished people of Mexico.*

My heart goes out to them. She thought of a recent lesson Liana had taught her.

"Whenever you see someone or something in need of help, send them gentle blessings which travel with the speed of love," Liana had said.

Kat took a deep breath and radiated a strong wave of love out to the families she had seen in their meager surroundings. An overwhelming sense of compassion and reverence overtook her, and she suddenly found herself blinking tears away.

Alex looked at Kat and, sensing a need for support, tightly clasped her hand. She cuddled up to him just as the guide started to relate the history of the Toltecs and the Mayan community. Kat tried to pay attention, but she couldn't rid her mind of the stark poverty she had just seen, so she continued her silent prayers until they arrived at the pyramid.

Chapter 47

"Pay attention, dear one," a voice said loudly in Kat's head.

Kat looked sideways at Alex, but he was focused intently on their guide who was describing the mysterious craters near the Yucatan peninsula of Mexico, now cited as evidence of the asteroid collision with Earth that killed the dinosaurs. She glanced around her, but the rest of the group was also listening to Manuel.

"There are no accidents. You're here for a reason," the inner voice said.

Kat blinked hard and came to attention as the group began to leave the bus and follow Manuel out of the parking lot and down a tree-lined path of vendors. They soon came out into a clearing at the base of the Pyramid of Kukulkán where Manuel waited patiently for their exclamations to die down.

"There were originally ninety-one steps on each of the four sides of the pyramid," he said. "If you add the platform at the top as a final step, there are 365 steps in total, one for every day of the year. This building demonstrates the Mayan knowledge of astronomy and their calendar. During the spring and fall equinoxes, the shadow of the sun plays on the stairs, creating the illusion of a snake moving down the pyramid."

He held up a large photograph of the pyramid, taken during the spring equinox. The crowd gasped at the sight of the snake of light which appeared on the north side of the pyramid steps.

"Notice how the snake's mouth is open and facing the Sacred Cenote or sacred well. It is a sinkhole in a bed of limestone which accesses an underground river and was a place where ritual offerings, at first precious objects and later human sacrifices, were made. You may want to stop by this beautiful well of water and make an offering of thanks that you made it to the top of the pyramid and came back to tell about it."

Manuel chuckled huskily, his white teeth gleaming in the sun. He took off his hat and used it to point toward a nearby bench surrounded by low bushes.

"I will return right over there an hour from now so we can continue our tour. Please meet me by the bench."

As the group split up, Kat and Alex opted to climb the seventy-nine foot wall of the pyramid while the more intimated tourists rushed off to see the ball court, the columns in the Temple of Warriors, and the other many buildings which made up the complex at Chichen Itza. The stairs on the pyramid were steep in height, but not deep enough in width to accommodate Alex and Kat's feet, so they turned their feet at a slight angle for surer footing and began their trek up the ninety-one steps, pausing to rest a few times before reaching the top.

The breath-taking view was well worth the effort. Soft expanses of grassy fields gave way to ancient platforms, carved statues, walls created out of human skulls, and a playing field where the winning male was beheaded and instantly catapulted into divinity, his mother elevated to a sacred status forever. After snapping

373

a few photos, Alex pulled Kat into a tunnel which wound them around to the opposite side of the pyramid affording a better view of the ruins with its spectacular columns, enormous walkways, and smaller temples decorated with carvings of warriors and plumed serpents. Taking in the sheer majesty of the sacred grounds, Kat was hit with the sudden realization she had been there before. Tiny tendrils of fear seemed to crawl up out of the stones she was standing on and wrap around her body like a boa constrictor. She grabbed Alex's hand for support.

"I've lived here before," she whispered, tucking her wind-tossed hair behind her ears. "In another life time. I died here, too. I was one of the sacrifices. Maybe at the well, but possibly here in the temple."

"How do you know, Kat? What makes you think that?"

"I just know. It feels all too familiar, and I have these flashes of being tied to an altar and drugged so I wouldn't feel my heart being ripped out of my chest."

"Wonderful," Alex said, a scowl forming on his face. "Why on earth would you want to come back to a place where you were murdered in a previous life?"

"I didn't know it until just now. Anyway, that's not the real reason why I'm here. That is."

Kat gestured with her chin to indicate a structure in the distance. Alex snapped open his tourist map to find out what she was looking at.

"The Observatory? That's why you came?"

"I'm pretty sure. Let's go check it out."

They scrambled down the pyramid steps holding on to a steel chain to steady their descent on the slippery, stone steps and hastily made their way to the southern side of the ruins. Kat read aloud from their brochure:

"Set upon two rectangular platforms, The Observatory, also known as 'El Caracol,' the Spanish word for *snail*, is a circular tower whose roof is crowned by a small structure with windows facing all cardinal points. This building obviously served the ancient Mayans in their observation and recording of celestial movements upon which they based their religious and civic calendar. The windows and shafts leading to the windows are oriented to indicate the azimuths for west and south, the equinoxes, and the summer solstice."

As they approached the grounds of the observatory, Kat felt the same prickly sensation in her stomach she had at the top of the temple. Some prior life memory had bled through somehow, triggering vague remembrances of having been there before. She nudged Alex toward the first set of stairs leading to the conservatory.

"There's a spiral staircase inside the top dome. I really want to look out the window there," Kat said, stopping at the top of the first platform to catch her breath. "Now I know why I should have gotten in better shape."

"It's time for both of us to sign up at a gym." Alex whipped off his baseball cap and mopped the perspiration off his face with a handkerchief.

At the entrance to the tower, both Alex and Kat were happy to take shelter from the sun. They ducked inside, leaned against the stone walls, and regarded the inner staircase ahead of them which would take them to the observatory dome.

"Ready?" Alex held his hand out to Kat to pull her toward the stairs.

"Yep, but you go first. Both of us won't fit on the same step together," Kat said with a chuckle. "Mayans sure must have been little people."

Alex took his cue and began to climb the inner stairs, pushing against the stoned walls with his hand to help propel himself forward.

Kat took her sandals off first, then followed. With each step the soles of her feet began to tingle with energy.

Mana! I can feel it stored in the stones. I wonder if the Mayan astrologers were really priests who knew the ancient magic, too.

The stairwell ended at a hallway which led out to the observatory windows. Kat went to the middle lookout point and gazed out onto the sky, trying to imagine what she might see on any given star-filled night. She took a deep breath and closed her eyes, asking her High Self to reveal the reason why she was there. She felt it had something to do with cycles, circles, solar phases, and inter-dimensional doorways. Her mind groped for the right word.

"Calendar," she heard her inner voice say.

"Calendar?" she asked out loud.

"Hey, Kat," she heard Alex call from one of the other windows. "Come look at these slots in the wall. The brochure says they were built into the tower to align with the location of Venus when it reaches the horizon at the most northerly and southerly extremes of its path through the sky. Why were they interested in Venus?"

"I don't know, but we could ask Manuel when we get back to the group," Kat said, still stymied over the word *calendar* which kept echoing in her mind.

"It's time we get back to them. Have you figured out why you've been so drawn to this place yet?" Alex took a swig of water from the bottle he'd been carrying.

"Only that it has something to do with their calendar," Kat said, splashing water on her face from her own bottle to cool off.

"One more thing to ask the guide. Let's go."

When they caught up with the group, Manuel checked his roster and let everyone know they needed to wait for three more people to show up before they could take off again. Kat and Alex approached him as he sat on a rock in the shade of a jacaranda tree.

"Manuel, we have a couple questions for you, if you don't mind," Alex began.

Manuel merely nodded and smiled shyly.

"We were in the old observatory just now and noticed the brochure said something about the Mayan interest in following the motions of Venus. I'm curious why they did that."

"Well," Manuel answered, his grin expanding to a broad beam. "We believe the planet Venus is the celestial manifestation of Kukulcan-Quetzalcóatl. Venus had great significance for the Maya who also consider it to be the sun's twin and a war god. Mayan leaders used the changing position of Venus to plan appropriate times for raids and battles."

"Interesting," Kat said, using her brochure to fan her flushed face. "What about the Mayan calendar? What can you tell us about it?"

Manuel's grin slowly faded into a more somber expression. He answered with slow deliberation as some of the others in the group who had been listening came closer to hear his answer.

"The Maya developed a precise and sophisticated calendar which they used to keep track of celestial configurations which occurred millions of years ago and as a way of projecting into the future as well. They used a count of 260 days and gave each day a name, much like our days of the week. There were 20 day names, each represented by a unique symbol. The days were numbered from 1 to 13. Since there were 20 day names, after the count of thirteen was reached, the next day was numbered 1 again. The 260-day or sacred count calendar was in use throughout Mesoamerica for centuries, probably before the beginning of writing."

"They were geniuses, weren't they?" Kat smiled knowingly at Manuel.

"We like to think so," he said solemnly.

"But they were practical, too," Alex asserted. "They used the calendar to predict the seasons for farmers and astronomical events, even for religious rites and wars."

"But what else is so significant about it?" Kat asked, her voice tight with anticipation.

"The most significant thing about the Mayan calendar is it ends in the year 2012."

"But...but if the Maya could project their calendar millions of years in the past and the future," Alex sputtered, "why would they stop at the year 2012?"

Manuel narrowed his eyes before answering and considered how he should answer the question. He opted for blunt honesty.

"We believe there will be some kind of world catastrophe at that time. The last day of the Mayan calendar is Dec. 21, 2012."

Kat gasped. "Are you saying something drastic will happen to the planet on that date?"

Manuel nodded and looked around at the shocked expressions on the faces of the other tourists.

"If the Mayan cycles prove true," he added, "I'd have to say yes. Some big changes which have already begun to start will have finished by then."

"The world won't end, will it?" Alex asked with a smirk.

Manuel blinked at him languidly, then spoke in a tactful tone.

"The Mayan calendar is not predicting the end of the world in 2012, but the start of a new era—the golden age."

"Oh, good," Alex said with a sigh. "I thought maybe life as we know it would be over."

Manuel laughed heartily and winked at Kat conspiratorially.

"But it will, my friend. It will," he said.

Alex stared at Kat, his mouth slightly open in protest and confusion. She stared back at him with worried eyes.

"Something tells me we've got to get back home."

"Yeah, while there's still one left!" he replied, rolling his eyes at Kat who merely sighed with deep concern.

Something's up for the Huna Warrior, Kat thought. *Something really big.*

Chapter 48

Only ten weeks left and school will be out for the summer, Kat thought anxiously. *But not before we tackle state testing and graduation. Then I can concentrate on looking into the 2012 mystery, not to mention helping Sean and Chelsea with their wedding.*

Kat pulled the door down on the airplane's overhead compartment and retrieved her bag of gifts from the trip before exiting the plane with Alex. Kalani greeted them as they stepped into the airport waiting area.

"Hey, cuz! Hey, Alex!" she yelled excitedly, flashing her beautiful Polynesian smile.

"Hey, yourself," Kat said, a laugh erupting as she gave Kalani a hug. "Where's Liana?"

"She's circling around outside. Airport security won't let her wait at the curb for you."

They merged with the rest of the passengers surging toward the luggage depot to pick up their bags.

"How was Cancun, Alex?" Kalani's long brown hair swayed as she walked.

"Great. The beach was incredible, the food superb, and the scenery amazing. We even got a chance to visit some ruins where Kat died in a previous life."

"Are you serious?" Kalani said, surprised the normally skeptical Alex would bring up such a esoteric detail with uncharacteristic candor.

"We toured the pyramid at Chichen Itza. Have you heard about it?"

"Actually, I have. Grandma has me doing research on all the sacred places around the world, like Ayers Rock in Australia and Stonehenge in England. Chichen Itza is one of them."

"Why would Liana have you looking up information on places like those?" Kat asked curiously.

"It's a long story, Kat. It has to do with my grandfather, Kahili Kingston." Kalani looked off into the distance, reluctant to go where the conversation seemed headed. "I'll let Grandma tell you all about it."

By the time they arrived at the baggage department, luggage of every size and shape had already begun dropping onto the conveyer belt which snaked around a large designated area crammed with passengers squeezing by each other to seize and haul their bags away. Alex deftly dove through the throng, grabbed his and Kat's, and led them on their way to the curb outside where Liana spotted them and waved. She pulled in tight to an open space on the curb a few yards down and popped her trunk open for Alex to stuff their suitcases in.

"Hi, Auntie! Good to see you," Kat said, sliding in the front seat to give Liana a hug.

"Even better to see you, my dear," Liana said, happily. "Lots to tell you, Kat. Later."

The ride home was filled with the highlights of Kat and Alex's trip, but nothing of importance was said until they arrived at Kat's door, and Alex left for his home across the street.

Once Kat had greeted and hugged Caesar, she quickly ushered Liana and Kalani into the living room where they could talk.

"Okay, what's really been going on? Tell me everything," Kat demanded as they settled on the circular sofa.

"Grandpa's power to see into the future came back now that he's recovered from being kidnapped and tortured. He said he saw a powerful tsunami hit the Hawaiian islands, Kat. Hit them so hard, the wave went to the base of the mountains. No one, except for those in the highest elevations, was left alive."

"My God," Kat shuddered. "When does he think it'll happen?"

"He doesn't know, Kat," Liana said softly. "But I, too, have been seeing scenes of devastation, only it's not specific to Hawaii. It's everywhere in the world. Earthquakes, volcanoes, floods, mountains disappearing, land popping up out of the sea. It's unbelievable."

"When I was in Chichen Itza," Kat said, her eyes wide with alarm, "I heard voices from the other side telling me to listen up, so I went into alert mode. Our guide, Manuel, told us the Mayan calendar was developed so precisely they could trace back the position of the stars millions of years ago as well as anticipate what the skies would look like way into the future. Here's the thing, though: Their intricate calendar stops in December, 2012. According to Manuel, that's when some world-wide catastrophe will happen. What if the Maya were predicting the same thing you and Kahili have been seeing? What if it's part of the same phenomenon?"

Kat sat back and rested her head on the back of the sofa. She thought for a while, then blurted out, "Well, whatever it is, we need to find out who else is foreseeing these calamities. See if they're picking up any timeline so we can warn people, if need be. It'd be great to consult with more kahuna, not just the ones in Hawaii, but all around the world. Maybe we need to all come together and talk about this."

"You know how good Grandma is at divination, right, Kat? Well, my grandfather, Kahili, is pretty good, too, although how he missed my father kidnapping him, I'll never figure out. Anyway, if he says a tsunami will hit the islands, it will. The thing is, can we warn everybody in time? What if they don't believe us? Especially if we can't tell them exactly when it's supposed to happen."

Liana put her arm around Kalani's shoulders to calm her down.

"We've been given this knowledge for a reason, most likely to prepare for the devastation we may be facing. But, you're right, Kat, about getting every kahuna in the world together so we can pray together and compare notes, so to speak, we could come up with a plan to face whatever challenges may be waiting for us in the future. We need to remember nothing is ever set in stone. We're still in charge of our destiny."

Kalani leaned in toward Kat, nervously chewing her bottom lip.

"That's why Grandma had me looking up the sacred sites around the world. Maybe they hold the key to preventing this disaster or whatever it is that's going to

384

happen to us," she said, excitement and trepidation brewing within her.

Kat nodded at Liana. "So what's the bottom line here, Auntie?"

"Kahuna and other spiritually advanced people of like mind tend to gravitate to the special areas on the Earth which store an abundance of mana," Liana said, her hands now folded calmly on her lap. "If we can get in touch with the others at these places who practice Huna, or who are spiritual seekers, we can get the word out we need to come together and address this impending upheaval. What's at stake is the future of life as we know it on this planet."

"But first we need to get a handle on what exactly we're dealing with," Kat said, her logical side kicking in high gear. "We could be getting all discombobulated for something which may not won't happen for decades, or may never happen."

She took a breath and closed her eyes as if she were tuning in to a wavelength in the outer reaches of the galaxy. She shook her head and grimaced.

"Oh my God, this is bigger than I thought. I'm hearing 'Urgent' in my mind. We have to do something right away."

Liana patted Kat's knee to comfort her. "Don't panic, my dear. We have time to work on this. Otherwise we wouldn't have been warned ahead of time. The main thing to remember is not to operate out of fear. We have to act out of love. Nothing can stand in the way of the heart. Nothing. All prophecy, all thoughts of what can happen in the future can be changed. We just have to use our own discernment, speak our truth, and use our hearts. The

385

future cannot be changed by using fear. Whatever we do must come from the heart."

Kat could feel the muscle tension building up in her body fade away as the impact of Liana's words registered its truth. Kalani stopped bouncing her knees together which she did whenever she was nervous.

"You're right, Liana. No need to get uptight and stressed out. What we really need to do is a Huna prayer for guidance and understanding. Then we'll know what to do."

Suddenly Caesar, who had been stretched out on the sofa next to Kat, jumped down and ran to the front door.

"Someone's here. I think it's Alex," Kat said. "Should we ask him to join us?"

Before Kalani and Liana could say a word, the doorbell rang. Kat looked through the peep hole and saw Alex pacing on the porch.

"Hi, honey. What's up?" Kat asked, a tentative smile on her face.

"I've got to talk to you," Alex whispered. "Privately. Now."

He pulled her outside, shut the door and walked with her to her driveway. Kat could see wrinkles on his forehead begin to crease as he started to speak.

Uh oh, Kat thought. *I hope it's not another break up because he's freaked out over Huna again.*

"Something's happened to me, Kat. I was unpacking my bag and putting some things in my medicine cabinet. When I looked in the mirror, I saw colors around my head and body. Blue and salmon-orange. What's going on here? Am I losing it?"

Kat suppressed a giggle. "Not to worry, sweetie," she said. "You just noticed your aura. It's an energy field around your body. Everybody has one, only not everyone has the ability to see it."

"I can yours, too," Alex said, his mouth gaping despite his best effort to hide his perplexity. "You're blue on top and green and pink on the sides. Kind of like a trout."

Kat burst out laughing and shoved Alex playfully. "You're so funny. Listen to me, Alex. You're not alone. Kalani can see auras, too. Lots of people can. You're not going crazy. You're just becoming more psychic."

"It's hanging around you, Kat. That's why I'm changing, isn't it?"

"Probably. Since being chosen as the Huna Warrior, my vibration's speeding up and changing yours as well."

"I won't speed up so much I'll disappear, will I?

"I don't think so. Hey, want to come in? We're getting ready to do a Huna prayer, and this particular request needs all the mana we can muster. You up for it?"

"Why not? I can see auras, can't I?"

Alex gulped nervously but followed Kat into the house. Kalani and Liana greeted him warmly and scooted over on the couch to make room for him.

"Alex would like to join us tonight for our prayer."

"Good idea," Liana said with a twinkle in her eye. "This room could use a little male energy for balance, don't you think?"

387

"Kalani!" Alex said with a surprise. "You're green and blue!"

Kalani squealed with laughter. "You're peachy and blue!" she countered.

"Is this a new ability, Alex? You see auras now?" Liana asked, studying him with keen interest.

Alex shook his head in disbelief. "I don't know how or why it happened, but, yes, I can see auras now."

"He thinks it's because he's been around me so much," Kat said.

"Ah, that explains it," Kalani said. "Like attracts like."

"Or maybe it's more along the lines of 'If one be lifted, all be lifted,'" Liana said, looking at Kat for confirmation.

Kat merely smiled, then went to the kitchen to get a chair. She placed it in front of the sofa where she could face the other three. Then she filled Alex in on Kahili and Liana's prophecies of Earth changes and why they'd be praying for clarification and understanding of what to do next. While Liana covered the steps involved in the Huna prayer, Kat lit candles and turned out the lights, creating a more relaxed atmosphere in which to address their High Selves with their requests.

Twenty minutes later when they had finished, Alex was the first to speak. "Wow! That was powerful! I felt much more energy than when we walked on the beach in Cancun."

"I taught Alex how to pull in energy from the earth," Kat explained. "The difference between then and now is there are four of us praying, and the energy grows

388

exponentially when we're all asking for the same thing together."

"Okay, so what message did you get?" Kalani asked, bouncing her knees together. She was like an eager puppy ready to go for a run.

"I got confirmation about gathering everyone for a conference," Kat said. "I saw hundreds of us meeting somewhere on one of the islands in Hawaii. Liana, which island had the hurricane Iliki?"

"Kauai did. Why?"

"That's where the conference will be held, then. In Kauai.

"I heard the words 'more research' and saw a computer," Kalani said.

"I saw Luly's list growing like a huge flower with roots like a banyan tree," Liana said.

"What about you, Alex? What message did you get?"

All eyes turned to look at Alex who seemed a bit non-plussed.

"Well," he said reluctantly, "all I saw was my own computer and the initials HRI on the screen."

"HRI? Alex, remember when you did all that research on Huna after I first told you about it? HRI is the Huna Research, Inc. organization in Missouri." Kat was pleased Alex had gotten such an immediate response following his first ever Huna prayer.

"Looks like we have a plan. Kalani, get on my computer in the office down the hall and see what you can find out about 2012 or the Mayan calendar. Liana, use my phone and call your cousin, Luly in Hawaii. See how she's doing with the list of kahuna living in Hawaii. She and her son will need to expand the list to include as many kahuna as possible in other states and in other countries, for that matter. Alex, you can contact the folks at HRI and see what they sense about 2012 and what resources and ideas they can share with us for bringing Huna practitioners into this. I bet they have a huge database of "Hunatics" who can help us. I'm going to put some water on for tea. Looks like it's going to be one of those long nights."

Kat headed for the kitchen, Caesar trailing her in hopes of a treat, meowing all the way.

Chapter 49

"I should have known he wouldn't be stupid enough to come back here," Hukui muttered to himself as he waited impatiently at his childhood home in Makawao, Maui.

He had been recuperating from being hit by the van as he tried to persuade Kalani to come back to Hawaii with him. His leg had been broken in three places, and a surgical pin was now holding his right hip together, putting his career as a diving instructor at the University of Hawaii on hold. When he got out of the hospital, he took the first plane he could book and jetted home. Kahili had disappeared from the old stone temple by the time Hukui had the capacity to check on him. From the looks of the chains, Kahili had help getting away.

"Wonder who found him? Well, it doesn't matter. He would have starved to death by the time I got back, so it's good someone got to him first. He won't be of any use to me dead. He's sure putting a strong shield around himself. No clue where he might be."

Hukui sighed. Talking out loud to himself felt pathetic, but the sound of his own voice, at least during the day, was all he had heard for the past two weeks. He didn't dare put a radio or television on for fear the noise or light would alert someone of his presence. The old, wooden house was set away from the main road, surrounded by fields of sugar cane, in the back country of

Hawaii. Every day the mailman came to drop mail through a slot in the door, but no one else approached during the time Hukui had been in hiding.

"I'm running out of food here, and it doesn't look like Father will show up any time soon. Better get back to my apartment and take care of business from there. Damn, I'm sick of these!"

Hukui threw his crutches down, his armpits sore from the pressure of his weight on the pads. He plopped down on the rug in the foyer of the house where Kahili's mail had been piling up and began to sort the pieces, bills on one side, letters the other. He stopped when he found a thick, cream colored envelope and carefully unsealed it.

"Well, what do we have here?" he said with a sneer. "An invitation of some kind."

He read from the card: "You are invited to attend a ceremony on June 9 to honor the late Leilani Kingston whose ashes will be scattered at sea. Meet at Pier 11, Honolulu Harbor, at 10:00 a.m. RSVP: 808-555-1895."

Hukui stuffed the invitation back in its envelope, licked the flap on the parts that still had glue and resealed the envelope. He mixed up the mail, shaping it into a random pile again, then retrieved his crutches and struggled to stand.

"This will work out better than I thought. No doubt Kalani and Liana will be there. Along with the so-called Huna Warrior. We'll have a great reunion, won't we, Father? I can't wait to see your face when I tell you how I killed Kat Romero."

The sound of Hukui's malicious laughter echoed through the house as he limped down the hallway to his bedroom to pack his belongings in a duffel bag he'd brought. Then he checked the other rooms to see if he had inadvertently left anything in them. His last stop was Kahili's office. As he entered the room, a strong energy web coated his skin. He gasped for breath and leaned against the door frame. The room was spinning, and he felt like he was suffocating. He backed up into the hallway and leaned against the wall until his head cleared.

"What was that?" he said aloud. "Did you put an energy shield around these walls, Father? It wasn't here when I looked in this room a few days ago, so you are alive and well after all, aren't you? Which means there's something in here you don't want me to find."

Hukui shook off the effects of the force field that pervaded the room, took a deep breath and barged in anyway, sending his own mana ahead of himself to clear the room. He yanked open the closet door. Nearly empty. He went to Kahili's desk and thumbed through the papers sitting in a metal bin. Nothing. Then he began pulling out the desk drawers, one by one, dumping their contents on the floor but found only standard office supplies. When he emptied the bottom drawer, though, he found an envelope taped to the underside of the drawer. It was from his father and addressed to him.

"Dear Hukui,

If you're reading this, you have broken the protective seal put in the room. You've broken my heart as well. But you haven't broken my spirit. I'm still here. You may not think I love you, but I do, Hukui. Even after all you've done to me. I still love you, the old Hukui, the real Hukui. I always have.

I may not have shown it because I was so absorbed in my own life and calling. For that I ask your forgiveness. If I could take back all the hurt I caused you, I would. I never intended to hurt you, but I realize now how much I ignored you as a child and how painful that was for you. I've never told you the real reason for my behavior, but here it is. You are not my biological child, Hukui. Your mother was already carrying you when I met her. I married her not long after meeting her and tried to raise you as my own. I can see now what a terrible job I did as a parent.

Listen to me, Hukui. You were never meant to learn the magic. My po'e Aumakua told me never to teach you the magic. They knew you'd misuse it. There are always bad consequences when that happens. Please understand, this is not a threat. This is the truth. You have heard of the saying, *What goes around, comes around.* When you use the ancient rituals to do evil things, that evil will come back to you. The prayer to murder someone only generates death to the person who sends it. Look at me. I used the 'ana 'ana to help your dying mother because I couldn't stand to see her suffer anymore. And as a result, you came to kill me. What you think of others becomes your prayer for yourself first.

You say you want to be the most dominant kahuna in the world. Why? For power? Control? Ask yourself this:

Why did you come into existence in the first place? To learn a lesson. If you came in to cause chaos in other people's lives, then you came in to learn the lesson of the purpose of control. Since our life on this earth is to learn balance, you came in to *be controlled* in some way. Don't you get it? If you continue down your path of destruction, you will be destroyed. Is that the lesson you came here to learn? I don't think so, Hukui. I think you came here to learn how to love. Just like the rest of us. I have learned many lessons in my lifetime. One of them being I didn't show you enough love. But believe me when I tell you I love you. The question is: Do you love yourself?

It's not too late to take stock of yourself and turn toward the light. You have been getting your power from darkness, but that's never going to serve you well, Hukui. That's never going to give you the peace you're seeking. Give your power to the light, and things will change for you. It's never too late."

Hukui wadded the letter up and threw it across the room. "Yes, it is, Father," he bellowed. "It's too late for me. And you. And the Huna Warrior. We have a date with destiny."

Hukui gathered his things and stormed out of the house.

Chapter 50

The excitement was palpable as Kat looked out over the sea of faces at Anthony High's first graduation ceremony. The football stadium was packed with proud parents, relatives and friends of the class of 2006. Balloon bouquets, leis, flower corsages, sequined mortarboards, homemade posters and painted banners, confetti, and streamers created a mosaic of color for the big event.

Something's going to go terribly wrong tonight, Kat thought, sitting with the rest of the faculty near the portable stage erected for the graduation ceremony. *But what? I've rehearsed these kids so much they could do this in their sleep. The band is ready, the board members are all here, and nobody brought their boa constrictor to pass around for kicks. The people in the stands aren't too rowdy. What is it?*

At a signal from Principal Stafford, the music director cued the band to play "Pomp and Circumstance." The crowd went wild as the graduating seniors filed in through a side entrance and marched out two by two to take their seats on the field. Some of the students fought with the wind to keep their caps from flying away, but their orderly procession prevailed until all the students were seated.

Kat tuned out when the speeches started, just like the rest of the audience may have, she suspected. She was preoccupied with a million other concerns launched by the disturbing results of research done by her "HW team" —

Kalani, Liana, Alex— on the subject of the Mayan calendar and its end date of December 2012. That topic led them into looking up a host of other subjects known in various terms as the Ascension, the Harvest, and the End Time. Their sources ranged from psychics to authors and scientists; their readings were found on the web and in printed books and in magazines. Source after source were predicting the same thing: the end of the world, as we know it, sometime in the early part of the 21st century. The urgent need for an international meeting of kahuna and other Huna practitioners resonated in every part of Kat's being.

The mounds of information her team uncovered staggered Kat. According to some sources, every 26,000 years, the Earth has changed its orbit. Whether it was due to solar storms or the earth's erratic heartbeat releasing vast amounts of heat from deep within, the earth's core and crust will be soon experiencing drastic changes. A contingency of authors, psychics, and scientists were all predicting a major change in the Earth's axis of rotation. Since the distribution of large masses on the surface of the planet will also shift, new lands will rise, as existing lands will sink or be altered during earthquakes, floods, and tsunamis. The human and animal population of the earth will be greatly reduced. A change in the magnetic field of the earth will result in the north and south poles reversing, a switch that hasn't occurred for 780,000 years. Because the planet will occupy a different orbit, there will be two stars functioning as twin suns in Earth's skies.

What irony, she thought, staring at the graduates as they began their own ascension up the steps of the stage to receive their diplomas. *They think their lives are just beginning, and they have all the time in the world to achieve their goals. But time may be shorter than they know.*

The good news is our kahuna conference is set for the weekend after next. If the group determines this is really the end time, then we've got to come up with a plan to warn the world, get people to believe us, try to minimize the repercussions of the earth's tilting, prepare for the worst, and pray for the best. Humanity can't be flushed away like a bad experiment thrown down the drain. Can it?

Memories of horrific, heart-wrenching disaster scenes from the aftermath of Hurricane Katrina suddenly surfaced in Kat's mind. She closed her eyes at the painful thought of so many of her fellow Americans crying out in anguish for help which was shamefully slow in coming.

The government was given a study years before on the ramifications of a possible hurricane hitting the New Orleans area. It was ignored. Just like Katrina, our scientists have known about the changing weather patterns, increases in flooding and tsunamis, more earthquakes than ever before, especially here in California, but the media squashes so much of the news. Last week alone there were 746 earthquakes in California, but only five were reported in the newspapers. Wonder if it's a cover-up of some....

Kat's stream of worry ended abruptly as her attention snapped toward the stage where Rosalind Jacarro had just thrown off her cap and gown and was standing nude in all her glory, naval and nipple piercing, notwithstanding. Deafening noise erupted from the crowd as Rosalind turned around to display the '06 figures painted on her derriere. Then she grabbed her diploma case and raced toward the stadium parking lot where a carload of friends were waiting to speed her away. The entire incident lasted about thirty seconds, but was enough to permanently destroy any sense of dignity or decorum the ceremony was supposed to have. While the students howled with laughter, high-fived each other and gyrated gleefully in their rows, parents screamed in outrage and covered the eyes of their small children. Shocked grandparents and older relatives voiced their deep disappointment in the younger generation. The ensuing disruption crushed Kat. She diverted her eyes and groaned in disgust.

Serge waited until the buzz died down to resume handing out diplomas, but the stunt had proven to be such a shocking debacle, the noise level remained high throughout the night. After what seemed an eternity, the ceremony ended, the crowd filtered out, and the lights were finally turned off. One parent chewed Serge out, tears streaming down his face, saying he had waited twelve years to hear his son's name read at graduation, but because of Rosalind's obscene behavior, he couldn't hear a thing. He demanded the school hold another ceremony since this one had turned out to be such a disgrace.

Kat and the rest of the staff walked out of the stadium, dejected and humiliated that one of their students had turned what was supposed to have been a time-honored tradition into a jeering circus. They would learn later, to everyone's dismay, the event had been videotaped and shown repeatedly on local TV newscasts with Rosalind's private parts blurred or digitally covered up.

Kat felt strangely responsible since she had been in charge of the graduation ceremony, and, instead of leaving the stadium in triumph and congratulating students and parents afterwards, she rushed away, eyes on the ground, head hung in shame. Sean caught up to her and put a protective arm around her shoulder as she hurried to the staff parking lot.

"I knew something bad was going to happen tonight, Sean, but, for the life of me, I never expected this!" Kat fumed, still reeling in anger from Rosalind's escapade. "How could she do this to us?"

Sean shook his head and squeezed her shoulders tightly. "You can't take it personally, Mom. I talked to some of Rosalind's friends just now and found out she did it because she wanted to make her graduation something she'd never forget."

"Well, she did that, now, didn't she?" Kat said, her lips pressed tight with tension. "But what a selfish thing to do! She made a mockery of the whole occasion. It was so disrespectful to her classmates and such an embarrassment to the staff. Her parents must be mortified."

"That's just it," Sean said confidentially. "Her mom was in on it. She encouraged her from the get-go to do something outrageous. Who do you think painted the numbers on her rear end?"

Kat was speechless. She rolled her eyes, took a deep breath, said good night to her son, and sped away in her car, for once getting out of the faculty parking lot before anyone else.

When she got home, the light was blinking on her answering machine. She dreaded punching in the play button because she felt it wouldn't be something she wanted to hear. She was right. It was from the superintendent, requesting her presence in a meeting first thing in the morning to discuss Anthony High's graduation fiasco and how to handle the press since the story seemed to be going national. Phone calls were trickling in from the major networks with requests for immediate interviews with Rosalind, her parents, and the school staff.

Great, she thought dejectedly. *He's probably going to blame me for tonight's "Rosalind Bares Her Soul and More" show. Who would have thought that sweet little Rosalind could be so self-centered and devious, especially after Mazie saved her butt from Rudy's bullets? Wasn't that memorable enough? By the way, my spiritual buddies on The Other Side—I could have used some help from you guys. A warning...a vision...anything in advance would have been useful, you know? My job's at stake here!*

Kat met with Sean first thing the next day to get more inside details on Rosalind's stunt, then drove to the district office for her meeting with Superintendent Purcell. Along the way she said some prayers and put a shield of protection around herself before she stepped into his office. Her heart leapt in her chest when she saw the others invited to the meeting: four of the five board members, two assistant superintendents, the PTSA president, and Principal Serge Stafford.

Looks like all the big guns are here to take pot shots at me, she thought miserably. *And maybe they should. I should have prepared better, but I've had so much on my mind, I just wasn't focused on all the things which could go wrong.*

401

Serge signaled to Kat to sit by him as Purcell walked in, followed by his secretary carrying a steno pad. The superintendent looked around the room, smiling grimly as he cleared his throat to speak.

"I think we all know what happened last night at Anthony's High's graduation ceremony," Purcell began in his usual gravelly voice. "Hell, most of the country, if not the world, knows about it by now. It's the most shocking disruption at a school event I've ever heard of. The question is, how did it happen and how can we prevent something like that from happening again? My phone's been ringing non-stop. I've even gotten calls from three of the national news networks, not to mention all the local TV and radio stations. I've got to tell the media something proactive."

He looked toward Serge and Kat and waited expectantly for an explanation. Kat, in turn, waited for a nod from Serge before she answered.

"From what I've been able to gather, Rosalind Jacarro planned this disruption weeks ago, at her mother's encouragement to make her graduation something she'd remember for the rest of her life. In fact, her mother was responsible for painting the ' 06 on her rear end."

Kat watched the shocked reactions on the faces around the room and waited until their murmurs died down before she continued.

"Right before the ceremony, I lined the students up in the cafeteria and checked to make sure they were all properly dressed and hadn't hidden any water balloons, rodents or other objectionable items underneath their robes. At that point everything seemed okay. In fact, I remember Rosalind was wearing a tube top and a skirt. I had no idea she'd wiggle out of them before going up onto the stage."

"So the other students must have known she was doing this. Those around her must have seen what she was up to, right?" Purcell asked, pulling on his moustache.

"Right, they were all in on it, and you know how kids are—loyal to each other. They'd never rat her out to any adults, and we had no clue she'd be the type of person who'd ever dream up something like this. In short, we were ambushed by Rosalind Jacarro."

Kat looked with sincerity around the room, appealing to the group's sense of reason and hoping they would not blame her for actions that were unforeseen.

"Well, I'll tell you one thing," PTSA President Becky Farnsworth piped up. "It's a good thing we have the policy to mail their diplomas home to them after the ceremony and their diploma cases were empty. But in Rosalind's case? I think we should insist she and her mother come before the school board to get her diploma in person and answer for her contemptible behavior. We can't withhold the diploma as punishment, though, can we?"

"Unfortunately, no," Purcell answered, shaking his head. "She passed all of the requirements and earned her diploma, so we have to give it to her. However, I agree she should have to face us first and apologize before we hand it over to her. I'm sure all of us would like to say a few words to her before she disappears from our lives altogether. I can't believe one student could have generated so much local and national press about our district—all of it bad. We're the laughing stock around here."

"I've been getting a lot of requests from parents to hold another ceremony," Serge said, wringing his hands unconsciously. "But I don't see how that can happen. School's out, and kids have scattered to the four winds."

"Right you are," Purcell drawled. "That's not going to happen. Tell those parents I said so." He straightened his bolero tie which had a tendency to coil, then looked sternly at each member of the group seated around the conference table, holding a longer gaze at Kat than the others.

"It's imperative we get this episode behind us as soon as possible," Purcell continued. "Remember, any and all calls from the media must be directed to my office. I'm trying to squelch the negative press that seems to be occurring so much lately. First, there was the unfortunate demise of Rudy Baker and now this graduation farce."

Kat's cheeks flushed as many in the room glanced furtively in her direction. She looked down at her lap, suddenly interested in cleaning a spot of food that had splattered on her skirt.

"Kat," Purcell said, his eyes like pinpricks on a wrinkled map, "what do you plan to do differently next year if you're in charge of graduation? How can something like this be prevented?"

Kat straightened in her chair and took a deep breath. *If? Was that a veiled threat,* she wondered. *Could I get fired over something I couldn't help?*

"Well, it's hard to predict what high jinx our kids will think of for next year," Kat said, grinning nervously to

404

lighten the mood, "but we could check the students twice, first in the cafeteria and then right before they get their diplomas. Maybe we could have them go through a doorway of some sort so the screening process can be kept private immediately before they go on stage. We'll have to let the students and parents know ahead of time and in writing, though, what specifically would disqualify them from participating in the ceremony and crossing the stage."

"Good idea," Becky said, smiling at Kat. "It's hard to anticipate all the crazy things our kids will want to do next year just to top this one, but I think Kat's on the right track. It wasn't her fault. She's not a mind-reader."

I could kiss you for that, Becky, Kat thought.

Glaring at Becky for siding with Kat, Purcell nodded reluctantly, then added, "Are there any other ideas any of you would like to share?"

Then, after a few seconds of what seemed like interminable silence, Serge spoke up.

"Assuming Kat's idea works," he said softly, "there really isn't too much more to be done. We just need to be on our toes and have antennas out for rumors of a repeat performance. Last night really came out of the blue and was so over the top and ludicrous, it still seems like a bad dream. Anyway, I can't promise something like that will never happen again. But I can tell you we'll take every precaution against history repeating itself."

"Good," Purcell said, rising to indicate the meeting was over. "That's it for now, unless anyone has anything else to add."

No one did and everyone quickly filed out of the room.

Whew! Kat thought. *That was easier than I thought it'd be.* She grabbed her purse and shoved in her chair before trying to exit the crowded room.

"Kat? Can I see you a second?" Purcell asked just before she got away.

Oh no. Here it comes. I knew it wasn't over.

"I didn't want to say this in front of the others, but in the past year you've been an administrator with us, the most bizarre incidents have happened at Anthony High. How do you account for that?"

Purcell squinted his eyes at Kat to study her, his lips and jaw jutting out like a horse reaching through a fence to get an apple.

"I really can't speculate on that, Dr. Purcell," Kat said, holding her head up and facing him confidently. "I've never had anything like either of those events happen to me before. I agree with you, they were truly bizarre."

"Yes, and the news media jumped all over them to discredit our district. I had plans to move into a county position soon, but with this negative coverage and the criticism I've come under lately, my colleagues are wondering what the hell is happening to my district and if they should still take a chance on me. Now it's strange to me both of those freakish things happened in proximity to you. You are the common denominator to both events. I can only conclude you must have brought these things with you, like some kind of dust cloud. You get where I'm going with this?"

"I think so," Kat said softly, her heart sinking in her chest.

"A word of warning. One more of these fiascos, and you're through in this district as an administrator, got it? You'll be back in the classroom so fast it'll make your head spin. Now get out of here and get back to work!"

Kat drove back to the high school in tears. She pounded the steering wheel in frustration. As if Mother Nature sympathized with her misery, a light rain began to fall, forcing her to turn on her windshield wipers.

That was so unfair, she thought, incensed at being threatened with demotion. *Is that how they treat their first-year administrators? Granted, being the Huna Warrior does bring its challenges, but how am I responsible for Rosalind's behavior? They warned me when I became involved in Huna, everything would fall apart first before it got better. Old patterns had to break before new ones got established, they said. So does that mean I just forfeit the job, go back to living in an apartment, and forget about my dreams of bettering my life?*

When Kat returned to her desk, there was an urgent message from Liana waiting on her recorder.

What now, she thought. *I can't take any more bad news. Why did I ever become an administrator? The problem with the educational system is that in order to rise up in the ranks, teachers have to give up something they're good at, like teaching, and then use an entirely different set of skills as administrators. Programmed failure.*

They lied to us in graduate school, making us believe they were preparing us well. But how do you get ready for a bomb suddenly detonating in your face? They told us to have nerves of steel and be armed for battle, but that advice didn't work. It takes fluidity and flexibility to withstand the onslaught of being an administrator. So what if I've doubled my salary? I can't remember the last time I had any fun. In the words of my linguistically challenged students, it's beginning to suck.

Kat punched the button to hear Liana's message. *Hukui broke into Kahili's house and opened his mail. He knows about Leilani's memorial service. Now what do we do?*

Good question, Liana, Kat thought glumly. *Good question.*

As Kat got up to adjust the blinds in her office window, she glanced down at her terra cotta soldier, standing firm, eyes knitted in a frown, giving her the answer she needed at the moment. Stand firm. Be calm. Gather the troops. You're not alone. The plan will all fall together, and you will be victorious.

I hope you're right, little man. I hope you're right.

Chapter 51

The following week Kat, Henry, Liana, Alex and Kalani were on a chartered boat in Oahu. The sea water splashed playfully over the sides of a 27-foot cruiser as it bounded out of the harbor at Pearl City. The early morning sun shone brightly on the spray, creating tiny rainbows in the air. Kat breathed in the briny air, enjoying the ride but trying to put herself in a solemn frame of mind for the scattering of Leilani's ashes at sea.

Kat looked over at Liana and blew a kiss toward her diminutive aunt who was clutching her carry-on bag protectively. Liana had lovingly wrapped and stored an urn containing Leilani's remains which she intended to offer to the goddess, Ka'ahupahau today. She smiled back at Kat, happy to be out on the ocean as well. It was a pleasant reminder of childhood days of summers spent with her father, Hui, a prominent fisherman and diver. Just before going on a dive for oysters, Liana would often help Hui throw into the water beautiful orange blossoms of the 'ilima which were sacred to the goddess.

"Are you thinking of your promise to her father?" Kat asked Liana who was staring in reverence at the turquoise water.

"How did you know?" she said, chuckling at her niece's perception.

"What promise was that, Liana?" Alex asked, always interested in learning any new tidbit about Kat's family.

"I made a promise to my father, Hui, to honor the goddess, Ka'ahupahau. When I was young, he told me the story of the goddess who was once human and how she and her son were transformed into "good" sharks. My father and some of his friends used to take care of these "good" sharks in Pearl Harbor. They'd feed them and look after them in exchange for protection from the other sharks. Hui never forgot to pay homage to the goddess, and you know what? He never got attacked by any of the sharks there, and, believe me, there were many. I saw them with my own eyes. But he trusted he'd be protected. We always thought of sharks as part of our family Aumakua or divine ancestors. So it seems the sensible thing to do is to offer Leilani's ashes to Ka'ahupahau in exchange for our safe-keeping."

"You never cease to amaze me, Liana," Alex said, appreciatively, looking around at the group one by one. "I'd like to write that story up some time, if you don't mind."

"I'd like that, Alex," Liana replied, smiling benevolently at him. "You certainly have my permission."

I'm so glad he likes my family, Kat thought, and they seem to like him. He makes a nice fit. Speaking of fit, I hope I make it into my dress for Sean's wedding. But how can I lose five pounds in two days? Especially in Hawaii....

Soon Kat, like the rest of the entourage, became lost in thought as the boat sped on. Fifteen minutes later, the engine slowed down to a sudden crawl, and the captain, a deeply tanned Hawaiian who had kept to himself the whole trip, approached Liana, calling her attention to a particular section of the ocean.

410

"This area right in here is a pretty good shark feeding zone," he said gruffly. "If you want, I could chum the area and see if any sharks appear. That way you'll see Ka'ahupahau and her *ohana* up close when you give them your daughter's ashes."

Liana turned to Kat for approval before nodding to the captain.

"If any of you want to help me throw these in," he said, pointing to a steel container of fish, "be my guest."

Kalani and Alex, eager to do some physical exercise after sitting for the long boat ride, jumped up to volunteer their help. They took turns throwing the fish in different directions so that the boat was surrounding by floating carcasses. Within minutes, Kat spotted the first shark fin.

"Look! Over there!" she shouted, pointing out the starboard side of the boat.

Her heart raced with excitement and fear as she and the others watched the shark speeding to its prey, then snapping furiously at the chunks of fish with its spiked teeth, thrashing wildly from side to side.

That was quick, she thought, unexpectedly nervous. *I don't care if they are part of my family. They still scare the heck out of me.*

Suddenly Alex saw two sharks approaching from the port side of the boat.

"Oh, wow, two more are coming this way," he yelled. "And more just to the right of them. We have a regular shark convention going on, folks."

"Okay, Liana, looks like Ka'ahupahau is here. Are you ready to do it, sister?" Henry helped pull her up from her seat.

411

"I'm ready, brother," Liana said.

She pulled the urn out of her bag, took off the lid and climbed up on the padded seat for added height while Kat grabbed her legs to keep her steady. Just as she began to shake the ashes out, the boat began to rock violently back and forth as if a sudden storm had focused all of its raging force on the small craft. Liana and Kat began falling, almost in slow motion, into the hull of the boat. Alex leaped out toward them to cushion the blow of their fall, and the three ended up in a tangle as the boat continued to pitch. Henry grabbed Kalani to prevent her from going over the side, and all of them looked at the captain for help. He was the reason for the boat rocking. He was intentionally yanking on the wheel erratically, turning it first one way, then another, saying nothing. Finally, he turned around so that they could see his face which was filled with a malicious sneer.

"What's going on, Kat?" Alex asked, blinking sea water from his eyes and looking around. "There's no storm out here. What's wrong with the boat?"

Kat simply pointed with her chin at the captain whose face was disintegrating before their eyes. A prosthetic cheek drooped off the right side of his chin while he pulled fake caps off his front teeth and ripped off his bushy eyebrows.

"Better yet, what's wrong with him?" Kat said, barely able to breathe.

Alex's eyes grew wide with fear.

"Who in the hell is he?" Alex demanded.

"Meet my father, Hukui Kingston," Kalani said, glaring at Hukui through her sunglasses. She shot Hukui a bolt of mana to his solar plexus, the equivalent of a punch in the stomach, hoping to throw him off balance.

Hukui merely laughed, unfazed and even amused by his daughter's feeble attempt at combat.

"You're no match for me, Kalani, so quit trying," Hukui said. "None of you are. Not even the great Huna Warrior."

He nodded at Kat who was now back on her feet, arms akimbo, staring at the man who had become her enemy over the past few months.

"At last we meet," Hukui said with a smirk.

"Oh, I've seen you before, Hukui," Kat said, her chin high in defiance. She smoothed back the hair that had fallen in her eyes so she could face him directly. She was good at sizing people up, and what she saw in Hukui brought back memories of Rudy Baker's cume folder. *Ruthless. Disconnected from humanity. Feels no remorse.*

"You've been my worst nightmare for several months now, Hukui," Kat said, realizing he was more formidable than she had first thought. "What an imagination you have—a house warming gift of a poisonous shell, Halloween trick-or-treating, not to mention glowing eyes in my hallway. I'll give you an A for creativity, though, when you possessed Rudy Baker."

"You're very observant, Teach," Hukui said with a malevolent grin. "But it looks like you've underestimated me. Bet you never thought you'd see me today."

Hukui reached into a side compartment, pulled a life vest out and put it on.

"I've got to hand it to you there, pal," Kat replied lightly. "You've outwitted the Huna Warrior. So what's

413

next on your "To Do" list? Oh, let me guess. You think you're going to be the number one kahuna in the world, and, in order to do that, you have to get rid of me, right?"

"Wrong!" Hukui bellowed. "In order to do that, I have to get rid of all of you!"

Hukui reached into a box near his feet and pulled out a gallon of gasoline he had hidden earlier. He opened the gas can and dumped its contents in front of him. It sloshed at his feet and ran menacingly toward the center of the boat where Kat, Alex, and Liana were standing. Kalani and Henry climbed up on the seat and clung to the railing. Alex tried to pull Kat and Liana with him as he jumped to the nearest seat, but they both stood their ground in the center of the boat.

"Dad, no!" Kalani screamed. "You're not gonna get away with this!"

"Why not?" Hukui retorted. "No one's stopped me so far."

"Why did you send the knife to Leilani? You knew she was in a weakened state of mind. Which you probably created from the start. Why did you kill my daughter?" Liana demanded, her usually soft voice forceful and sharp.

"She was a guinea pig to practice telepathy and teleportation on. I had her wedding ring, so I used the aka cords on it to send the message for her to do herself in. Then I materialized the knife. I didn't know she'd actually do it. I just wanted to test my power."

"The death wish you send to others is what you wish for yourself," Kat said, eyes narrowed as she glowered at Hukui. "Kalani's right. You'll never get away with this."

"Nothing you can say will change me, and nothing you can do can stop me!" Hukui snarled.

"Kat, do something!" Alex yelled, desperation in his voice. "You can't just roll over and play dead with this guy."

Kat pursed her lips and shook her head so minutely he almost missed it. It was her signal to him not to interfere.

Alex looked around at Liana, Henry and Kalani whose faces registered a stoic intensity, but, oddly enough, not the sheer panic he was wrestling with.

"Let him go, Alex," Kat said coldly, her usually expressive face blank. "He's won. He's the world's greatest kahuna."

"The hell he is," Alex growled and started toward Hukui, but Kat put her arm out to hold him back.

"Check out his aura, Alex," she whispered in a raspy voice. "And have some faith in me."

Hukui had opened a hatch door and pulled a deflated rubber raft out. He tied the rope that was attached to the raft on to a grommet on the side of the boat and tossed the raft over the side. Then he bent over to pull the plug that would automatically inflate the raft. Within seconds, he was sitting in it, his hand poised in readiness to release the rope from the boat. Two oars were propped up in the back of the raft for his getaway.

"Come on, Kat," Hukui taunted. "You disappoint me. You're not even trying to stop me. What kind of Huna Warrior are you, anyway?"

He pulled a lighter out of his pocket and flicked it until a flame was lit.

415

"Well, it's been fun. Bon voyage, losers!" he yelled.

Hukui untied the raft's rope from the boat, pushed off with an oar and tossed his burning lighter into the boat. Then he rowed quickly away, his eyes glued to the cruiser, fully expecting it to explode any minute. After a few seconds of silence, he stared confusedly at the craft which was still intact. Where was the fire? What about the explosion? Kat and the others were standing unharmed. She was laughing and whispering an explanation to Alex who was still trying to piece together what just had happened.

Leaning over the side of the boat, Kat shouted, "Who's the loser now, Hukui? Kahili can see into the future, remember? He told us what you'd be up to. He's also still a master at creating smells, making the water you poured in here smell just like gasoline. You really shouldn't have messed with your father. By the way, Liana and I did the shark ceremony for Leilani *yesterday*. Bye, bye, sailor!"

Kat waved at him as she started up the engine and swung the boat around. She put the engine on full throttle and sped away, leaving Hukui to bounce around in its wake.

He sat stiffly in the raft, dumbfounded, staring at the silhouette of the cruiser as it bounded back toward Pearl Harbor.

"Why didn't I think to put up an energy shield so Kahili couldn't read my mind?" he said out loud. "How could I have been so stupid? And what did she mean by *yesterday*? Oh, crap! If they're protected by the shark family, that means ...."

416

He shuddered as he spotted three sharks circling nearby. Using all of the strength he could muster, he plied the oars and concentrated on making it to shore.

"Come on, Hukui," he shouted to himself. "You can do this! It's not that far. Come on, man! You can't let a shark get you! You're the toughest kahuna there is."

After a few minutes the muscles in his arms started to burn, but he kept pushing on, sweat pouring down his face and arms. Without sunglasses which had fallen out of his shirt pocket as he had jumped into the raft, the sun's glare off the water made it hard for him to scan for shark fins, but he was vigilant, turning periodically to look around as he bore down on the oars. When, at last, it appeared the sharks were finally gone, he stopped to take a break and massage his tense neck and shoulder muscles.

Once he felt renewed circulation in his arms, he started up again, determined to get to shore. He closed his eyes to concentrate on locking into a rhythm with the oars. He didn't see the Tiger shark come up aggressively out of the water, looking at him with flat, dead eyes, before dropping down and coming up under the opposite side of the raft, pushing it high into the air. The impact popped Hukui into the air. He looked like a rodeo rider as he struggled to hang on to the oars and not fall out of the slippery rubber raft. He threw his weight to one side of the raft to counter-balance the attack.

"Get away from me, goddammit!" he screamed at the shark. "I'm not afraid of you!"

The raft landed with a thud back into the water. Frantically, Hukui rowed away from the shark, its fin still skimming the surface of the water. He could see some

417

sagging in the raft where the shark had torn a tiny hole in the rubber. As the air leaked out, water began to splash over the weakened side of the raft. Within minutes the water was up to his ankles, but it didn't register with Hukui. He kept his eyes on the island ahead of him and focused only on a safe landing.

"Gotta get home," he said. "Come on, man. You can do it!"

He gained some ground, but the shark returned and butted the raft again, this time with such a jolt that Hukui slipped from his seat and landed on his back on the bottom of the water-sodden boat. Enraged, he struggled to stand, then grabbed an oar with both hands and held it over the water. He waited until a dark shadow appeared under the oar. When the shark lunged to bite it, Hukui smacked it across the nose which such force, it split the oar in half.

"Take that, you bastard!" he roared, throwing the broken oar at his predator.

He watched in triumph as the shark sank back in the water and retreated into the ocean depths.

"Leilani and her family sent you after me, but nothing can stop Hukui Kingston!" he whooped. "Not the Huna Warrior. Not you. Not anything or anybody!"

He breathed a big sigh of relief and rested his head in his arms, feeling his energy return before taking up the remaining oar. The drag in the water increased, though, and no matter how hard he rowed, he didn't seem to be getting anywhere.

In frustration, Hukui threw the oar overboard and then dove into the water, abandoning the raft altogether.

418

He headed for shore with strong and practiced strokes from years of swimming and diving competitions. The water was relatively calm, land was in sight, and the adrenaline surging through his body made him feel invincible. He was fast approaching the coral reef formation which was a natural barrier against sharks.

"No one, not even the Huna Warrior, gets the better of me!" he yelled out.

He threw his body toward the shore and visualized landing safely on the beach and making it home. The beach would be warm and inviting glove which would hold his fatigued body in a loving, cupped hand. Afterwards, he'd make it back to his apartment somehow where he could rest and figure out a new plan to defeat the Huna Warrior. As he pictured himself reaching out to strangle Kat, the specter of Leilani stepped in front of her to take her place. He tried to shake the image, but Leilani remained in his mind's eye, looking at him with pity. She was talking to him, but he couldn't hear her. He tried to read her lips.

"What the hell are you saying?" he muttered. "I ...forgive... you? I don't get it, Leilani. I sent you the knife. I convinced you take your own life. How can you forgive me when I can't forgive myself?"

Hukui, wrapped up in the vision of Leilani, never sensed the second shark that swam up behind him, attracted by the motion of his legs as they pumped through the water. He didn't feel the first bite. It felt more like a strong undercurrent pulling him under. His life jacket bobbed him back to the top, but the second bite was strong, ripping his left leg to shreds, leaving only bone exposed. Blood pooled around him as he stared out in shock.

"Leilani, get him away from me! Please! I'm sorry! I'm so sorry!" he sobbed, flailing his arms weakly, still trying to swim to shore. "This isn't how my life is supposed to end. I'm the greatest kahuna in the world!"

Hukui lost consciousness as the shark tore off the other leg, twisting his body in angry rhythms of destiny. His bobbing torso was soon caught up in the grip of a strong undertow which deposited his remains onto an isolated beach a few hours after Kat and her party had landed safely back at Pearl Harbor. The relentless waves slapped at him, pushing his face into the sand in mocking punishment.

Chapter 52

Sean and Chelsea posed happily on their wedding day next to the fourteen-foot statue of King Kamehameha as the photographer searched for just the right angle for a perfect picture. A lei of maile and ilima flowers adorned Sean's neck. He wore a traditional white, long-sleeve, Hawaiian shirt and white pants. Chelsea looked radiant in her *holoku*, a white formal version of the muumuu. Instead of a veil, she wore a woven garland of island flowers, a *haku* lei, around her head and carried a bouquet of white orchids.

To everyone's relief, their ceremony had gone off smoothly near a rugged cliff of black lava rocks on the beach front of the GrandWailea Resort in Maui. Theirs was a sunrise wedding with a setting so breath-taking, no one objected to its early start. Chelsea's parents, brother, and an assortment of friends and relatives had arrived the night before and, like Kat and Alex, were staying at the Grand Wailea, while Henry, Liana, and Kalani had been invited to stay with relatives in Kihei, a few miles away.

The sumptuous grounds of the hotel afforded a dramatic backdrop for the wedding: majestic waterfalls, colorful koi ponds, lush gardens, bronze statues of Hawaiian dancers, and tropical flowers everywhere. When the photographer had finally exhausted the exterior scenic spots, the wedding party headed for a reception at the Japanese restaurant housed in the hotel.

"If I have to be in one more photo, my lips are going to freeze into a permanent smile," Alex whispered to Kat as they walked hand in hand over a Japanese bridge which covered one of the koi ponds. Kat stopped to admire a bright orange-and black-speckled fish which seemed to be following her, its mouth open for a treat.

"Mine, too. But I don't mind. It's a perfect day, and they both looked so happy," Kat said, holding her hand out to the fish. "Look how tame they are, Alex. Like you can reach out and pet them."

"They're hoping you'll feed them," Alex said, pulling a packet of fish food he'd gotten from the hotel staff out of his pocket. "Here you go, fella."

Alex tossed a small pellet at the fish which gobbled it quickly as a swarm of other koi surfaced around it. "Watch this, Kat," Alex said as he scattered the rest of the food all out at once. The water boiled with koi in a colorful feeding frenzy.

"You'd think they were starving, the big gluttons."

"Speaking of starving, I can't wait for this little reception," Kat said, pulling Alex's hand so they could catch up to the wedding party. "It's amazing how your appetite returns when no one's trying to kill you."

"What's amazing is how you figured out what Hukui was planning ahead of time. I wish you would have let me on it, but I know why you didn't. I'm not a very good actor. Can't seem to hide my true feelings. But where was Kahili during all of this, anyway? He's been Hukui's target just as much as you've been."

"Kahili's pretty good at divination, especially now that his stamina has returned. So he could foresee what

422

Hukui was up to. Plus, he knew Hukui was a creature of habit, and, when Manny Puanani turned up missing, he figured Hukui had taken him to the old temple and chained him up. Manny's the captain of the boat that Liana hired for Leilani's ceremony. So Kahili and Luly rescued Manny, much like Luly and Liana had rescued him—with bolt cutters. Manny went back to the boat in the middle of the night and substituted the gas can Hukui had put in for a new one filled with water, and Kahili permeated it with the smell of gasoline."

Kat shook her head in amazement at the memory of Kahili's unusual talent with scents. "I still don't know how he does that, but Hukui fell for it. All we wanted to do was get safely away and impress upon him we could anticipate his every move and counter any magic he threw our way. We never meant for him to die."

"Why not? He sure wanted you guys dead," Alex said, angrily.

Kat ignored Alex's ire and thought for a moment before speaking. "What he wanted was power and control. But everything he tried backfired on him. Like, chumming the water for sharks was his idea, not ours. He didn't know when we scattered Leilani's ashes, we had asked the help of the shark gods to protect us from her killer."

"Too bad he didn't think to conjure up some dolphins when the sharks came to attack him. They're the natural enemy of the shark. Maybe he could have made it back to shore in one piece. Although I'm glad he didn't. The man was pure evil."

"Come on, Alex," Kat cajoled. "No one is pure evil. He bought into the illusion of separation from God, so he felt powerless and wanted to change how he saw himself. Let's face it. Every harmful act committed on this planet is done by someone who, in some way, feels powerless. The irony is he would have made a masterful kahuna if he wanted to work with us instead of compete against us."

"By the way, remember when you asked me to check out Hukui's aura? He didn't have one, Kat!"

"I know. His aura had already pulled out of his body. He was getting ready to die."

"But how did you and Liana anticipate all of his lies and deception? I mean, that prosthetic mask was a pretty good disguise. You were able to stop him, without personally committing murder. Amazing. You must have had some major help from The Other Side."

"More than you'll ever know, Alex. We had the help of the ultimate Huna healer."

"And who would that be?"

"Think about it. Who was the biggest "Keeper of the Secret?" Who was the most famous kahuna the world has ever known?"

Alex crunched his face into a puzzled expression. "Give me a hint."

"Let me put it this way. In the Samoan dialect of the Polynesian language, the word for carpenter is *la-au* which means wood or a kahuna who works with wood. The root word *la* means 'light' while the root *au* means 'a self.' So, according to Max Freedom Long, the coded word for carpenter means kahuna—an enlightened self. Now, we know, with the exception of Kahili, most all kahuna pass on their knowledge to their children and train them to be kahuna. So who was the most well-known, powerful, charismatic son of a carpenter you've ever heard of?"

"Son of a ca...carpenter?" Alex gasped. "Jesus?"

"That's right."

"Jesus of Nazareth?"

"Exactly. Jesus was the ultimate Huna healer. Huna is the secret behind all of His miracles. So, doesn't it make sense, if we needed help from The Other Side to pull off another miracle, we'd enlist the help of the greatest miracle worker this world has ever known?"

"You g...got help from Jesus?" Alex stammered and stared open-mouthed at Kat, his eyes locked on hers. "Did you actually see him? What does he look like? Was he a spirit or did he have a physical body? Or did he send someone to help? Maybe you just thought it was him. Come on, Kat. You've got my curiosity going. What happened?"

Kat grinned at Alex and playfully punched him on the arm. "I'll tell you all about it. But not now. We've got a wedding reception to go to, remember? Besides, I'm still too exhausted from dealing with Hukui and death and the end of the world to even begin to get into it."

Alex pulled Kat into a grove of bird-of-paradise flowers and held her tight. "I have an idea," he said, kissing her lightly on the lips. "Let's take a break from this horror movie, shall we? I'm up for a romantic comedy, myself."

Kat laughed and slipped her arm around him as they resumed their walk to the reception. Just as they got to the entrance of the restaurant, she tugged on his arm to stop him.

"One more thing, Alex, and I'll shut up. Whether the so-called 'end of the world' is metaphorical or literal or even a little bit of both, it's still about the beginning of something new. We're creating the future right now with every breath we take and every thought we make. So as far as I'm concerned, whatever the future holds, bring it on. I'm up for it. All of it. Because you're in it with me. Liana warned me when I started to use Huna, my life would fall apart at first and then be rebuilt in a new way. And she was right. It's different and better than ever. I feel more awake and alive, and I love my life so much more now because you're sharing it with me."

"In that case, take my arm, Kat," Alex said, grinning from ear to ear. "We have a wedding to celebrate. Ours!"

"Ours?"

"As in you and me."

"Are you serious?"

"Would I lie to you?"

"When?"

"In Kauai next week. After the 2012 conference."

"Are you sure?"

"Kat Romero, I love you. Marry me."

Kat's eyes widened as she studied Alex, looking deep into his eyes. A slow smile grew upon her face.

"Of course I will, Alex Burkette. Through thick and thin?"

"Isn't that our usual MO?"

"You won't mind being married to a kahuna?"

"Not if you don't mind being married to a mere mortal with no supernatural powers to speak of."

426

"Well, you won me over, Alex. That makes you Superman, in my book."

"Great! Come on, Lois," Alex said, laughing gleefully. "Let's go take on the world, one wedding at a time."

Kat laced her arm through his, as they stepped into the restaurant, their hearts beating fast like those of the doves soaring that moment over the palm trees swaying in the gentle Maui breeze.

Glossary

Aka cord: When contact is made between two people, a long, sticky thread is drawn out between the two, like a thin spider-web, and the connection between them remains. Further contacts along the aka cord result in a strong rapport between the two persons. Aka cords can be sent out from an individual to search for objects or people.

Akualele: Flying gods or spirits sent to bring destruction on enemies.

'Ana 'ana: Black magic; evil sorcery by means of prayer and incantation.

Aumakua: Deified ancestral spirit worshipped within a family framework; it epitomized the wise parent and is a member of the great Poe Aumakua, the family of High Selves who are in constant communion with each other and who guide and protect us; called the Higher Self.

Gusano: Spanish word for worm.

Haole: foreigner, used in reference to Caucasians.

Heiau: temple; shrine.

Huna: secret or hidden. Often used to refer to Max Freedom Long's system of quasi-Hawaiian psychological magic.

Kahuna: expert in any of several professions. Popularly associated with sorcery, all were indeed priests or priestesses, since all professions were guided by specific deities, but most weren't sorcerers.

Kahuna aloha: Expert in love magic.

Kahuna 'ana 'ana: An expert in sorcery, including the act of "praying to death."

Kahuna haha: An expert in diagnosis.

Kahuna ha'iha'i'iwi: A bone-setting expert.

Kahuna ho'okelewa'a: An expert navigator.

Kahuna ho'opi'opi'po: An expert in causing sickness or distress by concentration and gesture.

Kahuna ho'oulu 'ai: An agricultural expert.

Kahuna kalai: An expert carver.

Kahuna la'au lapa'au: Herbal doctor.

Kahuna kilo kilo: An expert who observed the skies for omens.

Kahuna kuhikuhi pu'uone: Architects; experts who selected sites for the erection of temples, fishponds and homes.

Kahuna lomilomi: An expert massage technician.

Kahuna nana uli: Weather prophet.

Kahuna nui: Counselor to the chiefs; a specialized function of the kahuna po'o class.

Kahuna po'o: High priest; expert in all arts.

Kahuna pule: "Prayer expert" who prayed within the heiau.

Keiki: child; offspring.

Kuahu: Altar.

La-au: A kahuna who works with wood.

Lei: A garland worn around the neck, wrists, ankles or on the head.

Mana: Spiritual power or energy; vital force taken from food and air by the low self and stored in its aka body, but shared with the middle and High selves.

Serpiente: Spanish word for snake.

Ti: A plant used by the kahuna.

Uhane: The spirit, soul, and animating force of humans, associated with the conscious mind.

'Unihipili: the low self which is in charge of the physical body and is the seat of emotions and memory.

About the Author

Jennifer Martin is a writer, a former teacher and educational administrator, and a television host/producer of educational programs in northern California.

A published author since the age of ten, Jennifer is the co-author, along with Rosemary Dean, of *The Angels Speak: Secrets from the Other Side* and has stories in the best-selling *Chicken Soup for the Soul* series: *Chicken Soup for the Writer's Soul* and *Chicken Soup for the Teenage Soul Letters*.

Since 1983, she has been a member of the Huna Research Inc., an organization that promotes the Huna philosophy worldwide. Jennifer invites you to visit her website: www.hunawarrior.com.